BLACK BOTTOM SAINTS

BLACK BOTTOM SAINTS

ALICE RANDALL

THORNDIKE PRESS
A part of Gale, a Cengage Company

LIBRARY OF CONGRESS CIP DATA ON FILE.
CATALOGUING IN PUBLICATION FOR THIS BOOK
IS AVAILABLE FROM THE LIBRARY OF CONGRESS.

ISBN-13: 978-1-4328-8513-7 (hardcover alk. paper).

Published in 2021 by arrangement with Amistad, an imprint of HarperCollins Publishers

Printed in Mexico
Print Number: 01   Print Year: 2021

To Caroline Randall Williams, poet —
a granddaughter and
great-granddaughter
of Black Bottom

Resurget Cineribus
We shall rise from the ashes

INTRODUCTION

Camelot. Seven years ago, in late 1961, I
saw that musical in New York City. Detroit's
best-known songstress-daughter, Della
Reese, was booked on *The Ed Sullivan Show,*
which made the time right for a few of us to
fly to Gotham from Motown. Making my
way, in a yellow cab after *Camelot*'s closing
curtain, from the Majestic Theatre on 44th
Street to my Harlem home-away-from
home, the Hotel Theresa, on 125th Street,
and whistling the title tune, I was thinking
about Detroit, not Jack and Jackie. I was
thinking about Maxine Powell, John White,
Robert Hayden, and other Black Bottom
Saints who need their story told "strong and
clear."

And loud.

Nothing shines brighter than Black polished right. Too often we're too tired to get
out the rag. Our brightest people and places
get quickly forgotten and tarnished. Once

there was a Black Camelot. And right down the road from Black Camelot, otherwise known as Detroit, was Black Eden, otherwise known as Idlewild. Our resort town, Idlewild, Michigan, was a cross between Nantucket and Las Vegas. At the end of my life, a life that started in Chicago's Bronzeville in 1913, that whirled into gleaming hours in Harlem, St. Louis, Las Vegas, and Los Angeles, one place and time shined brighter than all the rest — Detroit City, from 1937 to 1967.

And, as quickly as I am writing, evidence of our shining hours, our shining places, our shining people is getting knocked down by the wrecking ball, dynamited to pieces in the name of urban renewal, singed in the embers of righteous rebellion, buried in cemeteries, locked up in an aging memory, and coughed out into oblivion.

I'm sick. I'm probably dying. Bad kidneys, bad prostate, bad heart, struggling lungs, but my memory is good. I remember all the tall tales and most of the facts. Memory and stories are powerful tools of rebellion. I have long been a rebellious man, and now I am quickly being disarmed. In my most lucid hours I type a few pages, while on spottier memory days I dictate to my new, young, and healthy wife, Baby Doll, and she embellishes.

I work from Kirwood Hospital, a Black-owned, Black-operated, and Black-staffed institution where I have been sequestered for going on three months as life — stealthily some days, boldly other days — evacuates the premises of my once-agile dancer's body. I continually thank my friend Dr. Guy Otha Saulsberry, who founded Kirwood in 1943 in a stately Motor City mansion at 301 East Kirby, not far from where I would later found the Ziggy Johnson School of the Theatre in a modest concrete box.

Comforting me, extending my last trip around the sun, always near, are the brown and tender well-trained hands, fluttering or poking, of nurses and doctors, able and ready to battle death.

My life began in a Southside Chicago shotgun apartment owned by an ofay. Now it's pleasant to anticipate dying in a mansion owned by a Black man and being in the care of doctors trained at Meharry and Howard.

Not every memory is pleasant. Like the plans that John Wooley and I had to buy the Rhumboogie and make it a club of the highest caliber, this last effort, to return to my school triumphantly restored to health,

11

fizzled. But before I fizzled, I burned bright.

For the past twenty years I have worn three hats — each of them dapper, and all in Detroit: writer, emcee, and dean.

Hat one: Following in the wake of the great sepian entertainment columnists in our papers: Sylvester Russell, Dave Peyton, and the inimitable Salem Tutt Whitney, I write a weekly entertainment and gossip column for Detroit's "colored paper," the *Michigan Chronicle.* I was in the inaugural issue of *Duke* magazine, the Black, better-than-*Esquire* men's publication. If you count the variations of my Detroit columns published in the *Chicago Defender* and the *Pittsburgh Courier,* I have published over a thousand articles. And still counting. Now, I am posting from this hospital room. If Jesus loves me, and if Ethel Waters prays hard, my last column will be published after I die, but before I am buried.

Hat two: I emcee at the swankiest club in town. For a long time it was The Flame, but now I'm presenting Berry Gordy's top talent in the Driftwood Lounge, the almost-private club hidden inside the very public 20 Grand. You may say, Hold up! You can't be a patient in Kirwood and the master of ceremonies at the Driftwood Lounge! I say

— I pick the acts, I write the intros, I scold whoever is too drunk to go onstage or too drunk to get off, even if Baby Doll must drag the miscreant to my sickbed for the scolding. I, following in the footsteps of Eddie Plique, am the emcee.

Hat three: I preside as *the* unofficial Dean of the Ziggy Johnson School of the Theatre, where I teach the breadwinners' children.

That word explains Detroit to me: *breadwinner.* The partying factory people were those whom I first noticed when I arrived in the late thirties. Large numbers of Black men who earned a good, steady wage, doing a skilled job, then returned to the homes they owned, ready to refuel, and to dress to the nines, to head out to hear fabulous music and drink good liquor.

I was the breadwinners' emcee of choice and producer of choice — and proud to be so.

Songs, lines of dialogue, beats of choreography that ofay and mixed audiences loudly applauded in Chicago, Los Angeles, or New York clubs were often met with silence in Detroit showbars. For twenty years I created my best work playing to a sepian Detroit audience of breadwinners and their entourages.

It wasn't just Black factory folk in the audience, but on most nights, in most places, most people in the audience were there *because* of the factory folk. Black doctors, lawyers, ministers, businessmen, gamblers, dry cleaners, hairdressers, barbers, restaurateurs, teachers, policemen, firemen, bus drivers, gas station attendants, car salesmen, newspaper columnists, grocery store owners, funeral parlor directors — we all lived off the wages of factory folk.

Back in the day, because of the breadwinners, Detroit could support all-Black hospitals, and all-Black private schools, and even exclusive all-Black beach resorts.

The factory folk — the breadwinners — drove the Black city. Black Detroit knew this. We gave the factory folk who worked in the automobile plants their proper respect. We loved those men who did that shift work that meant *eight out of ten Black families in Detroit owned the home they lived in* and could afford to go out to a club to hear live music any night they chose. Our breadwinners built this city. We remember when River Rouge ran twenty-four seven. Three shifts a day at the plants meant the showbars had two shows on Sunday and late shows every night, sometimes at 2:00 a.m., for those who got off the late shift. That was the opportunity that created caramel Camelot.

All-Black Detroit audiences were fire. They brought a rare light and a heat that rated Black achievement and performance by a Black yardstick.

It was nothing unusual for a breadwinner or a breadwinner's wife to go to 52 shows a year. It was unusual but not rare to go to even 150 shows a year. Some breadwinners went to over 250 shows in a given year. The breadwinners heard so much excellent music that they became experts. And the more expert they became, the more everybody wanted to play Detroit. It was a self-perpetuating cauldron of sepia excellence.

I stirred that pot.

I wanted to do something for the breadwinners' children because the breadwinners had done so much for Detroit — and there's nothing a breadwinner loves more than a breadwinner's baby.

I taught the breadwinners' babies, and I did not just teach them to be dancers.

Week after week, hiding behind practicing new steps and learning sophisticated choreography, I shared stories that put a limelight on the Black Bottom Saints — people who had suffered so much, and so differently, but who had each found a way, or made a way, to experience radical joy. In my classes I dropped bits and pieces about the Saints' lives like breadcrumbs that marked a path out of the automobile plant for the breadwinners' children. I did this to celebrate and honor what the breadwinners did outside the factory: make worthy and beautiful babies — and be worthy and beautiful their own sometimes-damned selves.

And once a year, always on Father's Day, my School of the Theatre presents the extravagant recital that Black Detroit calls "Youth Colossal" at the legendary Latin Quarter Lounge.

On that day, there are no white faces in the Latin Quarter. None. There are just our children on the stage, and everybody in the audience, looking at our boys and our girls, has the same thoughts: *He is the second coming of Christ; she is the next Virgin Mary; and Lord, don't all the bronze apostles look good?!*

Youth. The seven most radical words in the Bible: *And a little child shall lead them.*

From the day it opened in 1952, the Ziggy Johnson School of the Theatre was a citizenship school. I did not run a dancing school. We were rehearsing for the theater of life. I have seen Butterbeans and the little genius Sammy Davis Jr. perform. I well know we

16

don't need a school to learn to dance. From jump, it was my ambition to educate boys and educate girls to be dangerous citizens.

By the time we were open for a few years, I was focusing on the girls. In Detroit, the boys and men were doing okay or, at least, so I thought. The girls had it harder.

I have known too many young, brilliant, precise women with heads for numbers who never considered attending medical school, never gave two shakes for Meharry or Howard. And I've known women who could argue the paint off a wall and didn't dream of law. I've seen girls who got raped, blamed themselves not the man, then got talked into thinking sex was evil and they were dirty. And I have also seen women driving Cadillac cars wearing furs who have never voted. That's what I set out to change at the Ziggy Johnson School of the Theatre. Autonomy, ambition, renewal, pride, and creativity are the five basic positions we teach.

That is why the big performers — the Supremes, the Mills Brothers, The Temptations, Gladys Knight, and the marvelous Marvin Gaye — loved to step to the stage and play my kid show where they remembered and played for the little boy or little girl they once were who, if they wanted to sing just for home folk, had no place to

17

perform, except in a church or a juke joint.

All my girls will say, "I was raised by a village of Saints." They will say, "Ziggy filled our heads, his citizen girls, with the lives of his saints, who whispered encouragement, and clapped us forward, as we spotted to hard-won 'happy.' " They will say, "God doesn't make Saints — people do," when they ask for something and it is given. One will say, "Kidnapping, rape, and a Judas kiss were eclipsed by step-together, step-together, step-together-step!" Another will say, "It's not just us Black folk who need Ziggy's book — it's everybody!" The girls will say things I don't say.

Now, in my last days, I am wearing a fourth hat — Saints Day Book author.

"I wrote a Saints Day Book!" I don't know anybody else alive, Black *or* white, who's done that. Saints Day Books usually list feasts and dates, along with a little biography of the saint being honored. Detroit likes to do things a little different than they been done before. My Saints Day Book includes biographies, plus cocktails in celebration of the Saints, and provides recipes and instructions on how to make them. Regular Saints Day Books don't do a *thing* about helping you make a feast. They just tell you on what

18

day to do it. I'm not telling you exactly on what day to have your cocktail — but I *am* instructing you exactly how to make it, thanks to one of my favorite Saints, Thomas Bullock.

The best cocktail man I ever knew was Bullock. In Detroit, people spend a whole lot of time in bars drinking cocktails. Every bar I ever walked into was improved by my knowing that every bar in America owes something to one brilliant sepian, Thomas Bullock — the greatest bartender of all, and the first Black man ever to publish a cocktail recipe book. All Black folk — hell, *all* folk! — can be a particular kind of proud when they walk into a bar if they think about Bullock and all he knew about altering perception to improve reality.

Sometimes we start celebrating ourselves by celebrating the ones who brought us over. My Saints Day Book gives you precise ways to do just that.

I am not sorry to be dying. I was born with the gift of premonition. There are things I do not want to live to see. Martin Luther King Jr. will be shot down. I don't want to live to see that. With his dying, everyone will forget about me. That story will eclipse all other Black American stories — maybe forever — unless I do something.

I'm not worried about me, but I've got some saints to attend to. And I've got just the young person to help me do it: the kid we call Colored Girl, the one who got snatched out of Detroit.

Colored Girl will complete my task, by hook or by crook. She's not a breadwinner's baby, but that child *is* Black Bottom to the bone. And a child will lead us.

These are the lives of my Saints.

SUMMER
Robert Hayden (1913–1980)
Nancy Elizabeth Johnson (1887–1968)
Edward St. Benedict Plique (1896–1986)
Night Train Lane (1927–2002)
Joe Louis (1914–1981)
Thomas Bullock (1872–year unknown)
Cordie King Stuart (1924–2004)
Sadye E. Pryor (1899–1977)
The Reverend Cook (1900–1961)
The Reverend Clarence Cobbs
(1908–1979)
Bricktop (1894–1984)
Butterbeans (1893–1967) and Susie
(1894–1963)
Tim Moore (1887–1958)
Valda Gray (1914–1980)
Ethel Waters (1896–1977)

WEEK 1
FIRST SUNDAY
AFTER FATHER'S DAY

The poet known as Robert Hayden was born in Detroit's Black Bottom in 1913 to Ruth Sheffield and was named Asa Sheffield. When Asa was eighteen months old, he was informally adopted by his next-door neighbors, the Haydens. Sue Ellen and Will, austere Christians, raised the boy as their only child and began to call the future poet laureate of the United States of America "Robert." Ruth Sheffield, an actress who knew her way around a bar, remained in sporadic contact with the child she birthed, off and on vying for his affection and attention, while maintaining the Haydens ruse of formal adoption.

The eastern border of Black Bottom was the railroad tracks at St. Aubin Street. The western border of Black Bottom was Brush Street. The southern border was the river. The northern border was the southern border of Paradise Valley, the Black entertainment district.

For the first half of the 20th century Black Bottom was the commercial district as well as a residential district more important to and more delightful than any other to African-Americans in Detroit. Its opportunities, institutions, people, and delights lured thousands out of the South.

By the end of World War I, Black Bottom was established as a municipality (along with New York's Harlem and Chicago's Bronzeville) with a clear claim of being one of the three most economically, politically, and artistically powerful Black communities in America.

For decades, Black Bottom had three distinct advantages over both Harlem and Bronzeville: its close proximity to Henry Ford's auto factories; its close proximity to Paradise Valley, a Black red-light district where all the primary doors to ecstasy — music, gambling, prostitution, liquor, and drugs — stayed wide open for business twenty-four seven; and its close proximity to Canada.

When the world was still moving in thick, dark rivers from the farm South to the city North, Robert Hayden made the reverse migration. In 1946 he trained south from Michigan down to Tennessee to teach at

Fisk University. When Colored Girl enrolled as a freshman at Fisk in 1977, she arrived on a campus Hayden had departed a decade before, to return to the orbit of Detroit and teach at the University of Michigan.

Colored Girl didn't know this. She had forgotten Black Bottom Hayden and Fisk Hayden.

Robert Hayden

PATRON SAINT OF: *Poets, Orphans, and Migrants*

It's always hard to leave Idlewild on a summer Sunday afternoon, but Sunday, June 26, 1966, was harder than usual. If I hadn't had a confirmed date with poet Robert Hayden, I don't think I would have got gone on time.

First off, Baby Doll was refusing to return to the city with me. She claimed three hours on the highway at midday with the top down would fry her hair and crisp her skin like she was chicken in a pan. Second, since Detroit was experiencing a record-breaking heat wave and no one else wanted to go home either, Sunnie Wilson had decided, late Saturday night, to host a Sunday noon "Bermuda Shorts and Pancakes Party." The updated plan seemed to be: long breakfast/lunch/supper at Sunnie's on Sunday; early to bed in Idlewild; hit the road at 4:00 a.m. in the cool of Monday morning; make it to work in Detroit by 8:00 a.m. Third and finally, everybody was still talking about Youth Colossal '66 a week after that extravaganza, praising it as "the best ever!"

I loved hearing that, but I knew this: Colossal '66 had been the hardest show ever to produce, and '67 would be even harder. I needed a secret weapon and I thought the sometimes ornery, sometimes awkward, always brilliant Hayden might-could be it. My three second-tier teachers were tearing up the school vying for the top spot that was being vacated by my best teacher, Gloria, who was getting married after Colossal '66, and then planning to take a sabbatical. Thinking she was winning too much of everything (husband, wedding, and top billing in the program) either on purpose or by accident, the other teachers had sabotaged the costumes for Gloria's class by taking the measurements wrong and then writing them down as what some of my students called "wronger!" Only by the grace of Maxine Powell's imagination and George Stanley's sister's sewing did we pull off costumes that looked like something my

26

breadwinners should be dipping deep into their pockets to purchase. Toni Lewis, owner of a rival dance school, smelled blood in the water. She scheduled a dance recital at the hoity-toity Detroit Art Institute Museum the exact same time as my Saturday Colossal at the storied but *funky* Latin Quarter. Every bougie parent with a child on my rolls considered taking that bait and switching schools. I held on to most of my best students, save one significant defection. That baby did the right thing at the last moment (Gloria can be very persuasive) and came to dance a surprise star turn in our show, leaving Toni in the lurch.

When crazy older mamas weren't making hard things harder, wild young daddies were doing it. We have a daddy or two: Nual Steele, for one, just in his twenties, a pimp (who we've had before), turned drug kingpin (we hadn't had those before), taking on everybody, deferring to no one, not even the Diggs family, maybe not even George Stanley. Nual's got seven kids in the school brought in by three different mothers. When he's late with tuition, it hurts. His oldest kid is profoundly talented, so you can't keep him out of the show.

Speaking of shows, we're competing with Motown now. Why should a student re-

27

hearse with us when they can be working up a pro act and sell it to Berry Gordy? Actually, that's not finally. Then, there's this: After James Meredith was shot in Mississippi on June 6, four of my kids headed down south to "walk against fear." I couldn't tell them not to go. I tucked $100 into each of their pockets (Dr. Bob "Bodywork" Bennett spotted me those funds), prayed they didn't get killed, then moved up three understudies to fill their roles. Year after year, the challenge is securing a big-name act. After they are signed, it's always hoping up to showtime that they don't get called to a paying gig or a spot on a television show and do a last-minute bolt. All of that was between me and "curtain up" at the Latin Quarter last year. I was catching all that hell and probably a bit more the year coming up. It was enough to make me sweat out my curls.

Except: I had an idea about how I might keep Toni Lewis at bay (Robert Hayden) and who might-could bring Nual Steele to heel (Blaze Marzette). That realization put a funny smile on my face. Baby Doll asked me if everything was all right. I replied, "Everything's copacetic." And it was in fact "copacetic" — our word for "fine and dandy." For that second of Sunday, Idlewild was Eden. Detroit was Camelot. And I might-could be Prospero.

For *sure* I was wearing powder blue and sweet cream. So was Baby Doll. Except she had on beige Bermuda shorts and a blue shirt, and had me in contrasting blue Bermudas with a beige shirt. When we arrived at Sunnie's, we made quite an entrance, pulling up with the top down in that borrowed baby blue Pontiac GTO with shoreline sand interior.

The two-door coupe convertible was difficult to steer and tough to brake, but it went fast, quickly, and looked good doing it. It wasn't a long, long car, like a Deuce and a Quarter, or a great wide car, like a Cadillac; it was a short, strong car with great lines. Just like me.

Inside folks shook their heads when I told them I was leaving extra early to see Robert Hayden before my emcee duties began at the 20 Grand. The parents who sent their kids to Fisk where Hayden was a professor, the folks who had gone to high school with him, the people who had lived down the block from him in Paradise Valley — all shook their heads with particular vigor. Even people who liked Hayden thought he was likely not to like me; that he was color struck, stuck up, and nice-nasty. And those were the folks who liked him!

The folks who didn't said he had gone too far (this had been reported in the *Michigan Chronicle,* in the *Pittsburgh Courier,* and in the *Negro Digest*) when he read Yeats to the students and faculty at the Fisk writers symposium and declared he was "no Negro writer." He was a "writer, period." All over Idlewild, people were echoing the novelist and poet Margaret Walker, repeating, "That's like a rose saying I'm not a rose, I'm a flower." To cut that off I said, "Flowers don't talk. I love that poem, 'Winter Sundays.'"

I love Hayden. Sometimes folks don't know. You got to see for yourself. And this is what I had seen: Behind his thick glasses, Hayden has sweet, soft eyes. On top of that: I was emceeing a show in the Driftwood Lounge, one of three nightclubs inside the 20 Grand that shared space with a twenty-lane bowling alley. In 1966, the 20 Grand was the top spot in our Detroit. When you're in the top spot, you want the top emcee, and that was me — once I showered off the sweat of Idlewild and changed into linen long pants, a silk and linen sports jacket, and a crisp tie, held in place with a tie clip. Ninety-five degrees outside didn't change any of that.

Pros get on the road on time. I got. But I started to worry as I donned my driving gear: straw hat and sunglasses; worried as I pecked Baby Doll's cheek — letting folks who hadn't seen when we arrived see as I left how good we looked; worried as I headed toward the car, worried, as I slipped into the driver's seat and cranked the radio up loud. What worried me most? I knew Hayden better than *any* of them knew Hayden.

Sometime back, Hayden had returned to Detroit to give a reading shortly after Langston Hughes himself had come to the Motor City. Certain civic leaders (including my own Shirley McNeil, PhD; Dr. Bob Bennett; and Dr. Alf Thomas) believed that whatever had been done for Hughes should be done better for our own poet of Black Bottom. So a reservation was made at the Gotham Hotel's Ebony Room, Detroit's finest restaurant, where Hayden could be feted on white tablecloths decorated with cut roses and fed squab under glass and cherries jubilee.

I wasn't invited but managed to be meandering in the lobby when the party let out. Hayden, dressed in a tweed jacket and a white, button-down shirt and bow tie with

31

a sweater over it, wasn't hard to recognize. I had seen his picture in the papers and also in Ruthie Sheffield's wallet. He wore suede saddle shoes that I never saw any one of us wear. Someone told me W. H. Auden, his teacher at Michigan, wore the same shoes.

Soon, Robert was up in my room. I was looking for a picture of his mother to show him. Didn't know exactly what *he* was looking for. Could have been a final free drink. Could have been something else we had yet to discover.

There was a liberating privacy on every floor of the Gotham. There were so many good and clean reasons to enter any of the eight stories of the hotel, designed in the Italian Renaissance style that made it look like it belonged on Park Avenue in New York. You could discreetly disappear behind any number of closed doors, and explore so many ambiguities and quite a few illicit pleasures. I avoided most of the illicit pleasures, particularly the gambling. I savored so many of the ambiguities. Living in the Gotham made my single life simple.

Hayden and I settled onto the little sofa opposite my bed, and I took a good look at him as he prattled on about new poems. We were the same age. I had read his first collection of poems, *Heart-Shape in the Dust,* when it had come out in 1940. It was a birthday gift from the Natchez Belle. I had poked into *Heart* regularly in the intervening years. It was on many shelves in Idlewild. He took a breath. I quoted a line or two *of* Hayden *to* Hayden. He was charmed. I took a breath. He spat out words like others of us wore tie clips and cufflinks, as bits of gleam to attract passionate and positive attention. Soon he had mine.

There was a chip on his shoulder I wanted to knock off. I anticipated the fun of wrestling with him and having him discover he could stop observing "us," and at long last join "us" Black folk. As some beckon of invitation, I felt we needed something to look at before I tried to interest him in looking at me, so I opened my jewelry box. I wanted him to see I recognized fine things. I showed him my favorite cufflinks. They were ebony black and blood red on 14-carat gold. The jewelry man had said the pattern was "stylized feathers."

"Bought them in a pawnshop in 1932."

"Rich folks' things were going cheap."

"It looks like the Black Diamond Express."

"Makes twelve stops and arrives in hell ahead of schedule!"

"Or, it's an express to heaven?"

Robert tapped a cufflink.

"I think it's a train through hell. Those red bars are hellfire."

"Can you write that?"

"Yes."

It was the first "yes" of many that night. Most, I don't remember. The last "yes" I remember clearly. Hayden asked me if I remembered his "first mother." I liked the way he put that. "First mother." "Yes," I answered. "Yes, we shared a bottle or three, in a blind pig or two. She called you 'darling Asa.'" He nodded when I said that, then he took off his glasses and wiped his eyes.

"A bar is one place Ruth could be sure she wouldn't see Sue or Will Hayden."

I reached up to take his glasses from his hands and place them on my face as a way of being him for a moment. It was the wrong move. He jerked his glasses back.

"What?"

"Four-Eyes. The kids at school used to call me Four-Eyes."

Four-Eyes. They probably called him worse than that. Words hurt him more than sticks and stones — particularly, I realized too late, his birthname, "Asa." Hurt too much for him to hear. I tried to press the cufflinks into his hand as a kind of make-up gift, but he wouldn't take them.

34

Everything was hot and irritable once I got near the 20 Grand. Driving "home" from Idlewild, since the Gotham had been torn down, didn't feel like driving home. The modern high-rise apartment I shared with Baby Doll was a fine place with river views, but it wasn't the Gotham. I had a higher perch but a lesser home. I drove past my School of the Theatre; it was on Warren not far from the 20 Grand. The simple storefront looked sad, vacant, and plain, like it always did right after Father's Day. No shiny cars parked in front. No shiny-faced young people preening just the other side of the plate glass window. No beautiful model answering the phone. No big stars walking through the front door. No rich parents double-parked waiting for children to come out. No neighborhood kids running down the sidewalk to class, or dawdling to peek at the students entering my door. No breadwinners dropping off an early tuition check. No Mari skipping out to George's El Dorado, singing some song she had just made up.

The week after Father's Day is the only week of the year when the place is completely dead. Not for the first time I noted: You plan resurrection, sitting in ashes.

Hayden was formal. He acted as if he had forgotten our earlier encounter. I apologized for my Bermuda shorts. I invited him to stay later for a show. He declined. I offered him a drink. He declined. I offered him a seat. He sat.

"Massey wouldn't say why you wanted to meet," he began.

"And you can't imagine?"

"I can't imagine."

I got back to business. I had a show to emcee.

"You've heard of my Youth Colossal?"

"Seen more than heard. Pictures in the *Jet*. But Dudley Randall may have mentioned it."

" 'Runagate, Runagate,' and 'The Ballad of Nat Turner.' I want your permission to choreograph a dance to those. Maybe get Stevie Wonder to do the music."

"Stevie Wonder?"

"Stevie Wonder!"

"Stop. Just stop."

"I'm trying to help you."

He laughed. I had never seen Hayden laugh.

"You want to adapt my poems for your pickaninny minstrel show?"

36

"Pickaninny minstrel show? They eviscer-
ated you at Fisk. Now you savage *me*?"

"You know about that?"

"I read. We were in the paper the same
day. May 14, 1966, right next to a photo of
Aretha Franklin and right below a photo of
Sammy Davis. The *Pittsburgh Courier* ran a
bit in Major Robinson's 'On the Line'
column talking about Joe Louis talking
about me. Ticket sales for the Colossal were
a little slow this year, then Major Robinson
gave me that few inches of ink and we sold
out. It helped that there was a picture of
Aretha right by my name. Across from me
on that same page was an article about the
writers' conference at Fisk and how you
went crazy and said you were not a Black
writer and even Arna Bontemps had to step
back from you, his favorite. You in a mess."

"How would putting my poems in your
show fix that?"

"How more Black a poet could you be
than to have your poems performed in
Detroit, land of 80,000 Negro girls, at my
Youth Colossal with no white folks on the
stage or in the audience? Melvin Tolson
would have to tip his hat to that. That's
Black as the winning ace of spades Black."

We didn't say anything except the words
necessary to bring a second round. Finally,

37

Robert broke the silence.

"Pageant. Your Colossal is a pageant. Like a W. E. B. DuBois pageant."

"Why you say that other thing?"

"I'm a little crazy."

Hayden *was* a little crazy. He had a second mother, Sue Hayden, who had been born a slave in the last days of the Civil War. She had whispered to him stories of enslaved Africans in America who grew wings and flew home, dark men who knew all the stars of Africa. And still he kept thinking on the light, bright, almost-white woman who bore him and left to pursue life as an entertainer on the road, occasionally returning to her son and to Detroit. Night Train always thought about the woman who pulled him out of the bulrushes; Robert kept thinking about the woman who laid him down.

"You came for me."

"For Ruth's boy, Asa."

A year later, when Youth Colossal 1967 had come and gone without the Hayden-Wonder collaboration I said, "Next year," and I lifted a glass to Ruth and to Robert.

Yes, on the last day of my last summer, in August 1967, I drank to Robert Hayden, thinking about love's austere rituals and all the times I swept the dancing school floor at 7:00 a.m. so my girls would have clean shoes.

LIBATION FOR THE FEAST DAY OF ROBERT HAYDEN:
I Knew All the Stars of Africa

A riff on Tom Bullock's "Gin and Calamus." Calamus was a particular favorite food of Walt Whitman's; he even named an entire section of *Leaves of Grass* after the plant. The hippies down on Detroit's Plum Street, according to Hippy Dippy, say calamus lets them fly. It became illegal to ingest calamus in the United States in 1969. Gingerroot makes a fine substitute.

A piece of ginger about the size of your thumb
A bottle of good gin

Pour out one shot of gin, and drink. Add the peeled ginger to the bottle. Cap tightly and refrigerate for three days. Strain. Chill. Serve chilled straight up. See stars.

WEEK 2
SECOND SUNDAY
AFTER FATHER'S DAY

Every girl who walked into the Ziggy Johnson School of the Theatre received the same first instruction: "Chin up, make me believe you're ten feet tall." Some frowned, some walked particularly upright, some rose on tiptoes; every girl failed that first-day-of-class test. And Ziggy told them. He never withheld a useful truth. In 1962, on the first day of summer dance camp, a just-over-three-feet-tall three-year-old in black leotard and beige tights, calling herself Colored Girl, chirped "No one can do that!" Ziggy, five-foot nothing, standing tall in a silk knit golf shirt and summer wool slacks, challenged back: "I've known someone who could do that since I was smaller than you are now, the Natchez Belle."

A church-sanctioned campaign to canonize Augustus Tolton began in 2010, one hundred years after the Natchez Belle began her unsanctioned campaign. Colored Girl joined the campaign in 2012. The prayer for Tolton's canonization includes words that apply equally to Tolton, to the Natchez Belle herself, and even to Ziggy, "who labored among us in times of contradiction, times that were both beautiful and paradoxical."

Nancy Elizabeth Johnson

PATRON SAINT OF: *Mothers, Migration, and Black Belles*

Nancy Elizabeth Alexander Johnson — my mother — was born on February 18, 1887, in Natchez, Mississippi. I always refer to her as the Natchez Belle. Natchez was important to the lady.

The taproot of her connection to that Old South city was the Catholic Church, specifically Holy Family Catholic Church, the first congregation of Black Catholics in Mississippi. Holy Family, then called St. Francis, was founded shortly after my mother was born. She said walking up the hill to Holy Family, and then walking through the doors to see only brown faces in all the pews — even the first rows, even the center seats, even if there was a white face in the pulpit — was a first and vivid memory. Mother

41

liked to boast that she and Holy Family shared a childhood, and that Holy Family was not just the best church in Natchez — it was the best church in the whole world.

Her allegiance shifted as she matured and as the first colored Mississippians ventured north to Chicago and wrote letters home to Natchez. Mother learned there were colored Catholics in Chicago, that there was a colored Catholic church, St. Monica's, at the corner of 36th and Dearborn Streets, and most stunningly that in Chicago there had even been a colored priest, Father Tolton! The glinting possibility of Black in the pulpit and Black in the pews tugged my mother north.

For the Natchez Belle, migrating to Chicago was a religious pilgrimage.

It tickled my mother, who understood the holy family — Mary, Joseph, and Jesus — to be white, that there was a Catholic church named for Monica, whom she understood to be the colored mother of the colored St. Augustine. The public celebration of colored motherhood delighted Mama. That Monica was the patron saint for women whose husbands and sons had gone astray, she considered a strange curse. Mama accepted that the same person provoked delight as well as dilemma. I suspect she learned that by loving my father, but that is not something we spoke about directly.

She told me her parents had met in the big integrated Natchez cathedral, while sitting beneath the arching blue triangles of the vaulted gothic ceiling ornamented with 24-carat gold. It was a place where, in Mother's memory, fathers reeked of lavender water and orange and Mothers of the dishwater and shirt starch. It was a place where the Black folk sat in the back and off to the side, unless they were holding a white baby. The first official Black members of the church were the descendants of the white members of the church. Eventually this became too uncomfortable for both white wives and Black husbands. In 1894, Catholic Negro Natchez went its separate way. I always wondered if some of my yellow tone was a blend of lavender and shirt starch. All of it reminds me of incense and satsuma oranges.

My mother was a second-generation free woman, because her mother had been born free.

She grew up hearing the voices of the freeborn along with stories of the various struggles and delights of liberation, including the existence of Father Tolton, who was born a slave but lived to become an ordained priest, serving under the Bishop of Rome.

In 1913, when I was born, there were about seven million African-Americans. Two hundred thousand of us were Catholics. For Mama, being Catholic was a connection to Natchez and to the South. For me, being Catholic was a connection to a world beyond America; to a world where Blackness mattered differently, and where Augustine and Monica were saints; to a whispered world where the Apostle Phillip converted an Ethiopian — a eunuch of great authority — and baptized him, then rose up, and was rewarded by God for doing good work.

Catholicism promised a bigger net, hauling in a more motley catch of dappled fish. From my early days I was swept up in the promise of variety beyond established borders. Eventually, the stage promised a bigger and Blacker world, but I first learned the power of the dark sitting beside the Natchez Belle in a pew at a midnight service.

The power of that dark, the power of Mama's church, was not God. It was the address to all five senses. Church was my first place where the sight of beauty, the sound of beauty, the taste of beauty, the touch of beauty, and the scent of beauty all enveloped me at once. Eventually, I would translate the sight of stained-glass windows, the sound of choir songs, the taste of communion wafers, the touch of chasuble silk, and the scent of frankincense to the symmetric line of high-lifted legs, bent-note torch singing, aged Scotch, tie silk, and Arpège mixed with exhaled smoke from Winston cigarettes. Mama didn't anticipate getting translated. Mama taught me to savor the cocoon of the beauty that church provided. She taught me to trust five-sense pleasures as a promised balm in Gilead.

Then, when I was in high school, my mother got down on her knees and prayed to Saint Monica for me to be a priest. She believed her prayers were beginning to be answered when my older brothers left school to go to work full-time. With Frank landing a job as a shipping clerk after his junior year, and Charles landing a high-paying factory job after his sophomore year, I got to finish high school. Finishing high school meant I could go to seminary.

Over and over my mother had told me Tolton's story. How he had been born a slave. How, after all the places to study to be a priest in America turned him down, he studied in Rome at the Vatican. How he expected to go to Africa, but they sent him to America instead. How the white priests in Chicago tried to shame him and the Negro congregants tried to blame him. She never told me for what. He was walking home from the train one hot summer day in July 1897. He collapsed. Heatstroke got him. He was forty-three. My mother always ended the story with the same words: "And when he's dead a hundred years we will make him a saint — the first colored American saint."

Those words stayed with me for a good long while. Back when I was turning from a boy to a man, haunted and harangued by Mama's words, "And when he's dead a hundred years we will make him a saint," I started imagining things. I imagined a colored man dropping dead in the street at forty-three. I imagined a too-bright, too-bold, too-red sun. I imagined Tolton twitching as his life burned out. I didn't have to imagine being mad at God for making the sun too hot that day.

What I heard from my mother's wish for me to be a priest was permission *not* to make money and permission to wear extravagant costumes. I heard what I needed to hear.

Mama didn't talk much about Daddy. He

was a there-and-then-gone man. Mama talked about God. She told me God was my father and he was always "home." And then she took me to church and told me to get comfortable. Later, I confused stages with churches and never wanted a house. Eventually, the Gotham Hotel became my stage and my church. That is over and I am returned to my beginnings.

My beginning: A Catholic faith that embraced Mary as the go-between, buffering men and women from their Father and Creator, as well as a love of smells, bells, ritual, and rosary, is what my mother carried north from Natchez — and what separated her from many of the Black women in Chicago, who were much more likely to attend Baptist or African-Methodist Episcopal, A.M.E., churches than Catholic. But her Catholicism connected her to the New Orleans folk, as well as to Mobile, Alabama, folk, and to brown folk from other northern cities who prayed the rosary and had landed in Chicago. It connected her to her past. I was hungry for the future.

LIBATION FOR THE FEAST DAY OF NANCY ELIZABETH JOHNSON:
The Natchez Belle

1 jigger of bourbon
1 sugar cube
1 jigger of soda water
3 sprigs of mint
Orange slice
Luxardo cherry

In a tall glass place mint, then muddle. Add sugar and soda water. Muddle a bit more, then stir till sugar is dissolved. Add bourbon, then ice cubes. Garnish with an orange slice and a Luxardo cherry.

WEEK 3
THIRD SUNDAY
AFTER FATHER'S DAY

In 1951 Eddie Plique would be the first Black ring announcer for a world championship boxing match. He would call the Sugar Ray Robinson–Jake LaMotta fight. Ziggy would do his part to help him get that gig. Soon after the fight, a framed photo of Plique in his ringside tuxedo quickly took up residence on Ziggy's cluttered desk. In 1965 Plique crowned Ricky DePaul of Detroit "Queen of the Finnie Ball." On Halloween 1966, Colored Girl donned a boy's tuxedo and knocked on mansion doors up and down Black Detroit's famed Boston Boulevard, demanding candy with the words Ziggy taught her: "Trick or Treat! I'm Eddie Plique!" As late as 1971 Plique was awarding the trophy for best drag queen at Chicago's annual Finnie's Halloween Ball, as well as serving as promoter and publicist of the event.

Edward St. Benedict Plique

PATRON SAINT OF: *MCs, Queens, and Promoters*

1936 Chicago. Southside. Regal Theater. December. Friday Night. Good Fellows Club Midnight Benefit Show. Eighth Annual. Big doings. Huge audience. Three thousand turned away. Five thousand in the hall. Bright-white but Black, Eddie Plique was the emcee that night, and he was some kind of special.

I didn't know emceeing could be an art, till I saw Plique perform.

When James J. Gentry wrote about the Good Fellows Club Midnight Benefit Show for *The Bee,* then Bronzeville's snootiest paper, he proclaimed the show historical, "the greatest of its kind ever held here or elsewhere in the nation." And by "its kind" he didn't mean "colored," he meant "variety."

Holding the thing together, from midnight to 5:00 a.m., connecting pieces that otherwise wouldn't be connected, was Plique himself. He didn't just introduce an act, or, if need be, get an act offstage early. He could also rescue an act with his approving stance or a beaming glance. I arrived a dancer and a producer. After seeing Plique

50

work — introducing what turned out to be my three favorite acts of the evening: Louis Armstrong, Bobby Short, and Tanya the Contortionist — I wanted to be an emcee.

I wanted to be just like Plique. I wanted to rear back, stuff my hands in my pockets (revealing the gold paisley silk lining of my jacket), and tell some young person what Plique himself had whispered to me, behind the stage drapes, in my threadbare but "looks good from a distance" costume: "All we have from Africa, son, are the yam, the sesame seed, and the drum. We have lost the names of the places our great-grandfathers lived, lost our great-grandfathers' names. But some of us remember, or we find, the rhythms we used to celebrate, the rhythms we used to mourn, the rhythms we used to tie joy to sorrow. You one of the ones!"

This was my path: Biggest show of the year, and I was charged with finding, costuming, choreographing, and rehearsing the local talent, as well as performing on the stage as a dancer. By the time the curtain went up I was swelling with a young man's pride of possession, even in my wrong kind of shiny suit, having saved the best costumes for the rest of my troupe. Sacrifice was easy: I was leading my floor show, my girls, my band, to the limelight.

This is what Plique schooled me to: Benny Skoller thought I was taking his Swingland show, his Swingland girls, his Swingland band, his Little Ziggy Johnson onto the stage. Skoller thought he owned me because he paid me a wage. And yes, the local talent on our show also appeared on his Swingland stage — doing what I myself had taught them to do. Good man that he was — and he *was* a good man — Skoller was a white man in show business, and he had serious blindness when it came to seeing more than one side of Black folk. Most white folks that I've met never do that. (Tallulah Bankhead is my sole exception.) At best, ofays think they love you because they pay you; at worst, they confuse hiring you with ownership.

"When an ofay is paying," Plique admonished me to buy my own costume first. Then he encouraged me to stop and enjoy the show, shabby suit and all, because I might never see or be a part of another show "so big with so few ofays in the audience." Only then did he warn me about the dangerous ones roaming our neighborhood: "There are four reasons for white folks to come to the South Side: music, drugs, girls, and boys."

Me? I stayed away from half of that. But I

52

couldn't stay away from this: At the big fancy clubs in Chicago, I was staging shows for white audiences with my people lucky to be included on the fringes. I was dancing on stages where my people couldn't get a ringside seat in the audience. That was the world of the Bronzeville Black-and-tan. Colored people were just lucky to be included.

I already knew that. Just like I already knew, from the first time I tapped something on the sidewalk and my friend tapped back to me, that rhythm ties us to each other; that rhythm invites us to weave separate lives together into a danced tapestry of kin and friend that is an unbroken connection to Africa. But I knew it all better when I heard Plique tell it out loud.

Plique introduced Louis Armstrong as "Pops," then Armstrong with his amazing trumpet gave the audience "Pennies from Heaven." The song was still new, and the audience lapped it up. They would have loved that song even with a bad introduction, but Plique made the audience feel like a part of Armstrong's family. When it came time to introduce Bobby Short, Plique had the opposite work to do — nobody knew who Short was, so Plique called him "the Little Fats Waller." With four words he prepared everybody to love Bobby.

Today, a new nurse is here to take my blood pressure. I always request the new nurses. They are the only variety I get these days. I do not let the high numbers throw my train of thought off track. I got fifty-two Saints and maybe not fifty-two days. I need fifty-two years. Colored Girl got to give me some of hers. But not today. Today, this is my line of work. Let me jump back to it before the factory foreman in the sky calls "quitting time."

Young Bobby Short looked out at the audience and instinctively knew the slippery truth that at some great performances the audience feeds the performer before the performer feeds the audience. At that point in his career he didn't yet know how to use "them eyes" to get his audience to give him a room full of excited approval before he began to sing or play. Plique knew. He used his eyes and got the audience high on happy expectation. They fed Bobby applause before he even performed. Then Bobby sang and they gave him more. Short discovered on that stage with Plique that he could be either response or call. Plique had set Short up perfectly.

Finally, Plique introduced the boneless wonder, Tanya, a contortion artist. She actually had bones. She dislocated her shoulders and her hips at every performance. She could front bend and back bend. She had no God-given talent — she had a discipline and a conviction that "if I can just do this, I will be *somebody.*" Plique introduced Tanya using a somber tone that almost prepared the audience for the shock and awe of her performance.

After the show ended at 5:00 in the morning, Tanya and I shared a cigarette; she let me touch her spine. I gave her my pack and she let me put my palm on her back while she popped her shoulder out and into joint. Then an arm. Out of its socket, her arm just hung limp at her side. Ain't nobody knows where Tanya is now. She walked that line between artist, performer, and freak into oblivion.

Tanya, the contortion artist, insisted she was a dancer. Eddie Plique was one of the few people who agreed. His voice had a lot of sway with me, but ever after seeing Tanya perform, when I danced, it was no longer just this holy thing, sacred steps connecting me: to myself, to a community of artists, even to Africa; connecting me in a way the white world couldn't disrupt. Until Tanya.

When I saw Tanya's performance, I saw that my dancing wasn't only and always a celebration of community and a strutting of self. Watching Tanya, I found no way to not know that every Black body flexing on an American stage actually works right next door to a freak show.

I left Chicago to find out, or *fail* to find out, how far dance could get from a freak show, how close it could get back to the drum, and what more than a dancer I could be. I didn't want to go where the ofays went — except to the show itself. I couldn't help myself about wanting to go to the show — but I set out to find one where they wouldn't go.

I was going someplace where the audience was always and only colored. I didn't know where that was . . . but I was determined to find it.

That's how I got to Detroit. That's how I left the Natchez Belle in Chicago, following Eddie Plique.

LIBATION FOR THE FEAST DAY OF EDDIE PLIQUE:
Contortion Art

1 jigger of gin
1 pony of French vermouth

Place ingredients in a large mixing glass

with ice. Stir and strain into a cocktail glass.

WEEK 4
FOURTH SUNDAY
AFTER FATHER'S DAY

Not every girl who walked into the Ziggy Johnson School of the Theatre came from a perfect home. Colored Girl and whole lot of other girls walked through the door knowing her mother was what the old women called "different." Ziggy learned what he needed to know about "different" mothers from his friend Night Train.

Every girl who walked into Ziggy's school learned a technique Ziggy deemed essential for dance and life, spotting, the trick dancers use spinning through turns. The key, according to Ziggy, was to keep returning head and eyes to a fixed distant point, a chosen spot, increasing the dancer's control and preventing dizziness. Ziggy's Ballet Babes spent hours twirling across a studio spotting to an invisible point on a wall — and to their future.

In 1974 Night Train was inducted into the Pro Football Hall of Fame. He died in

2002. As of this writing his record of 14 interceptions in a single season, 1952, has yet to be broken.

Night Train Lane

PATRON SAINT OF: *Junkmen, the Adopted, Widows, and Widowers*

When it's time for me to go, I will only need one pallbearer: Night Train Lane. That particular six feet and one inch of Texas could hunch over, hike my casket onto his never-broken-back, and walk me solo to the cemetery soil. I won't need a hearse. Don't want six white horses, or a second line. Let the greatest defensive back who ever played the game, Richard "Night Train" Lane, tote me the last mile of my final trip.

Some say they called him Night Train because the NFL superstar was afraid to fly, so he took night trains to the next game. Some say it's because the song "Night Train" was popular when he was starting out in pro ball. None of that's right.

I called him "Night Train" because night trains are the most dangerous kind. They speed out of the cloaking dark and kill you. Delivered by my Night Train, the devil will be scared to see me coming. Everybody and everything is scared of Night Train, and

Night Train is scared of nothing. That's why I love him.

I had a weekend gig in St. Louis, helping a fellow out who was dashing Vegas to get married, at a time when there were a lot of stick-ups happening around Gaslight Square. At 2:00 a.m. when you're out of town, the walk from the club to the hotel can be a treacherous block. Not with Night Train. Fortunately, my gig was during the NFL off season. Night Train doesn't carry a gun, but there's a glint in his gaze that even jumpy young punks recognize, a glint that professional criminals cross the street to avoid faster than they avoid the shine on the barrel of a Smith & Wesson 60. The "I fear nothing" glint. The glint that says: "Nothing about moving on me, or my friend, will be easy."

Night Train throws an arm around my shoulder, and his courage is contagious. That's why I call him over to Kirwood Hospital anytime I suspect Bob Bennett is bringing bad news. I summoned Night Train today. If I wasn't in Kirwood, I wouldn't still be alive. They got a machine that's doing most of the work my kidneys should be doing that the state of Michigan doesn't see fit to use on anybody who's not a veteran and white — but anything can fall

60

off the back of a truck. Or maybe they rigged something up. They borrowed some time for me. I want to know exactly how much. Dr. Bodywork says there is no "exactly." He's trying to balance helping out my kidneys with helping out my heart. When I press, Bodywork says, "A month, two months, Zig."

Night Train drapes his arm on my shoulder, and I can't be afraid. Night Train says, "You ain't dying today. Today we smile. When you die, I'll do all the crying. You'll be upstairs with Nat King Cole and that pretty Elsie Roxborough you always telling me about, and you gonna have my Dinah on your lap." That's what Night Train says. We laugh until it hurts my chest. I keep laughing 'cause it's pure joy to laugh with Night Train, pain or no pain.

He was born in Austin, Texas. His daddy was a mack man, a pimp, called Texas Slim. His mother worked for his father. Three months after he slid into the world, the woman he slid out of (or someone close to her) wrapped him in newspaper and put him out with the trash. Later that day, a different woman lifted an infant from a junk heap.

Ella Lane was strolling down East 9th Street when she heard a strained, high-pitched cry. She dug through scraps and filth, thinking she would find a cat that needed to be choked out of its misery. She found a brown baby boy. Thinking of the princess who picked Moses up from the bulrushes, Ella reached down for the babe who would be my last good friend. She took him home, named him Richard Lane, and raised him as her own. This meant she beat him hard with a leather strap to teach him right from wrong.

Over time and pain, he grew hard and long. And he *did* learn right from wrong. His worst day had happened, and he had survived it. The one who rescued him was the one who beat him, was the one who loved him. He was coming on sixteen years old and six feet tall and still growing when he embraced that complexity.

He played Texas high school football. That's saying something. And he played it like you can only play with an unworried mind.

When you're not worried about pain, not worried about receiving it, not worried about inflicting it, not worried about when it will come again, because you know pain will always come again, you play Night Train's way. Accepting pain when it came, as a teaching tool, doling it out, when necessary, dispassionately, this was the essence of his maturity and the engine of his kinetic genius. He played like nobody with a worry or a fear, and that was almost everybody else. The local papers took notice.

Ella Lane kept a thickening scrapbook full of Richard Lane's clippings on her lap and a thin strap by her side.

The boy tried to make it in a junior college; he didn't hack it. Soon he was in the military, wishing he was on a football field. Then he was discharged and in California, working on an aircraft assembly line, wishing he was on a football field. He took his old high school scrapbook out of the back of his closet, tucked it under his arm, and rode a bus across town to where the Los Angeles Rams practiced.

He talked his way onto the practice field with the help of his Mama-made scrapbook. Then he caught and blocked his way onto the team with the help of Mama-made memories of Mama's strap.

He had come up all kinds of hard, but his ambition was green and vibrant, the way ambition can only be when the inside of a heart is soft. In the third month of his life he had been the center of a miracle: He had found the sweet in a hard woman's love, and he was ready to make the best of what he had been given, ever after. He never meditated long on the moment of being thrown away; he saved all his attention for the moment of rescue. He didn't focus on the mama who put him down in the trash; he focused on the mama who picked him up from the trash. He won for her.

The first year Night Train played for the Los Angeles Rams, he set records that are yet to be broken. He invented a kind of tackle that was so effective that they first gave it a name, the "Night Train Necktie," but then the NFL commissioners outlawed it. Said it was too vicious. Yet his opponents rose in respectful awe of him. They knew: You have to be a man to wear Night Train's tie. When you felt his hit, there was no hate in it — just the will to win for Ella, his mama.

I loved to watch him intercept. The ball will be going in one direction from the hands of a quarterback to a receiver, and Night Train gets between those two men, puts his huge body in vertical motion, arches his torso, and curves his arm high, eclipsing even the famous ballet dancer Nureyev, and plucks that ball out of the sky. Suddenly the game is going in a new direction.

Other men played out of rage, and anger,

and desperation. Night Train played out of love and ambition.

He was a man who wasted no time on self-pity. But more than this, he was a man who never got numb to pain, or took pleasure in inflicting pain, but rather a man who refused to be distracted by it.

Night Train never made pain the focus or the locus of connection, except on a football field. And with Ella Lane as his mama and Texas Slim as the closest thing he had to a daddy, that was no small achievement. I loved the man. Not for how he played a game but for how he taught me to think in new ways about living when I thought I was full-wise to life.

He was a small part of the reason I finally got married. Night Train insisted that wedded bliss was the highest high ever.

It was 1960 when I met him, after one of his first games as a Lion. My School of the Theatre was eight years old. I was forty-seven years old and Night Train was thirty-two.

I was dazzled from jump. Night Train was different than anyone I ever knew — tougher and more vulnerable — and I knew Joe Louis. I knew Sugar Ray Robinson. Night Train was wild wind blowing from the shore of hard Texas love, and he revived me. To thank Night Train, I introduced him to the most passionate woman I have ever known, Ruth Lee Jones, aka Dinah Washington.

Ruth Lee came up from Alabama. Like me, she entered the Chicago scene when she was a child. She was one of the original Sallie Martin Gospel Singers. I didn't pay too much mind to that. The first time I heard her, and paid attention, it was at Dave's Rhumboogie. Next time I saw her she was upstairs at the Garrick, and Billie Holiday was downstairs and she wasn't Ruth Jones anymore; she was Dinah Washington. By '46 she had a hit with "Ain't Misbehavin'."

Now *that* was just a lie. Dinah Washington never behaved. Always armed with a pistol, always immaculate, cussing and fussing and fist fighting. The woman sang like Night Train intercepted — brilliantly — but she didn't behave. At a time when people didn't get divorced, Dinah got divorced six times.

Raw wasn't the point for Dinah. Unexpected was the point. If she loved you, taking care of you before she took care of herself was the point.

She loved Katie Basie. After Basie married his Katie, she became one of the sidditiest of siddity sisters. Katie, aka Mrs. Catherine Morgan Basie, never met a social

66

or civic club she didn't want to join, never was invited on a club trip she didn't want to take, and never chaired a gala without setting out to break its fund-raising record. Sometime in the fifties, or maybe it was the late forties, Katie decided Dinah was the perfect person to record a specialty number for one of her pet charities. Dinah said yes. Then Dinah heard the call time for the recording session. Dinah said no. She and the world were attending a birthday bash the night before Katie's scheduled 9:00 a.m. session. Katie signed on some lesser singer not invited to the party. Katie arrived at the studio at 8:45 a.m. She was led into the dark control booth by the engineer, who flicked on the light. There, sprawled on a couch, sleeping in her mink, was Dinah. Ready. At nine she was at the mike, helping Katie shine.

Dinah was a falling star when Night Train came to Detroit town to play for the Lions in 1960. She had as many enemies as friends and a speckled reputation, except among those of us who had — like Katie — been the beneficiary of her speckled generosity. And those of us who appreciated what it meant to bend a note so that it bent time. Night Train appreciated the bending of notes as much as Dinah appreciated the way he arched his back to love her. A few years after I introduced Night Train to Dinah in Detroit, they got married in Las Vegas.

It was his second marriage. It was her seventh. I had known Dinah with all her husbands, and this was the one. They were so good together.

Dinah wasn't intimidated. And Dinah didn't have her hand out. Night Train wasn't intimidated, and Night Train didn't have his hand out. They were on their way to happily-ever-after when fate intercepted.

The first year they were married, just before Christmas, Night Train was sleeping peacefully beside his wife when she stopped breathing. Seconal and something. Dinah went to sleep and didn't wake up. She died younger than Bessie, younger than Billie. She was thirty-nine years old. From Alabama. A big girl. Big and brown and beautiful. And dead.

All the presents, carefully chosen by Dinah, were wrapped and waiting under the Christmas tree.

Night Train sent her upstairs in a bronze casket, wearing a mink. His tears rained down on that fur. In this life I have never seen anything sad-saltier than Night Train's face as he leaned, weeping, over his wife's open casket.

68

He would have run into a brick wall for Dinah Washington. But he couldn't stop her from taking diet pills because she feared she wasn't small and pretty enough to be a big star again and to keep him forever. She didn't know she was so much more than good enough. She was his best of the best. She hadn't been with Night Train long enough to see herself through eyes sharpened by loving and being loved.

Christmas swirled around and into the funeral. A dazed Night Train watched her children and sisters open gift and notes she had prepared for them. What was it someone said at the wake? "He took care of her and she took care of them." And someone else said, "At long last, someone was taking care of her." Someone bigger and stronger than Dinah was big and strong, indeed. What did she write in *Sepia* magazine? "I have been hurt, humiliated, kicked around, robbed, maligned by lies. Name it, it has happened to me, but I refuse to give up. . . . I'll go on giving, loving and searching for the happiness I want. And if everything else fails, as that famous song said, I'll give my heart to the junkman."

In her own way, she did just that. Night Train started off life wrapped in a newspaper set down into the trash. Sometimes these days, after his football season is over, not just after a game, if he gets deep in his cups Night Train will say, "I am the junk-man."

LIBATION FOR THE FEAST DAY OF
NIGHT TRAIN LANE:
The Junkman's Julep

1 jigger of Copper & Kings American brandy
1 bar spoon of Smith & Cross Jamaican rum
1 sugar cube
1/2 pony of water
Mint

In the bottom of a metal julep cup, place the sugar cube and water and slightly muddle. Next add 6 or 7 mint leaves and the brandy, then stir briefly. Top with crushed ice. Using a spoon, slowly churn the crushed ice to chill the julep cup. Be careful not to pull the mint out of the bottom of the cup. With clean hands place a final mound of crushed ice atop the drink. Onto this ice pour your rum. Decorate lavishly with mint. Serve with a straw.

SUMMER MOVEABLE FEAST
JUNETEENTH

Sometime between the announcement, in the last days of the 20th century, of the forthcoming publication of her first novel (a triumph that Colored Girl associated with Ziggy's insistence that her eighth birthday cake should be decorated with a frosting replica of Arna Bontemps's novel *Black Thunder,* because Ziggy knew Colored Girl was going to be a writer) and the arrival of the novel in hardback into bookstores, Colored Girl's mother was diagnosed with advanced lung cancer. Her mother called with the news. And a request for a visit. It had been over a decade since mother and daughter had been in the same room.

Colored Girl had flown into Washington, DC, alone for the visit. During the plane's descent she had had a view of the Lincoln Memorial, the Washington Monument, and the Tidal Basin. She had been eight years

71

old the first time she had seen these buildings from the air; back then she had believed that she was flying into a picture book as the plane circled Arlington National Cemetery.

When Joe Louis died in 1981, President Ronald Reagan waived the requirements for burial in Arlington National Cemetery, where the Brown Bomber was buried with full military honors. Colored Girl's father declared that act to be Reagan's single shining hour.

Joe Louis

PATRON SAINT OF: *Sons, Representation, and Filial Piety*

Joe Louis was born in Alabama in 1914, a year after me. I was his senior and had been born "up South" so I had those two points over him. Joe had all the other points on me. He was over six foot tall. Beautiful. He had the heart of the smartest, prettiest, richest Black girl in Detroit, Elsie Roxborough. More than all that, Joe Louis was a global hero. Got there in three steps. First, he was our hero, when he whupped Braddock. Then he knocked out Max Schmeling in 1938 and he was America's hero. Then with the Nazis walking out and about, trampling everything, and the rise of Nazism, he became the world's hero.

The way Louis knocked out Schmeling was the way Churchill wanted to knock out Hitler, the way France wanted to knock out Mussolini. Joe made the Harlem Hellfighters proud. Noble Sissle, a Harlem Hellfighter, told me that. And he knew Henry Johnson, the Albany, New York, train station porter the Germans called "Black Death" because he was so lethal.

Only once was it hard to look at Joe. When Max Schmeling knocked him out in 1936, a Black girl in New York City was so distraught about the outcome of that fight she went into a pharmacy and drank poison. That stayed with me. A decade and a half later, when I opened my school, I was working to give my students what Joe had and that girl didn't: the will to rise from defeat.

On June 22, 1937, Joe Louis fought James Braddock and won with a knockout. Let me tell you what my breadwinners say: "Louis hit Braddock with a left hook into the breadbasket! Then he took a stance, rooted his feet deep in an Alabama cotton field his daddy had worked, and he followed that left hook with a right to the kisser. Braddock went straight down, like the bones in his knees dissolved, then fell over on his right side, unconscious. They counted to ten and he didn't wake up. For two minutes Braddock was sleeping the sleep of the beat."

When President Kennedy was killed, a question arose in the world that will be asked until the last witness dies: "Where were *you* when you heard the news?" Our children's children's children will know where we were when we heard Joe Louis win. It had taken seventy-five years, but Louis translated Lincoln's Emancipation Proclamation into body language that everybody understood. That was the beginning of our new world. Sepians across the country broke up from little circles gathered around radios to celebrate and cheer all night long, into a first new morning.

That gets remembered. This gets forgotten: Joe at home watching television in his house shoes and robe, faded cotton drawers, and undershirt. Phone rings. A bartender calling from a little joint near Joe's, saying a girl is crying at a table with a bruise on her face and there's a man with her who won't leave. Two 45's don't drop in the jukebox before Joe blasts in, fancy Moroccan leather house shoes still on his feet, faded underclothes under a silk robe. He stopped no longer than it took for him to pick up the two rolls of quarters he kept by his front door in an ashtray. Joe didn't have to say a word. After he watched the man out the door, Joe put the rolls of quarters on the bar. "The juke is on the house tonight."

He heard us. And by "us" I mean sepians. He heard his mama tell him to pick up a violin. He heard his first sparring partner tell him to put the violin down. He heard John Roxborough tell him not to stand near white women. Not to fall into the Jack Johnson trap. To live clean. To wear nice clothes. To buy a lot in Idlewild and to stay at the little hotel nearby until he built his house. He heard me say how marvelous Marva was, so he married her. He heard Ted Rhodes talk about the joys of golf. Heard that so loud it lost him that first Schmeling fight. Heard Killerman whispering to him as he walked into the ring for the second fight, "Ten thousand of my own riding on this." The bartender, trying to shield a bruised girl. Joe heard us all.

If I am out and about in Idlewild at two in the morning, I'm moving toward the doesn't-close-until-dawn club El Morocco. And I am hoping that when I get there I will find Joe Louis.

If I find Joe Louis and he offers me the seat beside him and a Cutty Sark, dawn will come sweet. Joe Louis, the Brown Bomber, the greatest fighter the world had ever seen, is Idlewild glue. Everybody wants to sit with Joe Louis. The doctors. The doctors' wives. The hustlers. The policy kings. The numbers barons, and all their women. The dentists, the lawyers, the politicians. Our butchers, bakers, and candlestick makers (yes, I met an ironworker at Idlewild who made ornate fences and candlesticks), they all want to be with him, too. Proud Teddy Rhodes, who likes to travel solo, sticks so close to Louis that when they are in the same room we call them Siamese Twins.

And when our earliest breadwinners, the first wave of the Great Migration, men who worked the line at Ford, Briggs, and Dodge, our first factories, landed on the shores of Idlewild, renting rooms at the Giles Hotel or Rainbow Manor, these breadwinners wanted to be with Joe Louis, more than anybody else.

I have watched breadwinners' eyes caress the Brown Bomber. I have heard so many variations on the verse "He just like me. Up from Alabama, living in Detroit. Got it done. Whatever needed doing. Forged muscle into good life. Got after it day and night. Just like me." With fight tickets in his pocket, a breadwinner had a pocket full of gold.

Fifty-two knockouts in sixty-nine fights. Only three losses in his professional career. The way he punched it was art and church at the same time. His body, his mind, his soul all saying this one intricate thing: "I'm 'bama bad down to my Black Detroit bones, and that's as good as it gets."

Joe Louis won! When that's not enough, it's a very bad day. There have been more days like that lately.

LIBATION FOR THE FEAST DAY OF JOE LOUIS:
Dawn Comes Sweet

2 jiggers of Jamaican rum
1 bar spoon of molasses
1 pony of cold water

Place ingredients into a bar glass. Stir until molasses is dissolved. Add ice.

WEEK 5
FIFTH SUNDAY
AFTER FATHER'S DAY

An hour after she hung up with her mother, the oncologist called.

Colored Girl had learned that her mother was expected to live longer than four months, but no longer than two years. She heard the news in Nashville, sitting in Bullock's Black Bottom Bar. After stating the facts, the oncologist asked if she had any questions, to which she replied, "None that you can answer." Soon Colored Girl was back on the phone to make plane reservations and to rearrange her schedule and budget to make monthly visits to DC a new reality.

She was her mother's only child. She had questions she wanted answered. She had an object that she wanted to retrieve, if it still existed — if it had ever existed. And she wanted, at long last, her mother's love. She believed that if she walked the woman to her death, they might find their way to that peace.

On her first visit, the mother offered the daughter a chair opposite a large and charming box with an avocado, harvest gold, and orange flower pattern. The box was conspicuously marked with thick black marker, "Mari's Papers."

Seeing the box stung Colored Girl. The mother purred, "Someone is walking over your grave. You may die before I do." Colored Girl forced a smile and started wondering how near the closest bar was, whether it was too early to start drinking, and how long she had to stay before she could politely leave. She calculated she could manage 120 minutes.

Sixty minutes in, her mother abruptly stood and inquired as to when she could expect Colored Girl's next visit. She was dismissed. Colored Girl wasn't ready to leave. She asked about the box. Her mother replied, "We'll get to that." Colored Girl took her leave, offering the same deep bow of her head that she had offered as greeting.

She exited her mother's lobby wondering where the nearest bar was. She appreciated a good bar. As a native Detroiter, she appreciated any bar at all. Black Detroit from the end of the Second World

War up to the end of the Vietnam War was a city of taverns, showbars, and illegal after-hours joints, called "blind pigs." Colored Girl's father had been an alcoholic. As soon as she was out of high chairs she could balance on a barstool. A barmaid at The Flame invented a drink for her, after her father, before he got sober, backhanded a Shirley Temple off the bar top, snarling, "Don't be handing my child anything called a Shirley Temple!" Before long there were half a dozen bars in Detroit that served up an Althea Gibson (Vernors ginger ale with a maraschino cherry, and a drizzle of juice from the cherry jar), as soon as Colored Girl toddled through their door. When her father stopped drinking hard liquor, an Althea Gibson became his drink, too. All that ended the day her mother kidnapped her from St. Philip's Lutheran School and spirited her off to DC. Colored Girl checked her watch. It was noon. The nearest bar was on the corner. She ordered a Blue Blazer. It was a good bar.

Thomas Bullock published *The Ideal Bartender* in 1917. It has a foreword written by President George W. Bush's great-grandfather. The date of Bullock's death is unknown.

Thomas Bullock

PATRON SAINT OF: *Drunks, Drinkers, and Domestic Workers*

When I landed in St. Louis in 1939 for what was supposed to be a short stint that ended up lasting almost a year, long enough for me to live through coal-fog so thick street-lights had to stay on in the daylight, I immediately set out to meet Mr. Bullock. Everybody I asked knew about him. They knew he was a Kentuckian by birth, that his father was a colored Union soldier and an Exoduster who headed west only to get stranded in St. Louis because racist steamboat captains wouldn't take *us* across the Mississippi River. But no one actually knew him. They did know where I might-could find him, the St. Louis Country Club, a place I couldn't go unless I took up waiting tables or caddying.

I worked the Plantation Club in St. Louis. It looked something like a Moorish temple. It should have had white columns and magnolia trees. The entire audience was white — or passing. All the performers were Black.

That's the thing about St. Louis: On the map it appears to be located in the Midwest. In reality St. Louis is located in a segregated

81

South, filthy with paddleboat gambling, river mud, and hot white hate.

So many of my Saints played the Plantation Club: Billy Eckstine, Nat King Cole, and the Mills Brothers. Sarah Vaughan and Billie Holiday played there, too.

If any place was more opposite from Detroit and the Black Bottom and Paradise Valley bars and supper clubs, it was St. Louis and the Plantation Club.

What I liked least about the Plantation Club? They plastered caricatures of us, drawings of darkies with protruding lips and gawking eyes on every matchbook, napkin, menu, and newspaper advertisement associated with or in the Plantation Club.

Why? I suspect they hoped their filthy-as-homemade-sin visual lies would inoculate white folk from the shock of Black beauty. That left me, and many of the rest of the entertainers, exodusing for the inner sanctum of drunk.

Sometimes we got nasty-silly. There was the legendary night when chocolate-brown Tadd Dameron walked through the Plantation Club drinking out of the ornate wine glasses that decorated the club's tables, with Charlie "Bird" Parker following behind, smashing the filigreed drinking glasses to "protect" white patrons from drinking out of the vessels that Dameron had "contaminated." Bird loudly declared, "Get yo'self a jelly jar! Don't contaminate the white folks' wetter water." I loved Tadd for writing "If You Could See Me Now," for Sarah Vaughan, but I loved him more for putting his beautiful lips on those ugly Plantation Club glasses.

That was a joke that Thomas Bullock would appreciate. He was a country club bartender barred from tasting the drinks he mixed. Of course, he tasted the drinks, just not when ofays were looking.

I met Thomas Bullock by accident. Walked into a hole-in-the-wall that poured a fine tipple and saw him at a back table, drinking alone. He still resembled his photo in *The Ideal Bartender.* When I dropped Butterbeans's name, he invited me to sit. We would meet once or twice a week. From the first, he would step behind the bar and make me a drink that he served me from beautiful silver cups that he always kept in the large pocket of his overcoat, folded on the back of his chair. That overcoat was both garment and valise. It was a great privilege to drink from those cups. One was engraved in big swirly script, across the front, with the letter "T" and the other with the letter "B." On the bottom in small letters each cup was stamped "pc" and with some symbol I didn't recognize.

One day I found him at his usual table in our usual spot and I asked for a Blazer, and he said he couldn't make me one. He had lost his cups. We agreed on a different drink, a whiskey smash.

A few weeks later, I happened to see Bullock's cups in a pawnshop window. I didn't have the money to buy them back and also to send money for my daughter in my weekly letter to the Natchez Belle. Sometimes when you need a little help, God sends a belligerent drunk backstage after the show with a pocket full of money. Sometimes he sends an old woman in an expensive suit with a veiled hat on her head and diamonds bulging through her leather gloves. Sometimes he sends both. Sometimes God makes the sun too bright, then when you're just about to die from the heat, he sends one cloud, then another, leaving you grateful for belligerent drunks and for gloved diamond hands. Most of the time when you need a little extra money, you don't get any. I was grateful.

A few days later, I found Bullock at our usual table in our usual hole-in-the-wall. I took my usual seat, tucking an unusual tote sack beneath my feet.

"Week I had, I need a Blue Blazer. Make me one."

"I pawned my cups, Zig."

"Happy birthday, fool!"

I wish I'd said something prettier, but that's what I said. I had seen those cups in the pawnshop window and that had hurt me. Hurt me for him. Hurt me for *me*. So, I did what I did. I said what I said. Then I pulled two mottled gray cups out of my tote sack and pushed them across the little bar table toward Thomas.

"How?"

"Did what I had to do."

He didn't ask me what that was. He reached across the table and put both his cold hands on my face. Those hands that had — what did he say? — "opened doors of perception and windows of imagination and broken shackles of anxiety" were soft. He kissed me smack on the lips like a man kisses a dear friend who has done him a great service. Then Bullock pushed the cups back to me.

"You earned them."

"*You* earned them."

"Now they better than earned. They gifted."

"Thank you, Zig."

He took the cups and stepped behind the

bar. As usual, the bartender didn't stop him or ask him to pay. The bartender stepped back and watched as Bullock, with shaking hands, made me a Blue Blazer, the drink you can only make in metal cups, pouring the blue liquor back and forth until the flames go out.

I stayed too long in St. Louis.

LIBATION FOR THE FEAST DAY OF TOM BULLOCK:
The Blue Blazer

Two pewter cups or silver mugs
1 tsp. of bar sugar dissolved in a little hot
   water
1 jigger of Scotch whisky
Lemon peel

Ignite the mixture and while it blazes pour
it several times from one cup or mug into
the other. Top with a piece of twisted
lemon peel.

WEEK 6
SIXTH SUNDAY
AFTER FATHER'S DAY

Colored Girl visited her mother's sickbed on the first Tuesday of each month. The visit would begin with her mother giving her something from the flowery box that had once belonged to Colored Girl but had long ago been seized: a postcard from her grandmother, a childhood journal, a cardboard kaleidoscope.

The kaleidoscope was one of the few toys that migrated with Colored Girl from Detroit to Washington. The mother said the kaleidoscope had been a gift from Ziggy. Colored Girl didn't remember Ziggy's giving her the toy. She did remember the day that it vanished. She had broken her mother's DC house rules, she had called her father, after a new friend told the area code for Detroit and how to use it, not knowing phone bills existed and were snitches. Her mother waved the phone bill in her face, seized the kaleidoscope, and then stomped out of the room. Colored Girl could not avoid a new truth: The white world made Mean Mama meaner.

Tucking the kaleidoscope into the tote bag that tripled as carry-on and purse, Colored Girl mused that memory was too much like a kaleidoscope: the same old bits and shards fall into ever-new shapes, as you twist or are twisted. She shivered. Her mother smiled.

Each sickbed visit would end once her mother handed her carefully inked cards with updated medical information: most recent test results, current prescriptions, a list of unintended side effects that she was experiencing (from hair loss to foot fungus), and possible remedies, ranging from Rogaine and Lamisil to cold caps and vinegar baths. After the health update, the cards would be returned to their card box where they were organized by chronology, and the mother would want to talk about her will.

On every visit Colored Girl attempted to avoid these discussions, as her mother focused on "how my money will be dispersed, should you die before me." She had an explanation: "If I die first, there is nothing to decide. Everything goes to you." It was disturbing to look into the face of someone with purply-red spots blooming on her arms and legs, repeating as often as she could possibly work the words into the conversation, "if you die first, I want . . ." This would be followed by a laundry list of directives and requests that changed on every visit. During one visit the mother wanted Colored Girl to re-search the possibility of endowing a schol-arship to something her mother thought might be called "Cordie's Castle Charm School," in Indianapolis. "It will tick Cordie off to realize I have enough money to leave her some. Ziggy thought so much of her for rising from Water Valley. Water Val-ley was nothing so hard!"

The mother was wrong. Colored Girl might not remember being gifted the kaleidoscope; she did remember Ziggy telling her that Water Valley was an outpost of hell on Earth, that fire there burned hot-ter than molten lava but didn't destroy, that pain in Water Valley was without end. Water Valley was some place worse than DC with Bette. Long ago, that knowledge had stopped Colored Girl from feeling sorry for herself.

Cordie King Stuart

PATRON SAINT OF: *Impoverished People, Jet-Setters, and Alumni of Alumni*

My Mississippi was not Cordie's Mississippi. The Natchez Belle came from incense and church candlelight. Cordie King came from cotton fields and creosote smoke. When Cordie was born in 1924, Water Valley was a train depot town. She saw, and heard, and felt thirty trains a day rumbling in and out. From the moment she was born, circus cars, banana cars, timber cars all rolled through. The most memorable thing about Water Valley other than the fact Cordie was born there is that it was the site of a quadruple murder that involved two Black men and two of the town's most prominent citizens.

The Water Valley killings occurred in 1931 when Cordie still lived there. The way the ofay press told the story, there was a Black man, Sam Green Whitaker, who stole a gun from his white employer. The employer discovered the theft, slapped Sam, and told him to go home and come back the next day, when he would be whipped. Sam went home. Or so we think. We know he came back and killed his abusive employer, then killed the man's wife. Or maybe he killed

90

the wife with a knife, then killed the man with a gun. Maybe he was defending himself or someone he loved. His sister, Adelle, and his best friend, Emmett Shaw, assisted him in dragging one of the bodies to a ditch and talking through why the killing had to be done and why there was no use in trying to run. It is said that that all happened. By the time the cleaning woman, also Black, arrived the next morning, the folks she worked for, Mr. and Mrs. Wagner, were dead. Now, Wagner had been the president of the local bank and also had owned the Water Valley department store. Did he believe he also owned Sam Green Whitaker? Why did he think Sam would come back for a beating? And why were his sister and his best friend, Emmett Shaw, so willing to assist in the aftermath of dramatic death?

Police took Sam Green Whitaker and Emmett Shaw to the jail in Greenwood. When they dragged Emmett Till to his death in Mississippi in 1955, some of us said we didn't *need* any young Black men named Emmett anywhere in America! Some of us were remembering Shaw as well as Till. After the trial, Sam and his friend were hanged. The trial took less time than the hanging. The younger sister, brave and strong enough to help the boys move Mr.

Wagner's body, Adelle Whitaker, was sentenced to five years.

Cordie King became a witness that the world could change. That banker and his wife seemed untouchable. Sam Whitaker was hanged by his neck until he died — but that didn't bring Mr. and Mrs. Wagner back to life. The powers that be, don't always stay in power. Sometimes the untouchable get touched. That murder made a lot of things bad for a lot of Black people, because the whites got so afraid. But it was a light that showed some things. Cordie followed that light out of Mississippi.

The hangings took place on Friday, July 17, 1931. That was just about the time that Cordie's family moved from Water Valley, Mississippi, to Wilson, Arkansas. Cordie toted her memory of and questions about Adelle, the brave and strong, with her to Arkansas.

Cordie and her family, at least everybody old enough to walk, share-cropped in Wilson, working for the Lee family, who paid Cordie's stepfather with small circles of metal, some marked with ones, some with fives, that the Wilson family passed off as money. But this was script, only good at the store the Lee family owned. In Wilson, Cordie worked ten months out of twelve and went to school two. Her life was picking cotton and milking cows and sometimes having a little metal disc that someone lied and called a coin to show for it. She grew beautiful under that sun, and continued to side with Adelle and her choice to help her brother, even as Cordie began wondering, provoked by fragments of gossip she heard, if Mr. Wagner wasn't her father. She had also heard Mr. Wagner had tried to get on top of Adelle.

In 1941, at seventeen years old, Cordie decamped to Chicago. It would take her another eight or nine years to be "discovered." She didn't like to talk about those years. But one fine day, the little brown chef herself, Freda DeKnight, the *Ebony* magazine food editor, who was stepping beyond food into fashion and planning the very first Ebony Fashion Fair, saw Cordie — and the rest is history.

International beauty contests, an engagement to Sammy Davis, mentions in the papers, our papers, their papers, over 10,000 pictures of her taken. None of that changed this: Cordie King had arrived in Chicago grown.

Her worst day was behind her. She could lie down all the rest of her life, and at eighteen she would have worked harder than most people work in a lifetime. Before her hands were bejeweled, they were paws. She had been worked like a farm animal. As an act of revolution, she set about to create something of herself no one expected, someone fine. Someone who had nothing to do with the hard and greedy places whence she had come. She was determined to be beautiful on her own terms. She would be for others what Adelle had been for her: a colored enigma who inspired.

Cordie kept her thoughts, wild and unpredictable, the opposite of how she kept her body and her days. She gave me a calendar each year for Christmas and a new Timex watch each year for my birthday. She believed that a fiercely organized life could best contain rage and fear, and thus a fiercely organized life was the best protection of her fragile and tender hope. She was right. When I first met her, her eyes were animated with a thrilling and rigid complexity that announced that her sanity couldn't be deranged. Some part of her self-knowledge was so well organized that it could not be tangled or eclipsed.

She was hitched to the home truth of her own value and her own courage. She knew the immensity of believing "I am better than this." Better than Water Valley, Mississippi, better than Wilson, Arkansas.

When Cordie later founded her charm school, she always taught that the first rule of charm school was to be alert, and the second was to be loyal. Let people know that you see them, and that you like what you see — do that and people will be captivated. I also teach that.

Some beauties, their eyes are dead and their smiles are false. There are dull chorus lines with beautiful dolls, everything perfect, but their souls are empty. Cordie has the "singed-sational" soul of a phoenix. Looking into her eyes, some of us got a promise of being born again, more certain than we got when reading the Bible.

I knew before *she* knew that her face was pretty enough to be her fate and her future. I first saw her — not to meet her, mind you, just saw her — on a Chicago street shortly after she had arrived. That was, I believe, in 1941 or in 1942, when I came back to open the Rhumboogie. She was ten or eleven years younger than me. She was taller than me, and she was more beautiful than I ever hoped to be, but she didn't know how to use it yet.

A week later, she snuck into my dressing room at the Club Delisa. Too hungry to drink without eating, and too determined to stay model-thin to eat, she loved to sequester herself backstage where she could hear the show and curl in a chair with a copy of the *Defender* (she was hell-bent on bettering her mind) and a glass of warm water and lemon. If she didn't like or love you, Cordie didn't give away many opportunities to look at her in the flesh — the best you got was a gander at a photograph of her in the magazines or papers. Fortunately, she liked me. When I got offstage, we headed for a diner where we could drink coffee until sunrise and then eat breakfast — the one meal each day she allowed herself.

She did most of the talking over that first coffee. I did the looking — at her — and the being seen with her. To be seen with Cordie was an instant high.

She knew what she wanted. She wanted to be acclaimed, she wanted to settle down, and she didn't want children. She thought life in America was too hard for a Black child. But she wanted students and a husband — and she wanted that husband to be a worker, not so she need not work, but just so she could respect her man.

I paid the check. She wanted to pay the tip. She dumped her purse on the table. I was surprised she had a flask. It was full of mouthwash. She had bubble gum. There was a blood-red lipstick. A flat wallet. And there was a "sugar tit," a cotton handkerchief that had probably been washed and reknotted over a thousand times. The cotton handkerchief her grandmother had once soaked in sugar water and jerked into a knot, then handed to Cordie to accompany the child on the first finger-ripping day when she worked the fields. It was her most-prized possession. Last week I received a package in the mail from Cordie. It contained an ancient sugar tit, washed and perfumed, that now rests in my pillowcase with my pillow and soothes me.

In about 1956, she met Sammy Davis, and their romance was in all the papers, Black and white. Their engagement was even rumored. I wrote in the *Michigan Chronicle* that Sammy couldn't do better than her, but if someone would lay me eight to five, I would wager that that was a wedding that would never come off. Cordie had not the least bit of interest in living in a white world — and by the time she met him Sammy's world was white. And more than that, Sammy lived in a material world. Despite all appearances, Cordie was *not* a materialistic woman.

She was working as a model in a Fashion

Fair fashion show in Indianapolis when she met Matey Stuart.

In Matey, the richest man from a wealthy family, Cordie found a man who eclipsed her industry. He bought his first truck from a pawnshop. Never able to borrow money due to racial discrimination in "Naptown" banking practices, he washed windows in the middle of the night and cleaned the interiors of commercial buildings in the early mornings to finance the expansion of his company, moving from one truck to three. When he got the three trucks working good, he was able to pay for the expansion to a fleet that crisscrossed the country toting families from the Atlantic to the Pacific and even into Canada. Matey was on his way to being, or maybe he had just become, the biggest Black moving-company owner in America. He also owned real estate and a cab company. His daddy was a dentist; his brothers were undertakers. There was nothing about him or his that she had to apologize for, forget, or deny. His businesses were completely legitimate. And they were all in Indiana.

When Martin Luther King Jr. came to Indianapolis in 1961, Matey picked him up from the airport in his long, clean Cadillac and took him straight to Cordie's long, clean table. Every time after, whenever King came to Indianapolis, he would make a beeline to the Stuart home and Cordie would cook. King loved to tease Cordie about the *Ebony* magazine article in which she had first been profiled, titled "What Men Notice Most about Women." She had it all.

And she gave most of it away. One of my favorite gifts I have ever received was from Cordie: a first edition of Tom Bullock's cocktail recipe book, *The Ideal Bartender*. Cordie had learned about Bullock from *Ebony*'s food editor, Freda DeKnight. I never told Cordie that I actually knew Bullock before she made the introduction, or how well I knew him. It's important to accept gifts like Cordie did, graciously.

LIBATION FOR THE FEAST DAY OF CORDIE KING STUART:
Charm School

2 jiggers of dry sparkling wine
1 sugar cube
2 sprigs of bruised mint
1/2 pony of brandy
Crushed ice

Place sugar cube into the bottom of a

brandy snifter, add a splash of sparkling wine, muddle, add the mint leaves and further muddle, though briefly. Add the rest of the sparkling wine, the brandy, and crushed ice. Stir, being careful to leave all the mint at the bottom of the snifter. Serve with straws — preferably silver.

WEEK 7
SEVENTH SUNDAY
AFTER FATHER'S DAY

In 1904, five years after Sadye Pryor was born, the National Association of Colored Women's Clubs was incorporated with Mary Church Terrell as its first president and Mrs. Booker T. Washington and Harriet Tubman as early members.

Clubwomen . . . They have been dismissed as overconcerned with trivialities, including home economics and the "respectability" of the race.

Colored Girl saw the club women another way: as warrior women who fought the battle of making everyday and earnest Black living visible; as women working in the company of women, prizing the company of women, fighting Jim Crow with to-do lists and club meetings. Club Women were the DC mothers who reminded Colored Girl the most of Detroit mothers.

Ziggy had stock phrases that he repeated, classic lines that worked, so he recycled them year after year to different classes. One was "When I go, I'm not leaving you anything in my will, but that don't mean I don't love you! With warm hands I give you my sister Sadye!" She was in the center of the story passed down from class to class about the one time any students at the Ziggy Johnson School of the Theatre had ever seen Ziggy cry. He was telling the Tuesday ballet ladies about Sadye hanging her head and letting her voice quiver to win lifesaving lifeguards for the Black beach in Pensacola, Florida.

Ziggy said, "She played low not because she feared white men; but because she loved Black children." Ziggy added, "The Uncle Tom-Tap can be a powerful thing. Perfectly performed, it distracts ofays. When you get them distracted, you can steal them blind. But it's a costly show. Don't put it up unless you can steal something you need, not something you want."

When Colored Girl joined the Links in 1990, she was following in Sadye's footsteps. When she brought her passionate Black poet daughter in as a fourth generation Link, in 2015 she thought, "I am initiating my daughter into a secret cell, committing to lifting as we climb, waiting to be

102

activated." She thanked Ziggy right out loud for sharing his father's siddity sister.

Sadye E. Pryor

PATRON SAINT OF: *Teachers, Principals, and Librarians*

Sadye Pryor has been my secret weapon. More than one president of the PTA and more than one doctor's wife has encouraged a mother to send her daughter to a fancier, more formal dance school, a school where *only* the daughters of teachers and preachers were welcome, not the "riffraff" that the PTA president spat out that "came through the Ziggy Johnson door." I scared more than one bougie mama halfway to death when I told her my aunt was the actual Sadye Pryor. In the clubwomen world, Aunt Sadye was a queen.

Another place I love to drop her name? Around the pool at the Sir John Hotel in Miami. I started going there in 1957 when Bodywork Bennett treated me to the first vacation of my adult life. I was forty-four years old. Sadye was going on sixty. I was standing on a pool deck crowded with singers, models, colored baseball players, Black doctors, Black dentists, and Black lawyers and their wives when someone asked if I knew anyone in Florida. I answered humbly, "My aunt Sadye Pryor." The pool crowd parted like the sea before Moses. A silk-swathed matron in a turban approached, cooing, "Please beg your Aunt Sadye to run over for a visit."

Sadye does what Sadye chooses to do. Usually that's stay in Pensacola unless she's running to some national meeting. But once I drop her name, I am popular with the talented-tenth Negroes who typically sneer when they call my name. If I'm related to Sadye, they know I come from good stock.

What I know? We come from stern stuff. If Mississippi and Alabama are the belly of the beast that is Jim Crow, Florida is the beast's second stomach. Aunt Sadye taught me that. Born in 1899, she was raised around family who remembered being enslaved in Florida and was raised with even more family who remembered slavery's immediate aftermath.

The Pensacola of her family memory and childhood was both a city racked with race hate, yellow fever, and hunger *and* a cradle of political and economic opportunity for newly free men, women, and children.

Aunt Sadye has long said my father, her brother, moved north to Illinois hoping to land somewhere less contradictory than

104

Florida. Aunt Sadye decided to embrace the contradictions — then find respite from them on visits to the heaven she found in Detroit. Sadye loved Black Bottom.

Some people can't believe it till they see how much Sadye loves me. Why? We seem so different. From the outside Aunt Sadye and I could not be more different.

Sadye Pryor is a pillar of the Pensacola Mt. Zion Baptist Church. I myself see the inside of a church only when there's a funeral. Aunt Sadye wears glasses and frumpy sack dresses and looks studious. I was born dapper and will die dapper; I don't wear the reading spectacles I need. She is a librarian who's known for raising her eyebrows to get students to quiet down. I am a show producer known for raising my eyebrows to get kids to project louder. Yes, presidents of Motown PTAs have been known to question whether I am a fit example for our young ones, because I consort with show folk and gamblers and others associated with nightlife. Sadye Pryor maintains perfectly proper associates (fellow board members of the YWCA, members of the Eastern Star lodge she leads, fellow Sunday School teachers) and is lauded as an example of PTA-praiseworthy deportment. In Pensacola, indeed across Florida, and all around these United States. Sadye was born a virgin and by choice will likely die a virgin. Some folks call me the old reprobate.

But all that is from the outside. If I look at our goals from the inside, if I understand my business to be raising our small fry to be fully enfranchised citizens, Sadye and I share a common cause.

I have said that I have been jealous of Sammy Davis for having his father and his uncle making a way for him in his chosen profession. What keeps me from going completely green with envy? Sadye. I was born in 1913, Sadye in 1899. She was always just ahead of me, leading the way. My aunt began teaching in 1926. See it, be it. It was Sadye who showed me that teaching could be quietly political. Without Sadye I don't open my dance school.

Sadye, though she has been a classroom teacher as well as a principal, knows that the classroom, the schoolhouse, isn't the best place to catch a kid if you wanted to make the biggest impact. Church, dancing schools, and libraries were all better places to create high impact. She migrated to the library. I opened my dancing school. It might not have looked like it to anyone but us, but we were working in cahoots with each other.

People have often wondered how it came to be that I wasn't intimidated by Shirley McNeil. Sadye is the reason. Shirley had a PhD, but my aunt studied in the Ivy League, at Columbia University. Before she stopped collecting degrees, she had studied at the University of Iowa, University of Illinois, Columbia University, Bethune Cookman College, and St. Louis University.

For a time, I wasn't sure Sadye *got* me. In fact, I was rather sure she didn't. When she saw me down in Florida, on those rare occasions when I successfully persuaded her to join me poolside at the Sir John, promising to take her to see Nat King Cole or some other big Miami show she couldn't and wouldn't have gone to without me, I usually had a drink in one hand, a cigarette in the other, and some bikini-clad brown girl on my lap rubbing my shoulders trying to get cast in a show. This did little to raise me in Sadye's esteem.

Then she came up to visit Detroit in 1962. She saw me in action. Met some of my students. One night I took her to a bar where she had three cocktails and smoked a cigarette. I was stunned.

"They don't see it."

"What?"

"When they focus on our social climbing, they don't see the children we are lifting over the wall — hard, hungry, and able children prepared by us to make the Bible promise an earthly reality: the last shall be first."

"To the last being first!"

We clinked glasses and toasted to being complicit in each other's successful creation of cradles of sepian excellence. We were not coordinated but we *were* complicit. That night was the first and only time we got drunk together. She on three glasses, me on five. We saved the best toast for last.

This book was born in the aftermath of that toast. Sadye took a second sip, looked at the crowd, which included Massey, Bodywork, Shirley, Maxine, and Scatterbrain, and said, "They are not your friends, Nephew. They are your Black Bottom Saints. The way you talk about them inspires me to proceed."

Christmastime, three years ago. 1964. There was Sadye E. Pryor Night in Pensacola. I should have been there. But I was working, and had I attended she wouldn't have known what to do with me in one of my light-colored silk suits.

She was president of the PTA. She was the principal of Spencer Bibbs Elementary.

She helped found a Black YWCA and the C. B. Nelson Daniels Chapter #172 of the Eastern Star and was installed as a worthy matron. She was a national leader of Girl Scouts. If I sound proud, it is because I am, and she always played humble. Sadye knew Black girls made miracles — because she had been a Black girl making miracles. Every day, in every club, she worked alongside Black women who had been, but not acknowledged as being, shamans. Some came from hoodoo, some from conjure, some from vodun, but they stood on the shores of colored girl "mistery," that shrouded territory where misery is converted to mystery and power.

Watching Sadye work with her clubwomen sisters to finally win, in 1953, a beach that welcomed Black kids to swim, without also winning lifeguards that the white beaches had, started me on a road of discovery. Watching her continue to work against well-monied, elected, racist men eager to invite Black bodies into danger took me further down that discovery road as I heard about her grinding city commissioners down with silly questions, administrative technicalities, and treacle-sweet pleasantness. She had mother wit. It took mother wit to finally get the lifeguards the colored kids needed and deserved.

Girls and women will be increasingly the key to maintaining Black identity as we Black folk began to enter new predominantly white spaces with new difficulties and new dangers. Integration brought evil as well as good. Sadye saw this. Told me over drinks at the Sir John Hotel, "We need the magic box of your dancing school to intensify their soul-selves — their own inner magic box." She clutched the pearls at her neck when she said this next: "A string of pearls can be a shield. A dance school can be a lifeboat. So much gets diluted when we enter white space."

LIBATION FOR THE FEAST DAY OF SADYE E. PRYOR:
The Siddity Sister

1 jigger of Old Tom gin
1 pony of grenadine
1/2 lime, juiced
Lime zest
Mint sprigs

Place gin, grenadine, and lime juice in a cocktail shaker and shake with ice. Strain into a tall glass filled with ice cubes. Garnish with mint sprigs and lime zest.

110

SUMMER MOVEABLE FEAST: INDEPENDENCE DAY

Every time she disembarked from a plane in Washington, DC, Colored Girl found her right hand tightly clutching her left, as she squared her shoulders, straightened and lengthened her spine, pulled in her stomach.

In the cab from the airport to her mother's apartment, she prepared herself for the inevitable trauma: Small things jolted her back into the past. Once it was watching her mother file her nails with a Revlon emery board that triggered the memory of stinging abrasions. Another time the sight of Epsom salts made her gag. Once as the cab pulled to her mother's curb with the Fourth of July approaching, she shivered in the heat. Red, white, and blue bunting-festooned doorways. Street vendors selling flags.

Colored Girl and her mother had arrived in the Federal city in October in time for

Halloween. When they went to the store, the only costume left was Uncle Sam. The mother snarled dismissively, "You will look like nothing, like you belong in the Y Circus." If the Y Circus was nothing, the world, as Colored Girl knew it, had come to an end.

The Reverend Cook

PATRON SAINT OF: *Youth Group Members, Youth Group Leaders, Green Blacks, and Environmentalists*

If this is my deathbed, it's time to confess: I stole the idea for my Youth Colossal from Reverend Cook's Y Circus. Nobody much remembers what the Y Circus was, but that Kiddy-Show in St. Louis started more careers than the Apollo Theater in Harlem.

Cook was crazy about kids. The circus raised money to provide scholarships for Black kids from St. Louis to attend camp in Bourbon, Kentucky — the Rivercliff Camp if they were boys, the Derrycott Camp if they were girls. I was there for the second Y Circus. The first one happened in 1934. Count Basie, Cab Calloway, Duke Ellington, Louis Jordan, Nat King Cole, Pearl Bailey, Eartha Kitt, Earl Hines, Sammy Davis Jr., and me, Little Ziggy Johnson, all

112

performed in Cook's shows, along with hundreds upon hundreds of kids.

The Rev. Cook loved camping and camps. The green. The country air. The big dark sky so far from city lights. The provocative patterns of constellations. He didn't love the shows. He didn't love music. He was all about nature and self-determination. The Y Circus was his way of supporting his Black camp with Black money, Black creativity, Black effort and industry. He didn't talk about Marcus Garvey — probably would have said he disapproved of him — but Cook *loved* him some Marcus Garvey. Black St. Louis loved the Y Circus, loved the Pine Street Y, and loved Cook's church, if not for its sermons, then for its youth activities and programs. The larger Black show world loved the Y Circus as our cradle of eminence.

Cook's shows were James Cagney–Yankee Doodle Dandy patriotic. He used a lot of red, white, and blue flags, plus military titles to keep the group organized. Part of it was that he was afraid of anything that seemed soft or feminine. Sometimes I wondered if he wasn't scared of his own short, soft, pudgy, nurturing self. We weren't afraid of him. Everybody loved being in the Y Circus. It was a strange, all-in way of claiming "I

113

am America!" and "America better claim me!"

He made kids tough enough and connected enough to each other and to nature to endure what had to be endured. And he gave them the good sense to run out to the country from the city to revive themselves when they had to.

Cook died in 1961. He was up at that camp he loved more than the church he pastored. We all said it was the right way for him to go. If I go the right way, I will die the Monday after Father's Day.

LIBATION FOR THE FEAST DAY OF THE REVEREND COOK:
The Pine Street Y

1 lemon, juiced
1 tsp. of bar sugar
1 chilled bottle of high-quality ginger ale
Fruit and berries for garnish

Pour the lemon juice into a tall glass. Add sugar. Stir until sugar is dissolved. Add ice cubes. Top with ginger ale. Decorate with fruit and berries.

WEEK 8
EIGHTH SUNDAY
AFTER FATHER'S DAY

Colored Girl wasn't alarmed when her mother decided to buy, six years into their Washington, DC, life, a farm in the countryside, when after a whirlwind courtship her just-remarried mother was fortuitously widowed via a car accident. Colored Girl didn't know until they had spent what her mother termed "quality time" together on the farm that the mother believed Satan lived in the woods, and that mother would go truly crazy when she again lived in the only Black home in a white community, as she had decades before with her foster parents.

The mother's foster parents, the Jacksons, were descended from enslaved Africans who had made their way up to Canada in the 1840s. They migrated back down to Michigan, once freedom was proclaimed, establishing themselves as

115

the only Black family in the town of Farm-ington.

The Jacksons were not evil, but they were obsessed with evil. They prayed and attempted to whip the devil out of the foster child every time they saw signs of Satan's presence, and they frequently saw such signs. They were determined to provide the pale beige girl (who they speculated had a white father, so they also speculated that she had a Black whore for a mother) with a body that was a pure vessel for a pure heart. They succeeded in whipping the devil into the girl. This made them easy to hate.

This made them possible to love: Sixty rural miles west of Detroit, they were determined to provide a tidy home on a small vegetable farm in a town surrounded by dairy farms. In the winter the Jacksons dressed Bette in warm snowsuits; in the summer they fitted her out with ugly but skin-saving straw farmer's hats. When they were not praying, speculating, or spanking, Mrs. Jackson cooked meals fresh from the garden for Bette. Mr. Jackson delivered mail to earn the money to send Bette to an all-white-but-for-brown-Bette school, run by Lutherans, where she learned German and Latin as well as reading, writing, and arithmetic. The Jacksons were proud Black people living in a white town; Bette was something else. Over time and after many tears, the foster child graduated from the eighth grade of Saint Paul's Lutheran school, the virgin valedictorian of her class. If Colored Girl's mother had heard Clarence Cobbs preach, "Be nice to yourself," she might have done as she was told. Before she became an angry woman who demanded obedience and chilling ablutions, she was a sad, obedient girl.

Clarence Cobbs

PATRON SAINT OF: *Self-Care, Self-Respect, and Choir Singers*

Clarence Cobbs's Church of the Deliverance started off in his mother's basement. His first altar was her ironing board. I didn't ever attend Deliverance in that basement but heard about it often as we lived in the same Bronzeville neighborhood in Chicago.

"Pedigree." Cobbs liked to say he was from Memphis, as if his birth in the South provided credentials and pedigrees of wisdom and relevance. He often and loudly claimed Memphis was the capital of Mississippi.

He understood being born in the South as a kind of special anointing for the work he did in the North — that it set him apart in a superior way that he never let me forget. I was born in Chicago, and for Clarence that meant I was born in the second act of the Black drama. Born in the land of freedom where I flourished, I could never claim to be the one who delivered myself from the land of bondage. That pride belonged, for Clarence, solely to the ones who got on the trains, not to the ones who were born in the Promised Land.

There were those in Chicago who referred to preachers from the South as "jackleg" and who looked down on them and their storefronts. But those northern seminary- and college-trained ministers didn't get down in the streets to help God work through taverns and singers and policy shops to create redemption. That was Clarence's gig and genius.

Whores on the stroll quoted "Preacher Cobbs" to each other. Matrons whispered his sermons over the slumbering bodies of their beloved men and children. Children "played church" on the sidewalk and vied with each other to preach his sermon better. Southside children loved to imperson- ate Preacher. And when they did often, they would riff on this:

"There won't be any sermon today. Y'all have been working too hard raising money for the convalescent home. I want you to do something nice for your own self for a change. Hear me: Go on out and have your own self a good time. The dishes you've been saving for company — use them. Go on and eat off of them your own self. Go on out and buy yourself some records. Buy yourself a bag of apples and oranges and every night before you go to sleep eat yourself a slice and read yourself something good from the Bible. Be nice to yourself. Amen."

Be nice to yourself. It was a simple, radical instruction. And it was a delicious message that made me and so many others love the messenger. Love got "Preach" listened to, love got his church built, and love got him into a whole lot of trouble.

Preach took a hat factory and turned it into a church with two tall towers he nicknamed New Testament and Old Testament, with the help of Walter Thomas Bailey, the first sepian to be a registered architect in the state of Illinois. Some of the folks who worshipped in the church once worked in the hat factory. They lived the reality of how things change in unimagined ways. And I

119

think this experience inspired many to believe that people, too, can change in unimagined ways.

I rarely go to church, but I love to sit in Preach's pews and pray. I do not pray the strength prayer. An ox is strong. Steel is strong. I pray for places that break clean and pretty. I pray that after I am destroyed, I will have the will and the skill to reconstitute myself with new shimmer. In Preach's pews, that is a common prayer.

He has filled his church with bodies that others condemned as fit only for laboring, or for entertainment, or for sport — bodies that were only valued when they were strong or beautiful and discarded when they were broken.

In Preach's church those bodies are reclaimed and refurbished. He conspires with his congregants to turn their bodies into walking, talking sanctuaries of significant souls even if the body was out gambling, dancing, whoring, or just sleeping because it was tired. Clarence was always imagining and reimagining space and ways that spaces ranging from bodies to buildings could be used in new and different ways.

Kids on the street would perform this Cobbs sermon:

"You in the taverns tonight . . . You on the

dance floor . . . You in the pool rooms and in the policy stations, you on your bed of affliction: Jesus loves you all. And the Reverend Cobbs is thinking about you and loves every one of you. It makes no difference what you think of me, but it does make a difference what I think of you."

Preach was an arrogant man. According to the Natchez Belle, he was a blasphemous heathen. She understood his address to his folks in the taverns to indicate that he was equating his love to the love of Jesus. I heard something different. I heard, "Hate me and I will love you." That's a human sentiment. God don't anticipate being hated.

Preach wasn't perfect. I didn't love the way he was lifted up by women, because with the notable exception of his mother, his beloved Nana, he never gave women their due places of power within the church. Girls and women kept his coffers, his cupboard, and his pews full, propelling the church forward, largely unacknowledged by Preacher. I had to cuss him out loud about that a few times. Cussing didn't change much.

Billie Holiday once sang at Preach's church. She even brought her little Chihuahua, Pepe-the-gin-drinker, to the church and let him curl up in a pew while she,

Billie, raised her voice in praise song. Dinah Washington sang at Deliverance, too. But Cobbs didn't embrace those women as artists like he embraced Louis Armstrong and Lionel Hampton when they performed in his church. He used Billie and Dinah just like he used a B3 organ and a recording booth.

But maybe the women got the better end of the deal. For Cobbs, there were no lines between workmates and playmates. His loves and his lovers were all too often members of his church or of churches he was visiting. I never chose from my students. Never chose from those who worked for me. That wasn't who I wanted to be.

You can do a lot of wrong and still do some right.

Clarence created something. He snatched Saturday night out of the jaws of Satan and gave it back to the good angels, with the help of great music. I worked with Clarence to achieve that. And somehow, the way we did it suggested that what we were doing out in the clubs — making music, singing, swaying, talking love — was sacred, was part of what it meant to be sanctified.

Clarence taught me the importance of privacy. We all went to Idlewild. He went to Benton Harbor, closer to Chicago and more private. And when he wanted more privacy still, he went to California or Mexico. A picture he was proudest of was of his mother and other female relatives with him in Mexico. His mother is wearing a wondrous Mexican skirt.

These women have come far from Memphis. Clarence carried them like they carried him: silent, high, and with unshaking arms. The last time I sat beside his mother in one of his Chicago pews, I started to cough. As she passed me a little round red and white striped mint wrapped in cellophane, I realized he loved his flock the way Nana loved him — without questioning — all the hours of the day, present or away. To slip in his door, any door he opened, was to discover, again, that you were loved. This was whispered: Slip in his body and you were just outside of Earth and just inside love.

LIBATION FOR THE FEAST DAY OF CLARENCE COBBS:
Sleek Shelter of Deliverance

1 jigger of brandy
1 lime, juiced
1 sugar cube

Place sugar cube and juice into shaker and lightly muddle to break up and dissolve sugar. Next add brandy and ice and shake. Strain into a cocktail glass and serve.

WEEK 9
NINTH SUNDAY
AFTER FATHER'S DAY

Between the topics Colored Girl wanted to avoid — the farm, the will, and "your hoodlum father" — and the topics her mother wanted to avoid — Fisk University, Colored Girl's second marriage, Colored Girl's daughter "I'm too young to be a grandmother," and especially Colored Girl's bar — there wasn't a lot for Colored Girl and her mother to discuss, except her mother's illness and Colored Girl's writing.

It pleased the dying woman that her daughter had become a successful writer. Ziggy had predicted this when the girl was just two years old and scrawled the word "yellow" on a cocktail napkin without knowing what she had written. The mother hated the fact that Colored Girl owned a bar. She dismissed this act as "broke down" and "colored" and "Detroit crazy." Six months into Colored Girl's monthly visits with her, a national magazine published an article about Bullock's Black Bottom Bar. That changed things.

"Thank God you lied and said the inspiration for the bar was Bricktop. I can live with that. I loved the way you said the place was named for the Black Bottom neighborhood in Detroit, the Black Bottom neighborhood in Nashville, and the Black Bottom dance." Colored Girl's mother lifted up the paper and read this aloud: "that became an international craze rivaling the Charleston for popularity while shouting out to Ma Rainey, August Wilson, and Lloyd George Richards. The play *Ma Rainey's Black Bottom* is the one that brought playwright August Wilson to the attention of Lloyd George Richards, who would become Wilson's most influential and effective director." The mother finished by saying, "You remind me of Nellie Hill Trapp, the way you lie so fast and elaborate!"

"It's the truth, Mama." Colored Girl's mother dismissed this last as another pretty lie. She insisted on being pleased. "I have a postcard from Bricktop. You could frame it in your bar. She said Ziggy had told her I had moved to DC and I should keep an eye peeped to where she could open a DC bar and she would call it

66 Rue Pigalle. I've got some letters from your father you've never read. I got Ziggy's old column on Black Bottom. We should start to talk about me getting those things organized and when they might come to you."

Bricktop

PATRON SAINT OF: *Fish out of Water, Aging with Swagger and Audacious Ambition*

Bricky. When I sleep in Detroit, I dream of Arthur Braggs's Idlewild. When I sleep in Idlewild, I dream of Bricky's Paris. Bricktop. Like Bobby Short, she came from West Virginia. Like my own mother, her father was white and her mother was Black. When she was young, along with her bright red hair and freckles, she had the best legs in Paris.

Cole Porter loved her legs. Fitzgerald loved her legs. Josephine Baker loved her legs. Best of all: Bricky loved Bricky's legs! Who didn't love Bricktop's legs? Mistinguett! The great French courtesan and actress was, when Bricktop arrived in Paris, the highest paid woman in the world. Mistinguett's legs were insured for 500,000 francs. Mistinguett thought she had the most beautiful legs in the world, not only because of the insurance policy, because she heard that every night at the Moulin Rouge. And then she started hearing that the best legs in Paris belonged to a mulatto girl singing down in Montmartre. Mistinguett's world ended in 1924. She was still breathing but it was in a new world in which Bricktop had become the new standard of beauty. Our gal Bricky arrived and changed everything. She won an undeclared war without firing a shot.

But to go back to that red hair and those freckles: There was a lot of white in her — her mother had slept with an Irishman — but Bricktop considered herself true Black. And Bricky believed there was a lot of white in the world, but that her world was true Black, plain and simple. Bricky didn't live in opposition to anything. She enclosed everything. She enfolded me and everyone near and dear and admired by Bricky into her precious golden creases. Of everything I have ever felt, and seen, and tasted, and sniffed, and heard, nothing was finer than the inside of Ada Beatrice Queen Victoria Louise Virginia Smith. On a good or a bad day, her golden folds of body, of logic, of life, made me want to holler "Sweet Jesus!"

Like me, Bricktop started her show life in Chicago and, like me, her early days were marked by an exceptional performance of the Charleston. Bricky took the Charleston to Europe. And she taught the Aga Khan how to Black Bottom. Then, just like me, she moved beyond dancing to community building. Except she did it with nightclubs.

She always owned her own place. And it was usually called Chez Bricktop. For years it was at 66 Rue Pigalle. That was the only address most American sepians knew in Paris. It was the only address anyone Black needed to know. In the Second World War she closed that club and opened another in Mexico City. Later there would be a Bricktop's in Rome. How was all this possible? Cole Porter said our Bricky had a "unique talent to amuse."

All the ofay Café Society loved Bricky. I was in high school when F. Scott Fitzgerald published his story *Babylon Revisited* and Bricktop was in it. I didn't really know her then, but I was proud. We all were. She was taking us, our show people, into literature in her own way. She knew the Duke of Windsor and all his crowd, but she preferred us. Particularly La Baker, and here I don't mean my sweet LaVern, I mean Josephine Baker. Bricky mesmerized Café Society. What mesmerized them? Her disinterest. It was not feigned. It was not hateful. She was simply serenely committed to the life she had longest loved: sepian show life. Everything else was an amusing addition. She amused because she *was* amused.

When she was globe-trotting, I would call her more than she called me. I would dial her up from some phone in Idlewild, because everybody wanted to talk long distance to Bricky. It was an honor to pay that bill, and I couldn't afford to call long distance to France, or Italy, or Mexico from my room in the Gotham Hotel. She would usually end the call by demanding that I clip out six or seven of my recent columns and send them to her. "I want a big fat letter full of Zagging with Ziggy. I can get the gossip from folks passing through. I miss the way you tell it, Zig. And Jimmy sends his love."

No, he didn't, but I loved hearing all the lies that connected me to other of Bricky's more-famous and out-of-my-orbit loves. The center of Bricky's literary Paris was James Baldwin, who would come by for little breaks when he was writing *Giovanni's Room.* Bricktop, she loved her some Jimmy Baldwin. And I loved sharing space in Bricky's heart.

When she was at the height of her fame, when those magnificent legs supported two hundred fine pounds, Bricky would do a version of the "St. Louis Blues" that was unforgettable. A favored costume from this Bricky era is a brocade coat that looked like something a Mandarin prince might wear. When she proudly claimed, "I'm a big fat Mama, meat shaking on my bones, and every time I shimmy a skinny woman loses her home," we believed. Bricktop danced with a feather boa and you wanted to be that boa. And when she sang, "my hair is curly and my teeth are pearls," it wasn't a joke. We were seduced into believing what our eyes could not see: who she used to be.

"St. Louis Blues." Louis sang it. Bessie sang it. Basie sang it. Bricky sang it best. It was King Oliver who first discovered her and introduced her to Louis Armstrong. And after that, she worked for Jack Johnson, the fighter Joe Louis tried so hard not to be. The audacious, white-world-loving fighter. Bricky wasn't jealous of Jack Johnson's white women. She was sorry for Johnson that he couldn't have her, bronze Bricky.

Too much life at the end of the money is a hard blues to cure. When Blonzetta died last year, Bricky inherited her sepian sister's money. Their brother died early of tuberculosis. Their other sister got shot by an angry

Other Woman. Blonzetta stayed in Chicago, making money on real estate, always spending two less dollars than she earned, while Bricky always spent two more dollars than the big bucks she earned. Each woman appreciated the value of the other woman's approach. Catholic Bricktop buried Blonzetta back in West Virginia at the Greenbrier Baptist Church Cemetery.

When my girls go to Paris, I want them to make a pilgrimage to 66 Rue Pigalle.

LIBATION FOR THE FEAST DAY OF BRICKTOP:
66 Rue Pigalle

1 jigger of Old Tom gin
3 fresh large strawberries
I sugar cube

In a cocktail shaker, muddle the strawberries and sugar. Add gin, then ice. Shake and strain into a cocktail glass.

WEEK 10
TENTH SUNDAY
AFTER FATHER'S DAY

When Jodie Edwards died in October 1967, the *New York Times* ran an obituary. The obit included laudatory commentary from the composer Eubie Blake about Edwards's writing process and achievement and noted that Edwards had played the Apollo the year before his death, in 1966, using much of the very same material he had first written and performed on the vaudeville stage in the 1920s. It further noted that Jodie and his wife, Sue — the two being better known as "Butterbeans and Susie" — had appeared on *The Ed Sullivan Show* three times. Prodded by Ziggy, Colored Girl and her friends from the School of the Theatre had watched all three performances.

Butterbeans and Sue's original stage act was not especially child-appropriate. Their '20s duet "Switchboard Mama, Elevator Papa" is a salty discussion between two old lovers doing everything they can, using mouths, using hands, using everything they have, even as their aging bodies begin to fail, to make joy. They were not only better than Stringbean and Sweetie Pie, who preceded them on the minstrel circuit and whose influence they acknowledged in the naming of their act; they were better than the white act, Gracie and George, who came after them, stealing some of their material, building on all their material, migrating it to radio and to Las Vegas, appearing time after time on *Ed Sullivan,* never acknowledging that Butterbeans and Susie were the real pioneers of modern couples comedy.

At crucial moments, later in life, when Colored Girl wanted to give up on sex, or have too much sex, words she had heard in the Ziggy Johnson School of the Theatre, spoken by Ziggy himself, would echo through her head: "One hundred lovers is too many, and one is not enough." For a long, long time, Colored Girl didn't know Ziggy had learned that line from Sue.

Butterbeans and Susie

PATRON SAINT OF: *Married Folk, Sly Whisperers, and Witnesses*

They were my stage Mama and stage Papa. They taught me to keep moving until I got where I wanted to go. And they told me to take a few people with me, if I could, like they took me, like they took Moms Mabley, like they took Tanya the Contortionist.

At birth Butterbeans (in Georgia, in 1893) had been given the name Jodie Edwards; Sue (in Florida, in 1894), Susie Hawthorne. The world came to know them as Butterbeans and Susie, the "first family of Negro entertainment." They got married, the story goes, only because someone paid them $50 to tie the knot and do it onstage.

I never believed that. I believe Butterbeans conned some publicity agent into proposing the stunt, after he and Sue fell in love and decided to wed. Maybe they even had a small wedding in 1915 at the Greenville, South Carolina, home of the dancer called Peg Leg Bates. That's what the grapevine says. One way or another, the big public wedding happened in 1917 on the stage at the Philadelphia Standard Theatre.

They played with everybody from Silas Green of New Orleans to James Brown.

135

They played with Dick Gregory. They played with Josephine Baker. They even played with me. You can't be an American and stand on a stage and not owe something to them. They influenced too many people, in too many cities, in too many towns, for too long, not to have influenced somebody who influenced you, whoever you are. They came out of Oliver Tolliver's Big Show, or, as they liked to tell it, she came out of the Smart Set Review and he came out of Oliver Tolliver's Big Show. That was one of their soft kitchen jokes. She was "smart" and he was "big."

We who loved them called them Butter and Sue. You can't tell it from that kitchen joke, but they were astoundingly gifted comics, singers, dancers, and songwriters. This last is overlooked but they co-wrote "Construction Gang," "Deal Yourself Another Hand," "I Got Your Bath Water On," and, my personal favorite, "I Can't Use You." It's hard to find those old shellacked discs now, and when you do they're usually all scratched; most of them were released when I was still a schoolboy, but to hear them sing was to catch something raw and significant. King Oliver as well as Louis Armstrong and his Hot Five were proud to be called Butter and Sue's backing band.

136

I was in Chicago in high school the first time I saw them perform. Lord, could they dance! He wore a too-tight suit and a tiny odd hat; she wore a swanky evening dress. A lot of what they did, particularly what Butterbeans did as far as dancing goes, is what we call "eccentric dance." He is famous for a version he called the Heebie Jeebies. I call it "the itch dance." It involved syncopated scratching. I hated that trick, but it brought down the house so dependably that Butter performed it night after night for half a century.

I saw their show in Detroit, more times than anyplace else. Their act was all about the way they loved each other. It wasn't that they were bawdy — and they *were* bawdy — it was that they were tethered to each other with an obvious pride and respect. This made their act, whether they played beneath the canvas of the minstrel show tent or beneath the gilt and painted plaster ceilings of the vaudeville show stage, completely different from other acts in either tradition.

They were prouder than the other minstrels and dirtier than the other vaudevilles. Proud and dirty, Butter and Sue style, was delicious. Pride, respect, and sex were the snap, crackle, and pop that pervaded their onstage arguments and humiliations. Just when you thought they had gone too far with the insults and they would fall into the shit-pit of shame-fueled minstrel laughter, they jumped right back into the honeypot of love. Despite the itch dance and the blackface; despite his too-small bowler hat; because of her big hips, and his crazy lips: any fool could see what they bent the notes to sing — she had a roll and he had a hot dog that fit just it. Every audience was wooed into believing Butterbeans and Susie were luckier than anyone else in the world. And they made many a body in the audience believe they might-could be that lucky, too.

And they themselves might-could be loved. Butter and Sue's act was all about the war between the sexes, but it was also about the war between the races. Hidden in every Butter and Sue stage fight was a love letter that read: "We appreciate each other even when the white world doesn't."

And their act wasn't just about love. It was about sex. The church preached that sex will kill you. Butter and Sue preached, on the minstrel show stage, on the vaudeville stage, on the Apollo stage, that sex can save you. That was a radical sermon.

That sermon got me out of the pro audience and onto the pro stage. Butter and Sue gave me my first big job. That was in about 1932. Variety shows, minstrel or vaudeville, always have room for another act to be squeezed onto the bill. All through the years, Butter and Sue used their influence to secure spots for up-and-comers and falling stars. Everybody else had to help themselves. I left Chicago for the first time on the road with Butter and Sue. They were making $1,000 a week. I was making just enough to get by and learn. The first thing they taught me was to *see* my audience.

When Butter and Sue began working together in 1915, most anybody Black over fifty in the audience had been a slave. Anybody over sixty remembered slavery well. There were seventy-year-olds in the audience the first night I applauded Butter and Sue who had made babies enslaved, birthed babies enslaved. Butter told me that. Sue told me about looking out on an audience and seeing a brand on a face, a whip scar on an arm. In Chester, Pennsylvania, they met a man, after a show, who had a scar on his face from when he was a slave child and his mistress threw him into a blazing fireplace grate. When you are dancing, and singing, and cutting up for people who look like you except for the brands and whip scars, you don't hold nothing back if you are Butter and Sue.

He played the bones. She sang the funny songs. They had seen the slave scars. They worked in vaudeville, they worked in blues, in jazz, in R&B, but they always stayed connected to that old-timey minstrel show. Not because they wanted to shuffle along and step and fetch, but because they didn't want all that forgotten. Butter taught me that laughter was a narcotic that took away just enough pain to allow us to recall when and where we had been maimed. According to him, healing was a dance, and recall was its first step.

"Find a way to help the wounded laugh. And if the rest of the world laughs, too, so be it. Help ours get theirs." Butterbeans and Susie taught me that.

They taught a lot of showbiz lessons, but this was the biggest: Find a way to let your audience love you. Find that for them and you'll help them find a way to love themselves. Butter and Sue got me started right. From the get-go I wanted to find a way to help my brown and Black audiences love themselves.

They played so many Detroit clubs so many times, but in '45 there was a legendary midnight gala at the Paradise with Louis Armstrong and Stepin Fetchit. Topping the bill: Butterbeans and Susie. Black Bottom said that was the Detroit show for the century.

What had happened to make that show legendary? Some people were saying 68,000 workers (others put it at 150,000) — for sure it was a whole heap of a lot of folks — had just been laid off in Detroit in a period of less than three months. When Butterbeans and Susie arrived for that particular gig, nobody Black was smiling. Watching Butter and Sue perform, breadwinners started laughing. And they took those jokes out with them into the streets to the laid-off breadwinners who couldn't afford show tickets. Butter and Sue's jokes got told out in the city for days. They took to the stage to remind us of where our "get-up and go got hid — and it wasn't in the Willow Run plant!" It was in our hips and on our lips — ever available.

In '47 I mounted a show at the Club Paradise in Atlantic City. I put Butter and Sue on the bill. Count Basie was there, with his wife, Katie, taking a needed break from her many charity fundraising duties. It was a big show, lots of folk, so big that we fielded two rival baseball teams from one cast. We'd get up in the morning and play ball. Yes, sir! And in the afternoon, we'd go crabbing.

That was our Atlantic City. Sue loved all that. She and I would hold hands and scream whenever either team scored a run. At night the white folks would come to see the show. And we gave them a big show. *Variety* wrote it up. But when the white folks weren't looking, in Atlantic City, in 1947, we had us a very big time. All those years on the circuit we stole some good times.

Most times we traveled by train. We had to carry all the sets, the props, the backdrops, the showgirls, the main acts, everything and everyone. It wasn't like later when all you had were your clothes and you could travel by car or plane. Back then the boxcar was our ship, the rails were our sea, those little towns our ports. I was out there a good long while in the thirties, sending money back to the Natchez Belle in Chicago to help her take care of my daughter, Josette.

I got off the ship in Detroit. Like all good parents, Butter and Sue wanted more for me than they had for themselves. They thought I had found that in Motown. Nobody was happier for me when I stepped away from the Chitlin Circuit and flourished as an emcee at The Flame, or at the 20 Grand, or when I published my first column in the *Michigan Chronicle,* or when I moved into the Gotham Hotel. They loved Detroit and were thrilled that one of their adopted children was settling there and settling high.

And they loved Idlewild. Summer wasn't rolling until Butter and Sue showed up. When I am starting to feel low, I remember them out on the lake in a fast boat, Butter in a well-fitting cap, Sue with a silk scarf tied around her head laughing when Butter said for the thousandth time that "TOBA" didn't stand for "Tough on Black Asses," it stood for "Tough on Butter's Ass." Sue estimated they had logged over one million miles on the Chitlin Circuit, so she reckoned they could name TOBA for Butter. She knew by heart all the distances, in miles and hours. Sue and I swam across the lake together many an Idlewild morning. She loved splashing in the water like you can only love it if you grew up near the beach in Pensacola and were barred by law from entering the waves because your skin is brown. She loved my aunt Sadye for getting our kids access to that Pensacola Beach. As Sue backstroked gracefully, closing in on the distant shore, she hollered to me who was Australian-crawling in slow circles around her, "I traveled a million miles to get to Detroit, Zig, and it's only a thousand map-miles from Pensacola. Maps lie."

One year they came up to Idlewild right

after Youth Colossal. When they agreed with each other that my Youth Colossal was better than Reverend Cook's Y Circus, I started to suspect that I had done something. Butter and Sue didn't lie.

Susie died on December 5, 1963. I was at the Top of The Flame celebrating Bette Stanley's birthday and watching her admire the new restaurant's oriental garden with its waterfall and pool and the bartenders in their colorful Thai-silk uniforms. The place was built for Henry Ford, his kin, his ilk, and his immediate executive underlings. Bette was starting to venture into that orbit. Bob Bennett, my sweetest doctor, arrived at the Top of The Flame, so different from our Flame, the legendary showbar, that had closed earlier that year, with the bad news. Bob knew I would want to know, but he feared the shock of Susie's death might give me a fatal heart attack. He trusted only himself to inform me that my stage mama was gone.

There was a memorial show for her, with Dick Gregory presiding. Butterbeans himself died last year. Walked on the stage at the Dorchester Inn outside Chicago and just dropped. He had a heart attack. He had been performing for over half a century — the last five years without Sue.

When I get to heaven, when I get upstairs, I will see them. I want Diggs's funeral home to tuck a pretty silk dress beside me in my coffin to take up to Sue, and a starched silk handkerchief for Butter. Nobody looked better in silk brocade than Sue. Butterbeans deserves to have all that burnt cork wiped off his face by me. He wore it when none of us could bear to wear it any longer. He wore it, not to play low, but to call out to high heaven in witness of what we had been through, what we are still going through. When I start to forget but want to know how we made it over, I meditate on Butter. He was bright witness to affliction, and he was burnt-cork-faced testimony, that pain acknowledged is pain that can be transcended.

I do not forget the last time I saw them together. I savor it. There was Butter standing in the center of the lobby of John White's Gotham Hotel, one arm linked into Sue's, the other patting me on the back. Sue wore a fine but simple green wool dress and there was a small hat perched just-right on her head. Butter wore a well-fitted drab suit. They were posed in the perfect spot for the giant lobby chandelier to cast them in the most favorable light. You don't get to work on thousands of stages without learn-

ing how to find exactly the right light. Butter took it all in and declared, "Detroit is
some kind of heaven on earth!" I was as
proud as a peacock of my high-rise abode.
Prouder still when John White himself
entered the lobby, stood close by me,
greeted Butter and Sue, and called me
"friend." Sue got it. All of it. She leaned
into me, grabbed my hand, and whispered,
"You've arrived, son."

LIBATION FOR THE FEAST DAY OF
BUTTERBEANS AND SUSIE:
A Way to Let Them Love You

1 jigger of bourbon
1 sugar cube
2 dashes of Angostura bitters
1 lemon peel
1 Tbsp. of cold water

Start by placing a sugar cube into a rocks
glass. Dash Angostura bitters onto the
sugar cube, then pour water onto the
cube. Lightly muddle the soaked sugar
cube to allow it to break down and
dissolve. Add bourbon and ice, then stir
briefly to incorporate ingredients. Finally
zest a 2-inch-wide lemon peel over the
top of the drink and insert the peel into

the drink, allowing its tip to peek out
above the liquid and ice.

WEEK 11
ELEVENTH SUNDAY
AFTER FATHER'S DAY

Tim Moore didn't play Amos *or* Andy. He played Kingfish, leader of the Mystic Knights of the Sea, the fraternal lodge where Amos and Andy were members. Kingfish was always at the center of the story, and always, somehow, better than Amos or Andy when *Amos and Andy* was the most famous show starring Black people on television. And he was, according to Ziggy, better than the two white men who invented those racially stereotyping roles. Some actors can so infuse a character written as a debasing caricature with sly intelligence and felt humanity that the stereotype gets quietly slaughtered. Tim Moore, who played Kingfish, aka George Stevens, was one of those actors.

Ziggy told anyone who would listen about the single performance he "hated to have missed more than any other." The older kids would egg him on with ques-

148

tions like "Even more than seeing Bert Williams perform with George Walker?" Or, "Even more than seeing Bert Williams in the Ziegfeld Follies with you being named for Ziegfeld?" And some show-off would win an extra-sweet Ziggy smile with "Even more than seeing Aldrich playing Othello?" Ziggy always came back with, "Tim Moore's one-man show of *Uncle Tom's Cabin* — that's the show above all others that I missed but still yearn to see."

After Ziggy told Colored Girl about Moore's *Uncle Tom's Cabin* for the third time, she made up a little play called *Eden.* She played Adam, Eve, God, and the snake. One of the older girls at the dancing school helped her with the makeup and hair. Half her face had lipstick and eye shadow, and one long braid; the other half had no makeup and her hair pinned back. She used her arm to play the snake. When she was God, she put her hands in front of her face and talked through her fingers. She wrote all her own lines, and George Stanley insisted that some of them improved on the Bible.

Ziggy gave *Eden* a two-Saturdays run at the dance school. Four performances. Ten minutes each. Colored Girl got so much applause, she tried to do her show at her little Black Lutheran School. She got hushed. If she hadn't been George Stanley's daughter, one of the girls whispered, she would have been suspended. Apparently, some of the Lutheran School parents thought Colored Girl's *Eden* was blasphemous.

Tim Moore

PATRON SAINT OF: *The Innovative, the Misunderstood, and the Good Friend*

Tim Moore, the man we called Kingfish, was a singular sensation.

Young colored boys and girls dancing for pennies and nickels and sometimes dollars on street corners and stages in their neighborhood, and sometimes on the flatbed of a truck slow-rolling through their community — these actions were common between the Civil War and World War I. Born in 1887, "Kingfish" didn't just start working early, which so many of us did in those days. He started early and he started *internationally.*

Tim Moore worked England. He worked Europe. He hit the sea prematurely, at about ten years old, performing with a boy close to his same age, Romeo Washburn, along with a woman who toured with them while living off their labor — the vaudeville veteran vixen Cora Miskel. Moore and Washburn performed as Cora's Gold Dust Twins.

Their act was fueled by a broad audience understanding, established by soap advertisements, that the Gold Dust Twins were hard, cooperative, and eager-to-please workers, yet flawed by dusky skin that soap might-could fix.

The soap wrapper featured drawings of two boys of distinctly African heritage on its wrapper, the "Gold Dust Twins." Over time the wrapper evolved. The Gold Dust Twins started off as pretty boys. Over time their faces changed. The way Tim and Romeo played them in their stage show, the Gold Dust Twins stayed handsome, and clean. And they unexpectedly saved the day, time after time, even if the humor came from the fact that they always won despite the expectation that they would lose. Gold Dust Twins got the job done!

Tim Moore gushed with deserved pride when he told me, on his first visit to the Gotham Hotel, "Me and Romeo, we saw more of the world than almost anybody on the planet our age, Black or white or yellow or red." When we talked about all the theaters we knew and loved, he would always end the conversation one-upping me by concluding, "I saw The Royal when it was the largest theater in the world! And I saw The Royal before, when it wasn't so big, just like The Royal saw me, when I was in short pants!"

He loved to tell me about how the Prince of Wales played the banjo and how everyone in England was crazy for old-timey minstrel shows. And how the people were really just plain crazy, and how some of those aristocrats would pay ten-year-old Tim five silver crowns to teach them five new chords on his old banjo.

The last time Kingfish was in the Gotham Hotel, John White gave him the bridal suite, decorated with sleek Herman Miller furniture, a king-sized bed with headboards and footboards, side tables, a dressing table, a tallboy, and a desk. Every piece oiled and dusted.

Checking in, Kingfish asked the desk clerk if he could pay for all of that with a silver crown stamped with the face of Queen Victoria, which he pulled out of the pocket of his perfectly tailored suit.

The desk clerk smiled and replied: "Mr. White says that the room and the liquor are on the house with his compliments." The desk clerk got that silver coin, worth more than $10, as a tip. I got an invitation to mosey over from my room to his suite. Kingfish had always been one to share the wealth.

We posted up in that sleek and modern room and talked about everything we had seen and everywhere we had been. We could go toe to toe counting American towns and cities. When we left talking about these United States, Kingfish had me beat. The only foreign country I've been to is Canada. Kingfish had been to thirty-five countries. Me and that old man had much to chew over, and almost none of it had anything to do with *Amos 'n Andy,* the television show that made Tim, for a hot minute, a rich and also a reviled man.

The man who once chalked half his face white and corked the other half black to perform a sly, one-man show of *Uncle Tom's Cabin* that he himself had written, stood accused of being a stupid and self-hating coon. Thank you, Amos and Andy!

The NAACP had picketed his performances. Politicos didn't understand why some of us, including that little genius Sammy Davis Jr., who organized the fundraiser for Kingfish's widow when Kingfish died in Los Angeles at the age of sixty-nine or seventy in 1958, wouldn't speak out against him personally, even as we spoke

153

out against the role written for him. To understand this, you have to remember that when I was just starting out Tim Moore had already been performing for a quarter century.

When I'm alone in this hospital room, when Baby Doll is at that office working as a secretary typing letters with lots of carbon copies and fetching coffee and answering phones for some rich white man in an ugly gray suit, the kind who eats lunch at the London Chop House while his wife eats lunch at the Pontchartrain, joining him on Saturday nights for dinner at the Top of The Flame, and everyone else is somewhere else, I close my eyes and my most astonishing friend, Kingfish, comes to me.

He sits in the hospital room chair by my head and we talk. Just last night I got drowsy and he did one of his ghost bits for me — a ghost doing a ghost bit: that's Tim! He's got a lot of numbers that involve ghosts, so I guess that's why he likes to come back as one. Two nights ago, he did the one that involved a card game. Last night he did "The Black Scotchman," and I laughed so loud a nurse came in and threatened to get a doctor to put me on chlorpromazine if I didn't get ahold of myself and stop talking to dead people. Soon as she left the room, Tim did the bit that starts, "It was no night fit for man nor beast." Finally, he told me that one about an army camp on the Mexican border, and I started to cry because I knew his Black soldiers would be forgotten while the Kingfish was remembered, and remembered for the wrong things. Nurse came in and gave me a tablet, but I hid it in my cheek and pretended to swallow.

When Tim came back later, I told him not to do anything that would make me laugh or cry loud, so we just softly talked over the old days. He agreed with me that Jackie, meaning Moms Mabley, was the greatest comedian working in showbiz. Reminded me that Butterbeans and Susie had discovered Moms in Dallas and were the first to bring her out on the road. He likes to poke the "Ziggy-bear" and remind me that I wasn't the only one who called them their "showbiz Mama and Papa." Kingfish also told me about being in a show where Moms was in a skit with the writer Zora Neale Hurston and they played cheerleaders. I want to find and revive that chestnut and stage it in the '68 Colossal.

And, like usual, whenever we talk for more than ten minutes, we start talking about our close mutual friend Count Basie. Kingfish starts off with some of the corny things Basie is always repeating, like "There wouldn't be so many guys going hunting if those bears and deer had rifles and could shoot back at them." And the wise thing he often said: "If I've learned one thing, don't forget people! If you pass them going up, they're still going to be around when you pass them going the other way." We argue about which of us is closer to Basie. I try to win by reminding him of my daughter's cotillion ball and Mr. Count Basie taking my daughter for a whirl around the dance floor. I remind him of my buying Count Basie fruit when he was on a diet. What I don't say is "I'm closer because I am alive."

Kingfish has got all the stage history in his head. Butter and Sue are always looking out at the audience or at each other. Kingfish keeps his eye peeped at the other performers and on history.

And I don't tell him what Basie said about planning his retirement, when he told me, "Ziegfeld, I'm a happy man, off the lamb, invested in some property in New York, I bought Harris's Corner. I will be the daytime bartender and the nighttime band." I don't say that. And I'm glad I didn't. Because Kingfish died broke.

Kingfish didn't plan for his retirement. Once upon a time he made $700 a week. When he died, as I said, Sammy Davis Jr. said he himself had to shell out for the funeral. Sammy recognizes a debt. Baby Doll is my retirement plan. Which means the real plan is I need to hurry up and die while I'm still looking pretty good, before I make her pull too hard or too long. Kingfish chuckles loudly when I say this. The nurses don't hear that. Tim knows all about wives. He often reminds me that he died mad at his last one.

Over and over when he came to me, he wanted to try to explain something about shooting up his kitchen over a burnt roasted side of beef, terrifying his wife. He said, "I never hit a woman in my life." He added, "If I had wanted to kill her, she would be dead. All those ofays think I've changed from a fool to a brute."

He blamed his last wife for his having to go sit in Jack Parr's chair, on Jack Parr's TV show, and "coon" so the audience would stop fearing Kingfish the brutal Buck Negro and he could get back to work. He shouldn't have blamed her for that, because it was on him. Kingfish was more perfect than most, and also more imperfect.

The last time he was with me in the flesh,

he wanted to talk about writing. That's where we started, with me reading his words on paper — a letter to *The Chicago Defender* long before I met him — and then we moved on to talking in person.

His last, in-the-flesh words to me were "Tell your readers that Kingfish, Tim Moore, is a race man. If I thought anything in *Amos 'n Andy* was derogatory, I wouldn't have accepted a part in it."

I wrote a column and told my readers exactly that. I didn't have the inches to tell them this: that Kingfish had been a jockey and even once rode in the Kentucky Derby, thinking about the first jockeys to win the Derby and how they were all Black. He had starred in three feature films, including *His Great Chance,* with his wife, Gertrude, in 1923, and *Darktown Revue,* produced and directed by the great Oscar Micheaux in 1931. His *Boy! What a Girl!* was a 1946 movie that featured Kingfish in a wild female impersonation that eclipses some of the best of *Some Like It Hot* a decade before that classic hit the silver screen. He even sold jokes to W. C. Fields and hundreds of sepian and ofay comics; many more stole hundreds of jokes from him. But when I best remember Kingfish, I don't think on any of that. What I want my girls to remem-

158

ber: a face corked half black and chalked half white to create a profound and political performance. Kingfish dropped it like that.

LIBATION FOR THE FEAST DAY OF
TIM MOORE:
The Race Man

3/4 jigger of brandy
1/2 pony of light rum
1/2 lemon, juiced
1 sugar cube
1 slice of orange
1 slice of pineapple, or pineapple frond

Place sugar cube and lemon juice into shaker tin and lightly muddle to break up and dissolve sugar. Next add ice, then brandy and rum. Shake. Strain into a rocks glass filled with shaved ice, and garnish with orange and pineapple slices or a pineapple frond.

WEEK 12
TWELFTH SUNDAY
AFTER FATHER'S DAY

Long before the documentary movie on competitive drag balls called *Paris Is Burning* and the delicious television series *Pose,* there were three friends from the Brewster projects who started coming around the school announcing they wanted to become female impersonators. One of the older students new to the school announced that Ziggy would throw the trio out of the building when he heard their plans. Ziggy heard. With a silencing wave of his jeweled right hand, Ziggy loudly reminded everyone present in the dance studio that he had choreographed for the great female impersonator Valda Gray long before any of his current students were born.

The three friends, Tyrone, David, and Levon, kept coming around. One had a sister who could sew. If the Supremes had skirts four inches above their knees, she sewed skirts five inches above the knee and bought contrasting fishnet stockings, plus go-go boots with the tallest heels. Impressed by the trio's sartorial swagger, Ziggy demanded that the group do what they had been afraid to do: sing for him. They could sing. They could dress. But their faces were rough, even when made up, and the way they moved was all kinds of raggedy. "When you walk, you look like $20 all in loose change." "You got somebody can fix that?" "Valda Gray."

When Valda Gray arrived, she immediately renamed the individual artists Jackie, Lee, and Pat. "Those names," Valda explained, "mean you have to work harder. Call you Mary, Amy, and Ann, and the names do half the work." Then she pronounced the trio, Trio.

At Colored Girl's elementary school (St. Philip's Lutheran) weekdays and at her Grandma's church (King Solomon Temple) on Sunday, you were a boy or you were a girl. The thing that decided that was whether you had a pocketbook in your panties or a weenie. Everything was set after sex was determined. Whether you got pink or blue clothes. Whether you got a football or flowers. Whether you got an extra math class or an extra art class. On

161

Saturday things were different; at the ZJ School of the Theatre, gender wasn't just and always about what was in your panties or shorts, or panties *and* shorts.

At the Woolworth five-and-ten when they were out and about buying makeup for Trio, Valda, who was dressed as she had to dress to enter a store and make purchases, in slacks and sweater and having us call her Mr. Baker, pointed to a case of pink lipsticks. Valda said, "There are as many different ways to be a girl as there are shades of pink. Look at those purples! It's hard to tell if you should call them pink or blue. People want to think they *are* pink or blue. Everybody is really purple. Don't tell your parents I told you that! Don't tell your parents Ziggy let me take you to Woolworth's. Don't tell your parents anything. Most of them are nothing like Ruth Ellis's parents. Lie!"

Valda Gray was born in Indianapolis and given the name Harold Baker at birth.

Valda Gray
PATRON SAINT OF: *Self-Invention, Gender Nonconformists, and Exuberant Living*

I have not always wanted what I wanted, without regard to the ways others might as-

162

sign desire. Want *this* if you are a boy! Want *that* if you are a girl! Want *this* if you are white! Want *that* if you are Black! Want *this* if you are mulatto!

Valda Gray taught me to refuse all such instructions. I teach the art of this particular refusal in my School of the Theatre. It is one of my specialties. Female impersonating was Valda's.

There is a particular, public queer Black world where I have spent a good bit of time, a world largely created by the peerless sunkissed female impersonator Valda Gray. Valda produced shows, often starring in the very ones she produced. All her shows were solely cast with men performing as women. In the 1930s when I was just starting out in life and in my career, I choreographed for Valda and the amazing talent she gathered around her — Petite Swanson, Carole Lee, Frances Dee, either one of the Dixies (Dixie Jean or Dixie Lee), and Calla Donia.

The first show we worked together, Valda chided me when I referred to her as a *him.* I didn't do that again. I wanted her favor and I needed the work. And I liked being a part of the public queer Black world of 1930s Bronzeville — it seemed so shockingly new.

But that was only "seeming." Quiet as it's

kept, except at Halloween when it's an open secret and everybody came to the Southside to attend the big drag balls Eddie Plique produced, there has been a public queer Black world for as long as there has been a Black show world — and that goes back to minstrel show days.

I was there when Alfred Finnie was a queer street hustler and gambler who was just getting the big public fun started in 1935 at the first Finnie's Club Ball. Perhaps what seemed new at the time was the heightened sense of shared intoxication born of exuberant and unfettered public self-presentation.

Actually, there has been a private queer Black world since as long as we've been Black in these Americas.

I knew from the beginning what I announced without guilt, guile, or shame in my column: boys will be girls. I've known some boys who have been girls since high school. And many of them hung out at the Cabin Inn.

The Cabin Inn, called by some Chicago's *oddest* nite spot, by others Chicago's most *unique* nite spot, was called by Valda, and by much of queer Chicago, a second home. Eventually, she got put out of her second home and found others, my favorites being

Joe's Deluxe Café and the Club DeLisa. But for as long as Valda produced shows in Chicago, wherever she was putting on the show was the center of the public queer Black world.

Not everything improves over time. Once upon a time, there was less hate for boys who would be girls, and for girls who would be boys, and for girls, period, in our world. It isn't like us to hate. Valda swore that was true, and it jibed with what I knew. But now that hate is on the rise.

Inside the Bronzeville of my youth, inside our schools, our churches, our barbershops, our beauty shops, our houses, apartments, and hotels, bright lines between what a man does and what a woman does, what a man wears and what a woman wears, how a man talks and how a woman talks don't exist as absolutely and always polar opposites. Valda believed sepian maids toted ofay distinctions between the pronouns "he" and "she" home to us in apron pockets. In ofay homes, men do one thing and women do another: men swear and women don't; men like sex and women don't; he is he, and she is she, and the heshe, shehe that is so much of everyone's real life goes unacknowledged.

Valda impersonated no one. Valda Gray was always Valda Gray. Always queer, always

165

funny, always sepian, always femme, always fine, always vigorous, always powerful.

Want what you want. When people find it hard to do that, they should meditate on Valda. Discerning your desire is the first business of being human. Tall Valda in a demure gown with a bow at the neck, lithe and lovely, sweet-singing a song, or energetically running her way through all those shows she produced: "Anything Goes," "Doing the Jive," "At the Jazz Band Ball," "Turn on the Heat," and "Swing Patrol." So many are forgetting Valda and her most-prized lessons.

Valda fears that part of the price of integrating into the white world is losing a world where men can openly dress as women and love other men if they want, and also losing a world where women are valued. She says the white men hate to be compared to women for two big reasons, and both are ugly. First, they hate women, and second, they think that women are powerless.

Things are changing. At the Cabin Inn we prized eccentrics and individuality. Today, every Negro is being asked to conform, to wear suits and ties or dresses and pumps to the sit-in. Valda doesn't play that. Golf-sweater and silk-suit-wearing Negro that I am, I prize that. I prize Valda running around this world on heels in dresses, even with Dr. King preaching respectability so hard, so often, so loud, and so silently that somehow, now, it feels easier for me to get married and hide.

Valda doesn't believe many things are one thing or another. She thinks everything is just like her — mixed. I want my students to know Valda. I want them to know that most important things about themselves are a choice. They can choose their own names. Choose to know and announce their true sex. Choose who they work with. Choose a life of art. Choose to see when politics is failing. Choose to build community. Choose to be as vibrant as Valda. Or not.

My favorite times with Valda are not on the public stage. Our best time was semi-private and dim lit, those creole card parties of a late afternoon, those times when after working all week it would be someone's birthday and we would post up far from stage, in our kimonos, twelve or fifteen of us, eating gumbo, drinking cheap brandy, playing spades, and laughing like old biddies and steel-driving men. This was the time to remember the moonlight that had fallen on our shoulders and all the lips we had shamelessly kissed. In these moments we did not talk of caliber, we did not evaluate our performances; we talked of besotted love, of those times we had discovered that bit of boy in our girl, or that bit of girl in our boy, or that we were all-boy, or all-girl, so many delightful variations to be found when you boldly lose yourself in someone else. I can't tell my students about that. Part of Valda's power and joy was inhabiting a sensual life.

For years our female impersonators were in almost every issue of *Ebony* magazine and in all the Black newspapers all the time without apology or explanation. In Detroit they were in the *Chronicle.* Some of our best of our Detroit best? Valerie Compton, Priscilla Dean, Princess DeCarlo, Ricky DePaul, Lamar Lyons, and Baby Jean Ray. This, for me, was a sign that ours wasn't a pink-and-blue world. Our sepian world was many shades of purple, some closer to pink, some closer to blue.

Valda Gray would have had a little something to say to MLK, had she gotten the chance. Valda would have let Bayard Rustin stand at the front at the March on Washington. Others hissed he was homosexual and should be shunted to the side. Others were wrong. Bayard Rustin produced that show, the March on Washington, and he should have gotten to take a more visible bow. We pay many prices to be fully recognized as citizens of these United States. One of them should not be the sacrifices of Valda Gray and Bayard Rustin. And me.

A gesture I loved having seen? Valda snap a perfectly manicured finger and try to call Bayard's name in her singsong drawl, "You know who I mean, that siddity Quaker colored kid from West Chester, Pennsylvania, with a sweet tenor voice, sings 'Trouble.' What's his name? Bayard Rustin! I knew Bayard then and I stand with Bayard now."

Where's the place for Valda Gray in our civil rights dream? Why is Bayard way off to the side when the preachers start arranging the congregation for photos and television coverage? Why is there no place for Valda at all?

If Valda was here, she would say, "Don't pay him no mind, Zig. After they go in through the front door, one of them runs back to the kitchen and opens the back door for me. Acknowledged or unacknowledged, we always up in the house."

LIBATION FOR THE FEAST DAY OF VALDA GRAY:
The Art of Refusal

This riff on a Crimean Cup à la Marmora serves 10. Valda always moved in a crowd.

2 jiggers of Jamaican rum
2 jiggers of maraschino liqueur
2 1/2 jiggers of brandy
1 pint of Torani almond syrup
1 bottle (750 mil.) of Champagne
1 quart of soda water

Place all the ingredients in a pretty bowl. Pack the bowl in fine ice. When chilled, serve cold in fancy glasses.

WEEK 13
THIRTEENTH SUNDAY
AFTER FATHER'S DAY

Colored Girl's father gave her a copy of *His Eye Is on the Sparrow,* Ethel Waters's first autobiography, for her twelfth birthday. She kept her copy of it on the shelf of her bedroom in Middleburg. In 1972 Ethel Waters published a second version of her autobiography, titled *To Me It's Wonderful.* Colored Girl purchased a copy at Savile Book in Georgetown, DC, and spotted toward making Waters's words real.

On her thirteenth visit to her mother's sickbed, Colored Girl was presented with her copies of the Ethel Waters autobiographies. Tucked into the more-recent volume, she found an envelope that had been addressed to her and postmarked January 5, 1968. The slit-open envelope contained a typed letter she had never read:

Colored Girl, Colored Girl! It's your old friend Valda.

171

Typing you a letter on Ziggy's typewriter from Kirwood. Ziggy says if you get this letter call Ziggy. 313 555-1111. But don't worry about him none. He wants me to tell you he's "cocooned by every available luxury." Baby Doll, Bob Bennett, and all these Detroit people he's writing about in his Saints Day book are taking excellent care of your godfather. Detroit folk love them some Ziggy!

And I'm all about loving Ziggy, too, now that I read the first part of his book. Ethel Waters, Bricktop, Cordie King, and me — we some of Ziggy's summer saints. He's fallen asleep and stopped telling me what to write, so I'm just going to tell you about what I thought of when I read the part of his Saints Day book that stars me.

First, I don't know who is in the rest — but I'm glad to be in the kickoff: summer. And you in it, too! Ain't nothing

172

better than summer and
fifteen-cent five-decker ice
cream cones while watching the
kids play their last games of
tag until the street lights
come on — just about the time
I start thinking about getting up and eating chicken-
fried steak with gravy and
grits and going to work in a
smoky sweet club — that time
of night — you showed me that
once, Colored Girl, when the
neon shines bright and the
fireflies blink in mason jars,
that's the best part of summer. Girls across America were
playing school, and you girls
in Detroit played showbar, and
you, personally, made a flashing neon light by stacking
mason jars full of fireflies
one on top of the other. Only,
the first time you did it you
forgot to poke holes in the
aluminum lids and the flies
died quick. The next time, you
poked the holes, made a tall
stack with fireflies, topped
that one with an empty jar,

then topped *that* with another
jar full of lightning bugs.
Your sign flashed the letter
"I." Y'all made fun out of a
little bit of nothing.

Summer is root time in Detroit. The heat reminds all of
us old enough to have been
"born south" of Alabama, and
Mississippi, and Louisiana,
and Georgia. Most of Ziggy's
summer saints come from those
old places and old times. The
places and times we remember
when we see all the old roses
in all the east side Detroit
gardens, backyards with gold-
fish ponds in them and trel-
lises with pole beans curling
up them, right on Hazelwood
and Taylor, off 12th Street
with the blind pigs and those
streets near the Catholic
School, Roselawn and Green-
lawn. That's the roots of
where we been blooming into a
great big night flower. Cassius
Clay-pretty. Too pretty to
bruise or scratch. That's Motor City Summer. That's Ziggy

summer. I think he's writing this book so you won't forget all of that.

Ziggy says you curious. That's why he's gifting you his book. Y'all must be alike. Ziggy is curious as all get out. He never needed more than four blocks to have a million adventures. He falls in love with the sun when it rises; when it slips out of the sky, he starts wooing stars, while winking at the moon. Ziggy say you love nature, too. I'm starting to wonder if you ain't Ziggy's child. You more like him than Josette is like him, but we all know Ziggy sweet as tea and afraid of George Stanley, so we know that's not true. Ziggy tells everybody he can't afford silver spoons for his god-daughter, but he's leaving her the manuscript of his *Saints Day Book* in his will.

I wish your mama would bring you to Ziggy's bedside. The only two people he's tore-up

about not seeing one more time is you and Eartha Kitt. And Eartha ain't coming.
Begging you to beg your mama,
Valda
January 2, 1968 — Kirwood Hospital, Detroit, Michigan

After reading the letter, Colored Girl had a question for her mother. "Where's Ziggy's book?" Her mother smiled and replied, "I don't think I remember."

Ethel Waters

PATRON SAINT OF: *Twice-Told Stories, Having Your Say, and Abused Children*

Like my friends Eddie Plique, Tom Bullock, Bricky, Butter and Sue, and Kingfish, Ethel Waters was born in the 19th century. Unlike the others, Ethel, born in 1896, is now crazy religious. She gets signs and messages from God. Some of them are about Detroit. She thought this crazy mess was so normal, she talked all about it in interviews. If Jesus didn't hear her prayers, she hoped he might see one of the newspaper articles. On both channels Ethel told King Jesus that she would be ready and in Detroit waiting for King Jesus to provide material deliverance

176

in the form of pretty-plenty cash. Ethel was gigging in a Motor City showbar when she got the news that she was signed to play Berenice in *Member of the Wedding.* I was emceeing those shows. Oddly, the address of the club was "666" — the devil's sign. The place was so rough, we boasted of "protected parking" on the show bill. You called Ed Griffith for a reservation, and you needed a reservation. With Ethel singing and Fletch Henderson accompanying her on piano, topping the bill, all my breadwinners were coming out in droves. Sometimes they didn't even stop to change into going-out clothes; they came straight from the plant in uniforms and work clothes. Fletch and Ethel were something to hear.

She was married for the first time, in 1909, in Chester, Pennsylvania. She was thirteen years old and called herself "grown." I call her a child whose rape was sanctioned by the state.

She wrote an autobiography, *His Eye Is on the Sparrow.* That impressed me. When women didn't talk rape, *she* wrote about it. A mixed-race, middle-class man put a knife to her mother's throat and raped her. Ethel turned that evil into art. And she managed this other triumph: despite being conceived in a rape, she managed to love freely. She

177

had the will to resist believing that all people were as that one (evil) person had been, and the will to resist seeing herself as others saw her — unless they saw her (good and untainted) as she saw herself.

Something about Ethel touched folks in their innards. The first person I ever heard say that was Della Reese. Della claimed Ethel as her idol. Della was jealous of Ethel's body. How it was at first too thin, then too wide, and never a worry to Ethel. Della worried about her shape and her height. Della was only five feet and maybe two inches — in heels. Della said she envied Ethel's ease more than she envied Lena Horne's and Dorothy Dandridge's perfect heights and perfect shapes. I took Della to see Waters in *Mamba's Daughters* on Broadway. There was a scene where Waters's character tussles with the character played by Willie Bryant. After the show we gathered in Willie's room while someone rubbed his shoulders. Someone always had to rub his shoulders. Waters would get so into her role she bruised Willie every performance. When he took his shirt off, Della winced when she saw those blue, purple, and black bruises. Ethel was quick to reassure her. Between drags on a cigarette she said, "At least he got it for art, not love."

Waters landed a starring role in *Pinky,* a 1949 film about passing, poverty, and mother love, and for us hip to the show world gossip, white directors trying to control a Black star. All Black Detroit went out to the Nortown at 7 Mile and Van Dyke to see *Pinky* and maybe a bit of the back-stage drama, starting with: Waters hated the film's first director, John Ford. And Ford hated Waters.

Ford got fired and had to pretend he had shingles. He had been afraid-to-get-out-of-bed-to-face-Waters. Could be he really *did* have the shingles. Ethel had prayed so hard against Ford and believed so faithfully that "God's eye was on the sparrow" and God's eye was on her beautiful brown body, so maybe Waters's Sweet Jesus did strike that old white man down with a slash of red-oozing rash. You never know.

At the end of the day, Elia Kazan came in to direct, Waters starred, and *Pinky* was the biggest box office hit of 1949, the year Elsie Roxborough died. We were all mad the studio didn't choose Freddie Washington, or someone else pale and Black to play Pinky. Maybe even our Elsie Roxborough. All that loss was half-eclipsed by these gains: Waters taking down Ford, then taking on the other Ethel, Ethel Barrymore, acclaimed Queen of the Theater. *Our* Ethel and *their* Ethel went toe to toe, and Ethel Waters bested Ethel Barrymore frame by frame.

I used to love to go to the movies with Ethel. She would talk right out loud to the screen and say the funniest things. She could make a bad movie good with her commentary. People didn't tell her to shut up, they told her to talk louder. She was completely at home around movies on the screen or in the audience.

Sometimes you beat the drum with a shrug of shoulders and a lift of chin. Kazan tried to talk to Waters once the picture had wrapped, after he had been bludgeoned a bit by her anger and what he wanted to see as her paranoia, after she had sweetened him for the kill with her daily on-the-set morning kisses and a seeming compliance. Kazan, a smart man, asked Waters a question he stupidly thought she wouldn't have the courage to honestly answer.

Kazan asked, "Do you hate all white men?" With a flip of the tip of a curl hanging off the wig on her head, Ethel snatched back all the kisses she had used to scratch Kazan's patronizingly progressive ego. Waters replied, "I am suspicious of all white men. I love none of them." With a dozen words she got revenge for every woman who ever played "Mammy" on- or offstage. And better than that, she pronounced those words like this: "i-am/ SuSPIcious/ of ALL/ WHITE men." It wasn't just words. It was the rhythm under the words. She beat our ancient drum when she took him down.

When Ethel met my wife and discovered she had got her pet name from Kazan's '56 flick *Baby Doll,* Ethel hugged my bride and whispered, "You may persuade me to like director-boy Kazan."

LIBATION FOR THE FEAST DAY OF ETHEL WATERS:
The Twice-Told Story

1 jigger of rye whiskey
1/2 pony of curaçao
1 dash of Angostura bitters

Add all ingredients and ice to a rocks glass. Stir.

FALL

Tanya Blanding (1963–1967)
Charles Diggs Sr. (1894–1967)
Herman "Scatterbrain" Stevens
(1920–1967)
Milton Winfield Jr. (1919–1958)
Elsie Roxborough (1914–1949)
Artis Lane (1927–present)
G. S. (1930–present)
Minot Jelke (1929–1990)
George Stanley (1929–1996)
Tallulah Bankhead (1902–1968)
Martin Luther King Jr. (1929–1968)
Della Reese (1931–2017)
Billy Eckstine (1914–1993)
LaVern Baker (1929–1997)

WEEK 14
FOURTEENTH SUNDAY
AFTER FATHER'S DAY

Addie Mae Collins, Carol Denise McNair, Carole Robertson, and Cynthia Wesley were assassinated on September 15, 1963, while attending church services in Birmingham, Alabama. The blast was deeply felt in Detroit. Many Black Detroiters were born in Alabama, had ancestors buried in Alabama, or had family remaining in Alabama. Birmingham shrapnel made Motown bleed. When Tanya Blanding was killed in 1967, Colored Girl's father, born in Selma, told her, "It's open season on colored girls, Colored Girl."

After the mother's funeral, Colored Girl went to the DuPont Circle apartment. The mother had given her the keys. A copy of the will lay on the dining room table. According to the notarized document, the mother had left her entire estate, with the single exception of a box marked "Mari's

Papers" and "Ziggy's Book," to the Lutheran Church, Missouri Synod.

It wasn't a shock. Colored Girl knew her mother. All she wanted were the papers: the letters from her father, the photographs, and Ziggy's book. Her husband was a painter, she was a barkeep and a writer; with a girl to raise, she could have used the insurance money and the proceeds from selling the apartment. She had the papers. She was fine. With the papers, there was a chance she could remember who she had been before she knew who her mother was, and what Detroit had been before it imploded. She needed that.

The Earth Day–era green and gold flowered box was on her mother's white-linen-covered bed. Since Colored Girl last saw the box, the words "Ziggy's Book" had been scrawled in a shaky hand beneath the words "Mari's Papers." Inside the box she found dozens of letters written from 1969 through early 1977 by her father to Colored Girl. Letters she hadn't received. Some were still sealed. And there were letters from Colored Girl to her father that the mother had intercepted on their way to the mail.

Dear Daddy,
I am the most unhappy girl in America. Come get me.

Mari

Dear Daddy,
Can you help me be happy again?

Love,
Colored Girl

Dear Mr. Stanley,
Colored Girl is the most unhappy girl in America. The Black kids here say her mother is on a pancake box and the white kids say "Colored Girl" is a bad word not a nickname. I sleep beside her in the bed every night and hear her cry. Come get us.

Tanya

The mother didn't take all the letters being sent in either direction. Just enough, ten or twelve a year, to make father and daughter think the other lied about writing. At the bottom of the box was a smaller box marked "Ziggy's Book." Colored Girl opened the box. It was full of ashes.

Tanya Blanding

PATRON SAINT OF: *Violated Innocence, Civilians in War Zones, and Black Girls Creating Magic*

Not all my Saints are living. Tanya Blanding resided at 1756 Euclid Street. I had plans for that girl. On July 26, 1967, she was shot dead by a Michigan state trooper.

Tanya was huddled underneath the family dining table, the table on better days she twirled around. The window-unit air conditioner had given out, but Tanya was shivering despite the heat. Someone remembered that. Someone else in the room, one of the men, who was tired, from the sounds of gunshots, from being stuck in the house, from being full of fear, lit a cigarette as a way of taking a rest.

The child shivered in the heat, then went all over goosebumps. Perhaps she was remembering moving, her own way, around the table, taking two miniature steps, then a leap. She was so much other than the exhaustion or the folly of grown folk.

Tanya was four, and hungry for new surprises. She had seen the sun rise like a red ball of fire in the sky, and her eyes had glowed brighter ever after. She had been surprised by that big red circle where usually there was only blue and white. The surprises provoked a pleasant little buzz of girl-joy. I know all that because I know four-year-old girls, taught platoons of them. Already she could jump double-dutch. I know because I had seen her on the street. She would walk down to the corner store and buy a nickel's worth of lime Nowor-laters. Most girls choose strawberry and the boys choose grape, but she chose lime. I knew this because she had agile fingers that folded the little squares of wax-coated paper the hard-green taffy came wrapped in into a striking green chain necklace that she wore around her neck. Most four-year-olds can't do that. Already she could sing a large repertory of Sunday School hymns: "This Little Light of Mine," "Michael Row Your Boat Ashore," "He's Got the Whole World in His Hands." She could already tell her favorite Bible stories. She liked the one about Adam and Eve because she thought it was funny that they were naked. The grapevine told me that. One of my students said that Tanya was under the table because she was imagining she was Jonah, and she was in the belly of the whale, and it was a very safe place. Another girl told me Tanya was under the table just knowing she was Daniel-safe in the lion's den. They couldn't

189

know any of that. They were trying to imagine something good she could have been doing just before she died. Afterward, the rest of the summer of 1967, all that the girl students in my dancing school wanted to tell me about was Tanya.

What happened next? Uncertain. Maybe the flame from a cigarette lighter ignited the paranoia in a Michigan state policeman. Mortimer LeBlanc. The summer of 1967, crazy was contagious in Motown. Michigan State Police and National Guardsmen were patrolling the Detroit streets like they were still patrolling Vietnam's Iron Triangle, on a search-and-destroy, Rolling Thunder mission. That's what some sepian soldiers, home early from 'Nam because they were all shot up, were saying up and down 12th Street when they got drunk in some blind pig. And this: LeBlanc shot at a flash from a cigarette lighter and hit Tanya Blanding.

Twenty-seven bullets pierced her. Forty pounds, forty inches, four years of fast-growing future were cut down before she could twirl through my door. This is how the *Detroit Free Press* put it, and I memorized the lie: "the light was greeted by a fusillade of bullets from the outside." Bullets are not a "greeting." They are always a dismissal.

You walk into my School of the Theatre from a Detroit street that runs from a farm to a factory. You walked out of my school, if my magic worked, onto a path that connected a dance studio to a courtroom, to a surgical operating theater, to the Rose Room in the Algonquin Hotel, to someplace where you can change a few things. You walk out toward being a lawyer, a doctor, a writer, a labor leader. But not if you don't walk in.

All kinds of ways and all kinds of folks tried to interfere with me turning a ghetto dancing school into a launchpad that propels young sepian citizens into John Glenn's sky and into any other place they dream of being. I was prepared for most interference. Uniformed men shooting one of my girls down with a rifle I did not anticipate. That didn't break my spell, that broke *me.*

I sat at the back of the Rev. Cleage's church and heard him preach Tanya's funeral sermon. The eulogy hit me hard. Seeing the young boys carrying the tiny coffin hit me harder.

The riots. The death of Tanya. The funeral. July 1967 was the hardest month ever. These last months I worked, I worked longing for a student I will never teach — Tanya.

For twenty years I have taught a powerful

dance, the "girl walk" — a walk of self-reference that allows for syncopation with other self-referencing souls. It starts by not looking down. *Baby, keep your head up!* It ends with remembering. And in the middle? Sustaining delusion. Hearing the drum. When it's not there. Hearing Tanya's heartbeat. When the heart is not beating. The girl walk is the dance that allows living hearts to beat in coordination with the heartbeats of dead Black daughters who did not make it across the water. This is the dance I teach to all the girls who come to my school: the breadwinners' daughters, the thieves' daughters, the dentists' daughters — all of them. I can't teach it anymore.

The girl walk is not a victory dance; it is dance as victory. I lost that step when I lost Tanya.

LIBATION FOR THE FEAST DAY OF TANYA BLANDING:
The Girl Walk

Fill a large mixing glass 2/3 full
crushed ice, then add:

1 Tbsp. of bar sugar
1 lemon, juiced
Soda water

Fruit for garnish

Stir. Strain into a lemonade glass. Dress
with fruit and serve.

Week 15
Fifteenth Sunday
after Father's Day

It was the most shocking event. It was in all the Negro newspapers and magazines coast to coast. Charles Diggs Senior waited until his brother left the room, to get a drink of water or pee (the story is told variously), then jumped out the window of his fourth-floor Detroit Memorial Hospital room. He was seventy-five years old. He was one of the richest Black men in America. He was the pillar of Black Detroit. He was the father of the congressman who founded the Black Caucus. He was the son of a Baptist minister who had traveled from Mississippi to missionary in Africa. And he was dead.

He had survived a two-year imprisonment for accepting bribes while serving as a state senator. He had survived two strokes. He didn't survive the nightmares in which he relived these events.

"The war don't end when the last gun is

shot," George Stanley said. "That's the end of a battle. The war ends when you stop waking up shaking in the middle of the night. Too many men, Colored Girl, win the boots on the ground war then lose the war in they head when they're back safe in their bed. Be better than that."

After the mother's funeral, she started losing the war in her head. Her head hurt so much that she followed, and not for the first time, advice she had been given by Lucille Ellis, and went to see a therapist, this time one with "Dr." before their name. She thought she needed a prescription.

Colored Girl described dipping her dog's paw into pigment and signing a letter to her father. She thought her father would laugh and cry and then come get her. Ziggy always said laughing or crying helped people remember. But George didn't come. And now she knew he had never gotten the letter.

It should have been devastating, except it wasn't. Colored Girl had known when she pressed her dog's paint-dipped paw onto the paper that if George didn't come, he couldn't come, or that it wasn't safe for Colored Girl if he *did* come. And she knew exactly what she had to do if George didn't come. He had told her a thousand times:

"Hold the fort."

"Most kids," the shrink said, "would think their daddy didn't love them — if their daddy didn't come."

"Not kids from Detroit back then," Colored Girl replied. "In our Detroit, if one man didn't want to be your daddy, there were three men, starting with Ziggy, and maybe a grandpa, an uncle, or an older cousin, who wanted that job."

"Tell me more about that."

"Me, I didn't have to get further than George. If he didn't come, I just had to do what he taught me to do: hold the fort."

"And what do you have to do now?"

"Figure out how to disarm."

"How do you disarm when all the men you loved wore guns?"

"Ziggy didn't."

She had survived because of George. She loved movies like *The Professional,* about a contract killer and a little girl, because she understood what it was to be a hard man's daughter. If she was to thrive, it would be because she had figured out how to be Ziggy's daughter.

She bought herself a steno pad and made herself a To-Do list. She laughed out loud, thinking she was in this one way turning into her mother. She wrote herself a memo. She block-printed a goal at the top: "Don't be like Bette. Accept life as it comes, without attempting to control it." She crossed that out and block-printed a better goal: "Don't dive like Diggs. Be like Ziggy and George: Embrace and Enjoy a messy and dangerous world." She translated that goal into four short action items: Stay alive; know her mother; love her mother; get to hard-won happy. Next session, she shared this info with her shrink.

"What if you discover, when you come to know and love your mother, that she doesn't love you?"

"I already know that."

"So?"

"I want to know why, and how I can love her without it being humiliating."

"You think that's possible?"

"Ziggy did it."

Ziggy didn't know the mother as well as Colored Girl thought he did.

Charles Diggs Sr.

PATRON SAINT OF: *Mourners, Equestrians, and Fathers*

1967 The wingless descent of Diggs to the ground, when he leapt from a fourth floor Detroit Memorial Hospital window to his

197

death, unbuckled Detroit from some powerful mythologies. He had risen so high that we believed he had wings.

After graduating, in 1919, from America's top embalming school for Blacks, the Echols School of Mortuary Science, in Philadelphia, Charles Diggs came to Detroit and in 1921 founded the House of Diggs funeral home.

White folks do not embalm Black bodies. And even if they did, we would not go to them for that service. Sepians seek sepians to embalm our dead, to see us naked, to make the cheek soft for the family member who leans over the coffin to get that last kiss. These truths have made the Diggs family of Detroit rich.

In 1962 *Ebony* compiled a list of the 100 wealthiest Negroes in America. A good ten percent of the list were people related to the burying business — the other, quiet-as-the-grave, Black underworld and wealth engine.

Striding through the lobby of the Gotham Hotel, or on his way to dinner with political cronies in the Ebony Room, Diggs, who measured a height of a mere sixty-six inches, according to his tailor, was an imposing presence. On his seventeen-hand-high, jet-black Percheron, as he was frequently seen by sepian picnickers, on the bridle path of the park on Belle Isle, an island in the center of the city, Diggs was a literal ten-foot tall.

Whenever he left the city, a pillar of the town was missing — but the town didn't topple to the ground. Imprisoned, or at a conference, or vacationing, Diggs maintained a presence in Detroit by phone and mail and via his appointed surrogates, including his son. I got a note from Diggs in 1958 that was mailed from Tokyo advising me, and "all who could afford it," to visit the Orient. He said traveling in the East was a "new breath of freedom." When he determined to stay gone and killed himself, many, myself included, predicted the city would crash.

Charles Diggs liked to present himself as a great man in a circle of great men and women. One day he particularly treasured was October 6, 1962, when President John Fitzgerald Kennedy came to Detroit and spoke at a large rally calling on Diggs's son, the congressman, to help save America. Diggs was standing by Junior on the side of the stage when the president lifted up their family name. In that autumn of 1962, so much still seemed possible. We did not think the autumn leaves were dead; we thought them colorful.

Those days, those years, Diggs enjoyed such good fortune that he had to work hard to stay humble. He painted himself as the rule, not the exception. And he did it his way: He would talk about US Bonds, that embalming product manufacturer who was a millionaire based in Madison, Arkansas, who had built an empire that stretched from coast to coast. He didn't just flirt with the Chicago-cemetery-owning socialite Callie Broxton, whose father founded Burr Oak Cemetery, referred to by *Jet* in 1955 as "the Windy City's richest bachelor girl." Diggs sought out her advice and boasted of taking it, making her both more popular and more respected. He was proud of knowing the California civil rights leader and mortuary owner Aramis Fouche. He would say, "There are the Fords in Memphis, of course, and A. G. Gaston in Birmingham. There's Rayner in Chicago who showed Emmett Till's body without corpse-makeup or closed coffin. There's that fellow in Plaquemine, Louisiana. He doesn't make any money, but he saved John Farmer from certain death by hiding him in a coffin and sending out a decoy hearse, and then the real hearse, and got him safe out of Plaquemine. And then there's *me.*"

He wasn't the tip-top man, he announced,

just because he owned the mortuary, the cemetery, and the flower shop, or because the House of Diggs had its own radio show that often featured my favorite schoolmarm, Shirley McNeil. He wasn't the tip-top man only because he got himself elected to office and his son elected to even higher office. And yes, he created wealth and a web of connections that could be converted to political power; there were also others who did that. What elevated Diggs? Detroit.

Everybody knew Diggs had buried a lot of breadwinners. Most paid him. Some, he paid for. He buried the breadwinners during strike years and overtime years. When Diggs died, articles would be written that cited his ability to "walk with commoners and kings." Journalists were too polite to mention his ability to thrive both in jail and in his mansion, and some were unaware of his ability to thrive on the Belle Isle bridle path and on a faraway Tokyo freeway. Black Bottom knew all of this.

Black Bottom knew something about Diggs the world couldn't know: Diggs wielded the power of the Negro undertaker to keep ritual true to love. There was the time a long-married doctor ran off with a younger woman from somewhere out West and divorced his wife of forty years. That doctor shot himself on the first anniversary of his second marriage. The young wife was in charge of the burial. The sepian undertaker helped the young widow bury her husband where and as she wanted. But three years later, when the first wife died and the dead doctor's grown children wanted to bury their mother *beside* their father and the young widow refused, Diggs had a solution. By the light of the moon his men dug up the father's casket, put the coffin of his first wife in the bottom of the grave, then returned the husband to his eternal rest atop her, while leaving room for the young widow above — when her time came. He provided this service without charge and without informing the young second wife, who didn't understand a basic Black Bottom truth: Detroit makes a space at the center of the action for every beloved body.

Until it didn't. The doctor who ran out of the hospital to declare Diggs dead on the sidewalk reported, according to *Jet,* that his body "looked like a crumpled biscuit." It would have seemed impossible. He had had a second stroke. He could barely stand. But he stood. His frail arms wrestled open a window. Charles Diggs Sr. was a man to achieve the impossible. Detroit survived the blowup of the Gotham Hotel. Then Diggs jumped out a window. The death of Tanya. The 12th Street fires. Nineteen sixty-seven was a vicious year!

LIBATION FOR THE FEAST DAY OF CHARLES DIGGS SR.:
Bronze Casket

1 pony of cognac
1 pony of apple brandy
1 pony of sweet vermouth
Brandied or Luxardo cherry

Place the brandies and the vermouth in a mixing glass with ice. Stir for about 20 seconds. Stir longer for a slightly weaker drink, shorter for a stronger drink. Strain into a cocktail glass with no ice, and dress with a brandied cherry.

FALL MOVEABLE FEAST: LABOR DAY

Scatterbrain, shot dead September 10, 1967, was the model for *Super Fly*'s Youngblood Priest, played by Ron O'Neal. Though the film *Super Fly* is set in Harlem, the specific activities that inspired the construction of the cult-classic occurred in Cleveland, where the *Super Fly* screenwriter Phillip Fenty, the *Super Fly* actor O'Neal, and the *Super Fly* model were all raised.

After Colored Girl's mother's second (and white) husband died, leaving the woman a substantial life insurance payment, the mother stopped working for the federal government, started volunteering, bought a condominium in a prestigious building on Dupont Circle, then that farm near Middleburg, Virginia. This has been told. The mother took up hunting and target shooting. This has not been told. She bought Colored Girl rifles and riflery lessons. She insisted that they shoot together. One Saturday, after catching a glimpse of a red palm print on her brown cheek, Colored Girl was contemplating the need to stumble and discharge her weapon "accidentally on purpose." The most benign of Colored Girl's Middleburg daughterly duties included providing the evening meal. She had put ribs on the Weber grill before she left with the mother for target practice. The scent of fire, evoking memories of September backyard barbeques in Detroit where dry cleaners, doctors, lawyers, artists, and contract killers had often convened, stopped her from stumbling. She had known stone-cold killers and she wasn't one. She took her shot, hit her paper target, then put her rifle down.

Herman "Scatterbrain" Stevens

PATRON SAINT OF: *Chefs, Criminals, and Byzantine Brains*

I am almost embarrassed to love Scatterbrain, but this makes it easier. I play "September Song" and I remember that Moses was a murderer.

Nobody enjoyed a September Sunday in Motown more than Herman "Scatterbrain"

205

Stevens. In his hometown, Cleveland, he was a hardworking, high-rolling celebrity surrounded by people with their hands out and problems that needed solving that only he could solve. In Motown, he was the football fan grilling and giving away the best barbeque in town.

The world will say Scatterbrain was a heroin dealer. But he didn't deal in Detroit. He believed Detroit was the best place in the world to shoot the bull, pour the corn, leave all the white horses behind him. He understood Detroit was a place to get yourself a special kind of straight you can only get in the company of peers and friends and preferably at a Lions game! Sometimes that meant we went to the stadium; sometimes that meant we shared a couch at someone's house, preferably Lawrence Massey's, where we were warm, where old and gold liquor flowed, where plates of dry-rubbed and wet-sauced barbecue were plentiful; and sometimes that meant we listened to the game on a radio while driving around in one of Scatter's many Cadillacs.

He was the only person I ever knew whose favorite way to experience a Lions game was not to sit in his excellent seats on the forty-yard line but to drive around listening to

206

the game on the radio, looking at "Motown and all the pretty people in it!" Scatter worshipped Detroit City. The way "everybody had jobs, some people had two, some people had three." Scatterbrain loved to see the houses those jobs bought, the children those jobs clothed, and the cars those jobs built.

Scatterbrain loved cars. He was the first person I knew to have a phone in his car. And the first person I knew to have a burglar alarm on his car. That Cadillac with an alarm was, as Scatter himself described it, a barbeque-sauce red.

Shirley McNeil said Scatter had a byzantine brain. What I know? He figured this out: In 1933, Italy recognized the Vatican as its own country. When Pope Pius XI drove out of the Vatican, the country, into the country of Italy for the very first time, Pope Pius XI rode in a Detroit-built Graham-Paige put together by Detroit Negroes. Yes, there were Negroes in Detroit who claimed to have helped build the Pope's car, and Scatter knew them. Those breadwinners, who worked at the Graham-Paige plant when the Pope's car was being built, were the same breadwinners who later, during the Second World War, insisted that union monies not be used to pay for a trip to

Boblo Island because the boats to Boblo were not letting Negroes ride. Boblo itself was Negro-friendly, the boats were not, and Boblo was an island. Boblo was segregated until Graham-Paige Negroes desegregated it — without the help of lawyers.

If you were Scatter driving around Detroit and listening to a game, it meant you were able to gaze at some ordinary-looking old Black man and know he might be one of the retired breadwinners who had built the Pope's car, or one of the men who had brought R. J. Thomas, president of the United Auto Workers, to heel. Seeing those old ebony men who made global marks swinging heavy hammers, Scatter couldn't help but love him some Detroit City, and Detroit couldn't help but love Scatter.

Part of what Scatter was doing rolling around Motown was looking for a place to open a Detroit rib shack. In Cleveland, Scatter's Restaurant specialized in two affordable luxuries: footlongs, and fries topped with barbecue sauce. The footlong is the Cadillac of hot dogs; it's still cheap ground meat. Sauced French fries are little bits of cheap heaven; they are still potatoes. Scatter was experimenting with rubs and sauces for pork ribs, beef brisket, and steak filet. In Detroit, Black folk ate meat. We ate so much meat, one of the kings of the Cleveland barbecue scene, Eugene "Hot Sauce" Williams, had already opened a Detroit outpost of his Cleveland rib shop and called it "Williams World's Best Bar-B-Q." Scatter was working to top that.

Scatter said that when he got his ribs perfect, he was moving to Detroit and getting out of heroin. When he brought his ribs to Detroit, he was putting Vernors ginger ale in the sauce. And it was going to have a little sorghum in it because so many of the Black folk in Detroit had come up from Alabama, where they grew up on farms making sorghum with a big press and a mule.

For years, Scatter told everybody he knew that he wanted thirty Cadillacs in his funeral procession. He had fifty. Many of the cars came over from Detroit City. All were built in Detroit City.

Diggs, Tanya, Scatter — their deaths got my blood pressure shooting through the roof. When I got back from Scatter's funeral, Dr. Bodywork Bob wanted to put me in the hospital. I refused to go. He prescribed Resperdine, a mild sedative, that he said would help bring the pressure down and let me sleep. I said I preferred to try a little brandy. Fall of 1967, I was beginning to think it would be easier to die than to live.

LIBATION FOR THE FEAST DAY OF
SCATTERBRAIN STEVENS:
Fifty Cadillacs

1 pony of cognac
1 pony of curaçao
1/2 pony of Jamaican rum
1/2 pony of bourbon
1 sugar cube
Fruit slices for garnish

Put sugar cube and all the booze in a
cocktail shaker. Lightly muddle and stir
sugar to dissolve. Fill cocktail shaker with
crushed ice and shake briefly. Pour entire
contents into rocks glass and top with
more crushed ice. Dress with fruit slices.

WEEK 16
SIXTEENTH SUNDAY
AFTER FATHER'S DAY

From the time that she could toddle, to the week she moved to DC, on many Sundays while her mother went to church with the Lutherans and her grandmother went to church with the Baptists, Colored Girl and her father went driving in Elmwood Cemetery.

Shortly before his death in the early nineties her father asked Colored Girl to take him out to drive around Elmwood one last time. She thought he wanted to see the place where he would be buried beside his sister and brother, who had already gone.

"We all got to come to some negotiation with death, Colored Girl," he remarked. "I never allowed myself to be afraid of death. Never wanted you to be afraid of it, either. A person not ready to die is not ready to live." Then he started back in on telling the cemetery stories he had told her when she was a girl, starting with stories of long corteges. The father said the longest cortege he ever saw was Milt Winfield's — but the remarkable thing about that cortege was not the cars but the tears. "That was the one time I ever saw Ziggy cry. Never saw Ziggy shed a tear before or after, but at Milt Winfield's funeral Ziggy cried like a baby." Then the father moved on to the lives behind some of the tombstones, stories of week-long wakes, and onto recalling menus of fabulous repasts in days gone by, as he had done when she was a girl, but this time the stories had a different ending.

"All that's gone with the wind, like silk suits and mohair golf sweaters. When I die, cremate me and spread me Hippy Dippy style over the Detroit River."

Milton Winfield Jr.

PATRON SAINT OF: *Gamblers, Best Friends, and Barkeeps*

God took Milt, like God took Tolton. God did what God shouldn't have done. They say we are made in the image of God. I make plenty of mistakes. Maybe God makes mistakes, too. The Natchez Belle and my aunt Sadye both say God don't make no mistakes. God took Milt, too soon. If God don't make mistakes, God is against me.

There was only one cortege that made me cry harder than Scatter's, and that came ten years before. It was the cortege of the man I called Mr. Henry M. Stanley; he called me Dr. Livingstone. It was the cortege of Milt Winfield.

Milton was a policy baron's son. His daddy, Milton Winfield Sr., was called Beans. He was our Great Gatsby, so Milt was the "more than Gatsby" — he was what Gatsby didn't have: Gatsby's golden son. In Chicago, sepians were addicted to gambling on the policy wheel, and everybody fed off the addiction. Policemen, politicians, preachers — folk of every hue made money from the wheel. When a policy wheel was raided it was understood to be a message that somebody shouldn't run for ward committee, or someone's father-in-law shouldn't run for Congress. You didn't raid a policy wheel for no reason. In Chicago, policy was big business and the Winfields were near the top of it, making enough money to buy a house for themselves and a house in Idlewild for their son.

Milt Winfield spent a lot of time in Michigan. He may have been the one who said: "Idlewild is our Black Eden, sure as Detroit is our Black Camelot." Or maybe that was me. We shared so many ideas, words, and hours.

What was so different in Chicago and Detroit? In Chicago, policy was king and the Black policy barons rose high and ruled while serving white sovereigns. And the wheel was the main place Black and white met. Detroit was different. Our numbers racket was mostly all Black. Second, numbers *did* rule the Black city, but numbers were not the primary place where Blacks and whites interacted.

In Detroit, that happened in the plant. Al Capone and Henry Ford were very different men. Figuring out the labor movement took a different set of mental tools than buying off politicians and policemen and even rival policy-wheel bankers. Detroit gave the promise of less vicious interactions between Blacks and whites, and Detroit sparked the possibility of greater Black economic independence through the Black businesses created to serve our breadwinners.

Milt loved all that, which was why he loaned me without interest some of the money I needed to start my school. Milton J. Winfield wasn't yet forty, actually only possessed thirty-eight years, and he had it all going on. His official job was floor manager of Chicago's Archway Lounge, but he did so much more than manage that floor. He ran the big wheel.

It was not unusual for Milt to be up till 4:00 a.m. Sunday after a Saturday night. It wasn't even unusual for him to have a headache. It wasn't unusual for him to duck into Herb's on Garfield and buy a Coca-Cola and some aspirin. Coke and aspirin were the breakfast that Black southern mothers in the North fed their children who didn't want to eat and also the tonic they whipped out for overworked adult sons and daughters who were feeling puny. It wasn't unusual for Milton to swallow three aspirin and wash them down with Coke. Or to go back to his pretty car and sit behind the wheel and take a deep breath with his window rolled down. That was an ordinary early morning for Milton.

It was unusual, though, for him to fall onto the steering wheel and start hemorrhaging blood from his nose. By the time the car horn was blaring long enough to attract the attention of tavern patrons and early-morning strollers, he was all but dead. They officially declared the death at Billings Hospital, down the road, in the bright light of early morning.

We buried Milt out of Preach's Church of the Deliverance, but for once the name sounded bitter and lying. The funeral procession was longer than long, full of beautiful cars, all built in Detroit. White people gawking at the cortege asked, "How do they *do* it?" The ofays were really asking, "*Why* do they do it?" If I told the truth, that it was because it ensures the breadwinners a job, they wouldn't understand. Milt understood.

Bodywork Bob told me to hasten the pace of my writing. Ten days after Scatter's funeral, he made me take up residence in Kirwood. He doesn't tell me that I won't leave the hospital alive — but I know. Rice boiled in distilled water and fruit juices (supplemented by tasty snacks from the outside) are no longer working with the reserpine and the chlorothiazide he's added to keep my pressure down below what Bodywork Bob calls "Franklin Roosevelt" levels.

The day Roosevelt died, his pressure was at 300/190. Bodywork won't tell me what I'm at, only that it's better than Roosevelt's. He wants to try a pacemaker. I don't want to.

I am in the unending ugly of late autumn. I publicly claimed Milton as my little brother. When we called each other "Stanley" and "Livingstone," we were promising that one of us would travel a long distance to find the other. He's calling me to come meet him upstairs. Daddy Winfield has already gone upstairs or downstairs; I don't know which. He died in 1965, never getting over the image of young Milton in that car bleeding hard from the head. The leaves are off the tree that once stood in front of the Gotham Hotel that now stands before a vacant lot. Nothing and no one is getting better. Scatterbrain makes it to the shelter of his rib shop and dies. Milt makes it to the hospital and dies. That crawl from the cigarette shop to the rib shop is autumn. That ride in the ambulance to the hospital is autumn. Me being in this hospital is autumn. Autumn is the season when you know what's coming next is harder than what is now. In pale spring you look forward to bright summer; in hot summer to the cool of fall; in winter to the hope of spring. In fall, you watch what you have blow away.

LIBATION FOR THE FEAST DAY OF MILTON WINFIELD JR:
Money from the Wheel

1 jigger of brandy

1/2 cup of ginger ale

Place ice into a tall glass, add brandy, top
with ginger ale, stir briefly, and serve.

WEEK 17
SEVENTEENTH SUNDAY
AFTER FATHER'S DAY

Joe Louis was photographed by James Van der Zee. Ziggy received an autographed copy of the photo inscribed "To my dear friend Ziggy, a true champ" from Louis. Years later, Elsie Roxborough stole Ziggy's Joe Louis photograph after having torn up the copy Joe had given her. Following Elsie's death, the Roxboroughs returned the photograph to Ziggy. It lived on his dressing tables at the Gotham and later in the Lafayette Towers.

In the second month of his Kirwood Hospital stay, Ziggy stopped eating his new favorite snacks, tamales and Chinese food, which Baby Doll had been sneaking in, and stopped wanting to work on his book. Baby Doll bought the Van der Zee photograph to the hospital and used it to decorate Ziggy's bed tray and remind him to keep fighting. When Ziggy saw it, he lit up as if he had just walked onstage and found the spotlight. He looked like some-one who might, one day, come home to the Lafayette Towers. Then he spoke, and Baby Doll wondered if the pressure hadn't already damaged his brain past a point of no return: "Baby Doll brought me Elsie Roxborough." She thought she had brought him Joe Louis.

Elsie Roxborough

PATRON SAINT OF: *Unconventional and Invisible Blackness*

If I could bring one person back from the dead, it would be Elsie Roxborough.

Elsie was the first colored woman to go to the University of Michigan and live in the dorms. After his daughter was admitted to Michigan, Daddy Roxborough made her wait out a year to matriculate. He needed time to take the University of Michigan to court to force them to do right by the apple of his eye.

At Michigan, Elsie Roxborough was in the same class as Arthur Miller, the playwright. They both competed in a play competition. He won first place; she won third, but Elsie was right there in the mix with the future Pulitzer Prize and Tony Award winner. In those days he was called "Outstanding Arthur," a fine Jewish boy, born in Harlem, editor of the *Michigan Daily* college paper, who widely announced that Miss Roxborough was the most exciting woman on the Ann Arbor campus. To fully appreciate the compliment, you have to know Miller is the man who would one day marry Marilyn Monroe.

Elsie wrote four, or perhaps it was five, plays, and while still at college even produced one of Langston Hughes's plays. I've been told Lang had a picture of Elsie on his desk on the day she died. Probably kept it there to the day *he* died. Elsie was beyond special.

Joe Louis and Elsie had a thing. Her family and his pride broke that up. Elsie was only seventeen when it was reported that she and Joe were engaged. Soon there was another public announcement declaring the engagement off. Louis made a statement about Elsie's needing to follow her books; she issued a perfectly coordinated statement about wanting a career. Her family, who were carefully grooming Louis for respectability and Elsie for elegance, were satisfied and even pleased when they went their separate ways. And even more pleased when she was writing plays and she founded a company of actors, the Roxanne Players.

She wrote about what she knew. So few people knew her world that her plays were deemed preposterous. One of them was so viciously damned by the sepia press that she stopped putting on plays in Black Detroit. Instead, she moved to New York and began a new life as a white woman.

This took significant preparation, vivid imagination, and a flush travel budget — all of which Elsie, soon to be not-Elsie, possessed in spades. She didn't go straight to New York. She detoured to Mexico, to try out and polish up her Spanish and also to give herself a bit of time to get the details of her lying story straight.

John Roxborough was drinking fine Scotch when he dropped that dime. We were in the Ebony Room of the Gotham Hotel and it was very, very late. He didn't begin the tale with that day, that year, or with his daughter Elsie. He told me a story that began generations earlier, when the 19th century was turning into the 20th, about Roxborough men, Black lawyers and doctors, generations of them, who decided they had had enough of not making money. So they ventured out of the world of respectable Negroes, poor as church mice, and into the world of illegal gambling.

Roxborough put it to me this way: "Was I

too original? Did I raise her to be too original, too?" I could only answer, "Elsie is an original." He took her picture out of his wallet. He held it to the bar-candle flame. He let the flame burn his fingers as it consumed her image. He smashed out the last of the fire with the palm of his powerful hand. "They say Elsie's living in New York. Elsie's dead!"

I looked into Roxborough's eyes to see if he was sharing news or taking a stand. I wished I had not looked. I saw something in Roxborough's eyes that I had never seen there before: hate for his child.

John Roxborough, the numbers king, who had been so proud when Elsie published her first newspaper column just a year out of high school, so proud when she formed the Roxanne Players and produced the Hughes play she called *Drums Out of Haiti,* hated his daughter for being as wild as he was. I wanted to tell him that wasn't fair. But you don't tell John Roxborough anything about his family.

In New York, Elsie started calling herself Pat Rico, then Mona Manet. She started playing a new kind of role in Greenwich Village at 77 Washington Place and ended up at 865 First Avenue, somewhat in the vicinity of Sutton Place. That's where she

223

was living when she died from an overdose of pills on October 2, 1949.

In New York her "white" working life was spent toiling for one second-rate white magazine after another, covering stories in white Atlanta, interviewing white southern society folk, being embraced and entertained by them, all while launching double entendre jabs at white-middle-class habits and peculiarities from the pages of middle-brow white magazines. That victory makes me think her overdose was an accident.

And this: Perhaps her last way to show contempt for the mundane evils of the white social world was to wrap herself up in it, knowing she was superior in every way.

Elsie is the only woman I knew who had lived in the Black world and lived in the white world and lived in them both in a way that would let her know that her Black world was better.

How did our "It" girl, our more-than-Tallulah Bankhead, our more-than-Marilyn Monroe — how did it come to be that she found no place for herself in either world?

Can a person be destroyed by one bad review? Maybe if you were Elsie and so used to praise you could be. Maybe it was her fear of being unable to find her peers, the others as smart, as rich, as beautiful, and as

Black. Maybe being peerless became an unbearable isolation.

With me writing here in Kirwood with no impending date for my release, it is a time to shout this once-whispered truth — that while Elsie passed for white, she did not pass for white and completely vanish. She was only white downtown, only white in her other name. Uptown in Harlem, on the very rare occasions that she ventured north, she remained colored, observant, vivacious, and eager to see her very best old friends. I was pleased to be one of them.

Once Elsie called me from New York and begged me to come see her. I came. In the quietest Harlem bar she could find she told me that she was writing a one-man show for me. It would have a simple set and costumes. It would be cheap to mount. I would be sitting at a table, cig in one hand, glass in the other. From that perch I would tell the audience about my Black Bottom Saints. We would argue who should be included. When she was tired of arguing, she would kiss my cheek with a kiss as soft as Idlewild rain. And she would say, "Altar boy" — she called me "Altar Boy" — "I'm going to write that for you." But she didn't write it. Or, maybe she wrote the manuscript and it never made its way to me. What I know: When I left, she went downtown and she was white again, leaving me and everybody who loved her to wonder, *What happened to Elsie?*

I don't think it was some big thing we didn't know about. I think it was some small thing the impact of which we underestimated.

Like the way she really, truly loved Joe Louis, though her father or her uncle scared him off because he wasn't of the right class and Joe let himself be scared because he was beholden to the Roxborough family. Maybe being unable to forgive the Roxborough men became unable to forgive her own Roxborough self.

Maybe the fact that Joe listened to the men in her family, when she wanted him to listen to *her,* undid her completely, pulled undone, never to be tied again, the bow that tied her to the Black community beyond her family, and from her family.

Or perhaps, if she killed herself — and, sitting in this late autumn of 1967, I am starting to believe she did kill herself — I think it might have had something to do with Langston Hughes. Or maybe it had nothing to do with Langston.

If she did kill herself, I'd like to think it was because one day she decided she would like to see what was beyond life. Curiosity carried her forward, curiosity and confidence that a bigger, brighter, neither Black nor white, nor male nor female, adventure was waiting for her upstairs. I like imagining she was rushing off to heaven to attend some celestial party, eager to greet someone she had never had the pleasure of meeting on Earth. My Elsie would want to meet people from a thousand years ago and from the other side of the globe. That was the Elsie I knew, a woman going on an adventure boldly.

Probably it was some small family thing: say, the third person in the family who told her a Roxborough's going to jail was a far less worse thing than a Roxborough's passing herself off as "Mona Manet" and going around with second-rate white people.

When she died, friends who wished to argue her death wasn't a suicide pointed to there being stockings in the sink, saying that proved she wasn't intending to kill herself, that she was anticipating going out.

How I read the gesture? Elsie rarely washed stockings; she had a maid, but she wanted to do that common thing once again before she died.

Two of her relatives (women who could, but didn't, pass for white) went east to claim the body. They told the white friends the burial would be private. They kept her secret. The New York death certificate, according to the grapevine, had "white" written on it. We buried her Black in Detroit.

I wish I could have done for her what she does for me now: revive me. The other deaths make me sad. Elsie's death makes me angry. Angry enough to pull on my thick-and-thin silk stockings, tiptoe out of the hospital, and stomp back into the world she abandoned like a toy, showing herself at the last to be a silly girl — and from first to last a savior. Before she abandoned the world, she whispered to me across a round barroom two-top: "There is still bright mischief to be made, on a bed of fallen leaves."

LIBATION FOR THE FEAST DAY OF ELSIE ROXBOROUGH:
Stockings in the Sink

1/2 pony of white crème de menthe
1/2 pony of apricot liqueur
1/2 pony of apricot eau de vie
1/2 lime, juiced

Place all ingredients in a cocktail shaker and shake well with ice. Strain into a cocktail glass.

228

WEEK 18
EIGHTEENTH SUNDAY
AFTER FATHER'S DAY

In 2009, First Lady Michelle Obama unveiled a bust of Sojourner Truth in the United States Capitol. The artist who created the bust, Artis Lane, was described as a Canadian-born California artist. Colored Girl and her husband attended the unveiling. The husband had wangled the invitation, because he knew Artis Lane's first significant commission had been a series of portraits for Detroit's Gotham Hotel.

Artis Lane

PATRON SAINT OF: *Painters, Sculptors, and Offstage Artists of Life*

A fine mischief I could make would begin with Artis. That is her real given name, Artis, and she, Artis Lane — her married name — was born in 1927 in one of the all-sepian Canadian towns people don't talk about

229

much now, like they don't talk about how some Canadians did own slaves and how a dusky Canadian doll, Marie-Joseph Angelique, all but burned Montreal down in 1734.

Artis's hometown, North Buxton, was just over the river from Detroit. Her parents, the Shreves, moved to Ann Arbor, Michigan, with Artis when she was still small. She didn't return to Canada until she attended art school in Ontario, and then only briefly. Soon she was back in America at the Cranbrook Academy before landing in Detroit and painting twenty-seven oil portraits for John White to adorn my home, the Gotham Hotel.

If I had a pocket full of money, I would beg Artis Lane to paint me an Idlewild triptych so that Baby Doll and I could be up on the island in our downtown apartment. The first panel? An Idlewild morning. A World War I vet, the walnut-colored Sarge, passing through on horseback trailed by children just learning to ride, coming upon Diggs Sr. on that huge Percheron flanked by his son the congressman, with both Diggses nodding deferentially to Sarge. Second panel? Midday. Baby Doll, in a hot-pink one-piece, being towed on water skis across the blue-gray lake by a speedboat full of women sipping tiki drinks, driven by Anna Gordy in a muumuu. Final panel: Me coming upon Milt by accident, in the middle of the night, in the middle of evergreens and hardwoods. I love Baby Doll but she can't woo me back in love with life. Artis is who I need. Artis paints so good I am writing her the one and only begging letter of my life.

Dear Artis,
   We need a mural. Paint Father's Day. Paint how we shoehorned five hundred into each of three sold-out performances by forgoing the round tables that came free with the Latin Quarter and renting long narrow tables that we could drape with fine linens and set up perpendicular to the stage so everyone had as good a view as we could give them — and we could squeeze those extra folk in. Paint how in the half-light pulled up to the tables were solid wood framed armless chairs upholstered in a nubby dark-ruby fabric. Let the world see the chairs were

good looking and comfortable — just like my audience.

Paint the kids who didn't come for the weekly class but once a year were drawn to be a part of the pageant of Father's Day at the Youth Colossal by playing the role of "audience." Paint the boys in suits and ties, some with double breasted jackets, girls in repurposed Easter dresses, church dresses, and sometimes flower girl dresses, swinging tiny purses on supple arms. Paint the kinky beauty of their curls and the bows in their hair. On the tables, Instamatic cameras and paper cups. We encouraged the small fry from all the different neighborhoods to take pictures by calling them shutterbugs, offering a $5 prize for "Ziggy's favorite Instamatic photo." Every year we dangled in front of them the carrot of an exhibit of the twenty best photos at the School of the Theatre in September. Diggs would pay to have all their photos printed, then I would choose the best and tape them to the walled mirror behind the ballet bar. Finally, Gloria and some of the other teachers would paint frames around the photos and invite the world to see what the children of Black Bottom had made more important and more beautiful by their observation and their art. Paint that mirror, Artis. Please.

Paint the matrons and their guests who would be seated in the elevated boxes that flanked the stage. The stage itself had a wooden circular floor bordered by potted plants and lights. We kept the room very dark. In the boxes there were little, low, tiny lamps on tiny tables that held big drinks.

Paint backstage: the young and all-but-professional Ziggy Johnson Dancers, the Monday Ballet Class, the Monday Models, the Tuesday Modern Dance

Class, and the Exquisite Ones! Also, in that backstage tableaux the Friday Dance Class, the Saturday Tap Class, the Boys' Tap Class, the Saturday Ballet Class, the Ballet Babes, the Advanced Ballet, and of course Gladys Knight getting the girls into tights and lipstick with other stars darting back to help.

And when you paint the backstage, do *not* clean the checkerboard of red and beige, always-grimy tiles. No matter how clean it was when we started and how often we cleaned, with all that rehearsing that floor stayed dirty. Latin Quarter grime set off the shine of our costumes. We designed those costumes and had them locally constructed, some hand-sewn, some machine-sewn. In '66 I particularly loved our costumes. The Boys Tap classes wore creased white pants and three-button jackets striped black, brown, yellow, and beige, a sophisticated stripe with almost no repeat in the pattern, with thin black ties, white shirts, and beanies.

Can you paint a scent, Artis? Paint this for me, Baby. The scent I associate most with the Gotham: Arpège, Winston cigarettes, and fresh-pressed hair dabbed with Chex. If you can't paint that maybe you can just paint a bottle of Arpège and a pack of Winstons and a jar of Chex and it will help some folks remember that Arpège smelled like a rose with a little bit of dirt on it and that everybody in our world loved the jet-black round black bottle emblazoned with a gold mother and child — and that we musicians appreciated the name as a slight musical reference to celebration of broken chords.

When you get through with all of that: Paint the American Lotus that grows on Alf's island and how he keeps one in a fishbowl as a centerpiece.

It has no scent and must not be forgotten. Paint that.

Paint the Sir John Hotel in Miami. Let there be an aspiring want-to-be recording artist on the diving board fully dressed, crooning to all the beautiful browns lounging poolside in bikinis. The rectangular-shaped pool is dramatically striped with dark and light paint around all its edges so that drunken revelers didn't unintentionally plunge in fully dressed. The occasional intentional fully dressed plunge was expected and accepted. Paint the striped umbrellas with heavy fringe, and the lounge chairs. All of this is surrounded by two stories of hotel rooms connected by a wrap-around balcony. Always people in the water, always people sitting poolside, always people on the balcony. Always sun. Always palm trees. Paint the reservation clerk who always found me a room, Thora Keel, and paint her flirting with a brown and Spanish-speaking off-season baseball player.

Paint the Gotham. Paint it rising from the corner of Orchestra Place and John R. to a height of nine stories in all its gray and symmetrical glamour. Better yet: Paint the grand lobby with its patterned terrazzo floor and all the ceiling arches. Paint the massive metal chandeliers cascading down from ornate painted ceiling medallions. Paint the reception desk, glass brick and curved, with a hat or a purse resting there, as a guest signs the leather guest ledger. Paint the mahogany staircase leading to the second floor, that slash of anchoring wooden antiquity. Don't leave out the huge potted plants hiding cigar ash or the pretty bellman pushing one of the tubular aluminum rolling luggage carts. Take care with the fabric at the windows; don't omit the abstract geometric pattern on the fabric that signals a march into a smart and prosperous future. Paint my home true.

Paint *me*. Put me in a sports coat with a big pattern. In silk or wool or cotton. Padded shoulders. Nipped in at the waist. A wide tie. Silk, of course. Paint me in one of my light ties on a white shirt. Make my clean, heavily starched shirt jump from the canvas. Have my good Johnson and Murphy shoes shined. Make my creases sharp.

Creases count all seasons of the year. If you don't want to paint me in spring or autumn in a sports coat, paint me in winter when I have just come in from the cold wearing a suit, with a cashmere coat in the crook of my arm. Hat still on my head. Pocket square. Tie clip. All the Ziggy details in place. Or paint me in one of my shirts that let me wear a collar bar. Remind us that that is how, once upon a time, we did it. That ours was a world of pocket squares, and tie clips — tie clips were most important, as they held a dancer's tie in place mid-flight — and stick pins, and gold cigarette lighters and silver key fobs and money clips of metal or a plain rubber band, and cufflinks, and good hats, and mohair V-neck golf sweaters and fine tuxedos and Murine. Don't paint me dropping Murine in my eyes. Or me in my boxer shorts and white cotton V-neck shirt sitting at my dressing table in my room at the Gotham, my toes tickled by the wool wall-to-wall carpet. Or maybe paint that. How and where we got ready. And we were ready. Paint our readiness.

Know that a part of what I have done has been with the inspiration that, if I do enough and do it right, you, Artis Lane, will paint me.

Sincerely,
Ziggy

When they tore down the Gotham, Artis Lane's Detroit portraits disappeared. Some say they ended up in a dumpster. Some say they ended up in an attic. Some say they were still hanging when the wrecking ball hit. Artis didn't know where they were going, and soon we didn't know where she herself went. The men who sat for those portraits thought they had bought some immortality. They thought wrong. I hope words are harder to kill than paintings.

LIBATION FOR THE FEAST DAY OF ARTIS LANE:
My Favorite Canadian

No extra calories, costs, or time in this recipe.

A bottle of Canadian Club and a bottle of water
A clean glass

Pour as much of either as you think you should have. Drink. Get back to the art of life!

WEEK 19
NINETEENTH SUNDAY
AFTER FATHER'S DAY

Parkside, the street where Goldie Sparks, widely known as G. S., lived, was the Monaco of Ziggy's Detroit, a sunny spot for shady people. Colored Girl came home from the hospital to Parkside. Her father's oldest sibling, Sister, the seamstress, owned a Tudor-style five-bedroom, six-bath mansion on that storied street, surrounded by grass lawns front and back, a small fruit orchard on one side, and a bricked barbecue area with shading maple and ferns on the other. In summer Sister would pluck apricots warm from the tree, wash them off with the garden hose, and feed Colored Girl the still-warm, soft, yellow fruit-flesh while the child splashed in a puddle pool. In autumn Sister would sit beneath her maple tree on a hand-sewn quilt as Colored Girl ran around her collecting orange, yellow, and brown leaves. When the child joined her on the quilt,

241

Sister would tell her niece about an October house fire in Black Bottom that stole her only daughter and her youngest brother. How the white firemen did not come quick to Black Bottom. "That's crime!" Sister would say. When Sister saw G. S. stepping down the road with a white man on her arm and bottle-blond hair on her head, Sister would sigh and say, "It takes all kinds. When my husband died, I found stacks of money in the safe in his closet. So much cash, some of it had started to mold." There was a sewing room in the basement of Sister's house. The shell-pink silk dress that Colored Girl wore to the Copacabana when she flew up to New York with her parents to see the Supremes and the World's Fair, the same weekend the Beatles played Shea Stadium, was a miniature copy of something G. S. wore out on one of her sacred strolls. Nothing remains today of Sister's house that once stood on the corner of Parkside and the John C. Lodge Freeway. It has been estimated that one-third of the 139 square miles designated "Detroit" is now vacant-land-prairie. *That's* crime.

G. S.

PATRON SAINT OF: *Practitioners of Extravagant Body Art*

Schoolboy is still holding down John R. and Garfield. I'm still here, in Kirwood, but he's out there and that comforts me. And G. S. is still out there being blond-Black-and-beautiful, and men are walking around free who want to give her everything. That comforts me, too.

G. S. is the only woman I know who ever received a court case as a Valentine's Day card. Some things can't be denied; G. S.'s lovability is one of them. When the legal wife said, "He paid you!" and the IRS said, "Pay us!" you said, "No deal!" You put your hands on your fantabulous hips and said, "You can't buy this. You can't tax this. This is better than that!" You said, "You want to talk about the allowance, the charge cards, the cars, the house? That was the least of it. He gave me time. He gave me attention. He gave me adoration. He gave me gift he didn't give *you*!"

But that wife dragged G. S.'s brown ass to court. I can see that crumpled man sitting there, on a court bench mashed in with his legal family. G. S. looking like G. S., bold and bronze and good, like someone a man

243

could fall in love with and romance. There's an old rich white man's joke that I have heard a hundred different times, told maybe a dozen different ways, a joke about whoring, and it always ends with a variation on this punch line: "I don't pay the girls to sleep with me, I pay them to be gone in the morning when I wake." Nobody ever wanted G. S. gone in the morning.

Men loved G. S., and G. S. loved men — but when it came to "like" she always chose women. She liked to go around in a gang. At one time it was a threesome of G. S., Carrie Gore, and Helena Harris; at another time it was the Six Socialites. Put a bevy of buxom glamazons around her and who gets noticed? G. S.

I don't know why I love her so. G. S. almost drowned me. In Canada, no less.

As her deep-pink nails like talons had approached my chest, I was thinking, G. S. is going to straighten my tie, or she's going to smooth those lovely hands down my torso — something like that. Instead she pushed me into Lake St. Clair, in my foolish white bucks, in my only pink suit.

We had been standing face to face. She toppled me over backward. The crown of my head hit the water first. Between G. S.'s hand making contact with my chest and my head making contact with the water, I had the seconds necessary to catch my breath. I steadied myself by grasping on the mental straw of her nail polish color. It was all wrong. It should have been "Red, Hot, and Blue." Steadied, my next thought was "You'd better catch your breath!"

As I slipped beneath the water, I was not breathing, I was recalibrating. It wasn't the easiest thing to do. I had been out on the golf course all afternoon, with Elliott Rouse, drinking, as much as hitting. It was that kind of day.

Between Cliff Fears, my protégé, calling to say he was landing in Detroit early but wouldn't make the Surf Club till midnight and Rouse talking about one of his employees who had caught polio, the day had me shooting double bogeys. Nothing was copacetic. There would be a vaccine in '55 but in '52 it seemed somebody you knew always knew somebody who had just got polio. Every time someone I knew got diagnosed, I put on four pounds. Detroit was no place for Cliff to be that summer.

In 1952 there were over 700 cases of polio in Detroit. Dr. Bodywork Bob had told me that. I told Rouse; he bogeyed a hole. Polio was hitting families all over town, white and colored, rich and poor, center of the city and suburbs.

It was a jam-packed, jacked-up day. Break-fast with a fashion show. Golf. Time to rest before working the first evening show. G. S. had found me on my rest break. She was trying to convince me to put her in an upcoming Idlewild show as a dancer, but she couldn't dance. By the time we were halfway down the pier I was considering let-ting her try to dance. She was twenty-two years old. Tallish, shapely, country fresh, she was wearing this hot-pink, deep-rose color, on her lips and on her nails, that my female dancers loved, called "Everything's Rosy." So many years of Ziggarettes had been so wild about that color that I knew it had a slogan and could recite it by heart. So many girls had chanted it at me: "If shy men sigh and strong men fight for you, if phones keep ringing day and night for you, the only shade in the world that's right for you, is 'Everything's Rosy.' "

But it isn't. Rosy. Or maybe it's exactly *like* summer roses. Quick as they bloom, they fade. Ziggarettes come and Ziggarettes go. Pretty doesn't last. And figures fade even faster. It came to me in a sudden flash of summer lightning what G. S. should do. So I told her. I suggested that she find herself

an older white man to take care of her —
and she smiled, for a hot second, then the
smile vanished.

"Why shouldn't I have a nice colored
husband? I want a house on Parkside and a
little cottage up here, in St. Clair Shores or
in Idlewild. I want a winter trip to the Sir
John Hotel in Miami Beach. And a mink
coat."

"G. S., what you got to give that's worth
all that?"

"You know what I got."

"I know what you got."

"And I'm up here to find a rich doctor."

"None of us rich enough for all what you
want. You need an ofay."

"White don't marry colored."

"Who said anything about marriage?"

"My mama."

"Use what you got to get what you want."

"What I want?"

"You want your freedom more than you
will ever love some particular man." Her
hands came up. More words were ex-
changed. I don't know if she pushed me or
she slapped me, but I was headed to the
water. I came up looking like a drowned
rat.

I had had big plans for that suit. I wanted
Cliff to see me dressed and absurdly perfect

247

as I had seen him all but fully undressed and absurdly perfect. I wanted to take his breath away as he had taken mine. But he was standing on the pier as I climbed up the wood ladder out of the water. He shook his head and misread everything about the situation.

"You always got something going with some pretty woman, don't you, Daddy?" Cliff said, looking at me with the eyes of a child. There was nothing I knew how to say with him looking at me like that except "Yeah, I do."

My delivery was two seconds off. Cliff's eyes changed. In a single blink I went from rooster to capon. I was a short, round, beige man, in a wet and wrinkled pink suit; he was standing in swimming trunks looking like a brown god. G. S. had had the grace to run off and leave the scene without standing witness to my misery. Cliff looked at me more closely. The little bit of mascara I had dared use on my eyebrows had run. He stood so close to me and wiped it off with the clean heel of his hand and said, "So, it's like that." He had caught me in a moment of trying too hard — and failing. You are forgiven if you try too hard and succeed, but try too hard and fail and you are a buffoon, just another tragic Negro.

"Go find your friends, son," I told him. "I've got to catch up, and make up, with that woman. You know how they are. You know how *I* am." This time my delivery was excellent. Cliff walked back to the shore, sad he had arrived early.

I stripped off all my clothes. I jumped back in. I raised my hand to the sky. I yelled, "The water's good, come on in!" And some of them came. I was the master of ceremonies. Where I was, was the place to be. But Cliff didn't see that, didn't see how I did what I do, turn it all around. He saw what they wrote in *Jet:* that I drank all day and that G. S. pushed me into the water.

Years later, G. S. in fact had that house on Parkside. She followed my advice and found an older, well-funded lover who was besotted with her, and she was besotted with the life they built together *for* her. I forgave her, then thanked her for pushing me in the lake and keeping me from drowning my best chance of heaven on earth.

Cliff Fears. He was my protégé, and that is a pure thing when you let it be. I let it be. I have never dallied with one of my dancers. I honor boundaries. Cliff has danced in Russia and Sweden. When he leaps I am his feet. He told me that. He asks me about the girls, and it has begun to be a game we play.

What keeps us apart, it is prettier to think, is that he is queer and I am not, than to know that I was not young or pretty enough for him, by the time we met. I would not have him out of gratitude. And if he thought of me as a father, I would not cross the familial line. Mentors should mentor without detour.

Eventually G. S. and one of her crews, the Six Socialites, would change their public slogan from "Free, single, disengaged, and looking for someone to love" to "Free, single, disengaged, and not looking anymore." Joe Louis would beg her to marry him. Eventually G. S. would change her name and would marry, but first she took a patron — a patron of the one art she possessed: "being G. S."

She didn't really have a talent. She wasn't really a beauty. She was so sweet that hard life and hard knocks would make her old quick. She dreamed of being a typist, of working in an office, as Baby Doll did. She wasn't the sort of Black woman usually given that work. She was statuesque and she was sensual, like a mountain lioness, and there was about her none of the pedigree that colored doctors wanted for their wives, or the remarkable talent that showmen wanted for theirs. She was ambitious and she was brown in a world that was kinder to men and to high yellows.

I knew men, so I knew she could catch herself a big white trout, if not a whale, and feast on it for a good long while and tell herself it was love, and let it be love. She liked nice things. But G. S. was no whore. She was art. Then it got complicated: When G. S. caught her whale, she loved him, and he loved her. The lady was lovable. Except to the Commissioner.

The Comish claimed that G. S. owed back taxes for the years 1954, 1955, 1956, 1957, and 1958. G. S. said she hadn't worked in those years except for a modeling job in 1954 for which she was paid less than $600.

The Comish told a different story. He said she had earned $41,000 in 1956 and about $6,000 a year the other years. *Say what?*

"Comish, don't you know that the average income for a white man in 1955 was $3,400 a year? That the median for women was $2,400 in the highest sector? And that escorts get $5 an hour for the hours they work. You wanted to call our G. S. a whore — and you don't even know how whores are paid? There's not a woman working the streets of Detroit City ever took home $6,000 a year! Some pimps maybe, that oleo heir maybe, but women? Never!"

That man was in love with G. S. That big money proved it. He wanted G. S. to forget the difference in age, in race, in beauty, and spend the rest of her life with him. G. S.'s whale is still crying. If she had been for sale, he would still be buying. And if it had just been paid companionship, he would have had another G. S. None of that has happened. *This* happened.

G. S. was crazy. She pushed me into a lake, she called me "sweet," and I called her a "slut," but we both knew who was lying. The world knew the opposite, but we knew the truth.

LIBATION FOR THE FEAST DAY OF G. S.:
A Fine Thing When You Let It

Champagne
1 tsp. of bar sugar
1 slice of lemon
1 slice of orange
Crushed ice

Place the fruit peel and sugar in the bottom of a rocks glass. Let sit for as long as you can manage to wait, preferably at least fifteen minutes. Half fill the glass with crushed ice. Pour in

Champagne. Decorate with fruit and
serve with straws.

Champagne Dacquate with fruit and
serve with straws.

WEEK 20
TWENTIETH SUNDAY
AFTER FATHER'S DAY

Colored Girl's mother had many secrets,
the most benign being a crush on Minot
Jelke.

In 1972, the year after Arbus's death,
Colored Girl was entering her fifth year of
living in a Washington, DC, girl-world that
revolved around Arbus, Plath, Sexton, and
Zelda — a world where every other home
had a copy of Arbus's photo book with the
black-and-white picture of twin girls on the
cover. She was starting to appreciate Arbus, Plath, Sexton, and Zelda; it was
Colored Girl's second year of not being allowed to visit Detroit.

Away from Detroit, Colored Girl's mother
started to suspect that Colored Girl had
perpetrated a fraud on her. She had loved
Colored Girl and had given her everything,
because she thought Colored Girl was the
little colored girl who, she, Bette, used to
be; thought Colored Girl was little *her.*

Time revealed the child was someone else, a different Colored Girl who needed to be punished, albeit stealthily, for stealing little Bette's things. Unfortunately, this impostor Colored Girl had powerful allies in Detroit City. Everything on purpose had to appear accidental.

The day Colored Girl's mother brought home a copy of the Arbus photo book, the woman bragged about an evening spent in the company of Jelke and Nemerov after purchasing her jet-black mink. In her early days Colored Girl decided she would never eat margarine or wear fur. With small, rigid decisions she buckled herself to sane.

Minot Jelke

PATRON SAINT OF: *Privileged Devils*

Eleven married men and one bachelor sat in judgment of Minot Jelke and found him guilty of enticing Pat Ward and Marguerite Cordoba into a life of prostitution. Minot, who the girls called Mickey, was the ofay oleomargarine heir who had first come to the attention of the show world by throwing a punch at Humphrey Bogart at the El Morocco.

In Detroit, Jelke was the prime example of

a mack man who would be trotted out whenever ofays turned the conversation in a way that suggested "Negroes invented urban crime." We talked about Jelke. We snarled and signified against all pots that were trying to call the kettle black.

I make Jelke a saint because his life is proof that this formulation is a lie: They good, we bad. White folks invented crime in America and stay rolling around in it. Sometimes they even manipulate criminal acts into being labeled legal. But sometimes they don't bother to do that: Minot Jelke, trust fund baby, Ivy League educated, was a pimp. And one of his biggest johns was the father of the young, newly acclaimed photographer Diane Arbus. None of that came as a surprise to us.

We liked to make a feast of that conversation. I chewed over it in my column for many a week. Folks, all kinds and flavors, and all colors of folk, needed to be reminded that no one kind of folk has a monopoly on crime or goodness.

For a season, the mack men in Detroit were fascinated with the oleomargarine heir. Oleo is a very profitable food associated with political corruption. The oleo heir had many choices of what to do with his life. The oleo heir was running call girls. He had

$3,000,000 inherited, and he was running fifty $100-a-night girls. One of his customers was David Nemerov, who sold furs to kept women at his shop, Russek's. He was famous for it. I heard about him from our own G. S. She told me Russek bought whores from Mickey Jelke, but because he dressed the G. S.s of this world he knew the immense difference between a call girl and a kept woman.

Nemerov had a daughter who became a photographer, Diane Nemerov Arbus. I give Arbus this: Arbus made beauty out of what she was calling out as ugly. But in every picture of hers I saw, I was back on that stage with the boneless wonder, Tanya. For me, Tanya, the boneless wonder, is a more significant artist than Arbus. Tanya was canvas and painter.

Minot Jelke was a pimp for the ages. And like a lot of pimps he destroyed a lot of women's lives, directly and indirectly. Arbus was one of the indirect destructions.

I met Arbus once. On a trip to New York. G. S. made the introduction. She had bought a fur from Nemerov; so had Bette Stanley — a jet-black mink. This is what I figured out about Arbus's pictures: she saw what others made invisible. Every subject became her invisible freak self. I think there was something brave in that — and absurdly narcissistic.

I, too, can be absurdly narcissistic. We are alike in that one way. In every other way she was the most inscrutable offay I ever met. I never met Jelke.

LIBATION FOR THE FEAST DAY OF MINOT JELKE:
Privileged Devil

1 jigger of Old Tom gin
1/2 lemon, juiced
1/4 orange, juiced
1/2 pony of rock candy syrup

Fill a cocktail shaker with ice. Add gin, juices, and syrup. Shake vigorously. Fill a shorter highball glass with additional ice. Strain contents of shaker onto the ice in the highball glass.

Because she knew who her father was, Colored Girl couldn't tell the man who her mother was. He would have killed the woman or had her killed. As Colored Girl did not believe in capital punishment, she was in a trick bag. Nual Steele and his bodyguard were assassinated in August 1970 at Detroit's La Player's Lounge. The assassins, sent by Blaze Marzette, shot through their coat pockets after inviting Nual's bodyguard to leave. He declined. Colored Girl was on a summer vacation visit in Detroit when that happened. Her father cut her visit short and put her on a plane to DC the very next day.

George Stanley

PATRON SAINT OF: *Alcoholics, Badass Brains, and Ritual Makers*

Everybody in Detroit was afraid of George

Stanley except Mari. George came by intimidation honestly. The patriarch, Will, once knocked a man down with a crowbar for cursing in front of his wife. That man never did that again.

The story everybody tells about Mari and George is the time he took Mari over to Lafayette's house and let the eight-year-old scream at the self-anointed Snow King of Motown. Detroit's biggest cocaine dealer wasn't a bluntly dangerous man, but he kept himself surrounded by armed and bluntly dangerous tall boys. Lafayette let Mari scream at him. That's all you need to know about George Stanley. And this: His child could ride across town in a taxicab. Somebody tried to call George out about that one night in the 20 Grand. George lifted his hand and the table got silent. "There's not a Negro or a peckawood in the whole of Detroit City fool enough to touch my child. I would kill their children's children. I would kill their children. Then I would kill them. Even Nual Steele knows that."

George had strange ideas about everything, including parenting. He sent his daughter to my dancing school and put her in tap class for a very unusual reason: George hated Shirley Temple. George thought tap class would help Mari "take

260

Shirley down." He put her in the boys tap class, because he wanted to teach her to compete with and love Black boys. He bonded with his daughter over loving Black folk. He tucked a $20 bill into each of her shoes every morning. Any day she saw an older Black person or a very young Black person who looked like they needed something they couldn't afford, she was to take a shoe-money twenty out and offer it with the lie, "I think I borrowed $20 from someone in your family. Please take this." In that way, George taught Mari to be generous and taught his Detroit City to be glad to see his daughter's face.

Mari started each day with her daddy in one or another of his dry cleaners "making hangers," putting the thin cardboard sleeve over the wire that kept pants from getting an ugly crease, sometimes taking orders. He wanted her to see where the money came from and he wanted her to feel a part of making it. Shirley McNeil said George was practicing his own form of Montessori. When her "morning work" was done, they would celebrate.

George would make Mari a hot chocolate, using two vending machines: a coffee machine and a candy machine. First, he got a Hershey's bar out of the candy machine.

Then he would move to the coffee machine and put in a quarter and punch the buttons for a cup of hot chocolate then the buttons for extra milk and sugar. Then he would put in another quarter and punch the buttons for a plain black coffee. Next came her favorite part: He would pour just a little of his black coffee into her sweetened chocolate, then some of her chocolate into his coffee, back and forth, back and forth, until both cups were perfect and different, hers a mainly chocolate draught, George's a mainly coffee drink. Last but not least, George would break off one square of the Hershey's bar and float it on top of her chocolate. He would break up the rest of the bar and drop it into his coffee. Then would come what they both described as the best part: They would each make a wish. After the wish they would touch paper cups together, then gulp. If she was lucky, she would get a cocoa mustache that he would wipe off with the back of his hand. Only George could use a vending machine and the back of his hand to put extra tenderness in the world.

People would go out of their way to drop off dry cleaning early in the morning to see that daddy-and-daughter dance.

Breadwinners who worked at the River Rouge auto plant would talk about seeing them every so often at shift change. Could be any shift change, even the one in the middle of the night, George at the wheel of his Cadillac car, Mari riding shotgun watching thousands of workers go in and thousands go out as the shifts changed. Men who worked down at the *Detroit Free Press* printing plant reported that they sometimes saw them in the wee hours of the morning at the loading dock when they were throwing down the first bundles of the morning edition with the ink still wet. George would be there picking up two copies, one for himself and one for his daughter. Then they would be in the all-night diner at 4:00 a.m. and he would be reading the whole paper aloud to Mari, always starting with her favorite column, "Action Line."

No story told how much he loved the girl more than the story about how he had stopped drinking. George Stanley, who had drunk all day, every day, from the time he was fifteen, stopped drinking overnight, albeit with a three-week hospital stay, when he was just about thirty-five.

Mari was in the car with him and he was pulling up to park in front of a favored tavern. Just as he was leaning over to kiss her, Mari said, "Daddy, please, don't go in that B-A-R!" He didn't kiss the girl. He got out of the car, pulling his daughter after him. They entered the dimly lit, long narrow room holding hands. Silent. People remembered that. They had never seen that before or after. He usually left Mari in the car if he was coming for a quick shot. They came in chatting if they were coming for a daddy-and-daughter date. George had his last cocktail bellied up to the bar with Mari. He ordered a Cutty Sark on ice and a Coke with an orange and a lime. When he told the story it always ended with Mari sipping on a pretty paper straw and him saying the same thing: "I drank an ocean of whiskey and enjoyed every drop. I pulled up in front of too many neon signs if you can spell-out those letters. Pace yourself. Maybe you can drink for your whole life."

George had a genius for love. He took a moment when his daughter felt abandoned and turned it into the moment when a whole city saw him live the announcement: *My brown girl is worth more than all the gold, white, and brown liquor in the world.*

Right out in public he would thump on her head and say, "I'm going to take that brain of yours and give it a new home, in the skull of the Frankenstein monster!" Then she would do it to him. And they would fall out laughing. Nobody in the world knew what that meant — except that it meant he had made her too bold to be afraid of the baddest man in town.

LIBATION FOR THE FEAST DAY OF GEORGE STANLEY:
The Pace Yourself

1 jigger of orange juice
1 jigger of imported ginger ale

Shake well with ice and strain into a cocktail glass.

WEEK 22
TWENTY-SECOND SUNDAY
AFTER FATHER'S DAY

Tallulah Bankhead, the actress known for her biting tongue and for starring in Hitchcock's *Lifeboat,* was born into a white Alabama political dynasty: Her father was a congressman, an uncle was a senator, and one grandfather was a Confederate army captain then later a senator. She was best known in the wide Black world for shouting jeers and curses at Nazis from her ringside seats during the Max Schmeling–Joe Louis fight.

She was best known at Ziggy's School of the Theatre for being the weird white woman who would look at one boy in the tap class and say to everybody, "Doesn't he look just like John H. Bankhead II dipped in chocolate?" She looked at another and asked, "Do you have any people in Jasper, Alabama?" When one of the older boys said, "Not all the Negroes in Detroit have family in Alabama," Tallulah replied, "Of course not. But that child has my cousin Eugenia's mouth. The men in my family were, for the most part, rapists who preferred the company of dusky women. I would like to know my cousins, if they would like to know me. Do you perhaps have any people in Como, Mississippi?"

The first time Tallulah saw Colored Girl she said, "You've got a Pettus forehead and Moore eyes. Those eyes in a white face stole many a boy away from me." Ziggy said, "Let me help you here, Tallulah, before you say something that won't be good for your health. This child, my goddaughter, was born fully armed for battle from her daddy's head. Isn't that right, Goddaughter? And Tallulah, isn't it time for you to get over to the theater or somewhere?"

Tallulah Bankhead

PATRON SAINT OF: *Orphans, Big Mouths, and Ill-Folk*

I always call Tallulah Bankhead "the lady who knows no color" when I write about her in my columns, and I sang that song even louder after the 1951 trial of her maid. Tallulah charged the woman with kiting checks. The woman accused Tallulah of smoking marijuana and hiring gigolos. Tallulah was the one and only white woman I have ever been happy to see when I land in New York.

Evyleen Ramsay Cronin, Tallulah's check-kiting maid, a former burlesque dancer, transformed checks for $27.50 into checks for $327.50 with a squiggle of pen ink. Her defense: She used the money she made from kiting the checks to provide Tallulah with extravagances. Why were my readers so interested in this case? Tallulah was from Alabama and Evyleen, the maid, was white.

Everybody in Detroit knew that white ladies from Alabama have Black maids. It's how they do their part to preserve and announce the color line. They have Black maids as a way of insisting that Black folk are only fit to serve. Some white folk are not honest. So many reasons to forgive Tallulah her many evils and extravagances!

Hiring white maids was Tallulah's lived way of proving that Black people aren't in one fixed place and whites in another.

Willie Mays got me in tight with Tallulah. When Willie was playing, Tallulah never missed a Giants game. She would scream for him in the stands, hat on her head, tortoiseshell sunglasses perched on patrician nose, six or seven strings of small white pearls, wrapped around her neck, gold bracelet on one wrist, gold watch on the other, clasping her hands together in prayer when she thought the Giants needed it. I have sat beside her in the stands and witnessed this firsthand.

When Willie let it slip that he would often get up after breakfast and play stickball with the boys in his neighborhood *and* come home after a day game and play another hour or two out in the streets, she washed off all her makeup, took off all her jewelry, pulled on a pair of dungarees, and stood on his street corner, admiring from a respectful distance, with a cheap scarf around her head and huge cheap sunglasses obscuring most of her face. To be a part of his life out of the stadium, she made herself invisible.

We argued about Willie in 1954. She had published an article about Willie in *Look* magazine. I loved that she wrote Mickey Mantle was not in Willie Mays's class. Delighted when she dismissed Mantle as a "laddybuck," a word I had never heard but immediately understood and added to my arsenal. But why did she write this? "Negroes are natural athletes, dancers and musicians. They have grace, speed and superb reflexes."

I hated that. She insisted she didn't write those lines. Said all she did was let the editor tuck them in her article. She said, "I wrote, 'Willie Mays and Willie Shakespeare were the only true geniuses.' " I told her she should have insisted. She smiled. "It's sweet to hear you believe I can insist and have it matter. I'm fifty-two, Zig. Old women have no power to insist." Tallulah was honest as the day is long.

And fun as the night is short. That belle had the swagger to promise in the midst of all the politics that she observed and rejected, "I'll have fun, if *you'll* have fun, and we'll have fun together!" When she came to Detroit in '48 playing in *Private Lives* at the Cass Theatre, we would club-hop after her show until the sun started to rise. Then she would say, "I love zagging with Ziggy, but now it's time to go home." She would go back to her hotel, the Book-Cadillac, the tower the world said was the best hotel, and I would go back to the Gotham, which Tallulah acknowledged was the better hotel. That mattered to me.

Another favorite Tallulah sighting: September 20, 1955. I turned on the TV to see Tallulah on *The Martha Raye Show.* I know the date because I kept that page from *TV Guide* and taped it in my scrapbook. My students tuned in, too, because I wanted them to see Miss Gloria Lockerman, the twelve-year-old, brown, Baltimore brain, who had won $16,000 on the *$64,000 Question* quiz show by spelling "antidisestablishmentarianism" while wearing organdy and crinoline.

Gloria starred in a skit on *The Martha Raye Show.* My girls loved that skit. Gloria was smart as a whip. Her eyes flashed. She had one of those smiles that children get when they are raised by old folks, and that mirror the ways of old folks, a smile that doesn't give too much away. Tallulah played Gloria's good Fairy Godmother, "Twinkle Toes." Martha Raye was her bad Fairy Godmother. Or maybe it was the other way around. When the actors came out to take their bows, at the end of the episode, Tallulah, spontaneously, kissed and hugged Gloria. Martha joined in. My girls loved seeing a brown girl turned into a kiss sandwich on coast-to-coast TV by white women. A large swath of the ofay world went berserk. Letters flooded into the network. The NBC affiliate in Mississippi threatened to cancel the show. Revlon threatened to pull its sponsorship. It was the beginning of the end of Martha Raye.

We were walking up Seventh Avenue from

Minton's Playhouse to the Apollo when Tallulah said she would do it again. It was the late fall of '55. Some folks bird-watch. I car-watch. Rolling through Harlem were two-tone Bel Aire convertibles, in Sea-Mist Green and Neptune Green, in Shoreline Beige and Gypsy Red, in a whole raft of new colors the breadwinners were spraying that year. And on two-door hardtop Bel Aires, a fine old color, Surf Green. Looking especially good to me, Packard 400s in pretty, jewel-named colors, like Gray Pearl and Topaz, and, best, Raven Black and Torch-Red Thunderbirds. When you're from Detroit in 1955, one of the great years of new-car design, walking up Seventh Avenue, you are home proud. And walking up Seventh Avenue, I was starting to get a new Tallulah proud.

With our arms crocked together she purred, "It is past time everyone sees Negro girls can be touched by white hands without lust or anger. If Martha loses her show, that is nothing compared to what Negro girls lose every day when people don't understand that. Now, let's stop talking politics. I hate cracking bores, and I don't want to hate *you,* Zig."

The last time me or my girls saw Tallulah was on television, the *Batman* show. She played Black Widow. She wore a black suit. The suit's deep V-neck was trimmed with red. Her lips were also red. Her back was straight. She sported wonderful black leather gloves. But, best, she had a step, a turn — she could still do a turn — and when she walked away, you wanted to keep looking. It was a poem the way she shifted her weight as she turned. She was sixty-five, but she managed to look an old forty-five.

"There is nothing common about me," her character stated, and it was true about the actress playing the role. One of her lines was a big, wonderful little rhyme: "If you wish to live and thrive, let the spider run alive." She accused Batman and Robin of the fault she had accused me of: "You may be caped, and you may be dynamic, but you are cracking bores." Tallulah snuck her own words into the script! After my girls saw that, Tallulah's archaic put-down, "Cracking Bore!," echoed around the dancing school for days!

I've had pains in my chest today. I took a pill before I started to write. Used to be I would never do that. I'm thinking about "never" a lot now. I have never been to the Kentucky Derby — anyplace south with that many white folks was never my scene. Things change. Every year now, I'm waving goodbye to a few more carloads of brown beauties driving to the Derby and providing unpaid taxi service to more and more gaggles of bronze girls clutching boarding passes to Louisville in one hand and tickets to the Derby in the other. Our women are determined to see and be seen, at the "run for the roses," and to remind all who may have forgotten that the first jockey to win the Derby was a Black man, Oliver Lewis.

If I live long enough to see May, I'm going to the Derby. G. S. and her crew have been making that hatbox-and-mud-shoe-trip for too long without me. This is *my* year. There's a horse I like they call Dancer's Image. I saw him at the Woodbine Racetrack in Ontario, Canada. He's gray, and he's fast! If I make it to the Derby, I'm asking G. S. if Tallulah can tag along, too. And I'm betting on that horse with the stone Detroit, Ziggy Johnson's School of the Theatre, swagger — Dancer's Image.

LIBATION FOR THE FEAST OF TALLULAH BANKHEAD:
The Spider's Web

2 jiggers of bourbon
Chocolate syrup in a squeeze bottle with
  a fine tip

274

Fill a wide coup glass with a very young bourbon, then drizzle a circle, within a circle, within a circle, within a circle on the top with chocolate syrup. Using a toothpick, draw a straight line from a point on the smallest circle to just beyond a point on the outside of the largest circle. Do this at 12 o'clock, and at five other points on the circle, evenly distributed to construct a chocolate spider's web.

WEEK 23
TWENTY-THIRD SUNDAY
AFTER FATHER'S DAY

Dancer's Image won the Kentucky Derby in 1968. Two days later he was disqualified in a highly controversial ruling that became the basis of multiple litigations and much speculation. Dancer's Image owner Peter Fuller had announced, two days after King's assassination, that should his horse win the Derby, Fuller was gifting the purse ($122,000) to Dr. King's widow.

G. S., who had betting-slip proof she had put money on Dancer's Image to win, said she could feel Ziggy rolling in his grave when the horse was disqualified.

On June 23, 1963, Martin Luther King Jr. gave his "Walk to Freedom" speech before a predominantly Black Detroit audience of 125,000 men, women, and children. Ziggy brought Colored Girl, most of the dancing school, and many of the parents to the march. Hailed, at the time, as the largest civil rights gathering ever held in America, this event introduced language that would develop into the "I have a dream" speech as well as momentum for the March on Washington.

In 1964 King received the Nobel Peace Prize. As part of the official celebration in Stockholm, Ziggy's protégé Clifford Fears performed a solo dance based on the Paul Lawrence Dunbar poem "Little Brown Baby."

Martin Luther King Jr.

PATRON SAINT OF: *Racemen, Racewomen, Reverends, and Voters*

There was a year when everything started to be different, 1963. Father's Day was June 16, two sold-out shows, and the next Sunday Dr. Martin Luther King Jr. came to Detroit and marched down Woodward Avenue. I marched in the street with him, surrounded by students from my school, who were dressed in pressed or starched church clothes or, in Mari's case, drive-through-the-cemetery clothes. The week before, they had all been onstage dressed in sequins, feathers, fringe, and sharkskin.

When night fell that Sunday, I went to hear Dr. King at Cobo Hall, catching a ride with Aretha Franklin's daddy, whom King greeted from the podium as "my good friend the Reverend C. L. Franklin." This speech of King's chilled me, Mr. Chills, and not in a good way. When he said, "The hour is late, the clock of destiny is ticking out," I didn't hear him talking about our people, I heard him talking about himself. And I heard him talking about *me*. I heard him warning that the shining hour that was our Detroit, was actually swirled through with lead, with bitter difficulties — that our shining hour would be dimmed without coming to full fruition.

While I was working to raise young citizens capable of making the American Dream an American reality — working to make America, America — others had been working against me.

What did it mean if I helped one, if I helped twelve, twelve hundred, or closer to twelve thousand Black girls feel their own beauty, their own worthiness, exactly as they are — when one hundred thousand Black girls stared and listened mesmerized when every billboard and television show screamed they were not beautiful, they were not worthy?

April of '63 was not the first time I heard the Reverend Doctor King in Detroit. If the

278

1963 sermon chilled, the earlier sermon thrilled. I heard him in 1954, right around Valentine's Day, at Second Baptist. That time, King spoke about Jesus's parents leaving Jesus behind.

Youth shall lead us. My Ballet Babes, the little girls who measure themselves only against each other, and against their mothers, and against my teachers, these are the treasures I will leave behind when I die. My girls are so different from so many older Black beauties raised in the kitchen of white folks' houses, hanging on every flick of fingers and hair of white women, fighting every flick of the finger of white women, dodging the flicking fingers of white men, so different from my beloved Natchez Belle. I have created a powerful fun house, a place where all the mirrors are without distortion. A place where Black girls reflect and reflect upon each other. In 1954, with his sermon about the necessity of Mary and Joseph's accepting being left behind, Dr. King inspired me to keep on keeping on.

In 1963 I heard King thundering about little gods, about Cadillac cars and riotous living; I knew he would never understand me. C. L. Franklin was his good friend and was my good friend, too, but my path would never cross with King's. I had miscalculated.

My mission was not understood.

I feared that if King passed me on the street, he would have dismissed me and probably thought that I was one of the things that went wrong. He didn't think enough about the threat of billboards and TV. The Rev. Franklin and Mahalia Jackson both tell me I am wrong. They say King is humble in his heart.

That keeps me loving Dr. King. Mahalia told King about me. I had asked her to. When King last spoke in Chicago, my mother, the Natchez Belle, and my daughter, Josette, were there.

King doesn't preach as I would like to hear him on how we treat each other and ourselves. His mind is focused on how the ofays treat us. He works one side of the street; I work the other. King doesn't let himself get tired. Me, I'm tired of thinking about how white folk treat us, and that is why all year I work to create performances for an all-Black world.

King's best speeches end with a wish for inclusiveness, his wish for a place where brown, Black, white, and yellow play together and are judged by their character. I have created that place now, today, but to do it I had to throw all the white people out.

280

They would say they didn't want in. I know what I know. I know they wanted in — in our bodies (that is so obvious in all my yellow splendor) and, less obviously, they wanted in our minds. They wanted to be so in our minds that they are what we think about and long for when we are alone. I don't give them that. Never have. That was my genius.

And I defeated those incursions in my Ballet Babes' brains. That was my gift. Give me a child young enough and often enough and I will win the war for her imagination, for his imagination, for their imagination. My Ballet Babes do not dream of being Shirley Temple, they dream of flying higher than the Nicholas Brothers, they dream of hair like Lucille Ellis's between their fingers, or on their head. They dream of being as powerfully crazy as Little Miss Sharecropper. After a year with me in the ZJ School of the Theatre, *Ozzie and Harriet* and *My Three Sons* hold no sway for them! White television isn't a standard, it's a deviation. That's the war I'm waging — and losing.

Mahalia Jackson is King's friend. She's my friend, too. It's Mahalia who told him to "tell about the dream." He didn't have that in the speech before Mahalia told him to put it there. My girls love it when I let that slip. A few years back, I was there when they shared a pulpit-stage in Chicago. Mahalia had this preposterous wig on her head: the bangs went straight up six inches from her scalp and the sides fell down in a wild pageboy flip. She was wearing a suit with giant buttons, and Mahalia looked like nothing but a star. When she sang, "Joshua fit the battle of Jericho, Jericho, Jericho, and the walls came tumbling down" she was making a promise that art can make what politics cannot — that we will win. And not only *will* we win, we will know we can win, before we win.

That's an uncommon sepia satisfaction.

In the hospital, people bring me little gifts and tokens. Someone brought me King's new book, *Where Do We Go from Here: Chaos or Community?*

I liked some of it a lot. King is starting to talk about poverty. He is talking about new ways to see who's on your team and who is not — ways that go beyond skin color and creed — and about class and capitalism — but some of it is dead wrong. King thinks the race war has been won.

Like Prophet Jones, I make predictions. Unlike Prophet Jones, most of mine come true. The race war will be longer than we anticipated. It will last way into the 21st

282

century but it will be those who know we will win who will fight longest and hardest. The dour ones, the rational, strategic, and pragmatic ones, will be lauded. But it is the artists who will fight when all seems lost.

Mahalia knew this; Martin knew it, too. Mahalia could turn a congregation into an audience, and an audience is a more powerful thing than a congregation. That's why Martin wanted Mahalia by his side. A congregation is always supplicant. An audience makes demands. An audience is a collaborator who makes transformation possible by allowing itself to be transformed and by transforming the performer. The good life is a four-piece jazz quartet trading solos. You know it when you hear it. You feel it when you see it.

We will win. That is the promise I make on Father's Day. Now that '67 has come and gone, I fear I have been rearranging deck chairs on the *Titanic*.

LIBATION FOR THE FEAST DAY OF MARTIN LUTHER KING JR.:
Shining Hour

1 jigger of Old Tom gin
1 sugar cube
1/2 lime, juiced

1/2 lemon, juiced
Ginger ale

Place sugar cube into cocktail shaker and
muddle with juices. Add gin and ice.
Shake. Strain into a tall, thin glass with
ice and top with ginger ale.

WEEK 24
TWENTY-FOURTH SUNDAY
AFTER FATHER'S DAY

Time to tell this. There was only one bathroom in the Middleburg farmhouse her mother purchased in 1973. Every time Colored Girl used that bathroom in her nadir years, '73, '74, '75, and '76, years with no Detroit, so little father, and too much mother, she was subject to seeing "stuff" she didn't want to see. Colored Girl didn't want to forget what transpired between her and her mother, she wanted to organize it so it didn't disorganize her. She cleaned her mind like some women clean houses, one room at a time, singing along, loud, to music. Usually she played, over and over, Rosetta Tharp's "This Train." Sometimes she played Della Reese. Nobody in DC, at Fisk, at Harvard, or in Bullock's Black Bottom Bar ever understood why she liked that silly album *Della, Della, Cha, Cha, Cha.*

And she had to organize this: At the end

of her summer visit in 1971 (which consisted of a brief stop in Detroit before she was seconded to a camp in Northern Michigan), driving to the airport her father said this was her last trip to Detroit for "the foreseeable future, final decision. I'll see you in Washington."

"Final decision," in "Daddyspeak," meant no further questions entertained. Except this time there had been no questions allowed. Four times a year the father would travel to Washington, check into the Statler Hilton, and visit his daughter.

Della Reese

PATRON SAINT OF: *Battered Women, Exceptional Allies, and Those Who Would Be Lucky*

Though she would have a superstar group named after her, the Vandellas, and appear on *The Ed Sullivan Show* nineteen times, Della was no musical genius. She was the queen of preparation.

We worked together at The Flame. No one made that curved marquis with those five letters that spelled "F-L-A-M-E" in double rows of naked lightbulbs burn brighter than The Librarian. I call Della "The Librarian" because she was forever studying someone else's act. She treated The Flame like it was

286

a lending library and every performance was a book she needed to study. When she was opening for Nat King Cole, she would run off the stage, change into street clothes, then hide in the folds of the stage curtains to watch him from up close, three shows a night, night after night. One night the curtains closed, revealing Della standing on the stage scribbling notes. The band started to razz her about her strange behavior. Nat shocked everybody by rushing to her rescue, praising the effort she was putting into building an act.

He didn't praise her voice, mind you. Nat was a truth-telling man. That didn't matter to Della. This mattered: Nat realized Della needed an ally. And he became hers. The rest of us thought she was just a little too ambitious for her talent.

But we loved Della for being a hometown girl. Her daddy, Richard Thad Early, poured steel in a plant; her mother did day work and took in laundry. Because she was as industrious as her parents, from the early days an ever-grateful Della kept being booked in the Detroit showbars. When reporters asked who she most appreciated working with in New York, she'd give a real Black Bottom answer: "It's who I sang with in Detroit before I came to New York that matters."

Ella, Sarah, Dinah, Billy Eckstine, Miles Davis, Erskine Hawkins and his band, and Duke Ellington. Nat King Cole. That's who she sang with in Detroit. A lot of those nights, I was the emcee. These were the acts she studied to craft a performance that allowed her to do the thing she had been doing since, as she would gut-bucket put it, "the doctor slapped my ass." Sing.

The truth was, Della was a true scholar with both a head for theory and an excellent memory. In elementary school, her former teachers told Shirley McNeil, they had predicted she was destined for Fisk or Radcliffe.

But her mother died and her father started running the streets. At fourteen she found some kind of home out on the road singing with Mahalia Jackson. At sixteen, she started at Wayne State University with an ambition to become a psychiatrist. At eighteen she dropped out. "With Mama dead, there wasn't twelve years of money to see me through medical school and training," she said. She knew what resources medicine took and she didn't have them. She would be a singer.

Della started scuffling. Driving taxicabs. Driving vegetable trucks. Singing at The

Flame and getting on *The Soupy Sales Show* anytime she could. She did anything to keep hungry away, and a roof above her head.

In 1951, Della did a self-treacherous thing. She married Vermont Taliaferro. He was twenty-nine and reputed to be rising rapidly within the auto plant ranks. She was twenty and failing to move from opening act to headliner. It wasn't long after the wedding that Vermont started using Della as a punching bag.

"He's a Gemini," she would quip, like it was some kind of explanation. A few said Vermont began hitting Reese upside her head so hard and so often she feared he would kill her. Others said that was a lie, that he provided, not just food and a roof, but also diamonds and a car. Only when I saw a bruise blooming beneath her makeup one night backstage at The Flame did I ask, "You don't really believe he would kill you?" "Why *wouldn't* I believe it, Ziggy? The last lick I got almost killed me." Only one thing to say back to that and I said it. "Get the fuck out, Della."

She fled to her sister's attic apartment in River Rouge. Her sister and brother-in-law were big people, the sister six-foot-one, her husband six-foot-five. They had a teen boy almost six-feet and still growing. Vermont was fool enough to track Della to those folks' apartment. He begged, banged, and pleaded until Della's sister let him in. He was so abject in his misery that the tall folks let their guard down. Vermont came upon Della in the front room sitting on a yellow couch beneath a window. He said all kinds of pretty things. Della wasn't hearing it. Vermont swore if Della wasn't coming back, he was throwing himself out of the window. He started lunging. Della's sister, her husband, and their son grabbed hold of Vermont and struggled to keep hold of him. While they struggled to hold him back, five-foot-two Della opened wide the window. Vermont walked out alive — but without a wife.

Della walked out onto the world stage. She studied, she prepared, she marched straight into the breach between herself and thriving, never taking one step back, though she sometimes allowed herself a rearward glance toward exceptional allies from Nat King Cole to Ed Sullivan.

LIBATION FOR THE FEAST DAY OF DELLA REESE:
The Last Lick

1 jigger of rye whiskey

1/2 lemon, juiced
1/2 pony of simple syrup
1/4 or less pony of red wine

Place rye, lemon juice, and simple syrup in a cocktail shaker. Shake and strain into a cocktail glass. Float red wine on top. You should have an 1/8-inch layer of red atop an otherwise gold drink.

FALL MOVEABLE FEAST:
THANKSGIVING

Martha Holmes, the *Life* magazine photographer who nearly killed Billy Eckstine's career in 1949 with a single photograph, died a half century and a little more later, in 2006, at the skinny old age of eighty-three. In her obituary the *New York Times* reported that her 1949 portrait of Eckstine was her "favorite" photo.

Born in Kentucky, in 1923, the photographer well understood what her New York editors could not, that Down South the photo would be viewed as a Black man hugging a white woman, an incendiary proposition, and, as a white woman adoring a Black man, a more incendiary proposition. The photo worked because of racism, exploding racism, and fueling racism.

When Colored Girl's brilliant brown Fisk art history professor started quoting Susan Sontag to Colored Girl, she knew Sontag was a second white woman Ziggy might-could have loved.

Sontag knew what it was to be over-scrutinized. That's what let Sontag write, "To photograph people is to violate them, by seeing them as they never see them-selves, by having knowledge of them that they can never have; it turns people into objects that can be symbolically pos-sessed." Colored Girl believed that state-ment to be both true and not true.

Ziggy had dragged Colored Girl and a bunch of the students from his School of the Theatre through a photography exhibit off the lobby of the Gotham Hotel, noting, "A photograph can show you as you see yourself as the world refuses to see you. Van der Zee did that. A photograph can be your friend that sees you as you see yourself." Then Shirley McNeil chimed in: "A photograph can be your own mother, your own completing other. Free you from the gaze of everyone but your mind's eye." Ziggy made Shirley say that to his girls, twice.

Ziggy only needed to say this once: "Martha Holmes used racism to build up her career, not caring nary a thing about who or what she tore down." Then he said, "It always hurts the most when your own come get you. I ain't got nobody to send for her that look like her."

Colored Girl developed allies Ziggy couldn't imagine. A day late and a dollar short, Colored Girl sent Susan Sontag in to get Mr. B.'s lick back. She wrote an essay about Martha Holmes, concluding with a Sontag quote: "Just as a camera is a sublimation of the gun, to photograph someone is a subliminal murder — a soft murder, appropriate to a sad, frightened time." Detroit wins war. Remorseless witch called out. Boom.

Billy Eckstine

PATRON SAINT OF: *Black Brilliance, Sartorial Splendor, and Capable Charismatics*

Mr. B., Billy Eckstine. I want all my young people to know about him. Mr. B. translates better than anybody into the modern era. Mr. B. was destroyed by a white woman, an artist, a photographer. It was a kind of hit-and-run, where the hitter doesn't even know they killed somebody. But Martha Holmes killed Billy Eckstine in 1949. She took a picture of Mr. B. surrounded by these white fans, girls, white girls, and the women are smiling and one of them lays her head on his chest in a kind of casual but rapt adoration, and Mr. B. is cool. He plays it like "all this and everything else in the world belongs to me." Martha Holmes captured that look.

After that photo, all his bookings stopped. Everything stopped. I have heard Quincy Jones say if Eckstine had been white, the sky would have been the limit. Without Eckstine there is no Dizzy Gillespie, Miles Davis, Charlie Parker, no Sassy, no Sarah Vaughan, as we know Sarah Vaughan, without Mr. B. They all played in that big band of his he started in 1944. Bebop. They played Bebop in a way I had never heard before, and I had heard everything. Billy Eckstine invented that language.

With the click of a shutter that white girl killed all of that. And never looked back. But she couldn't take away the way he rolled his collar and made those ties snap to attention in a Windsor knot that a thousand million cool cats have tried to imitate. They can't take away the way we loved him for us.

Yes, I hope St. Peter saves the swankiest cloud for you, Mr. B. When I get upstairs, I'll reserve that for you, the swankiest cloud.

There are gunshot wounds that are less damaging than some photo shoots. The great Billy Eckstine had his career cut down with a single camera shot. Have I said that enough? Can you hear it on the lower registers? This little white girl, Martha Holmes, slaughtered Billy's career. It was 1949 when the photo was taken and it was 1950 when it was released. Martha received a lot of applause for bringing Eckstine down. That's one person I've wished evil on for the nonchalance of her response to the damage done.

Billy was stupid to be in the wrong place at the wrong time, surrounded by white fans, and letting that white girl rest her head on his chest. You would have thought it was the end of the world. At one point he was just about to open up a haberdashery shop in New York. That could have been a tragic thing. But Mr. B. would have turned that haberdashery shop into someplace that made a brown man feel more like a man.

LIBATION FOR THE FEAST DAY OF BILLY ECKSTINE:
The Swankiest Cloud

1 1/2 jiggers of Calisaya liqueur
1 1/2 jiggers of Plymouth gin

Place in a cocktail shaker with crushed ice. Shake. Strain and serve.

WEEK 25
TWENTY-FIFTH SUNDAY
AFTER FATHER'S DAY

LaVern Baker lived in the Philippines for twenty-two years, arriving in 1966 and leaving in 1988. She performed in a club called Cubi, a legendary watering hole frequented by warriors, diplomats, and spies.

The first thing a customer noticed walking into Cubi might be the garish red carpet that would have looked good in a Detroit showbar. Next, the phalanx of drunk aviators. After that, the "cat shot," a most peculiar mechanical entertainment: the cockpit of a fighter plane rigged up to slide into a water tank, unless you grabbed an almost ungrabbable wire before getting dunked.

Over stingers at Cubi was the first time Colored Girl ever heard about what La-Vern called "Ziggy's Saints Day Book." La-Vern told Colored Girl she had heard Ziggy had written one and Ziggy had left it to

Colored Girl in his will. LaVern was in the will, too, so she got sent a copy of the document that eventually found its way to the Philippines. Ziggy left LaVern a Flame showbar poster. The object didn't make its way to Southeast Asia. LaVern thought it was probably in Baby Doll's place up in the Lafayette Park apartments. "Baby Doll is a packrat." All this was news to Colored Girl. What was news to LaVern? Colored Girl had married "a bougie Black southerner, and a State Department officer." "How Lynette Taylor of you!" "No," Colored Girl lobbed back, "how LaVern Baker of me! You were always Ziggy's globetrotter." When Colored Girl rose to leave, LaVern surprised her with a kiss.

LaVern played Madison Square Garden in 1988. Colored Girl was in the audience. The baby daughter she had with her brown diplomat was there, too. Colored Girl was teaching her daughter the Girl Dance. You can't start teaching that lesson too early. And once you learn it you don't forget. Listening to LaVern in the Garden, Colored Girl started thinking about leaving her first husband and emancipating herself from a constrained, self-protective existence.

In 1990 LaVern received the Pioneer Award from the Rhythm and Blues Foundation. That year Aretha Franklin became the first woman voted into the Rock and Roll Hall of Fame. A year later, in 1991 LaVern became the second woman voted into the Rock and Roll Hall of Fame. "Jim Dandy," her signature song, made it onto *Rolling Stone*'s list of the 500 greatest songs of all time. George Stanley often said, "Time will tell." Time has told. LaVern, as Ziggy predicted, won the long game, leaving petty pretenders, pretending.

LaVern Baker

PATRON SAINT OF: *Globe-Trotters, the Robbed, the Resurrected, and Seekers of Resurrection*

There are all kinds of theft. Sometimes petty theft can be pretty. And there are lazy little larcenies with a killing sting. Sometimes it's just calling a theft petty that bruises. And every different kind of theft leaves a different taste in the mouth. My dear friend, my sweetest girl, LaVern Baker knew so much about theft, the sound, the sight, the taste, the feel, the scent of theft, that one day she stole herself. She left Detroit, left Motown, stole away to freedom, via a Far East Asia USO show.

299

Everybody knows about Josephine Baker, and I knew her, too, but my La Baker was LaVern, who started off in show business, in my first business, as little Miss Sharecropper. Lord have mercy, today! LaVern Baker started off as little Miss Sharecropper and she won't make it home from the South China Sea to say goodbye to me. But first and for a good long while, singing from the stage of The Flame she was the toast of Detroit City when Detroit was Black Camelot.

LaVern Baker's kiss, that is a girl kiss I will miss. When she started gigging, she was making $3 a week. I lived to see my La Baker banking $500 a week. I lived to see her have children completely unrelated to her named for her. I lived to see Al Green manage her or come as close to managing LaVern as anyone could do. I lived to see her opening in New York at the Baby Grand Lounge. Al got that for her, and he got her a spot on *The Ed Sullivan Show* in 1953, just before Christmas. December 3, 1953, was the date. The event was so important to me that even the fog of illness doesn't shroud that date, and that's without keeping a *TV Guide* clipping. I see clearly those four dresses, gorgeous garments that her devoted friend and manager Al Green had

made for LaVern, just in case Sullivan put
her in one more spot on the show than she
was promised. Or if he kept her around to
play the next week. But Ed Sullivan never
did right by LaVern the way he did by Della
Reese. Our LaVern wore the hell out of
those dresses even if she didn't wear them
all on network television. Even if you had to
be in the smoky room to see her, to hear
her, to dream, only dream, of touching and
tasting her. LaVern, she didn't give nothing
away, often or easy, except her sound.

The sound of her. That's where the trouble
began and how, eventually, somewhere in
the Far East, maybe Thailand, maybe Vietnam, maybe the Philippines, the trouble
ends. She has a thrilling voice. Even at the
beginning as Little Miss Sharecropper, it
was a voice that froze and thrilled a room. I
had a dream once (bet the number based
on the dream, and the number hit) that
featured LaVern picking cotton, a girl of ten
or eleven, working in an Alabama field, and
as she and the others around her worked,
LaVern started to sing high and loud and
everyone stopped picking cotton. And then
they got whipped for stopping and she got
whipped for singing. But LaVern kept singing and the other hands kept listening, swaying and crying, because LaVern's voice was

what we called then "true." Those Negroes thought they were hearing one of God's own bright and brown angels right in the middle of a hungry and dusty Alabama acre.

LaVern was troubled by the theft of her beauty. The sun had burned lines into her face, poverty had mangled her teeth and mottled her skin. I've seen her look into a mirror and say right out loud, "I got robbed."

If she got robbed, she must have started off richer than rich. I tried to tell her many times she was so beautiful. But all she would believe was that her voice was beautiful, and maybe sometimes she believed she *was* her voice. Oh, my dear girl, my Little Miss Sharecropper, my La Baker, my LaVern: You were so much more than your amazing, stolen voice. You are my favorite act of self-invention and self-reinvention. You are my North Star and you vanished when I needed you most — insisting, dear liar, that I didn't need you at all. You are gone and I am dying and I am not sure that is a coincidence.

And I am glad you are gone. Glad you did what you needed to do — not what someone else, even me, needed you to do. You became, in this last iteration, a flashing light of self-determination. I imagine one of my girls from the dancing school, one of my

Ballet Babes, will live a big and adventurous life that will one day lead across the world, to the South China Sea to kiss your cheek for me. When that kiss comes, LaVern, let it matter.

Let yourself remember sending me breathless postcards from Italy with directions to the postman, "D . . . liver . . . D.letter.D . . . sooner D better." You made your preferences known. You gave instruction. It was not an act of spoilage, it was a generosity; the postman was included in your conversation.

Somewhere in Europe you picked up a title. You came back calling yourself Countess. In that phase of your manifestations, Al Green gave you $200 to buy a French poodle. Twelve hours later you were crying because the French poodle had run away. I thought he had been stolen. Nobody wanted to tell you. Better to think the pooch had run for her freedom. You got a new dog and named him Tweedle Lee Dee and I can remember you walking Tweedle Lee Dee down the John R. You never let that pooch off his leash even inside.

You didn't cry over the large and obvious larcenies like in 1958 when Al Green died. God stole him from you. So many times, that man saved you from yourself. When you came back from Italy and you were playing the Apollo Theater and you hired a maid and a butler and I came to see you in your dressing room and had to explain to two strangers, the maid and the butler, who I was. No one could see you until they got past them. Then Al showed up and fired them. Al saved you from your pretensions.

And before that there was Georgia Gibbs. I hate Georgia Gibbs like I hate chitterlings that don't get cleaned right. Georgia Gibbs singing LaVern's notes and inflections are dirty chitterlings (something that should not exist, but does exist) that nauseate me.

Georgia Gibbs was a white woman who called herself a singer who copied note for note LaVern's songs and made more money copying LaVern than LaVern made being LaVern. Georgia Gibbs stole LaVern's sound. Stole her songs. Said they were her own. LaVern hated Georgia Gibbs almost as much as I did. But not as much. She was mad as hell at her. But she felt the compliment in the theft. If she had hated her as much as I did, she wouldn't have been so agile in rebuffing her. Hate makes you stiff.

In 1957 LaVern took out a life insurance policy and named Georgia Gibbs the beneficiary. Then my dear lady wrote Georgia a letter and called her out by her first name.

"Dear Georgia, inasmuch as I will be flying over quite a stretch of blue water on my forthcoming Australia tour, I'm taking out an insurance policy and making you the beneficiary. If I die, your career dies." But my baby didn't leave it at the humorous jab. She sued in court. She didn't win but she sued for copyright infringement. That is my LaVern. Most singers have no idea of what intellectual property is, or that their phrasing and singing creates something that they own. LaVern Baker understood this.

LaVern, in her own way, tone, and range, was a singer of the caliber of Ella Fitzgerald or Sarah Vaughan, my Sassy. But she didn't get the acclaim they deserved and got. Two years ago, I was supposed to go to Sassy's show. I wrote in my column that Baby Doll, Little Miss Office Worker, after a full day in the executive suite had managed to come home and fix ham hocks, string beans, and cornbread. After I had eaten my fill, while waiting to go out, I turned on *The Big Valley* to catch a little Barbara Stanwyck and I was off to slumberland. The point was, and no one got it, Stanwyck couldn't keep me interested. If LaVern had been on the TV, I would have stayed awake.

After her Al Green died, she moved from the Orchid Room in Kansas City to The

Flame showbar and then on to a homecoming of sorts at Robert's Lounge in Chicago — but it was a peripatetic and increasingly frustrating time in my LaVern's life.

Like when Rudy Rutherford had his clarinet stolen and he wanted the mouthpiece back and didn't get it. And in 1967, the year of the rebellion, I had a record player and speakers stolen from the school. I took it as a sign. I didn't take it in my stride like LaVern had taken all the thefts she had experienced.

Until she didn't. LaVern took off. I'm not sure how it was she had heard of the Philippines but that's where she told me she was truly headed when she left on that USO show. She had worked abroad, Australia and Italy, but I think it was a Black serviceman who told her about the Philippines and the good life she could have there. It was some strange kind of do-over. She would have servants that she could actually afford and new clothes all the time because help, clothes, and food were cheap, cheap, cheap in the Philippines. In search of an easier street, she went globetrotting.

She quit us. Chasing a place where Georgia Gibbs couldn't hear her. She quit us. She stopped recording. People in Detroit counted on LaVern to turn theft to beauty.

And she quit us.

She returned to singing in a room full of uniforms like she had done when she was first starting out and the soldiers were dressed for or returning from World War II. She discovered a place where war always seemed right around the corner, and a revolution, and a world of spies, and Muslims and Christians, a place more different than many from Alabama would think possible. A place where she could forget Georgia Gibbs, forget sharing a bill with Little Miss Cornshucks, forget once being Little Miss Sharecropper.

When she first started singing she performed in overalls and a straw hat, in the clothes she had worn when she worked the fields, to honor those still working in the fields who she refused to forget.

I am forgetting. My name has been printed on thousands upon thousands of poster bills. I have a single poster-bill in the apartment I share with Baby Doll. It advertises The Flame showbar. At the top is the word "FLAME" in those bold, burning letters and then the address 4264 John R. at the corner of Canfield. The Flame was right down the street from the Gotham Hotel. The name Tamara Hayes in the biggest letters, then Andre D'Orsay and Nellie Hill and Leonard and Leonard. My name is in a box, Joe "Ziggy" Johnson, Comedy MC. Our host was Morris Wasserman. Just above my name, letters that read: "Little Miss Sharecropper Back from a Coast-to-Coast Tour." And there was a number to call for reservations. Back in that day, people came out in droves to come see us. Don't let this get forgot.

We were an *us,* LaVern and I. We were an us. I wish I could see you one last time before I go upstairs. Slappy White says you're dead. I know he's lying. If you were dead, I would feel it in my bones, the way you are going to feel it when I die. We are an us. One of my girls, sometime not soon, will go out roving in the world, like I am teaching them to do, using you as an example, and she's going to stumble on you, and hug your neck one last time for Ziggy. Kiss my child for me. Did I say that already? Let me say it again: Kiss my child for me.

LIBATION FOR THE FEAST DAY OF LAVERN BAKER:
We Were an Us

1 pony of green crème de menthe
Crushed ice

Fill a cordial glass with crushed ice. Pour over green crème de menthe. Serve with a straw.

WINTER
Josette Johnson (1934–present)
Lloyd George Richards (1919–2006)
Ruth Charlotte Ellis (1899–2000)
Billy D. Parker (1920–2012)
Harold "Killerman" Johnson (1912–1966)
Bette Jean Stanley (1937–2000)
Lawrence Massey (1918–1966)
Dr. Robert C. Bennett (1911–1975)
Lucille Ellis (1919–1998)
Nellie Hill Trapp (1914–2015)
Skipper Mills (1885–1967)
Nat King Cole (1919–1965)
Lynette Dobbins Taylor (1918–2012)
Sammy Davis Jr. (1925–1990)

WEEK 26
TWENTY-SIXTH SUNDAY
AFTER FATHER'S DAY

In 1967, Ziggy spent Christmas in Kirwood Hospital. Upon Shirley McNeil's and Maxine Powell's suggestion, Guy Saulsberry ordered Ziggy's room transformed into a "Winter Wonderland." Using fishing line and tape, Drs. Bob Bennett and Alf Thomas hung no fewer than 123 shiny snowflakes of various sizes and degrees of intricacy from the ceiling of Ziggy's room while Shirley and Maxine pushed Ziggy through the halls in the wheelchair that Ziggy had inherited from Charles Diggs Sr. He was wearing a beautiful green cashmere robe and a red silk pajamas set, a gift from Anna Gordy. Blocks away, the annual Ziggy Johnson's School of the Theatre Christmas party was in full swing with its namesake absent but not forgotten. The most popular offering at the shindig was not the gift giveaway. It was the table where kids created yet another snowflake for Ziggy, cut from paper doilies then decorated with Elmer's glue and glitter.

That same year, Colored Girl discovered Christmas in DC was different from Christmas in Detroit. In her new DC neighborhood (a planned riverside community of stark modern high rises, townhouses, and luxury conveniences built on the rubble of a once-thriving Black community), the girls she met didn't jump double-dutch, do complex handclaps, know what song was number one on the charts, or know what song was number fifteen with a bullet, or ask for albums for Christmas. The DC girls she met sailed tiny boats in an immense concrete reflecting pool, rode hobbyhorses stuck in boxes of pure white sand, played fashion show with their Barbie dolls, and wanted Twiggy dolls under their trees.

Colored Girl's neighbor looked and dressed like one of the Twiggies. Early Christmas week, Apartment Twiggy announced, after nearly bumping into Colored Girl in the hallway (because her eyesight was obscured by a shopping bag overfilled with gaily wrapped presents), that she "hated snow, cold, and church" and so was spending "the holidays in the

Bahamas." She offered Colored Girl a dollar a day to feed and water her cat. Colored Girl added a second key to her new key ring.

Her first day on the job, Colored Girl was surprised to discover holiday cards taped to the refrigerator in the shape of a tree. Back at home Colored Girl cut sheets of paper into squares and drew ornaments on them. She taped the squares to her mother's refrigerator in the shape of a Christmas tree. When the mother saw the tree she said, "Sweet."

Christmas Eve, the mother laid out purple and gold caftans, appropriate undergarments and jewelry, and gold ballet flats for the next day's wear as mother and daughter munched on Jiffy-Pop popcorn straight from its aluminum pan. On December 25, there was one present under the paper ornament kitchen-tree for Colored Girl: Stevie Wonder's album *Someday at Christmas.* For the mother there was a poem Colored Girl had written.

For the rest of Christmas Day, they played *Someday at Christmas* over and over, ate fruitcake for breakfast, canned smoked oysters and sardines for lunch, and for dinner Welsh rarebit (which Colored Girl was relieved to discover had nothing to do with bunnies and everything to do with grilled cheese).

In the afternoon they did something they had never done in Detroit: They took a long walk by the river. As the mother talked about the thrill of getting a Christmas card from President Lyndon Baines Johnson (hand delivered by her old friend Ofield Dukes) and mused on how delightful it was to have the Veep (Vice President Hubert Humphrey) as her neighbor, Colored Girl hummed, in her head, the tune "The Little Drummer Boy."

She was starting to realize that despite the show of the fancy apartment in the fancy neighborhood, one present beneath the tree, the food they were eating, and no car at all, meant she was poor. "What do I bring since I don't play a drum?" she asked aloud.

The mother wasn't listening. She was talking about starting to help organize the Poor People's March on Washington, how many dignitaries would be in town, what a crucial role she would play, and how she hoped her blue-jeans-wearing crush would come.

She didn't know King would be assassinated, that the Poor People's March would still go on, deluged with rain, and that Dylan wouldn't show. Time hadn't told that yet.

Mother and daughter stopped walking and sat on a bench looking out on the Potomac. Mother, shivering in her black mink, said, "I hate winter." Colored Girl, in her gray rabbit fur coat, nodded "yes" while she thought "no." Colored Girl didn't hate winter.

She knew. Ziggy always said, "Winter is a pregnant woman carrying Spring in her belly." Ziggy said, "Be sweet to Winter and Winter will be sweet to you — and maybe let you kiss Baby Spring." Colored Girl was hoping for that. Till then she would enjoy doing something she had rarely done — spend some time with her mother. She was an adventurous girl.

Five days before Christmas, Josette Johnson, wearing a minidress, bright tights, and go-go boots, arrived at Kirwood Hospital toting both a cloth sleeping bag that would allow her to camp-in on a chair in her father's hospital room and the new Stevie Wonder album, signed personally from Stevie to Ziggy.

317

Josette Johnson

PATRON SAINT OF: *Daughters by Birth and by Adoption*

Josette left her little boy in Chicago so she could stay overnight with me. George Stanley will take Baby Doll out to a few parties tonight. That's his second Christmas present to me. The first? Early this morning George picked Josette up from the airport and brought her straight to Kirwood and me.

Josette beams in my direction as I type. And she tells her daddy all. Josette told me she asked George how he was doing and he said that he couldn't be too down because if Mari was alive somewhere and brokenhearted, he could feel it. And if she was dead, he could feel that. I've heard him say that. George says he doesn't feel nothing but sure that wherever she is Colored Girl knows her daddy loves her. He says, "Every time she hears 'Ain't No Mountain High Enough' Colored Girl's going to be lifted up." He says, "Wherever Bette's got her hid, they have radio. Get Colored Girl near a radio and she's going to hear a letter from home." George says, "Bette may break me, but she won't break my little girl."

318

My Josette published a short story in a literary magazine when she was just out of college. For a hot minute I thought she was going to be the next writer in the family — but that wasn't to be. It's my favorite short story. At my request she brought me a copy. I'm pasting it in my book.

ETTA, by Josette Johnson

Easy come easy go. I went to see my pawnbroker. Walked into the door beneath the three globes suspended by a bar with diamonds on my left pinky finger and nothing in my pockets. I left with naked hands, a bankroll thick enough to choke a horse, and a thin gold band tucked into my breast pocket.

The rubber band wrapped around my bankroll was loose. I was on a mission. I headed straight to South Center. I bought a lady's light gray wool coat and gave the counter girl a tip to get it wrapped in a box with a ribbon. I stopped in a florist. I bought a little spray of lilacs and an orchid for my lapel. As I shot down the street with my parcel tucked beneath one arm, my lilacs in my hand, my perfectly creased dove-colored hat on my head, wearing a gray gabardine coat and clean-shined black leather shoes, I caught my reflection in a plate glass window. I looked like Christmas coming early.

Looks can be deceiving. I was on my way to see a lady about a baby.

I didn't have much time. I was juggling four shows that night. Two at the Club DeLisa and two at the Rhumboogie. Late or not, I had to see Etta.

Bronzeville is a long narrow strip. Etta lived in a kitchenette on the boundary of a poor white area. I sprinted up the four flights of stairs leading to Etta's place thinking of my track merchant days at Wendell Phillips High School but panting like a lap dog. Finally, I was knocking on Etta's door. A few minutes later the dead bolt was tumbling out of the lock and Etta opened the door wearing a flowery house-dress.

"What you want?"

"Take you to lunch."

"Looking like this?"

She smoothed her hands over her hips. They were wider than they had been a month before. Her green eyes sparked in the middle of her coffee and cream face.

"I know some dark bars."

"Let me get my stockings and shoes."

"And some lipstick."

Etta opened the door wider. It was a simple "kitchenette," a one-room apartment with a bath down the hall. There was a single bed on three of the four walls and one in the middle of the room. The bed in the center was made. A dent in the bed clothing, a Bible on top of the spread, and an ashtray with a lit cigarette on top of the Bible told me Etta had been reading and smoking before I arrived, while the other girls slept. Brassieres, panties, and clean sheets hung on crisscrossed clotheslines near the ceiling.

Clean-faced, eyes closed, with relaxed hair pinned atop their heads then wrapped in silk scarves, her roommates looked athletic and graceful. As they gently tossed in their sleep the muscles of their brown legs and brown arms fired and flexed with the quiet power of showgirls that I find intoxicating.

With her hand Etta gestured that I should take a seat on the bed as she stepped behind a screen to struggle into her stockings. I handed over to her the box and was about to tell her to open it when she put a finger to her lips. Fortunately, she antici-

321

pated what I was about to say. She opened the box and pulled out the coat and smiled. I helped her into it, then pinned the lilacs to her lapel. The one luxury in the room was a pier mirror. As she buttoned the coat, she stood before it and stared at her reflection.

She looked so good she wanted to look better. She plucked a hat from its perch on a nail, then set it atop her head. We were off.

I am five foot five in shoes. Etta was probably five eight or nine, a real glamazon. As we walked past a coffee shop, we caught the attention of passersby. A man stopped to lift his hat to her. We walked without stopping or speaking. The third time a man lifted his hat, she spoke.

"You here to propose, Ziggy?"

"Maybe."

"I'll take maybe."

We arrived at a bar that wasn't too popular. It had just opened and wasn't yet known. We took a seat in the back. I ordered us both double Cutty Sarks.

"Have you told the father?"

"Big Doc? Not going to."

"What's your plan?"

"Find an unethical doctor I haven't slept with."

"You are too smart and too beautiful to throw away anything that's going to be as smart and beautiful as you."

"You want to marry me?"

"I'm not the marrying kind."

"Then that's just pretty words. I need a name, an address, and $200. You got any of that for me? Am I pretty enough to get that from you?"

Etta wasn't pretty, she was beautiful. I wouldn't have been there if she wasn't. She was like a Greek statue dipped in dark chocolate with grass-green eyes fringed with long black lashes. She didn't stir my loins but she took my breath away. It was like a statue had come to life with a big brain and a big heart. I reached into my pocket, pulled out the gold ring and slid it across the table.

"But you just said . . ."

"You want this baby?"

"I don't want to end up cooking in some white woman's kitchen and cleaning her house and her snotty kids. I don't want this baby that much. I don't want that baby. That's the baby I was, and I don't want that baby. But I don't think I can just scrape this baby out of me, flush it down the toilet, and forget about it. If we got married, we could do this. Maybe start a dancing school or a bar. I wouldn't work for white folks. If I have this baby by myself, I'll end up a maid."

"I'm not getting married."

"What's this ring fo'?"

"I want a baby. If I could carry it for you I would. But I can't."

I reached into my pocket and pulled out four $50 bills then pushed them across the table to Etta. It was a night of many gifts.

"Put on the ring. Catch the train down to Greenwood, Mississippi. Stay out in the country with my cousin. She sickly and needs help. Have the baby, wean the baby. Help my cousin. Call me when you and the baby are ready to part and I will come get the baby. Drink water and eat crackers and walk those country roads till you're ready to come back looking like something. I'll put you in the show as a Ziggarette."

"Who's going to raise my baby?"

"Me. I want to be a daddy."

"And you don't care nothing about being a husband."

"Nothing."

"You mighty strange."

"If that's your way of saying I'm original I'll take it."

"What's the coat for and the lilacs?"

324

"I want my baby to start off warm and sweet scented."

"And respectable?"

"Don't care a thing about respectable."

"You counting on me not being brave enough to snatch her back."

"I'm counting on you wanting to dance and wanting to keep Big Doc."

"You a sweet liar. Give me a cig."

I gave her a cigarette. She took it, plucked it with a lotioned right hand that sported perfectly polished fingernails. I grabbed her left hand and slipped my ring on it. She didn't say anything. Her eyes filled with water. She thought I was robbing her. I thought I was saving the baby and Etta from dishwater and toilet bowls.

I was going to have a baby. All by myself. I smiled to think of the sheer audacity of it. No man I knew had ever done it. I would have a baby on my own and my mother and brothers would help. I would have a baby as beautiful as Etta. I tingled with the excitement of baby needs new shoes energy. I was gonna have a baby with no wife at all.

I walked Etta back to the stoop of her kitchenette. I wrote down my cousin's name, address, and phone number and urged her to be on the train to Greenwood before the end of the week. I suggested that she tell Big Doc she had a sick cousin Down South and tell the girls with whom she shared the kitchenette nothing — except she had a sick relation. I said when she came back, she was going to have to forget she ever had the child. I was not sharing the baby. I told Etta to put my name on the birth certificate and write down her middle name and first name for the mother's name. Told her root doctors deliver babies down in the country and nobody would do any better.

"You think it's a boy or a girl?"

"A girl."

"Then I'm going to name her Josette."

Josette was born "grown." Josette never threw guilt or excess praise. She bought me the cashmere socks she could afford. Do I sound besotted? From the day she was born I have reveled in being Josette's father. And I have worried that I am inadequate to the task. And this time of year I have worried about making family and Christmas for my daughter out of the unusual building materials I chose. From the moment I thought myself grown, I knew I wanted to be a father and I did not want to be a husband. I built our family without regard to convention.

My best building blocks: unspent love for my own father. Unspent because he was often gone, then always gone; unspent because when he was present there were better men, my brothers, between my father and me; unspent because the Natchez Belle preferred to share her last child with the church and not with her husband. For these reasons much of the love I had for Charles Johnson went unspent until I lavished it on Josette.

When she was growing up, she could rely on me to provide much of what she needed and some of what she wanted. Weeks I couldn't send money home from the road or Detroit for something she wanted, or, worse, times when there was something she needed I couldn't afford, my brothers stepped in. I was gone a lot. I was never always gone. I was often loving Josette across distances. Except at Christmas.

We always spent Christmas Day together. And we would always waltz. When we started the tradition, she would stand on my feet as we danced. We would sing our Christmas waltz as we twirled. I wrote the melody and the original words. Over the years she changed some of the words but left the notes. We would cook Michigan chestnuts and sweet potatoes and eat turkey and dressing and I would drink white Russians. When she got old enough, we both drank white Russians. It would be Christmas even before the gifts — for her, a bottle, first of fancy bubble bath, eventually a bottle of Arpège. Eventually there were presents for her children and an envelope with a $100 bill always wrapped with instructions to spend it only on herself, only on fun. One year, I gave her a rhinestone wreath pin signed by Eisenberg. Every year we go to midnight mass with the Natchez Belle and the uncles and after they were born the grandbabies. We would spend Christmas Eve Day playing our favorite records of the year and debating which song would be declared "Joe and Josette's Best Song of the Year."

After 1946, once we chose our "official" "song of the year" we would always play our "always" "song of the year" Nat's "Christmas Song."

"There will always be Christmas, and the 'Christmas Song,' by Nat King Cole, and 'White Christmas' by Bing.' " That's how I opened the column December 25, 1965. The "Christmas Song." That's sepia America's *Christmas Carol.*

This was my big Christmas gift: I opened the School of the Theatre in 1952 so that I could be a businessman, a permanent fixture, a father to the neighborhood, whose reputation would elevate my daughter's stature. She wasn't a doctor's daughter but I could make her *a legitimate businessman's* daughter. I wanted to create something tangible my daughter could inherit. Problem was the Ziggy Johnson's School of the Theatre, conceived as the ultimate Christmas present for Josette, became even a bigger present for the small fry of Detroit.

Trying to be all I could be for her, I stumbled into her having to share me.

Christmas Party Day is my second favorite day of the dance school year. We hang tinsel from the ceiling and everywhere else and give the kids presents and punch and ice cream. There is no list for Santa, and no disappointment, just the unexpected gift picked by someone who knows what you might like, because they know you.

We know these kids. They spend every Saturday with us. They spend many weekday afternoons with us. Each year we spend 360 days preparing for the Youth Colossal. We know who's naughty and who's nice and they all get presents wrapped in red poinsettia paper, or red or green paper. This is just one of the things I hope they remember years from now when they are raising children of their own. I hope they wrap holiday gifts in red and green paper and leave the white Santa Clauses alone. I hope Josette sees that I save all the gold paper just for her. I believe she sees that. Girl and woman, she's always been a "water the soup and invite the troupe" kind of gal.

One of the older boys in the tap class claimed he knew just what Santa Claus looked like, that Santa was five-feet-nothing and yellow with slicked-back hair and he preferred to wear a golf sweater to anything else. He was talking about me and he didn't know I could hear him saying just what I wanted to hear.

That matters to me. When I started grown-dreaming of making Christmas, I imagined days with song and sparkle. The trees wouldn't sit in windows. They would dance around a stage. They would December waltz around a room. I would have a daughter and give her a rhinestone wreath pin and when she put that on it would be Christmas.

I have only had one better name than Santa Claus. And it was not Ziggy. It was not Joe Ziggy, it was not Stanley or Livingstone, Brother, Son, Nephew, Friend, or Mr. Johnson. I have loved all those names. My best name is Daddy.

LIBATION FOR THE FEAST DAY OF JOSETTE JOHNSON:
Baby Needs New Shoes

A superior Christmas tipple.

1 pony of bourbon
1 pony of rye
1 sugar cube
1 lemon peel
Grated nutmeg
Hot water

Place sugar cube into a vessel suitable for hot beverages. Pour splash of hot water over the cube, allowing the sugar to begin to dissolve. Lightly muddle and stir to expedite. Add bourbon and rye. Next add 4–5 ounces of hot water. Top with zest of lemon peel and grated nutmeg.

WEEK 27
TWENTY-SEVENTH SUNDAY
AFTER FATHER'S DAY

Early days in DC. Colored Girl had only small bits of proof that Detroit still existed. Monday through Friday, as *The Today Show* played on in the background and she got dressed for school and her mother got dressed to look for a job, Frank Blair, the *Today Show* weatherman, would give the national weather report and sometimes he would mention Detroit. The first days of 1968 had arrived and the only news Colored Girl heard from home was words and sounds floating out of the radio when she tuned the dial to 1450. New songs on the radio meant Detroit must still exist. If Detroit still existed, her daddy was coming for to carry her home.

"I Heard It Through the Grapevine" played, and she didn't tell anyone how Gladys Knight had once helped pull Colored Girl into her tights, brushed blush on her cheekbones, then used her own spit to slick down Colored Girl's hair to make her stage-ready. If she had told them, she wouldn't be believed. She learned that in the fancy DC sandbox.

That January, Colored Girl learned that the only connection the Black kids, the white kids, and the Detroit kids all had in common was that they loved Stevie Wonder. When Colored Girl told her new friends that she knew Stevie and that he had sung "Happy Birthday" to her at her last birthday party, one of them threw sand at her knees (she still wore dresses with matching shoes and knee socks) and gaily screamed, "Liar, liar, pants on fire!" All the others laughed at her until she chimed in, "Just joking!" and joined in the laughter.

"Lay in the cut, Colored Girl. Choose the moment to act, don't let it choose you!" The DC kids knew more words, but they didn't know the important words Black Bottom had taught. They didn't know "strategy." They didn't know "alpha and omega." They didn't know all the meanings of "cut." The father said, You are the alpha and omega of my life. Lawrence Massey repeated, We've got to have the right strategy. Strategy is everything. Ziggy said, Lay in the cut. She was Detroit born, and Detroit bred, and when she died, she'd be

333

Detroit-dead. She might not have much, but she had enough.

Then she didn't. June 14, 1971. An older girl she knew from Ziggy's school had been bound with surgical cord and shot. She read about it in the *New York Times.* It was the summer between sixth and seventh grades. She had completed three years at Paliprep, a progressive private school, integrated and innovative, that proudly refused to field a football team, grade student work, or ask students to call their teachers by their last name, but rewarded daily reading of the *Washington Post* and the *New York Times.* The short piece left her shaking.

Among the dead: Katherine Winston and Tessie Brown, both eighteen. They would have been thirteen or fourteen when Colored Girl left Detroit. Both of their names sounded familiar. She didn't know either of the girls well, but she thought she knew one. The event, described as a bloodbath, sounded so unfamiliar. Other girls had been killed, too: Sharon Brown, nineteen, and Katherine Basser. The newspaper reported that five handguns and five long guns were found on the scene. This was no surprise. Colored Girl was raised in houses with guns. This startled: The house where the massacre occurred was described as being "on a street that is lined with tall elm trees and big three-story houses most of which are fronted by rose bushes and well-kept lawns." The massacre was on Hazelwood. Colored Girl's grandmother lived on Hazelwood.

Ten days before her mother died, Colored Girl hosted a luncheon for her and a dozen of her friends. Her mother made the guest list. As the guests gathered around the dining table in the private dining room of the hospice, Colored Girl observed that all the guests (in a city of half a million that was over fifty percent female and over sixty percent Black), save one, were white.

When the guests were seated and wine had been poured, the mother made an entrance. Steroids had blown her once-svelte figure up to nearly 300 pounds. She wore an artisan caftan of raw silk and huge, jet-black spectacles with clear-glass lenses. She thought the glasses created interest and definition to her bloated face by returning some of the bold sharp lines that the meds had stolen from her. Covering her head was a turban, also of silk, but in a contrasting color. She wore a chunky geometric necklace. When the piece was complimented, she said she had found it in the Museum of Modern Art catalog. She did not look like her old self, but she achieved much the same effect; she looked beautiful, powerful, and proud.

The approach of death had removed the mother's few filters. When one of the guests referred to her as coming from Detroit, she clarified that she was from *Ohio.* "The only good thing that ever came out of Detroit was Lloyd George Richards." "What about your daughter?" "As I said!" Colored Girl forced herself to laugh with the group at what the others thought was a joke.

Though Ziggy lived to see a show that Richards directed on Broadway, he didn't live to see what more this breadwinner's son became after Ziggy's death: dean of the Yale School of Drama, appointed by President Reagan to the advisory board of the National Endowment for the Arts, and the preeminent interpreter of the works of August Wilson. Ziggy's girls, when they were women, saw that.

Lloyd George Richards

PATRON SAINT OF: *Fence Builders, Fence Menders, and Fence Jumpers*

Things I won't live to see? What all my breadwinners' children become. But I have seen one shining bright on the Great White Way: Lloyd George Richards. In 1960 Richards earned a place in the history books when he directed *Raisin in the Sun,* starring Mister Sidney Poitier, on Broadway. No sepian achieved that before Richards, a breadwinner's son.

Though he was born in Toronto in 1919, Lloyd George Richards is a quintessential Detroit kid made good. He moved with his parents and his siblings to Detroit in 1923 for the most usual of reasons: His daddy saw a flyer from Ford promising jobs and better wages. Settled into Black Bottom, the daddy became a breadwinner, an autoworker, who toiled on a Michigan assembly line, like so many of the daddies of so many of my students. Then tragedy struck. Albert George Richards died in 1928 of diphtheria. To help support the family, Lloyd Richards shined shoes and swept floors at a local barbershop, the quintessential Black Bottom boy job. Lloyd Richards went to Northwestern High School and Wayne State

University, like so many of my students. His early biography has many elements common to most young males in our world.

But it has a few uncommon ones, as well. Those are the key to how it was he had it so hard and rose so high. Lots of boys shined shoes in Detroit — George Stanley and Marc Stepp, to name but two — but none were soaked in the stories that bounced around between cuts and shaves like Lloyd Richards. He turned a barbershop into a storytelling school. He took something that could have beaten him down — sweeping floors — and turned it into a way to lift himself up. He told me that the barbershop became an opportunity to observe the ways different people spoke, what made people laugh, and the kind of stories people never interrupted.

His mother worked as a domestic, earning a dollar a day, until tragedy struck a second time and the mother woke up completely blind. Richards worked harder. The family was forced to go on relief, a blow they dodged until they couldn't. Richards leaned into his position as an observer and used it to shield himself from the identity of victim.

He had fallen deeply in love with sepian barbershop language, but the first chance he got, he cheated on that language and took up with the Shakespearean language he met in school. He told me he was prepared for loving Shakespeare because of all the time he had spent with the King James Bible in the Black Episcopal Church his family attended. He thought he wanted to be an actor. He went to Wayne State University and majored in speech. He came out scuffling: He was a disc jockey and he wrote and narrated a crazily popular religious radio show called *Little Church of the Air,* put on by the Detroit Council of Churches. He wasn't a breadwinner but he was doing that other Detroit thing: servicing the breadwinners and their families.

But when he did it, he put an original Richards spin on it. Richards was always noting little-known facts, like that the Lone Ranger and the Green Hornet both got started in Detroit, or that Detroit was a radio center third only to New York and Chicago. In 1945 he founded These Twenty People, which became Detroit's The Actors Company. Those crazies held shows in a great big house in River Rouge Park near the auto plant. By the very early fifties, the time I was settling down into writing a weekly column for the *Michigan Chronicle,* Richards was a bona fide legend in the

Detroit theater world and a recognized eccentric.

He liked to stop in to see my kids rehearse and hear our plans for the coming year's Colossal, toting an old copper shoeshine box, using the footrest piece as a handle. He said he saw the thing in an antique store window and couldn't not buy it. He wanted to polish my shoes. I let him. Stuck one foot on top of his shoeshine box. He had Kiwi polish; he had a rhythm. While he buffed, he talked.

"Zig, you're a Garveyite, you just don't know it." Now I knew his daddy was a Garveyite. And I knew I knew a lot of Garveyites in Detroit and in Idlewild. I didn't know why Richards thought I might be one. Or why he thought he should be shining my shoes. I asked him to break that first one down for me.

"Racial pride: check. Self-reliance: check. Negro economic empowerment: check. Activating children for a political purpose: check." Then he started talking about Marcus Garvey's newspaper, *The Negro World,* and how it connected Detroit to points around the globe like Afghanistan, Cape Town, Ceylon, Cincinnati, Cleveland, Cuba, Gary, Haiti, Jamaica, Jerusalem, London, New York, Nicaragua, Philadelphia, and

340

Uganda, and I put my other foot on the box.

By the time he stopped talking, his chamois had my shoes gleaming and I had decided I needed to become a card-carrying member of the Universal Negro Improvement Association. And I still didn't know why he shined my shoes. So, I asked him. He had an easy answer: "Wanted to see what it would be to do it, eye to eye, not looking up."

Then Richards was gone — off to New York. I would bop over to New York to see each play that he put up. And Richards always returned to Detroit and his mama, sometimes stopping in to see me, often staying long enough to put on a show. In the late fifties, every summer Richards returned to Detroit to direct plays at the Northland Playhouse, a geodesic dome-shaped building that eventually housed The Mump Club, a teen discotheque. I would tease him that I was still a Garveyite, a nationalist, working for economic and every other kind of independence, and that he had moved away from his roots and became an integrationist putting on plays with live goats in them. All his plays had goats. He just smiled that shy smile that he half hid in his beard and let his eyes twinkle half hid behind wireframe glasses. But I sent my kids to see

341

him directing those plays at Northland and so that's how they got to know all about the Chinese Theater of Lao She and his play *The Teahouse* when that work was still new. When Richards opened his acting school in New York, I told folks he was copying me.

New York has always been cold for your Mister Chills. It was warm for Lloyd George Richards. When he did *A Raisin in the Sun,* written by the brilliant young sepian Lorraine Hansberry, starring a brilliant brown cast, I told him he was returning to his Black Detroit Garvey-nation roots. He said, "Zig, I never left. I just went out to do a little reconnaissance." I believed the man: He was the breadwinner's boy made good.

LIBATION FOR THE FEAST DAY OF LLOYD GEORGE RICHARDS:
These 20 People

2 jiggers of red wine
1 pony of Jamaican rum
1 pony of simple syrup
1/4 lime, juiced
2 jiggers of seltzer water

Place red wine, rum, simple syrup, and lime juice into a red wineglass and stir.

Add ice. Top with seltzer water and top with crushed ice.

343

WEEK 28
TWENTY-EIGHTH SUNDAY
AFTER FATHER'S DAY

In 1952 the American Psychiatric Association, in a flash of bigotry, designated homosexuality a sociopathic personality disturbance. The next year, President Eisenhower, believing homosexuals were a danger to national security, signed into law the ignorant Executive Order 10450, which banned gays from working for the government — including the military and federal agencies. The Daughters of Bilitis, an organization founded in San Francisco in 1955, is often credited as "the first-known lesbian rights organization." Black Bottom would beg to differ. Black Bottom knew Ruth Charlotte Ellis, and knew her as her own walking, talking, under-the-radar, lesbian rights organization founded in 1938 in Detroit, Michigan.

In 2000, Ruth, at the age of 101, attended the opening of Detroit's Ruth Ellis Center, an official hub of young Black queer life and resources. She died shortly after. Her former home on Oakland is now a part of the Detroit prairie.

Ruth Charlotte Ellis

PATRON SAINT OF: *The Courageous, the Salon Builders, and Those Who Look Out for the Kids*

Ruth Charlotte Ellis was born in 1899 to parents who had been born enslaved in Tennessee. In freedom the parents migrated to Springfield, Illinois, where Ruth was born the only daughter and last child in a family of four children. Ruth announced she loved women in 1915. In the late 1920s she announced she loved Cecilene "Babe" Franklin. Ruth and Babe moved to Detroit as a couple about 1937 or 1938, drawn to the city, like so many of my Black Bottom Saints, by the promise of factory jobs.

After trying her hand at factory work, and not liking it, Ruth invested a small inheritance (her wise father did not make the common mistake of disinheriting his daughter for knowing her heart) and established herself as the first female owner of a printing company in Detroit and as the premier hostess and social-work-central of Detroit Black gay life. She ran her print shop out of her home at 10377 Oakland. When her guests got a few drinks into them, some described her fondly as the first "Lavender, colored, woman in the history of the world to own a printing company, and it could only happen in Detroit City."

It was in Detroit, and only in Detroit, that my dear friend Valda Gray felt welcomed into a world beyond the world of entertainment, and so Valda, like so many others, made the pilgrimage to Detroit as often as possible in the forties, fifties, and sixties to come to Ellis's parties to savor this truth: In Detroit the queer world overlapped with the entertainment world, but it was rooted in the world of everyday working folk, of the breadwinners; it was rooted in the life of a "journeywoman" printer. Ruth claimed a place at the center of Black Detroit labor and life, then she radically shared it — with all comers.

Ruth and Babe created a legendary salon that was a haven for young queer people when there were few such places. They didn't just provide food and shelter and community, they provided money for college and schoolbooks. When necessary, the hostesses could turn into unpaid caseworkers. When the couple broke up, Ruth's social activism increased and the party continued;

but she never lived with another lover.

Today, Ruth came by Kirwood to see me. She barely leaves the compound that is her house and shop, but she hears all the East Side and West Side news. Everything. Today, she put a hard question to me. "Is there something they can do you ain't letting them do?," like she doesn't know the answer to that question. Ruth has been trained by Massey not to ask a question she doesn't know the answer to. I pout and I don't answer. Ruth starts humming some old hymn. I ask her what the temperature is outside.

Ruth responds, "Minus eight." I ask her to open my window. She looks at me crossways. As she opens the window she acknowledges, "This room is as hot as a greenhouse." Ruth stands ready to pounce and intercept should I attempt a Diggs Sr. I take in one deep, cool breath and then another. I gaze from my bed to the street. I love seeing our people fight the Michigan cold with shovels, tire chains, remnant pieces of carpet, table salt, and gravel. The Saints of Black Bottom winter know how to get ready. They understand the power of hibernation. They create wells of resilience from cold sky and bare boughs as our children

347

make snow angels, build snowmen, and wage snowball wars. They gestate. Like muscles twitching unseen beneath a heavy sweater and heavy coat, energy gathers hidden in winter, and the Saints of Black Bottom know how and when to wait. The nights are long in winter. I find strength in the night life even when I cannot go out into it. Minus eight reminds me there are things that I want to do and dying is not one of them. "Ruth, you can tell Dr. Bob Bennett I'm going to get my pacemaker. He should pay you double for his next set of business cards."

LIBATION FOR THE FEAST DAY OF RUTH ELLIS:
Printer's Ink

Bourbon
Blackberries

Fill a cordial glass full of blackberries. Top with bourbon.

WEEK 29
TWENTY-NINTH SUNDAY
AFTER FATHER'S DAY

Billy D. Parker made the national news in 1970 when he received the first-ever "strike check" issued by the United Auto Workers. A picture of a smiling and gap-toothed Parker brandishing the check was picked up on the AP wire and appeared in newspapers coast to coast. Parker's check was drawn on an account funded to the tune of 120 million union dollars.

Brenda Parker, Billy D. Parker's daughter, was in Colored Girl's ballet class. One day when Colored Girl arrived at ballet class wearing a new red leather coat and matching hat, Brenda said, "I'm jealous of you! My daddy's favorite word is *frugal*." Colored Girl said, "I'm jealous of *you*! Your mama isn't sometimey."

Billy D. Parker

PATRON SAINT OF: *Fathers, Breadwinners, and Audiences*

Shining brightest in my pantheon is a saint you ain't heard of, Billy D. Parker. Billy started working for General Motors in 1952. He was just back from the Korean War. For a hot minute he worked for De-Soto. He helped pull the last Custom off the assembly line, and the first Firedome. He didn't like the looks of the Firedome so he left DeSoto for General Motors. As I dictate to Baby Doll, while convalescing from pacemaker surgery, Parker is now a fifteen-year veteran of Cadillac Local 22, and I know he's going to see at least two live music shows this week.

Billy D. Parker is a breadwinner's bread-winner. Parker doesn't just build cars. Parker and his six sons built my Camelot. Billy is a philosopher of sorts. Once he explained it to me at the Chit Chat lounge: "Boring, profitable work will send you out to a club. At the end of your working hours as a porter or a domestic, you may not want to see any more people. Work on an assembly line and you're hungry for human interaction. And all that going out meant everybody wanted to play Detroit." Plenty pretty money to be made in so many Black-owned showbars, corner bars, lounges, and supper clubs. Get Scatterbrain, Parker, and Massey at a table and they might-could get the North and South Vietnamese to a truce table and end this killing of so many of our boys.

More than a worker and a negotiator, Billy D. Parker is a music connoisseur. His favorite artists are country-as-burlap Rosetta Tharpe and smooth-as-silk Hazel Scott.

Butterbeans and Susie did not marry because they were paid to — but Sister Rosetta Tharpe did sell tickets to her 1951 wedding in Griffith Stadium. It was 15,000 people paid $1.50 to $4.00 to see her husband promise to honor and obey her. A lot of breadwinners went to that wedding.

Parker and Scatterbrain could break down a Sister Rosetta song. The first line of my favorite Sister Rosetta song goes, "This train is a clean train." That seems simple, but to hear Parker tell it, it isn't. After telling us that the train is bound for glory, she makes a true list of who can't ride the train: liars, false pretenders, backbiters. After a laid-back but powerful guitar break, she follows the true list with a false list. She says that the train doesn't pull winkers, while winking, crapshooters, while shooting crap,

351

whiskey drinkers, while drinking, jokers, while joking, and tobacco chewers, with an apparent plug in the side of her jaw. By the end of the song we know Rosetta's train is a "her" and it's a clean train but not the way most folks define *clean.* Rosetta's train is a clean train because it is true, because it is authentic, because it nurtures, because it hauls everybody — but; but not the liars, false pretenders, and backbiters. Billy D. Parker loved all this, but what he loved best about Rosetta was that when she sang in Detroit, she sang Alabama, she sang Mississippi. The breadwinners loved how her country sound rang in their mamas' ears.

Hazel Scott, Congressman Adam Clayton Powell's second wife, sang citified and the breadwinners loved how her sound brought light of new horizons to their daughters' eyes. A classically trained Juilliard pianist, Hazel didn't come to Detroit as often as Rosetta. When she came, she played a grand piano and sold out concert halls. If a breadwinner owned an album with classical music on it, it was likely to be Hazel's, *A Piano Recital.* More likely they owned her classic jazz album, *'Round Midnight.* Billy D. Parker owned both. Kept *'Round Midnight* propped up beside his hi-fi and not just for the sound of it. He loved the photograph of Hazel on the cover in a chrome-blue strapless gown sitting at a piano. He had a gown like Hazel's made for his daughter to wear to her prom.

This is what most ofays never see: When a man, a sepia father, is driving down the street in a Cadillac or a Mustang, or whatever he's driving, he knows that a Black man, and if it's Detroit some Black man he knows, helped build that car. This is the pride the breadwinners know. I clap loudest for this.

And this: Driving to see Josette in Chicago or driving out to Idlewild, I get on a lonely stretch of flat and straight and put the pedal down and let the engine roar and that car glides and doesn't shake. Those miles, I'm alone but I'm not just driving myself, I'm driving some other Black man's sweat and prosperity. Some other Black man's competence. And the next week that man will be sitting in my audience. His approval will matter. By just driving I'm sending some other proud papa's kid to dance lessons, and music lessons, to a Black private school, to camp. That's the world the breadwinner built and that's the Detroit world I choreographed for.

They say 8,000 Black men were working in the factories by the end of World War I, almost 2,000 at Ford alone. The work wasn't easy or pretty. These first men were janitors and cleaners. Most of the ones who came next never got beyond the paint room and the foundry. They worked in the belly of a new beast, and the beast was a giant blast furnace. *But* they worked rain or shine, worked like you can't work on a farm. And they knew how much money would be in the check when it came. It may not have been what the white fellow got — hell, it wasn't — but it was the same every time. Knowing that, you could plan. You could buy a house with that, get to Idlewild, maybe buy a second house, have a night out at the clubs where some singer, some dancer, some barmaid could make you forget all you knew about the belly of the beast after you crawled out of it; and you could plan how it was that your son and your daughter would never crawl back in.

On a farm Down South, it looks like your children's children will be planting acres and fighting rain and weevils and every kind of plague forever. In a factory, you worry about losing a hand, or getting killed right off, but you know your child may not have to go into the factory — if you do it right, and long enough. You know there's a university down the road and your child just might-could get there. Yes, I worked to give the breadwinners a treat — but I worked harder, if more surreptitiously, to do something else: to nurture female citizens who questioned authority.

Back then in Detroit, a breadwinner was almost always a man. There were women behind the breadwinners: wives, mothers, daughters, but also artists like Hazel and Sister Rosetta; and there were some women who worked in the tire factories and some in the car factories, often pushing heavy mops, but most of the good plant jobs went to men. Women were left to hustling and scuffling, creating their own small businesses, beauty shops, catering, or a small funeral parlor, or working for some shop or another, earning low wages. To thank the breadwinners for making our audiences shine bright, I decided to do what I could to make their sons and daughters shine bright, but particularly I wanted to help the daughters. I had one. Billy Parker had one.

LIBATION FOR THE FEAST DAY OF BILLY D. PARKER:
The Dangerous Citizen

Based on Bullock's El Dorado Punch.
The Eldorado was a Cadillac

manufactured for half a century, from
1952 to 2002.

1 pony of brandy
1/2 pony of Jamaican rum
1/2 pony of bourbon
1 sugar cube
1 lemon: 1wedge and several slices

Place sugar cube and lemon wedge into
a cocktail shaker and muddle. Add
brandy, rum, bourbon, and ice and shake.
Strain into a rocks glass with ice. Dress
with lemon slices.

WEEK 30
THIRTIETH SUNDAY
AFTER FATHER'S DAY

"Culluds can't afford to goof." That was something the old folks said after they had been relocated from Black Bottom to the 12th Street neighborhood that included Hazelwood. Colored Girl goofed. She arrived early the morning after the luncheon, hoping to get some time alone at the hospice with her mother. The nurse waved her in. Usually she had to wait behind other visitors.

The mother said she had a box for the daughter. Finally. A box full of the letters she had received from the father, postcards from other family members, photographs, the early stories and poems that had been left behind when they suddenly parted. And she said she had a book Ziggy had written, *Lives of the Black Bottom Saints,* and she, Mari, was in it. The mother told Colored Girl she could have the box with the letters and the book

357

manuscript, if Colored Girl kissed her.

"What?"

"On my forehead."

"Your ring?"

"You want the box?"

"Yes."

"Kiss my face."

She had promised herself on October 15, 1977, that she would never willingly touch her mother's body again. She wanted those papers. Wanted her daddy's letters. Wanted her kidnapped words. Wanted Ziggy's book. She kissed her mother.

Harold "Killerman" Johnson

PATRON SAINT OF: *Cagey Corner Men, Versatile Allies, and Other Able Motivators*

Comfortable goes with baby. Challenged goes with grown. I have been no one's comfortable baby since I left the Natchez Belle's home. The honest hustle. I have watched money swirl around me and I have rarely tried to catch it. Not big money. My pockets have an almost magical way of coming up empty.

Harold "Killerman" Johnson and I went to Chicago to see Sugar Ray Robinson fight. I picked up the tickets. Then I dropped by

Mother's and asked the Natchez Belle to sew a button back on my coat. When we got to the gates my pockets were empty. All Killerman said was, "Ziegfeld, you have goofed." It was a simple statement of truth.

Everything else about the event was a mystery. Had someone in my mother's house taken the tickets out of jealousy? Out of spite? Had I dropped them on the street? Had someone picked my pocket, "boosting" the tickets?

Or maybe I sold them and lied about it.

What I knew for sure: I felt like Moses looking down at Israel but never making it to the promised land. How could I come that close and not make it to the arena?

Killer left me on the sidewalk and got into the fight. I don't know if he pickpocketed someone, or found a friend with an extra, or just talked his way in. I do know he was more fortunate than me. And we were friends after. He didn't hold our misfortune against me and I didn't hold his good fortune against him. We were copacetic.

I once put this question to Sugar Ray Robinson, the greatest boxer after Joe Louis. I asked Sugar Ray, "What does Killerman whisper in your ear when you come down the aisle toward the ring?" Sugar Ray whispered the answer to me low, like Killer talked to him on the way to the ring, "Sugar Ray, Sugar Ray, pick up on the beautiful dolls on your right!"

Think about the love, not the death. Empty pockets. I've been thinking about death too much this fall. That's empty pockets. This winter I'm thinking about love. Thinking about love? That's a pocket full of gold.

Culluds can't afford to goof. We don't live in a land of second chances. Rematch, maybe. Second chance, no. When you leave Black Bottom, when you leave Caramel Camelot, when you return to the wilderness some call the world, we are still cullud, and culluds need a friend like Killerman.

Thanksgiving 1962. The best game ever. Me and everybody in Detroit claimed it wasn't just the world that was watching, it was "Jesus and the twelve disciples watching that game; only God and Mary didn't come." Lombardi's Packers were undefeated. Bart Starr was a rising god in the football pantheon. He was sacked nineteen times in that game before Lombardi pulled him out. Every time Night Train stepped on the field, Killer would chant, "Hang 'Em High!"

White Detroit papers had predicted a six-point Packers win. That afternoon the book-

360

ies got burnt in Black neighborhoods. They said it couldn't be done. They said that Lombardi and the Packers were invincible. Killerman said "invincible" was our word for us. Our magic word and we would not let them have it. Black people believed Night Train could snatch that word back into our world.

All over, radios were turned up loud. You had to either be at the game or hear it on the radio. It wasn't on television. Black folk believed a locomotive called Night Train was going to give us a taste of victory. Nobody believed it more than Killer. "Roasted like turkeys! Roasted like Italian turkeys." He was gleeful with the knowledge the Mafia that had done so much damage in the Black world would on this day get burned — because they would have to pay out to believing Black folk who refused to concede victory to Bart Starr, an Alabama cracker.

Game day. Killer in the stands in his cashmere coat, leather gloves, a wool muffler, argyle socks. The temperature never dropped below freezing. He had a flask in his breast pocket. And beneath the flask, under his skin, he had a heart full of hate for Bart Starr. Starr had played at the University of Alabama when Governor

George Wallace was standing in the school-house door. It was rumored in the Black world that Starr's daddy ran the prison work gangs for the Alabama highway department. What we knew for sure was that Lanier was the million-dollar white high school that opened in 1929. In 1930 there were some 30,000 African-Americans living in Mont-gomery, Alabama, the capital of the state, *and there was not one Black high school.* Hank Williams and Zelda Sayre Fitzgerald both attended Lanier. Detroit knew all that. I had put it out in the dancing school. The kids took it home to their parents and the parents took it to the betting shops. Killer whispered it in Night Train's ear. Urban legend said Killer whispered it into the ear of 300-pound Roger Brown, who sacked Starr on one of the first plays of the game. Starr would be sacked eleven times and lose 110 yards.

Thirty-two million people watched on television. Watched without seeing how powerful Killerman's whispers were. It was reported in the press that 57,598 watched from the stands. No one counted how many listened with me, gathered into the Ebony Room of the Gotham Hotel waiting to buy drinks for Killer and Night Train and to hear what the radio announcers didn't know or tell.

Killerman died in 1966. He had asthma and died of pneumonia. Dick Gregory got there the day before and kept Killer laughing on his deathbed. Gregory had Rose Bowl tickets in the breast pocket of his topcoat, tickets he had purchased intending to take Killer to that big Pasadena game.

Everything about that game was awful. Killer was dead, his seat was empty, and Michigan State was defeated by invisible distractions and lost to UCLA. I'm glad Killer wasn't there to see that. Wasn't there to see Bubba Smith get beat. Killer loved the kid from Beaumont, Texas.

When the fans chanted, "Kill, Bubba, kill!" Killerman said they were chanting for him and for Bubba.

I went, like so much of the sporting world, old and new, to Chicago for the service at the First Church of Deliverance.

The world came out to say goodbye to Killerman. That was a credit to Killer. We would have expected that back in the Joe Louis days or the Sugar Ray days, but there's a new nursery rhyme the Ballet Babes have taught me: "They said the best was Sugar Ray/ but that's before they all saw Clay." Yet they all came out to see him, even Sonji Clay, Cassius's wife, wearing a long blond mink. Gregory was wearing a leather coat over his suit. All that was good. Killerman appreciated a sharp-dressed man and a sharp-dressed woman. Legions of them came out to send him upstairs. Proves we have memories. Proves love is the strut and hate is the stumble.

LIBATION FOR THE FEAST DAY OF KILLERMAN JOHNSON:
Copacetic

1 jigger of cognac
1 pony of curaçao
1/2 lemon, juiced
1 sugar cube
1 orange peel

Place sugar cube and juice into the bottom of a cocktail shaker and muddle briefly. Add cognac, curaçao, and ice and shake. Strain into a cocktail glass with no ice. Zest orange peel over the top. Twist orange peel to sit on the rim of the glass.

WEEK 31
THIRTY-FIRST SUNDAY
AFTER FATHER'S DAY

Colored Girl's seventeenth birthday went horribly wrong. She thought she had gotten beyond her mother's reach by planning a whitewater rafting trip in the high waters of the upper Yough River. She invited four of her most athletic friends. When the mother decided to come, too, Colored Girl wasn't alarmed. Keeping up appearances was important to the woman. She was probably coming along because one of the girls was a senator's daughter. The first day, they shot the easy but scenic upper section of the river. The sports team athleticism of the girls eclipsed the older woman's gym-chiseled strength. They slept in a primitive cabin by the river. In the morning Colored Girl was awakened before dawn, stunned to find the mother caressing one of her breasts with a shimmer-polished finger. The fingernail polish, pale and shiny and the only remaining vestige of Detroit and the sixties, looked anachronistic at all times. In the cabin light it was repugnant. The mother put her hand on the girl's mouth. The daughter could have screamed and the whole room of girl-women would have come to her defense, but they would have also known. So, she said nothing. Moved nothing. Left her mother to worry if they would get caught and beaten and prayed over. Eventually, the daughter rolled out of the bed to brush the mother out of her teeth and start the day for the ninth time. At the drop-off into the run of the lower part of the river, the guide warned about the treacherous Dimple Rock that must be approached from the right, from precisely the two o'clock angle. The mother, who didn't believe ordinary rules applied to her, approached Dimple Rock from the left, flipped out of her raft, and vanished. Heads were on swivels as the guide hollered for all to look sharp for the woman overboard. Soon the daughter was laughing. The guide thought it was the laughter of the daughter's hysterical fear. The girl felt something poking, pushing up on the rubber between her legs. The mother was trying to come up for air. To free her, the daughter had to paddle hard. She had to speak and let the others know where to locate the drowning woman. She was too tired to paddle, too tired to speak. She dropped her oar into the water.

Bette Jean Stanley

PATRON SAINT OF: *The Unforgiven, Bad Mothers, and Narcissists*

Bette Jean Stanley was something else. Cerebral and audacious, a quick study and innovator, Bette was a pure original. And she was peculiarly private.

Every other woman I knew who was anything like her wanted to do what she did for the stage or the screen. Bette Jean did it for the pleasure of being Bette Jean. She preferred to be her own audience. She rarely troubled herself to critique others. When she did, her most common vicious hiss was "That was an A-1 performance." She hated seeing anyone desperately try to connect by ratcheting up the humor, or the pathos, or just the sound, looking for an audience.

She didn't have to look for an audience. Bette attracted attention. She was tall, but not too tall, five foot six and one half, creamy skin that was just brown enough. Her eyes were large and dark. She had naturally straight black hair that she liked to wear cut short, which was particularly provocative because she had sloping shoulders and full breasts and shapely legs. Her stomach was soft, her arms were perfectly plump. She looked good in an Idlewild bathing suit. Bette was something akin to Lena Horne or Gina Lollobrigida. But, and this was the best part, Bette was the kind of beauty who wasn't sold to the world, because she didn't have to be. She just sold herself to George and kept on stepping. For herself and Mari.

She didn't follow the styles, she set them. She read and studied fashion magazines, particularly *Vogue.* After someone told her about it, she even managed regularly to get her hands on *Women's Wear Daily.* She discovered Pucci the first year his clothes were available in the United States. But better than reading to stay ahead of what she saw in the magazines, she would drive down to Detroit Metropolitan Airport and sit in the terminal watching people arrive, studying the fashion jetting in from everywhere. She would go to the car show and look at the colors and the shapes. It was looking at those colors and those shapes that helped her discover her love of shine — she liked frosted polishes, pale pinks, silvers, not apricot. She wore nude lipsticks before they were common; she considered painting her body all over in gold but heard about a model who died trying that stunt. She would go to the Detroit Art Institute and get ideas from paintings for new color combinations for slacks, sweaters, and scarves. She was the one woman in Black Detroit who dragged a shiny black mink. Most others wanted pale champagne or sable brown. She wanted jet black and got it.

The woman shopped as performance art. There were three pillars of her well-curated wardrobe. The first was menswear that flattered her curvy body. She was wearing pants before Mary Tyler Moore did on *The Dick Van Dyke Show.* Once she met George (he saw her standing at a bus stop on her way to her fancy job at the phone company), she would have his older sister Mary Frances do the retailoring. Before that, Bette did her own alterations by hand. Hooked up with George, she bought haute couture at Hudson's that became the second pillar of her wardrobe. The third pillar was exotic costumes. Before other people were doing it, Bette and Mari sported ruanas, saris, and caftans. Some days they looked like they had just stepped off the pages of *National Geographic* magazine. Whatever she wore, it was in the palette she had established for that season's wardrobe, and it fit her perfectly. You could tell an outfit was a Bette outfit when it was still on a hanger.

She loved details. She loved organization. Her shoe boxes were always labeled and stacked in alphabetical order. To poke into one of her closets was like peering into a clothes library.

She was hard to get close to, chilly, aloof. Some whispered she was color struck, but that wasn't it. She simply wasn't interested in anyone but herself. She was so profoundly and so effectively interested in herself that she was often a pleasure and occasionally a help to others — if they could help *her.* Her mind moved in mathematical and linear ways. She was never distracted by emotions, relationships with men, or dramas with other women. And now I have lost her.

She arrived in Detroit out of thin air. I believe she said she came from West Virginia. She had a story about her father being a coal miner and her mother being an Indian squaw, and this was believable because she had a Navajo kind of nose and Cherokee straight black hair. But there was something about the way she thought and acted that had a whiff of plantation about it that made me suspect a far simpler story. Maybe she was some white Alabama judge's daughter who had been suddenly smuggled north by family who didn't want to keep the wild and beautiful young Bette around the house. She ended up at Eastern High School, which she navigated the way strong men manage jail. The first time anyone tried to take anything away from her, in this case a kiss, she slapped him so hard she scared him.

Bette's slap wasn't a coquettish tease. It was a shock of pain that knocked its victim back to the day they were born. When Bette hit you, it revived the sense you have been thrown out of one world and landed someplace that wasn't meant for you. I know this because she hit me. You can't be much around Bette and not sometimes get hit.

What that boy saw in Bette's eyes scared him. What Bette discovered, emboldened her. The kiss-stealing boy fled, all six foot of him, moved quickly out of her sight and beyond her reach. Then Bette forgot him, immediately, like she forgot everything that wasn't real. Few people were real to Bette, except Bette. I was one of the few.

She took a fancy to me because I was useful to her. I see that now. I taught her how to walk, and how to turn, and pose, and just a bit of how to work the camera, and yes, she liked appearing in the column, but

371

not too much. She was no G. S. She had zero interest in being the center of general attention. She only wanted to be the center of attention to the ones who were specifically useful to her and to herself.

She wanted the baby. I had thought, like I had wanted Josette. It may have been more like a little girl wants a baby doll for Christmas. Desperately. George didn't want a child, but soon enough, Bette had Mari and George's money. All the baby's clothes came from Saks Fifth Avenue. Every piece. She bought so much clothing for the baby from Saks, the store sent her a charge card without her applying. Every season, twice a year, she bought an entire wardrobe for Mari. The child was an important accessory.

And a disappointment. She was surprised Mari wasn't more beautiful, was just pretty. I said she was beautiful enough — as beautiful as she had to be. George Stanley's child had a place no one could debate or best in Black Detroit. That made Bette jealous. I was always sorry I told her that.

It was such a pleasure to go out walking with Bette on my arm, so useful to hear Bette's ideas about how an act should dress, or a song should be edited, so helpful to have George's untraceable cash to throw at rising inconveniences or a political campaign, eventually so pleasant for Baby Doll to have another pretty young friend. I embraced Bette's friendship and accepted the pleasure of a moment with her as a high form of performance art, even while fearing she had become or would become a dangerous mother. I kept Mari close for quite a few reasons.

Then Bette left. Didn't say a word to me. I mentioned it in the column. Didn't mention her by name but I referenced the lady's transit. When Baby Doll told me, that day in October, that Bette was gone, it was like a punch to the head. It was like Bette knew the end of our world had come, knew that Detroit wouldn't survive the summer of 1967. Bette was getting out while the getting was good.

What were the "Detroit Riots" to me? A rebellion, an uprising, not a riot, but this rebellion was not my rebellion, not my revolution. My revolution was contained in the fires of the forties. Those made me proud. These shamed me. I wanted to build myself up. Wanted to dance. Wanted to play beneath the sun. Wanted to have, not what they had, but what I wanted. And up rose a sea of young folks more bent on stripping them of their power than on building our own beauty. Folks that don't understand that our safety is born of their not seeing who we are and what we are, as long as we see ourselves clearly and understand that their chatter about us is fully ignorant and not to be considered. The young folks who are hurt by words cannot be redeemed by gestures. We have created a world in which the dance, in which the drums, fail to matter. I did not know that world could be constructed until I was called upon to try to breathe in it.

Bette was one of these gifted and bewildered new young people.

I didn't believe Bette was gone until I saw her little honey-gold Mustang sitting in the used car lot. They only gave her $800 for it, and then it was sitting in the lot and the man was asking George for $2,000 to buy it back. Bette always was a fool about money.

Nobody knew where she had gone. George interrogated everybody. He hired Massey, and Massey hired detectives. And all anyone knew is that Bette took the daughter and left him the larger of two dogs. He came home and found the immense Bouvier lying despondent on the royal-blue rug all alone where Mari, the poodle, and her canopy bed used to be. Everybody else had that bed set in white trimmed with gold. Mari's was

374

white trimmed with a perfect gray-blue. Bette had taste. And then she vanished. I suspected she had help from white friends. If she had been helped by anyone Black, within a week we would have known where she was.

It took George nine weeks to find Bette in Washington, DC. Massey found her on New Year's Day. Never ever would have thought she would go to DC. Makes some wonder if she didn't have something going on with Ofield Dukes, who used to work for the *Michigan Chronicle,* then worked for Motown, then moved to DC to work for the vice president of the United States, Hubert Humphrey. Leaving George for anybody would be strange, I know she didn't leave him for no Ofield. Baby Doll says Bette had her cap set on Bob Dylan.

My best step? Changing trauma into transcendence, in the scented waters of my bath, in the holy aloneness of the Gotham. Bette couldn't do that backward and in heels, but I was teaching the steps to Mari and she was coming along fast, even if the lesson had been interrupted by Bette, her beautiful beloved nemesis.

LIBATION FOR THE FEAST DAY OF
BETTE STANLEY:
Honey-Gold Mustang

Bette's perfect drink-time accessory
matches the color of her skin.

1 pony of Spanish brandy
1 pony of dark crème de cacao
1 pony of whipping cream
Nutmeg for garnish

Add all ingredients to a cocktail shaker.
Shake well and strain into a stemmed
cocktail glass. Grate nutmeg over top.

WEEK 32
THIRTY-SECOND SUNDAY
AFTER FATHER'S DAY

Colored Girl's father admired lawyers and wanted her to become one. Attempting to inspire, Father chanted a peculiar litany: "Speak for those who cannot speak for themselves! When someone's out on the corner, in trouble with the police, they don't pray to God, they don't holler for Superman, they dash into a phone booth and call Lawrence Massey. Someday that's going to be you. And you going to use your words to put a blindfold on justice." The father did not get that whole wish. Colored Girl became a journalist, fulfilling, she hoped, the part of the dictate about speaking for those who cannot speak for themselves.

Lawrence Massey

PATRON SAINT OF: *Lawyers, Fixers, and All Who Use Language to Advocate for Others*

Lawrence Massey cleaned up other people's honest messes. There was the time Dinah Washington was driving her Chrysler Imperial, minding her own business, when two deputies, Stephen Book and Walter Bates, pulled her over. The officers violently yanked a fur stole from her shoulders, marking her neck. But that wasn't the worst part. The worst part was, they snatched the stole while loudly claiming they were checking to see if the fur piece was stolen.

What could they check? Discovering nothing, they returned the garment to Dinah. The damage was done and it was more than a neck bruise. Then the traffic stop escalated. There was an unpaid lien on the car. A nightclub had come after Dinah, enlisting the Music Union's help, when she had to cancel an appearance due to illness. The union had fined her $1,000, which she was paying. Unions are not always good. Sometimes they get your Imperial seized and the bruise on your neck overlooked.

The case ended up in court, where Lawrence Massey turned the tables. Massey said the seizure was illegal because Dinah was making payments — then he sued the city of Detroit for $1,000,000! Dinah was no longer a damsel in distress; she was a diva watching her own back.

He also worked the Massey magic for Little Richard, when his manager put him in a trick bag — making it seem like the genius had done something strange with some change. It wasn't so, and Lawrence proved it. And somehow when that fiasco ended, thanks to Massey, there were a few more pennies in Little Richard's pocket.

And more than pennies. Lawrence's genius was making people who felt a little illegitimate, a little brilliant but busted, know they were brilliant and flawed — but still worthy of their fair share, their fair day in court, their walk in the fair air, despite their flaws and freckles.

This is not common knowledge. Massey was often labeled crazy, but he made sense to me. He offered uncommon solutions to common problems. He thought the way to solve the heroin problem was to license hypodermic needles. He thought the way to end prostitution was to stop prosecuting Negro prostitutes and start prosecuting white johns. Massey made the case for this in language a child could almost understand. I had heard him make this case at a wake, several different house parties, and holding court at a side table during the rehearsals for the Youth Colossal.

But, best, he liked to make the case at one of his legendary house parties. Night Train Lane, Charles Diggs, Bob Bennett, G. S., George and Bette Stanley, Marc Stepp, Hobart and Lynette Taylor, Maxine Powell, Anna Gordy, Alf Thomas, and me — we were all regulars at Massey's parties.

We didn't come to see each other. Didn't come to see the visiting stars, like Count Basie and Joe Williams. Didn't come to see the colorful denizens of Detroit's dusky demimonde who could be found lounging at Massey's whenever he threw his front door open wide. On Massey's couches and barstools, certain Black Recorder's Court judges, traffic court referees, and even some hustlers had reserved and designated seats, but none of us came for the VIP treatment.

We all came for the same thing: Massey's ham hocks, cornbread, sweet potatoes, pole beans, ribs, and potato salad. The brother could burn almost as good as he could argue.

He talked about wildlife. "Everyone knows the mating habits of rattlesnakes, and whales, but they don't know why rich white men come into certain Negro neighborhoods." He was quoted as saying that. Somewhere else, while defending someone accused of running numbers, Massey was quoted as blaming the legal racetracks, proclaiming, "If they didn't have racetracks, there wouldn't be any numbers! Start by closing y'alls' racetrack down!"

But best of all, he defined Black Bottom. I told that in one of my columns.

ZIPPING WITH ZIGGY
by Ziggy Johnson

Last Saturday, two of my best students at the ZJ School asked me to settle an argument. One chap insisted Black Bottom was "a real place, like Indianapolis." The other insisted it was made up, "like the North Pole." I said they were both right *and* both wrong.

Black Bottom was a real place in the state of Michigan; now Black Bottom is a state of mind.

My medic pals rattle off specific streets (Hastings Street, St. Antoine Street) and north-south boundaries. My friends in the labor movement, attentive to competing constituencies, note that what many are remembering as Black Bottom was once two distinct neighborhoods, Black Bottom

381

and, just north of it, Paradise Valley. My showbiz kinfolk insist, "I don't care what the map says, or the taxi drivers say; if you were standing in the lobby of the Paradise Theatre or the Gotham Hotel, you were in Black Bottom." George Stanley says, "Don't try to talk about Black Bottom and not include Chene Street, where the original Stanley Dry Cleaners stood on a block between a Polish bake shop and a jewelry store, a city mile to one of Mr. Ford's factories."

My favorite schoolmarm, Shirley McNeil, PhD, says, "Zig, you can't say what Black Bottom is unless you say what year you're talking about. If you're talking 1850, it's farmland, with fertile black soil that gave the neighborhood its name. If you're talking 1900, it's Jewish people come over from Eastern Europe and Russia, and Irish folk, and some of us. Now, if you're talking 1920 or later, it's us, lusciously us. And after 1964, it's gone, gone, gone."

Old folks liked to say that Black Bottom "stank in the summer and froze in the winter, but don't mind that, down by the riverside, two, three, four families, crowded in a wooden house, with rent paid by factory jobs, we feasted on opportunity and hope." Young guns claim, "Black Bottom is paved over, long gone, and don't matter." I love me some doctor men, but on the definition of Black Bottom I side with my lawyer, Lawrence Massey. "Black Bottom ain't a place. Black Bottom an attitude. A Detroit attitude."

Yep, Massey got to the champion heart of the matter. Black Bottom is a defiant, inventive, modern swagger that has everything to do with being efficient, exact, ambitious, proud — and Black.

The efficient and exact part comes from the assembly lines. The inventive part comes from the breadwinners, too. We didn't get credit for all that we invented in the factories — from processes and tools to paint colors — but we invented in the factories. In Black Bottom, we celebrated what we invented as loud as we celebrated what we built. And we celebrated what we finna do loudest.

Straight up from Alabama you might walk down Hastings Street and ask, "What you know good, Son?" Spend a year on Hastings and you learn to ask the harder, sharper, sepia Detroit question, "What's new?" And when you have become a citizen of Black Bottom, your greeting will be "What I need to know, to do what I want to do?"

Black Bottom is walking tall, chin up, fist

balled, brain firing on all cylinders. Black Bottom folk got steel in their spines, steel in their jaws, and steel in their will. But it wasn't always an attitude. Before it was razed, it was a place.

Hastings Street ran north from the river and was Black Bottom's commercial spine. Hastings Street was a shiny black ribbon of a road flanked by one- and two-story brick buildings with thick plate glass windows. The sidewalks in front of the stores were studded with sheltering elm trees that towered above the buildings and electric poles equally beloved by the Black community as the elms for the modernity they promised even if some of the houses didn't have electricity — yet.

But Black Bottom's Hastings Street wasn't just commercial. Churches and other houses of worship, bars, and movie theaters that tended to the souls and spirits of Black Bottom's diverse and increasingly dusky denizens stood tall on Hastings Street.

Every bar on Hastings Street, every single one, had a piano; that's just the way it was back then in Black Bottom. Just like every church (be it a storefront church or a grand church in an old theater or a synagogue or a purpose-built building) had a piano and a choir.

384

Some of the bars had sawdust on the floor. Some of the bars you ordered a beer they would also give you, if you were a lady, a dip of snuff. Black Bottom was country. Some of the bars had silk hanging at the windows. Black Bottom was also city. If you wanted to fight but didn't want the other patrons to run out the door, you went to Mary's Bar. If you wanted to see a movie the rest of the world had seen fifty years before, you went to the Willis Theatre. Want a place to sleep and don't have a room? Go to the Castle Theatre, with sleeping hours until 5:00 a.m. A man called Detroit Count told all about that in a 1948 record called "Hastings Street Opera." Black Bottom buzzed every hour of the day and night.

Massey is the only one I ever told this: The first time I ever saw Black Bottom, I was in short pants. It was the early twenties. Back then the residential streets of Black Bottom were flanked with a hodgepodge collection of two-story wooden clapboard rental houses, some in a Queen Anne style with modest bay windows; others rose above the sidewalk, looking like New Orleans shotgun cottages; some even boasted second-story balconies. Many of these houses had porches and lawns spotted with dandelions.

The river and the wooden houses gave Black Bottom a distinct southern rural flavor while the tall downtown buildings of white Detroit, visible from points on Hastings Street, the electric poles, and the neon signs all spiced it up with "citified."

Mother and I stayed with second cousins who shared, with three other families, a two-story clapboard house that had a balcony running across the second story. From that balcony the neighborhood was on vivid and contrasting display.

Horse carts coexisted with cars on Hastings Street. I watched rag-and-bone men go house to house, some with a handcart, some with a cart pulled by a horse or a mule, buying bones, rags, and old clothes from housewives. The rags were turned into paper, the old clothes into industrial rags. The bones were turned into glue or sometimes carved buttons. The cousins explained all this. Watermelon and other fruit and vegetable trucks rolled through the neighborhood. Dry goods dealers, knife sharpeners, and all manner of street vendors plied their trade in Black Bottom.

Standing on the cousins' balcony was an exotic joy. In one of Bronzeville's all-city stone row houses, which were cut up into tiny kitchenette apartments, I had to press

386

my ear to a thin wall to hear a conversation I wasn't supposed to hear. And when I did, I only heard the single language of the current next-door neighbor. On the cousins' Black Bottom balcony, I heard so many languages the cousins could identify: Alabama English, Toronto English, and Irish English, as well as Lutheran farmer German and Berlin Jewish German, Yiddish, Polish, and even Greek.

And I saw this: Black Bottom sidewalks were full of brown boys and girls who held their heads higher and walked taller than brown girls and boys did in Chicago.

My cousins' house was within walking distance to the very bottom of Hastings Street where I could stand in America and look out to what I was told was Windsor, Canada.

Perched on an edge of America, looking across a blue river to Windsor, Canada, Black Bottom was one part small southern hamlet and one part global border town.

Pretending to nap on a pallet in the cousins' front room, I heard grown folk debating whether it was "the wind off the coast of Canada," the "regular payroll checks," "the 'can-do' influence of the Jews and Poles on Chene Street," or "deep roots in the strengthening red Alabama clay" that made Detroit Negroes so bold.

In Black Bottom, charm and squalor, nature and industry, opportunity and obstacles, citified and country-time, got all shook up into a strong cocktail that made a person believe they could do what they wanted to do, they could be who they wanted to be. I returned to Bronzeville from Black Bottom a more global and radicalized young citizen. My feet hadn't gotten to Canada but my gaze had. My cousins had been to Canada. My oldest cousin, Jerome, said, "I ain't letting this country treat me any which way. It treat me wrong, I'm over the bridge."

My mother overheard that conversation and decided it would be a very long time before we visited Detroit again. I decided on that same trip that one day I would live in Black Bottom.

Massey and me, we are spiritual neighbors.

LIBATION FOR THE FEAST DAY OF LAWRENCE MASSEY:
The Uncommon Solution

1 jigger of bourbon
1 pony of sweet vermouth
Club soda
1 lime, juiced

Begin by juicing one lime into a cocktail shaker. Add vermouth, bourbon, ice, and shake. Strain into a cocktail glass or a Champagne flute and top with club soda.

Begin by juicing one lime into a cocktail shaker. Add vermouth, bourbon, ice, and shake. Strain into a cocktail glass or a Champagne flute and top with club soda.

WEEK 33
THIRTY-THIRD SUNDAY
AFTER FATHER'S DAY

In 1975, Dr. Bob Bennett died of a heart attack in Detroit. He was sixty-four. At his funeral, Bennett's corpse, displayed in an open casket, was serenaded by a band of white gypsies. When he could no longer beat death like a drum, he eclipsed death with a memorable art gesture. In 1965, the apogee of Detroit as the Black Camelot, Bennett was chief of staff at Kirwood Hospital, on the board of directors of the Detroit Race Course, the medical examiner for the Michigan Athletic Board, and a governor of the Bell Clair Surf Club, where Ziggy was famously pushed in the water by G. S.

Dr. Robert C. Bennett
PATRON SAINT OF: *Fighters, Hypochondriacs, and Medicine Men*

When I whispered his name to myself in the

scented solitude of my tub, I referred to Dr. Robert C. Bennett as Bodywork. When you get your car into a crash, you need a mechanic to fix it up good, pull out the dents, and put on the new paint. If you have a regular car you can go to a lot of places, but if you have a Cadillac you want a magical mechanic — a man who could disappear the crash with hyper-proficient bodywork. A boxing match is a lot like a two-car collision. When it's flesh and bones smashing into flesh and bones and you can afford the very best, you didn't *call* Bob Bennett, you had Bob Bennett *standing by ready* to start stitching. Bob Bennett is a fight doctor, and he's also my doctor.

People think that I think life is a dance or life is a joke. That I'm Ziggy Johnson, the comic emcee — Ziggy Johnson, some lesser-and-lighter Sammy "The Little Genius" Davis. Bob Bennett knows me different than that. He knows me as a fighter. He knows I know life is a fight. And that's why I love him. That's why I have him standing by to get me back into my ring — the stage — and get me back pretty.

Bennett is the man who has seen me most often naked in the daylight. In these my hospital days, he is the friend I see the most often. He's the person who has the clearest

391

sense of how many days or hours I have left. When I breathe my last, he will be the one putting ink to paper to name the hour and minute of my death. He will heal me until he can't, then he will be my final witness. The way this goes, in the end he will fail me. I will not be healed. I will not be in another fight. We both know this.

I got the pacemaker. I also got the flu, and now pneumonia has set in. Bodywork is doing a fine job of keeping the pneumonia in the corner, but he hasn't got it knocked out. I should have better honored his embargo on visitors. But that pacemaker had me feeling too good.

I love Black hospitals. Hospitals are a part of what makes sepian Detroit shine brighter than any other sepia city. Detroit has so many great Black hospitals, and great Black doctors. They got trained other places, often Meharry or Howard; but they came to Detroit and founded hospitals and found thousands of patients who could pay — autoworkers, autoworkers' wives and children, the show folk who entertained autoworkers, that wonderful interlinking built-by-breadwinners beehive.

With my pneumonia, a new embargo on visitors has been established. I say, embargo or no embargo, I want someone to get

Eartha Kitt on the phone and tell Eartha to come see me, pneumonia or no pneumonia. Bodywork says for a day or two, or maybe a week, the embargo stands.

Bodywork can't embargo Dr. Guy O. Saulsberry, our mutual friend who founded Kirwood, so that old Kentuckian comes and I pump him for news of Detroit, his adopted city. I haven't missed a deadline for my column in fourteen years, and I wasn't ready to start now. With the embargo including Baby Doll and all my usual sources, I'm news-dry. All Guy wants to talk about is Kirwood. This is what I get: In 1967 Kirwood had a staff of 125, conducted research, and catered to all races but mainly to the Black and brown and beige and yellow. With help from one of my sepian Florence Nightingales, I put that in my column and the colored paper prints it up right in that pretty-pale green. That column is one of my favorite columns. But I don't get to tell this in the green pages of the *Chronicle:*

A hospital is the opposite of a cotton field, a boxing ring, a bad bedroom — those places where Black bodies get hurt, worn down, injured. In the hospital Black bodies get tender care, get noticed, get respected, get healed. I feel a special kind of safe at Kirwood. Almost like I've joined a monas-

393

tery or an abbey somewhere selective, sacred, and safe; someplace that keeps me in and keeps the world out. Cloistered.

Bennett announces that I am a hypochondriac because I love the tender care of this place. I say, "Hush." The closer I get to death, the less I edit myself. Guy tells Bodywork not to joke about "the reality and malignancy of essential hypertension." Says too many ofay doctors misdiagnose the pains of high blood pressure as problems of the mind. "I know Friedberg and that crew call chest pain psychoneurotic. Zig's pain is real. Zig's hard pulse is real," Guy says. Bodywork comes back with, "I just called Zig a hypochondriac because I thought it might make him feel better to think all the bad stuff was in his mind." We all had to laugh loud about that. To live is to gamble. I have bet on the right place and men.

Quiet as it's kept, Bob Bennett was also my banker. He helped me with money to open the Ziggy Johnson School of the Theatre. Milt *loaned* me funds; Bodywork *gave* me the funds. In 1952 when I published the names of those who helped me get my School of the Theatre started, I put Bob Bennett at the top of the list. After him, I listed attorney Hobart Taylor, Sunnie Wilson, Richard Austin, and Jose Alvarenga. I wanted to give those men thanks and praise, but I also wanted to poke at them with an inside joke.

None of those men cared anything about girls, particularly nothing about girls they couldn't sleep with or show off, or claim as their own, and yet by getting them to go in with me on the dance school I had tricked them into helping me create a launchpad for girls, a pad to launch our girls out of the worlds of entertainment, and nursing, and housewifing, and daughtering, and clubs, and into the worlds these men inhabited — medicine, law, and business. I did that. In the plain light of day and with nobody but the little girls noticing. Not even Bob Bennett. And he noticed a lot. My girls notice more.

One day just before she left, Mari was sitting in my office and I was trying to make payroll and rent and Bob Bennett came by and I got some money from him and later from Hobart Taylor. Mari said, "You've got a lot of big mules working for us little girls." That child heard and saw everything. "Who taught you that phrase, 'big mule'?" And she said, "You." I smoothed the top of her head with my hand, then kissed her head. "I'm counting on you, Mari, to take it all in, and tell it all back. You my Miss Immortality," that's what I said. Mari frowned. I said, "Repeat after me, copy me, like it was a step and we on the stage, 'We are artists of life.' " She looked a little scared. I gave the scowl that made my students leap higher than they thought they could leap. She finally said, "We are artists of life." I kissed her on the head. Now she was smiling. Her smile was hard to win, and I had won it. We *are* artists of life.

Bob Bennett didn't quite understand that. But he helped me raise hundreds of girls to be this — just what they wanted to be: smiling only when they felt like it. Pretty, only if and when they wanted to be. He helped me raise women who could oppose him.

After the Cassius Clay and Sonny Liston fight, the *New York Times* quoted Bob Bennett in an article about the bout. I read the story aloud to some of the girls in my school. The *Times* described Bennett as an "authority," then quoted him as saying, "I think Liston's problem in the fight was that he swung and missed, rupturing his shoulder." There were a few more details but the word I pointed out to the girls was the word before the quote, the word "authority." Dr. Robert C. Bennett, our Bodywork Bob, the physician of the Michigan boxing commission, my best friend, and cofounder with me of their dancing school, was being proclaimed an "authority" by the *New York Times*. My girls wouldn't believe that newspaper was as important as I said it was. They had a hard time believing any newspaper was bigger than their beloved *Michigan Chronicle*. That was my knockout!

Bennett was a double-edged sword, a sharp blade. A healer and a wounder, but he never wounded me. Bob Bennett was a fight doctor who served as personal physician to two of the greatest fighters of all time, Joe Louis and Sugar Ray Robinson. When I was so sick, first round, just after Bette left and stole Mari, in October, Bob Bennett whispered in my ear, "Death ain't nothing but another motherfucker you've got to knock down, Zig. Healing starts in the mind. You knock death down, then I patch you up. You the finest fighter I ever known, and I have known the very best. Let me see you beat death like a drum." I fell deeper in love with Bob Bennett when he whispered those words in my ear.

"Let me see you beat death like a drum." That he knew I was a fighter was part of it. But a bigger part was that, during all those years I had palled around with him in our little gang, I had been hating on him a little, too, thinking of him as the man who got our friends ready for the ring, who said they were ready when they were not, who was that contradicting thing: a fight doctor. But when he whispered to me, "Beat death like a drum," I heard a different tune. I heard we were all in the fight and he was promising to be a witness so close that the blood spattered on him, a support who stood so close that he put himself at risk to provide encouragement. It wasn't about fixing us up. It was about being there with us as we fought. It was about seeing the blood and the bruises so we didn't have to see them alone. He didn't think he was God. He knew we healed ourselves, or didn't, then he did the stitching, humble like a seamstress making a patch.

LIBATION FOR THE FEAST DAY OF DR. ROBERT C. BENNETT:
Get Me Back Pretty

1 jigger of cognac
1 pony of Kahlua

Add ingredients to a cocktail shaker with ice. Shake and strain into a cocktail glass with no ice.

WEEK 34
THIRTY-FOURTH SUNDAY
AFTER FATHER'S DAY

Sunday mornings at eleven, Colored Girl's grandmother sat in a pew at the King Solomon Temple Baptist Church; her mother sat in a pew at St. Philip's Lutheran Church; and Colored Girl and her father rolled through the cemetery in a basildon green Cadillac.

The living family thought they were visiting dead family. That wasn't true. The father was teaching his daughter to steer. The girl's legs were not long enough to reach the gas or brake pedal, but her hands were big enough to grip the steering wheel. She sat on her daddy's lap. Her hands were on the wheel; his foot was on the gas, or on the brake whenever she was driving them into a tree. They started slow. By the time she was eight, her father would press down on the accelerator and she would be taking those curves at sixty miles an hour, with all the windows rolled down and the radio cranked up loud, Daddy and daughter singing and laughing, except when Daddy was yelling "ring hand, ring hand," or "naked hand, naked hand." He didn't yell "right" or "left," he yelled "ring hand, baby, ring hand!" or "naked hand, now!" When she steered with confidence he'd say, "You got it, Shango!"

Lucille Ellis

PATRON SAINT OF: *Trick Bag Inhabitants, Psychotherapy Clients, and Shrinks*

March 1948. The Cass Theatre. Detroit saw a new kind of body, a new kind of dance, a new kind of beauty. Lucille Ellis came to town and danced as "Shango."

Lucille Ellis danced on bare jet-black feet, all dressed in white, to the sound of hand drums. To be in that audience was to receive a jolt of visual liberation. Lucille's body — sinuous, tensely coiled and released, not in sex, torture, or in slavery, but in art and self-chosen sacrifice — was something new.

I have spent my life looking at people who were called beautiful, and the only truly beautiful face I have ever seen is Lucille Ellis's face. Her eyes were jet. Her skin was ebony. Her nose was a perfect triangle,

400

flared and full and chiseled, wide and high. Her lips were this kind of perfect: shaped with just enough pillow to make them lush. Her face was a thing of perfect proportions and strength. Muscles and sinews were visible in her forehead. Often, she painted her eyes to look like Egyptian-goddess eyes. I loved to look at her because she looked like no one else.

Cordie King was a perfect version of a thousand different faces; Lucille's beauty was wholly original.

When I saw Lucille on the stage of the Cass Theatre, she was a woman of thirty who had used years of training, first in tap, then in classical ballet, and finally in Dunham technique to carve for herself a body that flaunted the beauty of muscle and darkness.

I never knew for sure if Lucille had been born in Pine Bluff, Arkansas, or in Chicago. I heard her tell her beginning story both ways, but I know she was born about 1919 and when she stepped onto the Cass stage that night in 1948, she strengthened bonds between Motown and Cuba, Motown and Brazil, Motown and Haiti, and Motown and Martinique. She danced the syncopations, sounds, and gestures of what my Shirley McNeil called the diaspora, and created a

401

hunger in the Detroit audience for those syncopations, sounds, and gestures. That was a hunger I would feed in my dancing school.

After the breadwinners saw Lucille dance, they believed dance was an art that mattered to their lives — was a way of gathering and telling our history, a new way of making us proud, a new way of healing the blues out of our souls. And some women saw in Lucille's beauty the possibility that a woman could look "nothing like no ofay ever" and be the most beautiful woman in the world. Detroit took one gaze at Lucille and fell in love. Which is why Lucille loved her some Detroit City.

Lucille's body was a sharp-angled revelation. Long thighs and arms, hard and ribboned with muscle, and a perfectly flat belly lined with muscle, did not charm, they mesmerized.

Lucille was a dancer and she was the administrator who, behind the scenes, kept Katherine Dunham's famous troupe going for three decades. She turned love into administration, and she turned administration, the day-to-day taking care of business, into art. She lived art and business and didn't cheat either.

I knew Lucille Ellis from the Regal Theater. Lucille was a tap dancer. And she was a mighty fine tap dancer. Back then she was nineteen and getting bored with the simple tap dances poor girls who work for soup beans got to do on Black Chicago stages. She heard about a group of rich colored girls, all of whom had had some ballet training, most of whom spoke some French and some Spanish, who paid two quarters for dance lessons that married tap and ballet (when Negro women were earning, at best, a dollar a day as housemaids) in a carriage house on 48th and Vincennes. Lucille was curious. She started asking around and discovered that the teacher was somebody nobody much knew, Katherine Dunham, or "KD," who was sashaying around Chicago saying she was going to invent a new dance style that was part ballet and part something else that she wouldn't name. Lucille signed up, wanting to find out what the something else was and maybe see that sashay up close.

Katherine Dunham came to say that Lucille was her muse; Lucille liked to say she was the housekeeper. Lucille did the grunt work (took the tuition checks, paid the rent, mailed the light bills, identified the raw talent) and danced; Katherine did the scholarship, the writing, the publishing, the choreographing, the fieldwork research, and danced. When KD returned from her first trip to Haiti, she stopped having a piano in the rehearsal room, introduced drums, and started the entire company drumming.

That was heaven for the young hoofer Lucille. Tap is a form of percussion. She had been drumming for years. Lucille came to believe that KD had created a dance form, a dance practice, a dance lexicon, a dance therapy, and a dance choreography to reflect and sustain Lucille. For Lucille this meant Black as the ace of spades with no cream in the strong black coffee of the art. It meant creating a dance form that had little to do with white spaces, white bodies, and white ideas of beauty until it had nothing to do with them — even when white dancers participated.

Lucille got hooked on the post-Haiti KD like folk get hooked on gambling. Lucille's drug, KD's dance, never did her wrong. One day she's waiting tables and living with her mama, and not long after she's in Norway dancing for white people who couldn't speak English and whose grandparents never owned anybody.

From 1938 to 1962 or thereabouts, the company had performed in fifty-seven countries on six continents. I loved it when they came through Detroit.

But Lucille didn't do Detroit completely right; she stole Clifford Fears from the city. Without Lucille, Clifford would have never danced in Stockholm when Dr. King won the Nobel Prize. Without Lucille, Clifford wasn't prepared to come back to Detroit to take my school to the next level, something I still want to live to see. She did for Cliff what she did for Alvin Ailey and what nobody had done for her: facilitate the move from teen dancer of promise to the international stage. In Dunham's troupe, she was playing at Ciro's in Hollywood, a place at the time that was none too Black-friendly. Somehow, she met up with teenaged Alvin Ailey and had him in the wings at every performance, taking it all in. Backstage after the performances, Lucille watched him when he wanted to show off his steps, his first choreographic gestures. KD connected the past to the present. Lucille connected the present to the future — and some of that, via Clifford, she did in Detroit.

She would write me letters, from the Far East, from South America, from Haiti. I always heard from Lucille and loved to share her letters with the girls in my school. They loved to hear about "the continent." Loved to tease me because she called me "darling." But they always smiled with me when she wrote something like "Your boy Clifford is doing a magnificent job. You'll be proud of him."

I am no Robert Hayden, but I try to write poetry from time to time. The poems I've finished are about brown nurses, but the one I keep starting is about Lucille. I can't decide if it is in the voice of Clifford, or in Katherine's or even Alvin's voice. Or maybe it's the voice of one of my girls who will go out into the wide world, but it starts like this: "On this bridge called your back I have walked across the water."

Lucille was a bridge. Dark women in the audience who had to traverse the killing waters of believing they were not beautiful walked across Lucille's back and found a place where they knew they were beauty true.

LIBATION FOR THE FEAST DAY OF LUCILLE ELLIS:
Fifty-Seven Countries

Tom Tom is the name of the world's only journal dedicated to female drummers. And it is also a cocktail in Bullock's cocktail book. Fifty-Seven Countries is a *Tom Tom* variation.

1 jigger of cognac
1 pony of white crème de menthe

Add ingredients to a cocktail shaker with
ice. Shake and strain into a cocktail glass
with no ice.

Colored Girl's relationship with her father entered a Renaissance period in the spring of 1978. The world, the father perceived, had turned enough times for her to return to the banks of the Detroit River for part of her spring break from Fisk University. As a belated high school graduation gift, the father had booked adjacent rooms in the new seventy-three-story Detroit Plaza Hotel in the shining, tall, mirrored Oz that was the Renaissance Center.

From her room she couldn't see Detroit. She saw the river and Canada. Walking on the grounds around the hotel she barely saw Detroit. Only when prowling through the twenty-five-story J. L. Hudson's department store did she have any semblance of a physical return home. She was poking into a Maurice salad seated across from her father in Hudson's thirteenth floor dining room when she said the word that she, who was never afraid of her father, had been afraid to speak.

"Why?"

"The Hazelwood Massacre."

"The Hazelwood Massacre?"

"You held Fort DC, I held Fort Detroit."

"I wanted to come home."

"You were already home. Anywhere my baby stands and breathes is Detroit City. You Black Bottom to the bone."

"Detroit is gone."

"Not gone. Scattered, hibernating, licking wounds, hiding."

Colored Girl went on exchange from Fisk to Harvard during her junior year so she could study under Eileen Southern, the first Black tenured woman and full professor at that university. Her father had given her Southern's book *The Music of Black Americans* as a way of keeping his daughter connected to Detroit. In Cambridge she met and befriended a sophomore, Reggie Hudlin, an aspiring film director from East St. Louis. They both knew Lucille Ellis. Reggie convinced Colored Girl to enroll in a class on classic Black Cinema. Soon, Colored Girl was entering into the world of Oscar Micheaux, a world that provoked a suppressed pining for her lost Detroit. In this white environment Colored Girl's experiences with her mother, at bay while at Fisk, now rushed to the front of her memory, cluttering her head and her dorm room. Clothes, books, papers, and food wrappers piled up, creating a buffer between Colored Girl and those shard-sharp memories. Reggie found a chink in the buffer wall. He whispered that Lucille Ellis herself was coming to campus for a panel and that he had invited her to dinner. C. G. didn't want to see Lucille. She decided to hole up in Widener Library until she was sure Lucille was gone. Lucille wanted to see Colored Girl. After the panel, she arrived at Colored Girl's room without invitation. When her knock wasn't answered, she walked into a room so messy she couldn't navigate from the door to the bed. Lucille guessed Colored Girl never turned out the light. Neat as a pin, Lucille cleaned up that room as Colored Girl worked in a carrel in Widener Library. C. G. returned just as Lucille was finishing. All Lucille said by way of greeting was "Let's find Reggie and eat." Didn't have to say, "Clean kills blues." She was a dancer. She showed her.

Over stewed octopus, Lucille said, "The

best thing a Black girl can get out of Cambridge is an hour on a Black analyst's couch. You don't have that in Nashville. You don't have octopus, either."

"I don't think that's for me."

"What's the paper you're working on about?"

"Nellie Hill."

"How you know about Nellie?"

"Ziggy."

"Just like how you know me. Listen to me like you would listen to Ziggy: Get you some therapy."

"Listen to Lucille," Reggie said.

"And send me that paper that you writing. It's gonna tickle Nellie. I'm going to take it to her, next time I go to Detroit."

"Listen to Lucille," Reggie said.

Nellie Hill Trapp

PATRON SAINT OF: *Beauties, Informal Adoptees, and Using Talk to Advocate for Self*

Once upon a time, Nellie Hill was a sepia cinema star. Playing two different women named Lola, she exuded class and sass and intelligence, first in 1941's *Murder with Music,* then in 1948's *Killer Diller.*

I call Nellie Hill Trapp my showbiz daughter. When she was sick, I stayed on my

411

knees. She was sick a lot in 1965. In and out of Henry Ford Hospital. I visited her each time. I don't let Nellie come visit me here at Kirwood. She's too frail to take the risk, unlike our mutual friend Eartha the vigorous, who should be showing up at my bedside but says she's too busy. Nellie would come if I let her. When Nellie finally got back to feeling good and looking good, I wrote in my column, "I'm glad you're well because my rosary won't stand much more praying."

The opening of the 20 Grand entertainment complex was what I liked best about 1966, and what I liked best about that opening was seeing Nellie step out onto the stage to emcee the fashion show. A good daddy is always proud to see his daughter walk in his footsteps and best him. Nellie is a fine emcee. In my will, I'm leaving Nellie my address book with all the phone numbers of the best acts in the business — some of them are still alive — and my three best jokes. One of them still gets a laugh.

If you begin her story in New York, Nellie started at the top and worked her way down. By the time she moved to Detroit in 1950, she needed a parent who was going to get that rosary out and work it. I was the man for the job. What I prayed for hardest?

That Nellie would find her lost ability to squint.

Like me, Nellie started off in show business by winning a dancing contest. I won mine dancing at the Appomattox Club. She won hers dancing in a Richmond, Virginia, factory.

If Nellie keeps announcing fashion shows, I'm going to let her inherit the gig of announcing at the 20 Grand Club, and emceeing the shows, even if I have a complete recovery.

When she was nineteen, Nellie Harrell met Wesley Hill from the Southern Sons — a sepian gospel quartet. Wesley was handsome and talented and bold. The first time he ever saw Nellie, he gave her a ring. He knew from his first meeting he wanted to marry her.

Nellie took that ring home and hid it in a trunk at the foot of her bed between the pallet quilts. She didn't want her mother to know she had been talking with a man. She was a nineteen-year-old virgin and still getting whupped by her family when they thought she didn't do right. One day, after they started into whupping her, she ran found the ring and slipped it on her finger. Then she ran off to find Wesley, a minister, and married life in New York.

She spotted herself to the memory of Maggie Walker, the Black self-made woman who owned a bank and an insurance company. Playing Lola, the pretty Miss about to be a Mrs. whose fiancé, a Black businessman, buys a $1,000 string of pearls, Nellie made her audience believe the giant paste pearls were real and elegant and, more importantly, that monied brown women were also real.

I adopted Nellie as my showbiz daughter for selfish reasons. I loved the idea that someone who belonged to me was a sepian queen of the movie screen, then the father-love got real and things changed.

When you get a child by birth or adoption, you find yourself talking to God in new ways. You stop negotiating for yourself and you start negotiating for her. Early prayers are easy and exuberant. You start with, "Let her have *everything* and you can do *anything* to me." When God doesn't accept that deal, you find yourself delighted to make bad bargains. You pray, "Give her *something,* and you can take *everything* from me."

The God who struck down Father Tolton drives hard bargains. George is suing for custody of his daughter. Massey got an expedited preliminary hearing. Massey says George will lose. Men don't get daughters.

And Bette will say George launders more than clothes. Shirley McNeil says the fight with her mother is a fight Colored Girl's got to fight for herself now. Maxine says, "She'll fight. And I'm betting she will win. And when she does win, it is going to have more than a little something to do with you, Ziggy. And a lot more to do with George. But mostly it will have everything to do with Colored Girl. And it's going to have a little something to do with Nellie Hill, and Massey, and everybody you put before her and all your Colored Girls, Zig. What did Massey call us, 'Walking talking Aesop's fables'?" Everybody started to laugh loud. It was about the noisiest my hospital room ever got. Everybody but me was drinking. Finding out Colored Girl wasn't coming back had us blue. Hearing she was alive and strutting out in the big world that was Washington was a tickle of hope in that drunk blue. Massey jumped up. "Don't put that on me, we're not fables, we Saints. Ziggy's Black Bottom Saints. That's what your Aunt Sayde called us."

I've got fifty-two Saints and Nellie's my only siren of the sepia screen. Nellie got two all-Black movies with all-Black casts that played to all-Black audiences. She worked on films with Noble Sissle, with

Moms Mabley, with Nat King Cole. Then the era of the race movie ended. No more movies with Blacks playing the good guys *and* the bad guys, the cops *and* the robbers. Nellie started singing in nightclubs.

Some people believed Nellie was just sexy. She had a voice of her very own and the sense to use it. She was all gumption and no whine. It wasn't just looking at the girl.

One reviewer said about her first appearance at The Flame, "Nellie's not a nice singer, she's an incendiary one." It was an around-the-block way of saying Nellie was a slut. I wanted to slap that man. Nellie was nice. And Nellie was sexual. She divorced Hill in 1952, maybe because he couldn't satisfy or accept her appetite. That was his problem, not hers. By 1953 she was on the cover of a magazine and billed as "The Girl Singer for Men Only." To add another layer of complexity and invitation the other headline on the cover was "The Intimate Lives of Paraplegics." In some quarters she was understood to be a woman selling sex in her songs. She wore a strapless gown that displayed her petite shoulders and her perky and pert breasts.

Soon she was married to James Edward Trapp and having babies. The dancer, actress, and singer added her favorite job title to the list, "Mama," on her way to adding that final title, "Emcee."

When Nellie got off the stage, her acting skills kept improving. She put her improvisation skills to peculiar use in October 1958. She got robbed in her own home. One moment she was opening the door for what she believed were welcomed guests, the next moment she was being tied up with neckties, and a gun was at her husband's throat. The robbers, she reported, found and stole over $3,000 in cash and $600 or $700 in coin.

Nellie shook her shoulders, jiggled her breasts, then told the police she was saving that money for Christmas and small bills. I didn't know until then that the woman could think that fast on her feet. She had concocted a quick lie.

That was "numbers money." That was money that could put her husband in jail. That was money that could turn the romantic comedy of her life into a tragedy. Nellie wasn't having it.

LIBATION FOR THE FEAST DAY OF
NELLIE HILL TRAPP:
The Lady MC

1/2 pony of Bénédictine

417

1/2 pony of Crème Yvette
Ginger ale

Fill a tall, thin glass with ice and add
ingredients. Serve with a straw.

WEEK 36
THIRTY-SIXTH SUNDAY
AFTER FATHER'S DAY

A Mills Brother never stood on the stage alone. They always had each other. Sometimes they were the only Black faces in the room. In 1981 the Mills Brothers celebrated their fifty-sixth year in show business with a European tour. Four-part harmonies had changed to three. They started their set with "Autumn Leaves" and ended with "Bye Bye Blackbird." They snatched that song back from vicious segregationists who sang it like they swung ax handles in schoolhouse doors, and they renewed that old tune with the promise of return home — if only a return to home in heaven. For an encore they sung out the secret of life: "You're Nobody till Somebody Loves You."

They loved each other. They performed the overlooked truth that brotherly and a hundred different loves count as much as romantic love, and often more.

In 1987 Colored Girl's father walked into the Nashville hospital room where she had given birth the day before, swinging a little vinyl weekender suitcase decorated with pop-art lavender, magenta, and turquoise flowers and whistling "Bye, Bye, Blackbird." The man was wearing black silk pants, a black silk shirt, and a bright red golf sweater.

Her father helped her open the suitcase: *The House of Dies Drear, Island of the Blue Dolphins, The Egypt Game, I Know Why the Caged Bird Sings, The Autobiography of Miss Jane Pittman, 100 Years of Solitude, For Colored Girls, The Color Purple,* and *Their Eyes Were Watching God;* all of Colored Girl's favorite books, the copies he had read in Detroit, as she read them in DC, were packed into her old suitcase as gifts for her new daughter. Nursing her infant daughter, Colored Girl sang, "Bye, Bye, Blackbird."

Skipper Mills

PATRON SAINT OF: *Bearing the Unbearable, Blacks in White Institutions, and Fathers*

Skipper Mills was both the manager and the father of the Mills Brothers. For Skip, singing was a family business not unlike

420

working a farm. You work together, eat together, sleep together, every day of every year. When his oldest boy, his namesake, John Mills Jr., died in 1936, Skipper became the bass voice in the quartet. They made twenty years of shows and post-show parties after John Jr. died — and there were years before he died. They crisscrossed the States too many times to count and made five trips across Europe.

They could imitate a whole orchestra using only their voices and a single guitar. It was a gimmick and a good gimmick. People told the story — maybe even the Mills Brothers told it, perpetrating the fraud — that one of them forgot their instruments and that's how they began imitating instruments. I believe it was a Skipper Mills plan. His sons' nonmusical ambitions ranged from those of John, who aspired to be a bondsman, to Don, who didn't have one iota of an idea of what he could be; with Herbert, who aspired to be a brick mason, and Harry, who wanted to own a string of shoeshine shops, in between. Fueling all these and greater ambitions: Skipper and Mrs. Mills — both musicians, who owned a barbershop in Piqua, Ohio. They believed their shop could be home base for the most successful barbershop quartet the world had ever seen. They achieved that.

It's hard for young people coming up now to understand what a phenomenon the Mills Brothers were. In 1934 Paley (William Paley, the president of CBS) put them on the radio, and they were the first sepian act to have a national radio show. This meant they were the first act to be dramatically bigger than all other acts.

And it wasn't just radio. It was film: They were featured in the film *Twenty Million Sweethearts.* It was live performances: They broke all the attendance records at the Howard Theatre in Washington, DC. People stood in lines that were blocks long for hours to buy tickets to one of the five shows they did each day of a week-long run. The first show was at noon; the last ended at about 2:30 in the a.m.

Between shows they were harassed by white citizens screaming as they drove past in their Cadillac, "Get that damned thing off the streets!" and calling them "darkies," assaulting the brothers so viciously that a beat cop arrested the ofays and took them to a police precinct. On another night the brothers attempted to go to a club, the Prudhom, and were refused entrance. They were refused a lot. Skipper said, "Jim Crow is the fifth Mills Brother; he travels with us everywhere we go."

Negro matrons, not understanding the rigor of their schedule, would sometimes grumble about the brothers' not accepting social invitations. Skipper didn't let this bother him or the boys any. He told his sons to throw that weight on their manager, himself, Skipper Mills. Then Papa Mills got folks who tried to stir up trouble for the Mills Brothers skewered in the Black social columns for unrelated infractions. Sometimes I helped with that.

When newspapers wouldn't cover racist incidents as news, Skipper used those same social columns and entertainment columns to call out whole cities' and states' Jim Crow practices. They called out Kansas City. Called out California. Called out London. Skipper Mills had a heavy toolkit filled with musical and nonmusical skills. It was a clean show but they were not quiet men.

Before World War II the Mills Brothers played London frequently, making the journey by boat, appearing at the Palladium, the Holborn Empire, the Gaumont Holloway. Mrs. Mills sat with the royal family in the royal box at one performance. Skipper arranged that. Trying to get out of London during the start of WWII, they ended up in Australia and away from America long enough for some folks to begin to forget them.

The city of Detroit has not forgotten. How could we forget? Without the Mills Brothers there's no The Four Tops, no Miracles, no Temptations.

So much of what I do for the kids in my school, is what I saw Skipper do for his sons. The best thing he did? Teach his sons how to venture into the white world, Skipper Mills–style: Don't go alone; holler when you have to; and, if possible, get the press on your side.

LIBATION FOR THE FEAST DAY OF SKIPPER MILLS:
A Whole Orchestra

1 jigger of Old Tom gin
1/2 lime, juiced
2 dashes of grenadine

Fill a large mixing glass with lime juice. Add gin and grenadine and shake. Strain into a cocktail glass and serve.

WEEK 37
THIRTY-SEVENTH SUNDAY
AFTER FATHER'S DAY

Natalie Cole recorded the album *Unforget-table . . . With Love* in 1991. The first single, a posthumous duet with her daddy, was Record of the Year. Seven million copies were sold. In 1992 the album won the Grammy for Album of the Year.

In 1992 Colored Girl divorced her first husband and married her second, a portrait painter originally from Detroit, a man who didn't grimace when she said she was more interested in writing than cleaning the house. And he also didn't grimace when she whispered that she was lost in the woods on the way to finding her way to radical joy — but she was determined to get there. He said he was lost in the same woods — with the same determination. Saturday morning, while Colored Girl's daughter was at dance school, they put Natalie Cole's CD on, and together cleaned as much as could get cleaned in as long as it took to play the whole disc. Colored Girl was starting to embrace a messy and dangerous world radically unarmed, as her daughter started to twirl her way into and through a conventional southern ballet class, bringing with her a bit of disruptive Detroit swagger.

Nat King Cole

PATRON SAINT OF: *The Woke and Wise, and Addicts*

My favorite public Nat King Cole sighting in Detroit? Briggs Stadium. July of 1954. Twenty-five thousand in the stands and he arrived in a convertible that circled the field three times before he strode to the stage. That was an entrance. Perry Como was on the same bill. Cole walked onto the stage, lanky, earthy, and elegant, took a stance and started to sing, making Como sound like a little bit of cotton-candy nothing. Nat King Cole was especially beloved by the sepia denizens of Detroit because he was just like us: country time and citified, all at once.

He played Detroit so many times at so many venues: The Paradise Theatre. Downtown Theater. The Fox Theatre. Olympia Stadium. That Briggs Stadium gig. The Masonic Temple. The Riviera Theatre.

Baker's Keyboard Lounge. And last, but certainly not least, the Michigan State Fair Grounds. September 3 through September 12, 1954. They put his picture in the center of the poster. He was the main event, not any of the ofays. Not the promised Thousands of Agricultural and Industrial Exhibits. But more than playing Detroit, Nat King Cole *was* Detroit. Nat King Cole, though born in Chicago, just like me, had a Detroit soul, just like me.

Chicago and New York Negroes go all city when they get a bit of money and education. In Detroit we liked to stay rooted in that red Alabama clay, in the Mississippi Delta, in the Florida muck. We like to get close to trees, and plant a garden, in between heading out to shows and to the factory. We let our kids run out proud to the watermelon trucks rolling down the roads of the East Side and West Side with little fists full of factory quarters. We serve grits and cornbread, sweet tea, and that old red Alabama snapper, not in nostalgia but in triumph. Up south in Detroit we eat beyond the gaze of white folks. There's such a thing as Black-Dixie-born-bad-to-the-bone. That's chin-up swagger that blooms best in Detroit.

When you're " 'bama bad to the bone"

and you got factory job spirit whether or not you got a factory job, you take risks. You come hard. No one can outwork you. Or insult you. Or scare you. You got a house, a car, and a gun. You got out of Alabama. You know miracles happen. You lived it. And so did your man, Nat King Cole.

Harlemites, talented-tenthers, and siddity legal-eagle Negroes might have turned on him; Detroit breadwinners don't turn our back on home folk. We understood Nat King Cole was a freedom fighter. We never veered from Nat's side like some folks did in Harlem and Bronzeville.

Let me tell you our version of Nat's Birmingham fiasco. Everyone agrees Nat was down in Birmingham, Alabama, playing a show. He had the local ofays all riled up. A Birmingham newspaper, called *The Southerner,* ran pictures of Nat and his white audiences, with captions that said things like "Cole and His White Women" and "Cole and Your Daughter."

The day for Cole's show came. April 10, 1956. It was an all-white audience, and he was on his piano bench. Now, Thurgood Marshall and Roy Wilkins and a whole lot of other folks thought Nat should not have been on that stage playing to a segregated, all-white audience. What they didn't understand? Nat was laying a trap, using himself as bait. He knew the Klan wouldn't be able to resist attacking. And when they came for Nat, because he had an international audience, it would be an international story.

Some people say that the Klan had come to kidnap Nat; others say they came to kill him; the rest say they just came to beat and humiliate him. Whatever the reason, they came.

The show started, Cole was singing a song about little girls, when one of the Klan's men let out some holler, a rebel yell, or a coyote howl, something loud, and supposed to be scary.

Nat wasn't scared. He kept playing. Didn't leap up from the piano bench. The Klansmen rushed the stage, knocking Nat off the bench.

Eventually the white boys were arrested. Eventually the audience wanted Nat to go on with the show. He refused. His mission was accomplished. The next morning, he flew out to Chicago. Some say Frank Sinatra got the Mafia involved to help get Nat out. Maybe that's true. For sure he got called an "Uncle Tom" and a coward, maligned as someone who had to run to the white folks to get saved after he got caught in Alabama doing something he shouldn't have been doing in the first place — playing for a segregated audience — when he should have been leading a boycott. Some Harlem brothers started breaking Nat's vinyl albums — cracking them into twos and threes on street corners. I started defending Nat in the pages of the *Michigan Chronicle.*

Let me go a step further than I could go in the *Chronicle:* Crooning was his radicalism. I say getting all those white women to show up in his audience was what George Stanley's pal Malcolm X calls "disruption of the power structure." Nat might have been playing in front of white audiences, like Black folk had long done, but Nat was doing it completely different. He intended to disturb, not amuse — even as he entertained.

He was gentle. He was near-jet black and asymmetrical and he was beautiful. He was elegant, understated, and powerful. All of that was crazy-making and world-disrupting for the ofays. It was world-making for sepians.

I say, Nat King Cole knew how to lay in the cut, how to choose the right moment, the right place, for the right action. After Birmingham, Cole stopped disrupting with his art and his presence and started being straight up political. Joining in Detroit, he bought himself a life membership in the NAACP, and refused to play in front of segregated audiences.

Nat was willing to let Thurgood Marshall and Roy Wilkins rebuke him publicly because that rebuke was powerful political theater that goaded real Toms to change — and we've got some in our communities who need to change. In 1961, Cole played the JFK inaugural ball. All had been forgiven, if not completely understood. Sometimes a freedom fighter must stay in deep cover.

Who did Henry Ford invite in 1960 when he gave his daughter Charlotte's debutante gala, the party the white press said was the party to end all parties? Nat King Cole! And what did Nat King Cole do? He played that party, enraptured those guests, then came across town and sang better for us. He saved the best for us and we relished his best with pleasure.

If you are Black and wise, you know Detroit is the largest and most important city in Alabama. Detroit eclipses Birmingham. After what happened to Nat in Birmingham, he got patched up in Detroit City. Once upon a time I was from Chicago. Nat and I went to Wendell Phillips High School together, where I had the lead in our senior show. That was long ago. Now I am from the half candlelight of the vanquished Gotham Hotel. Detroit is my Camelot. Detroit is Nat's Camelot. The Gotham, our Pompeii. We await archaeologists.

Until then it's Murine in the eyes, witch hazel with ice on the face, King Cole in the ears. A short haircut and a tux out of mothballs, and soon I am good to go into one more dim-lit winter night.

LIBATION FOR THE FEAST DAY OF NAT KING COLE:
Awakening Father

1/3 jigger of dry gin
1/3 jigger of Italian vermouth
1/3 jigger of French vermouth
1 slice of orange

Add all ingredients (including slice of orange) to a cocktail shaker. Stir. Strain into a cocktail glass.

Colored Girl's freshman year at Fisk, she was shocked to discover she had been assigned a white roommate — Sophia Hayward, a tall black-haired girl who came from a Republican "first family" of California and arrived at Fisk on an exchange from Pomona College. "Like Candy Caravan who wrote 'We Shall Overcome,'" explained Sophia, who was obsessed with Motown music, Jimi Hendrix, and Al Green. Colored Girl, the rooted in Detroit music aficionado that she was, liked that Sophia would venture out to dive bars such as Skull's Rainbow Room and the Modern Era, which served up great music that other Fiskites avoided. The young women soon became such good drinking and listening buddies that Colored Girl started calling Sophia "Tallulah." Sophia called Colored Girl "C. G." Together they agreed no white person should be calling any Black person "Colored Girl."

A few weeks into the term, Colored Girl's mother announced, via a long-distance hall phone, that she was coming to Nashville to receive a service award from one of the many organizations where she volunteered.

There were four at the table: Sophia, Colored Girl, her mother, and her mother's colleague. During the appetizer the mother put her hand on Colored Girl's thigh. Colored Girl left the table. The mother was smiling. Sophia excused herself and followed Colored Girl. When Sophia found her, Colored Girl was shaking, having just vomited. Sophia gently asked her friend if she was bulimic. Colored Girl started laughing. Sophia pulled a flask out of her purse. Colored Girl took three big swallows, shook herself, then told Sophia about "quality time" on the farm. "Today. It has to end today," said Colored Girl. Sophia said, "As soon as we get back to the table, just say that."

They returned to the table. Colored Girl sat down. The mother chastised them for staying so long in the restroom. They ordered food. When the waiter left, Colored Girl said, "This has got to stop." The mother played it off as if her daughter was talking about her being an audaciously demanding mother, wanting A's, annoyed that Colored Girl decided to go to Fisk when she could have gone to an Ivy. Colored Girl jabbed, "You know what I'm talking about." Her mother followed with a stern, "This is not the time or place." Colored Girl stammered back, "This has got to stop." The mother's friend asked, nervously laughing, not knowing what was going on, "Are you quoting the Van Morrison song?" Pouncing on the possibility that the older guest's ignorance and innocence made candor more difficult, the mother asked, "What *are* you talking about?"

Colored Girl said nothing. She was drowning in shaming silence. Sophia wasn't having it. "You. When you threatened her with foster care? Or with her father killing you and him ending up in jail? Stop. You touching her. She's eighteen and I have a trust fund. She's not going to foster care and you might go to jail. Stop!"

The mother stood up. Lifted her chin. Smoothed her skirt. "That was an A-1 performance. This lunch is over. I've written my last tuition check. Both of you leave." The mother thought the public dismissal would provoke Colored Girl to panic, to fight, to defiantly insist on staying. But Sophia's words had dazed Colored Girl. Sophia rose, rested a hand on her friend's shoulder, then led her out of the room.

That night in Jubilee Hall the two young people drank Hennessy straight from the bottle and danced around a dorm room with a 45 of "Stop, in the Name of Love" playing on repeat.

Before they called it a night, Colored Girl declared her mother "dead" and gave Sophia a new nickname, L. D., for Lynette Dobbins. Then C. G. told L. D. a story about two kids who didn't drown and a parent who did, long ago in Alabama.

Lynette Dobbins Taylor

PATRON SAINT OF: *Rescuers Who Refuse to Be Victims, Ironic Alliances, and Clubwomen*

The world knows Lynette Dobbins Taylor as Mrs. Hobart Taylor, the first Negro lady to dance with an American president at his Inaugural Ball.

There were five balls, and the biggest was at the National Guard Armory. Harry Belafonte sang. Rudolf Nureyev and Margot Fonteyn leaped. Louis Armstrong blew his trumpet. And Lynette danced.

436

When Lyndon took Lynette out on the dance floor, the cameras flashed. She had a soft pretty face, perfect lips, straight teeth, a little double chin, and freckles under her eyes. Her dress was perfect. A shiny brocade with a demure sweetheart neckline, cap sleeves, and a matching wrap — all very proper matron-who-was-once-a-debutante. Her hair fell in waves. Her earrings were slender dangles of real gold and fine diamonds. In the photograph most papers carried you couldn't see her single strand of appropriate pearls. You could see her worried pretty face, a woman's face, a sister's face, a church lady's face.

I have seen a lot of dances. I have seen Black women dance with white men. But I have never seen a brown woman like this dance like that with a white man. That dance changed things. It was a warning shot. I loved what those two amateurs did on that dance floor.

Lynette had come a long way from robe-and-road Alabama and she had come via Detroit.

Most of the breadwinners who came from Alabama came from cotton-and-coal Alabama, from working in the cotton fields and the coal mines and the kitchens of the people who owned the cotton fields and the coal mines. There is another colored Alabama, robe-and-road Alabama. Lynette Dobbins Taylor hails from that place.

Robe-and-road Alabama was a world of people who have worn graduation robes, a world of Negro teachers, preachers, professors, and doctors. The more prosperous lived in one of the few nice houses in the colored section of some poverty-stricken hamlet or clogged white city. Others lived in faculty housing in some Negro college town. A few lived in a manse beside a church.

Denizens of robe-and-road Alabama were a peripatetic and studious set who stayed connected to each other by frequent road trips to fellowship, worship, dine, drink, and talk with like-minded souls who now taught at, or perhaps once had attended, or certainly were connected by fraternity, sorority, or lodge ties to, Tuskegee Institute, Alabama A&M, Miles, Oakwood, Stillman, Talladega, Selma Normal, or Alabama Lutheran. Some were transplants who had studied at Fisk, or Howard or Hampton, or Natchez Seminary or Walden Seminary, or Meharry, and any one of the institutes, normals, seminaries, and medical schools where we went to become teachers and preachers, professors and doctors, the places where we lived for two or three or four years in brilliant brown communities, until they were cast out across Alabama like beads on a broken string waiting to be collected at house parties, picnics, revivals, meetings, weddings, and funerals.

May 17, 1954, when the Supreme Court announced, "In the field of public education, the doctrine of 'separate but equal' has no place. Separate educational facilities are inherently unequal," robe-and-road Alabama began to vanish, but not before it produced Lynnette Dobbins Taylor.

July 4, 1933. In that year, cotton was selling for six cents a pound. In 1920 it had been selling for 42 cents a pound. The Agricultural Adjustment Act of 1933 was paying white farmers not to grow cotton. Black sharecroppers were not getting the government bailout and they were not getting the work; they were particularly hard-hit.

Black coal miners, about half of all coal miners in Alabama, were doing a little better if they could ignore headlines like "Negro Miner Meets a Horrible Death" and "Miners Entombed in Mines Near Tuscaloosa: No Hope for Buried Men" and "All the Men Working on a Short Night Shift Die in Mine at Moffatt" and "Colored Miner Killed." It was reported that in 1933 no Alabama men died in the mines. They died in '32, they died in '34.

It was this summer of cotton-and-coal and robe-and-road Alabama: Fighting fear of falls, fire, entombment, the possibility that cotton prices would never rise again, and lynching. Three Blacks were lynched in Alabama in 1933. Colored Alabama teachers understood teaching to be a revolutionary act that might help someone have a choice besides cotton and coal. They treasured the respite that the summer break provided.

In July of '33 Lynette was fourteen years old and in a month would be headed to college. She had raced through high school, at the head of her class, and would have a college degree and be teaching in a classroom of her own by age twenty.

But first there was a picnic out by the lake. Lynette attended with her parents, four siblings, and friends and neighbors from both her worlds, coal-and-cotton, and robe-and-road Alabama. Some had traveled three hours by car to get to the gathering, and some had walked from the colored section of one of the model villages developed near the coal camp.

The Fourth of July. This is how I tell it: Lynette swims in Seven-Mile Lake with her

440

youngest brother. He starts to flail. She tries to help him. Her brother pushes down on her and she goes under the water. Luckily, she thinks to dive even deeper. He lets her go. She swims beneath the water, emerging out of his reach. Then swims back to him. He attacks her once again. Once more, she dives deep, swims away, but this time when she comes up she yells, she waves her arms. She screams. Her brother is not screaming. He is drowning. Her father is wading in. He's a strong swimmer. He reaches his son, but his son doesn't reach back or swim away. He flails at the father. His son pushes him beneath the water. His son gets high enough on his father's back to spit water and scream. She waits for her father to break her brother's grasp to dive beneath the surface as she had done. But he won't risk bringing his boy back under the water. A stick floats on the water. Beneath the water the father prays. Lynette knows her father, so she knows this. And she knows what he's praying. She grabs the stick. She hits her brother with the stick. He stops screaming, and he doesn't struggle. She grabs her brother's dazed, Daddy-rescued, body from behind and starts swimming him into shore. There is no time to look behind her, no time till she gets her brother safely to shore. When she looks, all she sees is water. It will be hours before her father's body is found.

There will be a funeral. People will come from all the college towns. Her mother, the widow, will move forward with five children and land in Detroit.

What was the Fourth of July to the Negro A. G. Dobbins, elementary school principal? It was the day he projected, in a flash, what would happen if he didn't go into the water. He saw two of his children drowning. He imagined dead bodies carried out from the water. He wasn't having it. When he ran into the water, that teacher who never cursed was hollering, "Hell no!" And when Lynette swung that stick, she was weeping and whispering, "No, Daddy, no!" A. G. was happy to die. He had not married a fine woman to give her five children and then ask her to stand with him to bury two. He wouldn't let his Louise lose a son and a daughter in a lake, at a picnic on a pretty day. The Fourth of July was the day the Negro A. G. Dobbins taught his daughter to do whatever she needed to do to survive. Her survival and her brother's survival were so essential that he was willing to buy it at the price of his life and the price of her innocence.

The way I see it, if her father had not ᴅ Lynette likely would have settled dowɴ serve and live in Alabama. But he did dᴢ So, she married at twenty, divorced, theɪ married again at twenty-five. After two divorces she married again at thirty, a Black millionaire's son from Texas, Hobart Taylor. She lived in a fourteen-room house on Detroit's Boston Boulevard with Hobart and she rose to become a principal just like her daddy, and like her daddy started saving lives in classrooms. Lynette Dobbins was our first female elementary school principal in the Detroit public school system. She had a master's in education from Wayne State University. In 1958, it was Lynette who chose the models and the music for the March of Dimes Fashion Extravaganza and Lynette who attacked the production of the show with the professionalism of a great Broadway entrepreneur. She had the marvelous Maxine Powell on her side working in a variety of capacities, not limited to director, model, resident psychologist, and stagehand. But the March of Dimes was The Lynette Show.

People will say her father rescued her brother. She will let people say that. And when she is dancing with LBJ, she will be thinking of how far she and her little brother

came from the waters of Seven-Mile Lake because her father made a sacrifice that bought them both seconds of crucial time, time for her to think, time for her brother to spit and breathe.

Sacrifice, that's what Lynette was thinking about on January 20, 1965, when Lyndon Baines Johnson, the thirty-sixth president of these United States, dressed in white tie and tails, whirled her around the ballroom floor. That and this: Earlier in the day, some 200 colored people had been arrested in Selma when they tried to register to vote in the Dallas County Courthouse. As she moved around the dance floor, she feared she would get whiplash, but she kept stepping.

In Washington, Black power was on the rise. The Civil Rights Act had been signed. I predicted it would prove to be a death knell to Idlewild and to so much more, including many of our beloved historically Black colleges and universities, but we were ready to accept the loss to achieve the coming gains. Hobart was cochairing the inauguration, another Black first. Rumor had it that more than 5,000 sepians who had gone "all the way with LBJ" were striding into the nation's capital to celebrate the victory. Things were different in Alabama, which meant things were different in Detroit.

Lynette was thinking about how she could mobilize her robe and road and cotton and coal troops as she twirled through LBJ's Inaugural Ball.

In January of 1965 it seemed that a phrase Hobart Taylor had coined, "Affirmative Action," when he first went to Washington and started working with then–Vice President Johnson down an Old Executive Building hallway from Ofield Dukes, would become an affirmative reality under now President Johnson.

In Detroit we understand the phrase "Affirmative Action" a little different than they do in the rest of the world. In Detroit it means: Take a step, don't step back, don't talk, don't wait — *act!* Knock your brother upside his head and drag him through the water, but save his life. Affirmative action is a lifesaving dance.

When Lynette Dobbins was just fourteen years old, she saw her daddy die and got over it. Affirmative action. I've got a schoolhouse of gals learning that Black girl dance. That's Motown Magic, too.

LIBATION FOR THE FEAST DAY OF LYNETTE TAYLOR:
A Dance That Changes Things

1 jigger of Old Tom gin
Ginger ale

Pour gin into a tall, thin glass. Fill with ice
and top with ginger ale.

WEEK 39
THIRTY-NINTH SUNDAY
AFTER FATHER'S DAY

Colored Girl's mother did not keep journals, she kept steno pads, spiral wire bound at the top, dated in ink on the front, and ruled down the middle. There were hundreds. A single steno pad marked "November 1992" was packed in with the box of papers Colored Girl inherited. She removed one entry and threw away the rest of the pad.

Colored Girl doesn't know why I left Detroit. I like confusing her.

Part of it was Bob Dylan. Ziggy helped me get to the March on Washington. That changed everything. Washington intoxicated me. I wanted that boy who sang "Only a Pawn in their Game." When Dylan came to Detroit, in October of 1964, and then again 1965 at Cobo Hall, I was backstage. And I believed if I could win George, I could win any man. Dylan was a lot less than George, at least that's how it looked in Detroit in 1964 and 1965. I planned on seeing him when we went to the World's Fair in 1967 but that didn't happen. But from the first we were together, I knew if I got the chance, I could keep him for a while. I thought my chance was in Washington. I didn't realize how good Dylan thought Detroit looked on me. When I saw him in New York he had moved on.

Everybody was moving on. When they first dressed the Supremes, they dressed them to look like me. In 1961 I was the most elegant woman in Detroit and they were . . . well, ghetto girls. By 1965, they had been to London, and Glasgow and Hamburg, and Paris, and I had been nowhere but Detroit. The summer of 1967, about the time we headed to the World's Fair in New York, things that should have been happening in Motown were happening in Hollywood, like it being announced that the Supremes were no longer the Supremes — but "Di-ana Ross and the Supremes." According to the grapevine, one or more Gordys were looking to buy a house in Hollywood, Bel Air, or Beverly Hills, not Palmer Park. And back in Detroit the bougie ones who didn't invite me into their fancy lady clubs, who were married to doctors and lawyers, were dancing with presidents and kings in other cities and coming back to brag up and down Boston Boulevard. George couldn't give me any of that. What I learned from Dylan? Change your name. Change the way you talk. Change your history. Change your clothes. Shoot for the stars.

I took the girl, because as long as I had her, if I needed Detroit, Detroit would save me, to protect the girl. Without the girl, Detroit would forget me. Simple as that. She was an insurance policy. That's all I intended. But taking Colored Girl did more than that. It killed George's sister. It wounded George. And it hurt Ziggy more than I thought it would. Ziggy tried to use the wound to his advantage. He left his book to her and sent it to me. He said he was getting the book out of Detroit because Detroit was busting up. Said it would rise again and the book would be one of the seeds. If I could have done that for Ziggy, I would have. I loved that little man. But I couldn't keep that book. Everything I told Colored Girl about Detroit was defeated by Ziggy's book. Everything she believed or suspected about Detroit was affirmed by Ziggy's book. I told her Detroit was shit. I told her Black Bottom was mud. I let her know her daddy wasn't anything more than a man born to clean other people's dirty clothes. If she didn't believe me, she stopped saying otherwise. Ziggy's book would have changed all of that. I burned the thing, kept the ashes, and tickled myself by thinking of what she would think when she saw those ashes. What didn't kill her would make her stronger.

I always thought she was me. It's never wrong to touch yourself. Colored Girl doesn't think she belongs to me. She says, "I'm your daughter, I'm not your slave." I am very angry at Colored Girl. That's the only thing we agree on: I am very angry at Colored Girl.

My shrink says, because I felt powerless as a child, I try to exert strict control over my daughter so that I might create an idealized version of a family that can never exist. I say it came very close to existing in Middleburg. Then she almost killed me in West Virginia. After West Virginia I mainly left that girl alone. There is more George Stanley in Colored Girl than one might think. She used a river and a rubber raft to half choke the life out of me with water.

That doesn't matter now. Clinton's just got elected. He'll get sworn in in January and before he's out of office he's going to appoint me to something big. Board of the Kennedy Center. NEA. NEH. Something. Diana Ross beat me out. I beat out Florence and Mary. That's why I left Detroit City.

The way Ziggy felt about Sammy, Colored Girl felt about Josette: jealous. A daydream that traveled with her from Detroit to DC was that she and Josette were sisters and they had two daddies just like Sammy had: Josette's daddy, and Colored Girl's daddy. One of the daddies would have all the vices except those that were unforgivable and none of the virtues except those that were essential. The other would be Ziggy.

Will Mastin lived to be 100 years old and died in 1979. Sammy Davis Sr. died in 1988 and was buried beside Will. Sammy Davis Jr. died in 1990 and was buried beside his father. In death, the Will Mastin Trio was reunited.

Sammy Davis Jr.

PATRON SAINT OF: *Peerless People, Performers, Veterans, and Other Wounded*

Sammy is without peer. My favorite performance I have ever seen on television, my one for the ages, was Sammy Davis on television on *The Milton Berle Show*. What was that, 1955? He was with his dad and his uncle. That was my Old World meeting the New, and nothing was ever the same.

Sammy is an artist who puts the green in my eyes. Closest I ever came to being a true intimate in his circle was when he was engaged to my dear friend Cordie, who threw him over. Sammy and I were almost exact opposites. We were both small, but Sammy stayed chiseled. And there was very little girl in his boy. I think that's why he loved women so much. He was especially hungry for what they had because he had so little of it himself. Sammy was all action, muscle, what the Eastern people call *yang* — he was the fiery sun. I think that's why he liked the desert and Las Vegas so much.

I was the moon. And I was no genius. But that is not why I was jealous of Sammy.

Why am I so jealous of him that I stumble on my words as I try to tell you about him? Sammy had two daddies; he had his daddy,

452

Sammy Davis Senior, and his uncle, Will Mastin. Sammy didn't start out in this life alone or with someone trying to exploit him, or like me, with a loving parent who didn't know the business; he was born into, then cradled by, two unselfish geniuses. I always wondered whether or not Will Mastin and Sammy Davis Sr. were actually blood relations. I don't think they were. I think they had a closer bond. What is certain: that Big Sammy, Little Sammy, and Will were a family.

Folk get this wrong about Sammy Davis. Many think he prefers the white world to the Black world. It isn't quite like that. It was like this: In the Black world Sammy felt like a pup who always saw Big Sammy and Will Mastin as top dogs.

I got this from Cordie. Sammy wanted to conquer the white world and find a bit more space for himself. He lived and loved and worked the first part of his life in a sepia bubble where there was only room for two men, Big Sammy and Will, and one short boy. There never was room for Little Sammy to stand up tall in our sepia universe — because of the deference he and we gave to Big Sammy and Will. In our world Sammy Jr. could never be fully grown. He ran out into the white world for space to stand and be a man, but he always returned home, to Will and Big Sammy. His fathers, the dance, and the song were his life. Cordie said there was no room for any woman of any color in Sammy's bubble. That's why she left him. And she left him stunned.

And there was this: You can read all about it in *Yes I Can,* his autobiography that he launched in Detroit. When he was in the army, white soldiers tried to make him drink pee as beer. Told that. Told about the car wreck and his eye dangling out of his head. Then he rose as high above vicious hate and hard luck as his feet rose above the ground when he danced Bojangles.

Sammy rises highest when the moons of winter shine into sheltering dark spotlighting our sepia capacity to make something out of nothing at all.

In 1965 Sammy was performing at the Fisher Theatre in Clifford Odet's play *Golden Boy.* The show was in Detroit both before and after it was on Broadway. During one of the performances he got injured in a fight scene. He had played that scene so many times and didn't get hurt. What do I think happened that second run in Detroit that caused Sammy to get injured? I think it was looking at all those white folks in the Detroit audience that got to him. Sammy depended on coming to Detroit and being with only us. And then he was too much with *them.*

He had earned some respite from their hate, earned time with us to give him a chance to fall fully back in love with life. "I need three weeks in the Gotham, but the Gotham's torn down," Sammy said. I said, "You got Big Sam and Will. You don't need a damn thing. You chiseled by love."

LIBATION FOR THE FEAST DAY OF SAMMY DAVIS JR.:
Stay Chiseled

1 jigger of Old Tom gin
1/2 pony of grenadine
1 lime, juiced
2 chunks of pineapple, muddled, or 1/2 pony of pineapple juice
1/4 orange, juiced, or 1/2 pony of orange juice
3 sprigs of mint
Seltzer

Place all ingredients except seltzer into a cocktail shaker and shake well. Strain into a tall glass with ice cubes and top with seltzer.

SPRING
John White (1909–1964)
Anna Gordy (1922–2014)
Maxine Powell (1915–2013)
Marc Stepp (1923–2016)
Shirley McNeil (1928–2001)
Bubbles (1902–1986) and Buck
(1903–1955)
Detroit Red (unknown) and Moms Mabley
(1894–1975)
Clifford Fears (1937–1990)
Arthur Braggs (1913–1992)
Dr. Alf Thomas (1906–1968)
Baby Doll (1937–present)
Ted Rhodes (1913–1965)
Ziggy Johnson (1913–1968)

WEEK 40
FORTIETH SUNDAY
AFTER FATHER'S DAY

On March 19, 2002, Colored Girl returned to Detroit City for the first time after her father's death. Straight from the airport she took a cab to 315 East Warren to the Charles H. Wright Museum, named for and founded by the Meharry trained obstetrician who brought her into the world. 301 East Warren was the location of the Ziggy Johnson School of the Theatre. The museum was built on land where once the school had stood. Walking around the imposing circular structure on the last days of winter in 2002, Colored Girl released the ashes of Ziggy's book.

John White
PATRON SAINT OF: *Club House Founders and Vertical Integration*

Old pals are calling me to new adventures. My kidneys are failing. No one calls louder

459

than John White.

I lived the best part of my life cloistered high in a tall and exquisite space — a suite at the Gotham Hotel. In its heyday the Gotham was owned by John White. The esteemed sepian poet Langston Hughes devoted an entire column to the enterprise, concluding with "A good Negro hotel should not be a minor miracle, but right now it is!" The future "Dean" of Motown's famous charm school, Maxine Powell, moved to Detroit in 1945 inspired by the presence of the Gotham. She read an article about the place, planned an eleven-day visit, and stayed long enough to redecorate a few suites and to teach Diana Ross how to enter and take command of a room. The day the Gotham was torn down was the day I decided to get married. I no longer had the privacy required for my single life.

In 1960 John White gave me J. A. Rogers's *Africa's Gift to America.* It's the one book I brought with me to the hospital. He inscribed it "To Mr. Ziggy Johnson, famous guest at the Gotham Hotel and personal friend of mine for over twenty-five years. May it last for fifty! Best wishes, Always, John White."

There was a bull's-eye on John White, his hotel, and his gambling enterprise as he wrote that — but he didn't know it. The Gotham would be raided two years later. Some 160,000 betting slips, $60,000 in cash, and thirty-three adding machines would be seized. Forty-one people would be arrested. When the verdicts came down in January of 1963, only fifteen were convicted and the fines were small ($50 for some, $100 for others) but the fatal damage was done. In June of 1964 a wan John White attended Youth Colossal. By July, John was dead.

John White's obituary appeared in the special, July 23, 1964, issue of *Jet*. No mention was made of the recent unpleasantness. His fortune was described as having been built on real estate, insurance stocks, and "other enterprises."

The issue, featuring a special report on Mississippi, had a black-and-white and blood-spattered red cover. No issue had ever brought so much bad news.

The courts say John was a criminal. I say John White was a saint. White used numbers to create jobs, to create wealth, to create community, and to create modes of invisible communication. The first person to discover that some old lady had had a stroke and called the ambulance? Often a numbers runner. Person to realize somebody needs a

461

handout to buy insulin? Often a numbers runner. Person putting some girl or young man through medical school, or law school, or some Ivy League college? A numbers kingpin.

John and I had many things in common. This was one of them: Our political resistance went unnoticed. In certain quarters we were dismissed as icons of the sporting life. Yes, we dressed like we just stepped out of the pages of *Duke* magazine. Baldwin published in *Duke.* I published in *Duke*'s very first issue. Wrote a music column. Who remembers that? Who understands that dress itself can be an art and a performance that liberates and protects the self and the soul? Who noticed I published these words in a gossip column all of four years before *Jet*'s Mississippi issue?

Catherine Fowler has a car so pretty that if she drove it back down to her little town in Mississippi, they would hang the car.

John White noticed. John White said, "You called out an ambition hidden in every lynching: a desire to slaughter our beauty. Ofays are made crazy by our beauty." I have committed to be beautiful as often and as publicly as I can. And I have determined to help more of mine see and be their beauty.

John White conspired with me to achieve this.

And we did. I have arrived at spring. Everything is blooming now. These days, in this hospital room it's a memory hit-parade. What comes back to me most vividly, my final spring, my spring come early? Halcyon hours of pleasure.

A best day in my life? Belle Isle. Willow tree by the water. Blanket on the ground. Atop the blanket: folding chairs. We both, John and I, wore linen suits and white shirts. I sported a gray tie, he sported pink. At our feet was a watermelon. In our laps: big shoe boxes, the kind boots come in. "Let me guess," I said. "Fried chicken, boiled egg, salt." He shook his smiling round bronze head, "Naw, Zig." Opened my box. Cold lobster, whole, and cracked. A split of Champagne. A hard-boiled egg. I got off my chair and sprawled on the blanket. He followed me down. This was a feast too good for eating sitting upright in a chair. We ate. We drank. We talked. He took cards from his inside pocket and we played spades. Motoring across the bridge to Belle Isle, we had been jawing over the reason for our celebration, me hitting the number big. I had $1,000 in my breast pocket when we crossed the bridge. On that blanket on the ground, in the middle of the game, I take off my sunglasses, lay on my back, with my eyes closed. To feel the sun and see the orange light leak through the skin of my eyelids is copacetic-squared. Sight sated, I put my sunglasses back on and we went back to playing cards. When John has won every dollar off me the game is done. He puts a rubber band around bills, then tucks the cash into my hip pocket. John put his arm around me, pulling me close. He has something important to say that must be quiet kept. With the taste of lobster and Champagne in my mouth, I am elated to have my thousand back, and honored to keep his secrets. John says, "Moses did not make it to the Promised Land but we made it to Black Bottom!" Nothing was missing from the moment. Nothing. Nothing is missing.

John was always good for the little favor that meant some sepian could keep on keeping on. John White lent Leroy Jefferies, veep of Johnson Publications, his chauffeur and Lincoln to ride out to Jefferies's appointment with a Chrysler executive in the hope of winning the Chrysler account. Jefferies won it. John White traveled with Burrell "Junior" Pace to Accra, Ghana, when Pace longed to see Africa but couldn't conceive

464

of taking on the role of witness alone. Rumors that John would sell the hotel started in '55. While those first for-sale rumors swirled, I was given new furniture for my suite. John White wanted to console me.

I savored all the tender care I received from Bea Buck and the staff at the Gotham. It was a congenial, marvelous, and ever-changing crew. Desk clerk James Nixon, a true eccentric, came to work each day dressed head to toe like an Ivy League collegian. Altogether different and old-timey: Smitty, a very formal bellman who would use the service elevator to informally slip a guest up to my suite. Bellman James Wiggins was known to get amnesia when he loses a bet or owes someone, also conveniently forgot who he saw leaving my room. My very favorite Gotham staffer was Sonny Cox, who one year had three of his small fry graduate from school on the same day. We all knew he had to shell out the loot for that, so we sympathized with the poor fellow — and slipped him an extra dollar or two. John White slipped him an extra hundred.

In 1954 White was keeping the Ebony Room of the Gotham open until 4:00 a.m. for late diners. Our Detroit was booming that year. The lobby, I wrote in my column, looked like the first tee of the Rackham golf course. Every December in the Holiday Room, White hosted wild-game dinners for the regulars. And every year there would be the March 16 birthday club party. I loved that group, particularly the deep, sweet Malissa Carr. Up and down the halls, running and skipping and laughing like their uncle owned the place — and their uncle *did* own the place — John's nieces and nephews Sarah Louise, Katherine, Margaret, Nancy, Susie, Donald, and Charles would come to visit from out Gallipolis, Ohio, way, talking about Edward Alexander Bouchet, who had graduated from Yale and was the first Negro to earn a doctorate in America. For years he served as the principal of the big high school in Gallipolis, the one everyone went to, and not exclusively the Blacks. I think hearing about Bouchet from the nieces and nephews from out Gallipolis way inspired James Nixon to dress the way he did. It should have inspired him to apply to college. Anybody's college.

Other things I love about the Gotham? The Shutterbugs (the Black photography club), holding their annual photo exhibit in the outer lobby. Sammy Davis Jr. was a Shutterbug. We loved to see Sammy in the

Gotham — he would take the whole sixth floor and invite the world. When some of the gents come home from "college" some of them ask if they can stay in my house. And this time when I write "college" I mean jail. The truth protects me from uninvited guests. I've got no house. I am a hotel man.

November 10, 1962, is a day that will go down in Black Detroit ignominy. The police invaded the Gotham Hotel in what newspapers called the biggest numbers raid in Detroit history. Not long after the hotel was raided, Lou Sarko (a man referred to in the press as Detroit's own "Barney Rubble," and identified as a close crony of the mobster Tony Jack Giacalone) was hired to demolish the building. With a single payment the Detroit City government simultaneously destroyed evidence of Black Camelot and enriched the white Cosa Nostra. A dying era no longer had a tombstone.

That doesn't matter. The steel and shine of the Gotham was reincarnated into the spines and charms of a thousand girls. We did that. The Gotham stands on toe shoes.

When I was late with the rent, I would hear someone say, "John White, your landlord, has a padlock on your suite." But they never padlocked my suite. John White was my landlord, but John White was my friend. And friend trumped landlord. I never wrote about the gambling in the Gotham and he never padlocked my room, paid rent or unpaid rent. The Gotham rolls in a wheelchair down the halls of Kirwood Hospital.

LIBATION FOR THE FEAST DAY OF
JOHN WHITE:
Hotel Man

1 jigger of Old Tom gin
1/2 pony of French vermouth
1/2 pony of Italian vermouth
Pickled onion for garnish

Place the gin and vermouths into a
large mixing glass and stir with ice.
Strain into a cocktail glass. Dress with
a pickled onion.

WEEK 41
FORTY-FIRST SUNDAY
AFTER FATHER'S DAY

As a fiftieth-birthday present to herself, in 2009, seven years after she let Ziggy's manuscript ashes fly, Colored Girl decided to attempt to re-create Ziggy's hagiography by using his columns, archives, and interviews.

It was harder than Colored Girl expected to get her hands on a microfilm copy of the *Michigan Chronicle.* Eventually the spools arrived. She spent hours in a university library's Special Collections room with her head bent over a microfilm reader. Other hours she photographed and copied, page by page, the columns for future study.

Some days, working with Ziggy's columns to re-create his Saints Day Book, Colored Girl felt like Ziggy's last editor; other days like his first curator; other days like a bit player in the drama of his life.

Anna Gordy

PATRON SAINT OF: *Putting Family First, Living in the Present, and Black Enterprise*

There was one brilliant Gordy man at Motown: Berry Gordy. There were four brilliant women: the Gordy sisters, Anna, Esther, Gwen, and Loucey. Anna, born into the middle of the pack, was my favorite.

Anna's public story starts in the fifties at The Flame, where she worked taking and selling photographs and cigarettes. Her sister Gwen worked with her. Gwen was point-and-shoot. Anna was an artist.

"Let me make your picture, baby," Anna would coo. When Anna took your picture, she would create something that surprised you. Anna could find that little twitch of muscle, that shine of a shoe buckle, the hat cocked jauntily to the right, that shadow in the décolletage — the place where beauty, and power, and money hung together on a body. Anna sought, saw, then caught the swagger and the elegance that proved that the person portrayed understood themselves as worthy of respectful regard — even if they were only discovering they were worthy of respectful regard by experiencing Anna's brown eyes watching them with pride and joy.

Her private story begins with her being born one of eight children to Pop and Bertha Gordy. After graduating from high school Anna headed west to California. Berry followed her out there in an effort to realize his dream of being a boxer. They didn't find anything in California equal to what they had in Detroit. Both returned home.

When the fellows down on the corner tell the story of Motown, they praise Berry Gordy, whom some remember from an assembly line, but mainly they talk about the sisters.

Esther, born short and bossy, stayed short and bossy. Full grown she was four feet eleven. Every team needs a naysayer; Esther was the Gordy family's. Berry had to get around Esther to get his seed funding from the family to start his record label. But she's so much more than the naysayer. Esther manages artists. Little Stevie Wonder depends on her in so many ways, and she hoards all the bits and pieces of paper and pictures Motown accumulates. Gwen, the youngest of the girls, is a hit songwriter who helped pen "Jim Dandy Got Married" for my LaVern Baker and a whole mess of Jackie Wilson hits. Loucey has already left us. She was fancy, she was smooth. Born cool, she didn't need Maxine's charm school. I thought of making Loucey the saint that represents the Gordy family. She started an equestrienne club for sepian ladies in Detroit. Loucey ran the Motown music publishing company until she died of a brain tumor in the summer of 1965. But Anna is my Gordy saint.

There was a word that was coined about Anna when she was still young, when I first came to Detroit in the late thirties: *swellegant.* They said it about a dance she danced in 1938 at Las Society des Jeunes Filles. *Swellegant* is glamour, power, originality, and more. *Swellegant* is graceful power completely unaligned with God or this world's ethics. *Swellegant* is bursting with the pagan joy and pagan pleasure of being beautiful and fruitful. It is ancient and it is new. It was Anna.

Anna is the will to reseed in a field of ashes watered by tears. Anna is seeing the ash field bud and bloom anew in *swellegant* spring.

Berry Gordy founded Motown in 1959. A year *before,* Anna and Gwen founded Anna Records. "Money (All I Want Is)!" with the call numbers A-1111 was their first release and first hit. That single makes an A-number-one-Anna-anthem. Anna Records begat Motown — then quickly got forgotten.

Motown has rapidly become the largest Black-owned company in America. In no small part thanks to Anna, my spy in the house of Motown. I am not fully on team Motown. Only Anna knows. When Berry talks about "the Sound of Young America," he's talking about the sound of young Black America becoming the sound of white America. He thinks that will make us one America.

I think that's a whole lot of water on the fire of the Black audience. Berry risks taking us back to the Plantation Club and the Cotton Club, those places where we are performing for white folks and white folks are diluting our art. Anna gets this. Anna does nothing in response to, for, or against whiteness. She lets Berry dare that.

Anna's not interested in the white audience. She always has one audience and it is all Black: Fuller, Esther, Loucey, George, Gwen, Berry, and Robert, her siblings, plus her parents, Berry and Bertha. Later she added Marvin.

Every spring on Father's Day Anna would gift me her whole audience. How sweet it is to be loved by Anna. Big sweet. Some people are so sweet you can't hold the thought of them and trouble in the same mind at the same time. A secret of life is to love you one of these people.

Berry wants to build an assembly line for the art. Anna wants more. Take "Dancing in the Street" as an example. Anna's husband, Marvin Gaye, who for a time worked as a clothes-presser for George, was one of the writers on "Dancing in the Street." Berry wanted to think it was a party record. Anna knew what Marvin put into it, because *it was what she encouraged Marvin to put into it:* a shout-out to Black youth in chocolate cities to "burn, baby, burn." Dancing in the street is a coded invitation to rebel. Goes straight back to the cakewalk and those patchwork quilts pointing the way to freedom. I love me some Anna!

For a season, the sound of young America was the sound of a striking match. That was Anna. There were many fires in those summers when that song was ringing in the air. We await all the phoenixes that will rise from all the ashes.

In 1966 seventy-five percent of Motown records made the charts. That doesn't happen without Anna getting those first records on the charts, unblushingly, unblinkingly, using everything she had to get those records played. Whatever she did, she always walked out laughing and clean.

It was Anna who encouraged Berry to start Black Forum, the record label that released works by Martin Luther King Jr. and Langston Hughes. Everyone always talked about how Marvin cheated. Anna cheated, too, but she didn't bother with a boy or a man. She cheated on Marvin with life. She knew, step follows gaze. I taught her well.

LIBATION FOR THE FEAST DAY OF ANNA GORDY:
Step Follows Gaze

1 jigger of Old Tom gin
1 pony of orange juice
1 dash of orange bitters

Place all ingredients in a cocktail shaker. Add ice and shake. Strain into a cocktail glass and serve.

WEEK 42
FORTY-SECOND SUNDAY
AFTER FATHER'S DAY

1959, the year Colored Girl was born, Ziggy wrote in his column that his wish for the New Year was that the "sepia model take her rightful place in the field of commercial advertising," acknowledging that "there are so many right here who are being stymied." The only two people who wished that more ardently than Ziggy were Cordie and Maxine. Coaching other women to be beautiful may provide a longevity benefit. Cordie King died at the age of eighty, holding corporate seminars on self-development and etiquette up until the end. Maxine Powell died in 2013 at the age of ninety-eight.

After three summers spent reading and rereading and researching over a thousand names mentioned in Ziggy's columns, Colored Girl arrived at a preliminary list of 100 likely candidates for Ziggy's Black Bottom Sainthood. From those names, she created several potential lists of fifty-two saints. Privileging creativity, she got one list; grit, another; self-sacrifice and generosity, yet another. Sometimes Cordie was on a list, sometimes she wasn't. Sometimes she didn't even make the 100-likely-candidates cut. Maxine Powell was on every single list.

Maxine Powell

PATRON SAINT OF: *Charmers, the Masked, and the Unmasked*

Friendship is the only drug where the more you do it, the higher you get. I got all kinds of true friends. Only one, Maxine Powell, is my soul twin. You search all your life and can fail to find your soul twin. I found Maxine.

In Black Bottom, in our world, beauty was a necessary work tool. In the white world, beauty was a natural resource, given abundantly to some, withheld from others. It was that way in Black Bottom until Maxine Powell arrived in Detroit. Maxine could make "real pretty" out of "butt ugly." Some called her "the magician." I called her the alchemist (thank you, Robert Hayden!). She was a model, a model agent, a beautician, and a charm school owner. Everyone she worked on left fully equipped, if not factory-equipped, with allure. Starting with Maxine.

Maxine hailed from Texarkana, Texas, and she joked about having been the kind of butt-ugly baby aunties kidded about having to keep a hat on so the family would know which end to feed. However that was, she arrived pretty in Detroit, via Chicago. She was just a little younger than me, and just a little shorter, five-foot nothing. The secret to Maxine's success as a model and a model agent may have been that she was born plain but lived attractive. In her presence it became almost impossible to see she wasn't exactly a flesh, bone, and blood beauty.

Maxine's skin wasn't light or dark. Her eyes were not small or large. Her nose was handsome. Her mouth was just on the edge toward too small. She had no cheekbones at all. Her magnificent whole was so much greater than the sum of those parts.

It was an excitement to be in her presence. Her eyes shined bright with her ever-present confidence that she was somebody of importance and grace, and they shined brighter with her promise that *you* were somebody of importance and beauty. Her over-trained speaking voice, which exaggerated and extended every syllable and pro-

nounced every end-consonant, was something you didn't quite want to hear but
couldn't stop listening to, like scratching an
itch — horrible and delicious at the same
time.

The longer you were with Maxine, the
more your focus shifted from her freckles to
her capacity for connection, the audacity of
her self-invention, and her always-evident
ambition to be midwife to any change you
wanted to make. All this conspired to keep
folks spellbound.

Maxine was a fun house mirror that read
"See Great, Be Great." She believed that, in
some way, everybody was born to be great.
She believed if you did what she told you to
do, you would remove the obstacles to your
greatness. That was the beauty of Maxine
Powell.

It was a beauty founded on religion. Maxine didn't believe God would create anything or anyone ugly. She believed that old
saw about God not making any mistakes.
And she got her students to believe it, too.
Once she got you to believe you were
beautiful, she helped you cultivate manner-
isms that brought attention to your beauty.
Her gift was an ability to chisel away whatever made you appear less attractive than
you were born to be. She taught you how to

mesmerize by the way you crossed your ankles, held a cigarette, chose the length of your false eyelashes. There were a thousand ways to frame yourself to best display your true allure. Maxine knew and taught them all.

But there was one essential move: unmasking.

Long before she landed in Detroit, experience had led Maxine to discover how to unmask — how to let masks of fake emotion, or the masks of feigned lack of emotion, drop. Mask dropped, Maxine's raw and real feelings played vividly upon her face. Raw and real emotion, counter-pointed and framed by her polished charm and polished manners, became Maxine's infallible recipe for allure.

It was a recipe she could teach, providing herself as an example of startling transformation. At the start of a charm class Maxine would wear a mask, perhaps a false smile, or anxious nonchalance. While she wore masks, she would look like nothing much. In the next beat, she would drop the mask, summon her raw and real, then summon her charm and manners. Suddenly everyone in the room was looking straight at Maxine, a wholly original woman you wanted, or wanted to be. Artists filled up her classes wanting to learn the basics of unmasking, charm, and manners.

Maxine rented out rooms at the Ferry Center where our community could host elegant wedding receptions, teas, dances, and fashion shows. From the Ferry Center she organized a wide swath of annual and one-off events, ranging from Spicy Omnibus (a cavalcade of exotic models at Broad's Club Zombie) to the March of Dimes Fashion Extravaganza with our Lynette Taylor. Before Lynette danced with LBJ she was hosting fashion shows with Maxine. Under the umbrella of "Finishing School," Maxine offered etiquette lessons, modeling classes, and seminars on charm; a Gordy woman was even one of her original students. The Gordy family's business was her original printer. Maxine was a joiner of clubs and a founder of clubs and a hostess to more clubs than any one woman could, or should, join. If you needed a room, and she liked you, you had a room.

Her Ferry Center was an outpost of my School of the Theatre. And Reverend Cook's Y Circus was the inspiration. If I wasn't dying, I wouldn't tell that. The Ferry Center was located at 275 East Ferry Street, just down the street from the Merrill-Palmer School, where Shirley Ann McNeil was doing her thing with Piaget and where all those psychologists and that school itself got credit for changing a lot of lives. This doesn't get said: the Ferry Center held down the other end of the street, and its parties and affairs changed more lives than Merrill-Palmer and its psychologists.

Maxine Powell turned an obstacle into an opportunity. In the mid-forties, when Maxine arrived in Detroit, people were coming from all over the world to the Detroit car shows. Car shows are big-time in Detroit. Those car shows announced what colors and shapes would roll down our roads, appear on walls in homes and in fabric of clothes, and even influence lipstick colors. Everybody wants to look good riding in their car, and "good" means your lipstick doesn't clash with the paint finish. Detroit car shows established the palette for our spinning globe. Standing in front of the cars are models from Paris, models from New York, the best in the world. When Maxine arrived, all the models were white. After Maxine opened her modeling academy, she marched on the Big Three. Soon Maxine's models were standing in front of Pontiacs and Packards, Dodges and Chryslers. That was huge. That was Maxine. That meant corporate bigwigs from all over the world saw the most beautiful women on the planet were brown and from Detroit City. Our breadwinners loved that!

We built the cars. We drove the cars. And because of Maxine, some of our daughters were promoting the cars at the Detroit Car Show, which meant people went back home to Rome, Paris, London, and Tokyo, talking about our brown Detroit City girls as the world's great beauties.

At Motown, Maxine was the magician. She could make the plain pretty; she could make the pretty gorgeous. She took the Supremes, Smokey Robinson, The Temptations, Tammy Terrell, and Marvin Gaye to intergalactic gorgeous. Yep. In the sixties she closed down her modeling school on East Ferry and created the legendary Motown charm school at Hittsville USA.

But she didn't quit the Ferry Center, and she didn't quit me. She liked me. From jump. In 1948 Maxine was living in Chicago doing a little bit of everything, working in a pickle factory, working as a maid, working as a hatmaker, working as a manicurist to support her struggling career as a talented but not exceptionally talented dancer and model.

She also wasn't an exceptional manicurist. She wasn't even a good one. Her customers complained their fingers hurt. Determined Maxine signed up for classes at the Madame C. J. Walker School of Beauty. With training she became proficient with file and clippers. After reading about the Gotham Hotel, she booked a short Detroit vacation, which turned into a Detroit lifestyle that she found superior in every respect to her Chicago life. Like me, she took up residence in the Gotham where she set up a nail shop. I had seen her onstage when she was acting with the Negro Drama League, but it was over a soak bowl at the Gotham that we first met and discovered we had many friends in common, including Joe and Marva Louis. Maxine was expertly filing my fingers for the very first time when I told her the difference between Black Bottom and Bronzeville: that Black Bottom knew how to be Country and Modern at the very same time.

She loved me from that moment. We became fast friends. Many of my best students were referred by Maxine, after they participated in some event at her Ferry Center, and showed up and showed out strong. Maxine regaled potential parents and potential students with effusive "Ziggy stories." Some of the best costumes in a Youth Colossal act were made by Maxine.

She could design, sew, steal, or forage a costume. For years and years I knew the Youth Colossal was going good when we moved into the Ferry Center, pro bono, and started rehearsing under her watchful eye. She could see what I couldn't see until she showed it to me: that every one of the girls in my school was beautiful and every one of them was capable of achieving a captivating appearance — that beauty did not depend on good luck but on the confident claiming of your authentic flesh-and-bone originality.

Where and when we claim our flesh-and-bone originality is bloom time.

Maxine came to see me today. No one embargoes Maxine. First thing she said was what she always said first, before she kissed my cheek: "What you know good, baby? What you know good?" The sicker I got, the more country she got. Country revives. Then she asked, "When's Eartha get here?" like she was worried it wouldn't be soon enough. I said, "I don't know," hoping it didn't sound like I was worried, too.

Nurses were fluttering about and they also seemed worried. Maxine shooed the nurses out, trimmed and buffed my nails, then dyed my eyebrows with dry powder. While she brushed my brows, she said, "Sometime the only good news some little chap, some

485

little nurse gal gonna get all day is seeing you raise these pretty brows, don't let your arches go gray! Don't deprive that lil chap, that lil gal! Now, let's see if someone pretty wants to take your pressure."

I told her to hold up on that. I had a request. I wanted Maxine to promise to make sure Diggs gets my makeup done right and my hair waves tight. Wanted her to promise to touch up my corpse when I'm in my coffin, before they let the mourners in. Maxine shook her head, No. "Ain't nothing dead, pretty Zig, except a flower, and you ain't no flower. You the most beautiful man in the world, you Ziggy Johnson."

Now, I know Maxine has dabbed powder on Marvin Gaye, Harry Belafonte, and Pretty Cassius Clay, so upon reflection, I know that she was lying to me. Looking in her eyes, I believed the woman. When I leave this world, I will be happy and holding Maxine's hand.

LIBATION FOR THE FEAST DAY OF MAXINE POWELL:
Fun House Mirror

This excellent punch, like Maxine's young stars, requires significant advance preparation.

3 bottles of Tokaji wine, 500 mil. each
1 cup of brandy
3 ponies of green Chartreuse
1 jigger of Jamaican rum
1 cup of fresh peaches
1 cup of fresh pineapple
3 oranges, sliced for garnish
2 lemons, sliced for garnish

In a vessel large enough to contain all the ingredients, but small enough to fit into your refrigerator, place all the above ingredients. Cover with plastic wrap and refrigerate for at least six hours. When ready to serve, prepare a punch bowl with one huge ice cube. (This can be made by freezing water in a gallon container.) Strain punch from refrigerator into punch bowl. Dress the ice with the fruit. Serve, using a ladle, into punch glasses.

WEEK 43
FORTY-THIRD SUNDAY
AFTER FATHER'S DAY

On January 18, 1968, Eartha Kitt sat down at a formal White House luncheon hosted by Lady Bird Johnson in a room with yellow walls. Gilt chairs surrounded round tables ready to hold the fifty women from across the country whom the First Lady had summoned to her first "Doers Luncheon" to share "practical, positive methods" to combat urban crime. Eartha Kitt was one of the chosen. Before the event was concluded, Eartha had confronted both LBJ himself and Ladybird with her observation that the cause of youth unrest was snatching boys from their mothers and sending them to die in Vietnam. The White House had sent a limousine to bring Ms. Kitt to the White House. No car was waiting when she left. Legend has it she walked, until a Black taxicab driver, recognizing Eartha Kitt from her Catwoman role on the *Batman* TV show, picked her up and drove her back to the Shoreham Hotel.

Jimmy Hoffa disappeared on July 30, 1975. Hoffa's body has never been found. It is believed by law enforcement that the legendary labor leader was murdered. From 1974 to 1989 Marc Stepp was vice president of the United Auto Workers, leading the Chrysler Division. He served in an era when union leaders were receiving death threats and even getting killed. At his death at the age of ninety-three in 2016, Stepp was credited by the *Detroit Free Press* with being the first Black to lead negotiations with a Detroit automaker. Ernie Lofton, Marc's contemporary and colleague, is mythologized for walking into Ford wielding a baseball bat; Marc Stepp was widely understood by auto manufacturers to be the more-dangerous opponent.

Marc Stepp

PATRON SAINT OF: *Union Members, Collective Bargainers, and Hardballers*

Bette Stanley brought Marc Stepp into my circle and made him a friend. Met him and said, "I'm going to put some of George's money behind that man." Now, Stepp didn't take any of George's money and Stepp didn't get elected to the Common Council

— but I don't believe we have seen the end of Marc Stepp. And I don't just mean all my girls filing their fingernails with his campaign-give-away emery boards.

Eartha Kitt had the chance to be accepted into the world of ladies who lunch at the White House and chose instead to stand up for all the young Black men being shipped off to Vietnam to be killed. Three times during a formal White House luncheon, she spoke for those who could not speak for themselves, spoke for the brown boys, without regard to her place in the white world, without regard to her place in her Black family, without regard even to the fact *Ebony* had once declared she was disliked by Negroes. She spoke up and a world of rage fell on her little shoulders.

She called me from the Shoreham. "All I've got standing with me here in Washington is Detroit. Hobart Taylor and Ofield Dukes may be the only people I know in this city who are still speaking to me. I'm coming to you, Ziggy."

Eartha had almost not gone to the White House luncheon. She had almost come to visit me instead of going. She didn't enjoy pomp and circumstance. But the White House pressed, offering to make the hotel arrangements and provide chauffeurs. She suspected there was something (she didn't quite know what) that she could do at the White House that would be a perfect gift for me. Instead, she almost killed me. And she knew it. Eartha told Hobart she was afraid that watching the news coverage of what was being characterized as "her rabid attack" on the First Lady might cause me to stroke out. Hobart responded that if it did, her presence would revive me. A few days later, just about noontime, I was roused to consciousness from my midday nap by the sound from a radio that was mixing with a dream, "Ziggy, Baby, wake-y, wake-y, wake-y, wake-y up, Ziggy, Baby, wake-y, wake-y, wake-up!" I opened my eyes. The radio wasn't playing. On the kitten heels of thigh-high suede boots, Eartha walked into my hospital room, looking as good in real life as Eartha looked in the opening scene of that picture she starred in with Sammy Davis Jr., *Anna Lucasta,* which means as good as any woman ever looked on film or Earth.

Seeing Eartha walk is a joy-jolt. She was swinging a mod faux-leopard-fur trench coat with a Nehru collar that zipped down the front and had leather pockets and cuffs. When she unzipped the coat, a dark leather minidress, matching her coat pockets, clung

491

to the essential points of her high-breasted, high-assed beauty.

"How are you, yellow man?"

"Perfect." And I was. For the first time in a good long while.

"If this kills you, I will regret it."

"You never regret anything, Eartha."

"I *won't* regret it. I will know you died happy, knowing your Eartha, impeccably dressed, arrived by limousine at the plantation mansion we call the White House, and there, after politely greeting the First Lady of the United States, loudly declared the war that was killing my Ziggy's boys, obscene."

"Obscener than anything that has happened to that body of yours."

"You heard what I didn't say."

Eartha leaned in and bit my ear. When I thought no one would ever nibble my ear again. It was a pleasant surprise until it made me think of Orson Welles biting her lip, or tongue, onstage till it bled. She must have thought of the same exact thing at the same exact time. She stopped biting and kissed my nose.

"I love the way you use me, Zig."

"Use you?"

"Everyone uses me."

"Not me."

"Yes, you. When I was a girl, I was used like a toy, like a slave, like a rake, by blood relations."

"We're done with talking about that."

"*You're* done."

"You've gotten over things people think they can't get over."

"And you've used me to let your girls know they can get over anything."

"I used you well."

"Purrrfectly well."

She bit me again.

"Why you here, gal?"

"Where else should I be? Hobart Taylor and Ofield Dukes say LBJ is coming for me. If the president of the United States is coming to destroy a Black woman, the safest place she can be is in Detroit City, by Ziggy's side."

I called Marc Stepp. When your favorite kitten's tail is in the tightest crack that will ever squeeze it, and you are me, you pray to a very particular Saint: Marcellus Stepp from Versailles, Kentucky, horse and whiskey country.

On Marc's first day in Detroit, he was nineteen years old and found a job shining shoes in a bar. When they figured out he was too young and too clean to be in that bar, they threw him out. Soon he had

493

another job shining shoes — this time at a barbershop in Highland Park near the Chrysler factory. Then next, my man Marc had a job *in* the Chrysler factory.

It was 1942. He was making fifty-seven cents an hour unloading gun barrels. He was one of the 700,000 residents of Detroit working to provide arms, armaments, and other tools for war. Soon he would be drafted. In the war he saw a lot of racism. Around Detroit, sepians said they were looking for a double V-Day — a victory against fascism abroad and a victory at home against racism.

Marc Stepp did as much as anybody to get that double win. When he came home, he returned to the Chrysler Highland Park factory. Sooner than most would have thought possible, he was a shop committeeman, and quickly in succession deputy chief steward, chief steward, finally he was VP of Local 490. In 1957 he formed the Trade Union Leadership Council to fight for better representation of Blacks in and by the UAW. In 1960 he did the impossible. He got elected president of Local 490 and won by fifty-four votes. Just last year, in 1967, he was appointed an international representative of the UAW, Region 1B. And it was all because he hadn't liked the way he was

494

treated in the army.

That's the thing Marc Stepp and Sammy Davis Jr. most appreciated about each other. Many Black men didn't like how they were treated in the army. Sammy and Marc came out and made something sweet out of that bitterness.

For a while, it looked like I loved me one failed politician. Marc failed to get elected to the Common Council. It soon became apparent that it was more important that Marc Stepp rise to be a prince in the union than a princeling in the city. The city — our city — is the breadwinners' town, and a seat at the table determining how the breadwinners get treated is more than a seat on the Common Council; that's being the mayor of Black Breadwinners Town.

I love a mayor come up from the bottom. Marc was in the plant for nineteen years. He entered in '42, the year Black women were first beginning to fight for their right to do the jobs to help save the country by working in the Detroit war factories. Black men went out on strike for that right, and I believe Marc Stepp was one of them. He was certainly the one who told me there were 25,000, maybe even 28,000, Black women available to work in 1942 and that the white folks had barred the war factory door. By 1943 an acute labor shortage was declared in Detroit. Wasn't no shortage. It was white KKK up from the South keeping Black women workers out — even if it meant we lost the war.

When we fight for ourselves sometimes, we fight for the nation. Marc and Eartha understood this most keenly. Thirty percent of all the hardware we used to fight World War II, ranging from aircraft engines to air-crafts to tank guns — everything — thirty percent of all of that came from Detroit, and we risked not providing all that because of racism. But our women, some of them, got in those factories, did those too-hard jobs; some of our men even got promoted. As Marc said, "The union called bullshit on a lot of white hate-strikes winning my loyalty." And Marc won mine.

Last I heard, thirty percent of the people working for Chrysler now are Black. And we know one daddy in a factory can earn a year of college tuition in less than a month. My breadwinners thank him for that. That's the man I called to help get Eartha out of LBJ's crosshairs.

Marc couldn't do much. What he could do, he did. And it will be enough. Quiet as it is kept, breadwinners live in solidarity with our most-singular selves. Our eccentrics, our artists often have no better friends than a union of ordinary folk who understand that sameness and normal are ideas constructed to restrain us and contain us.

Marc Stepp understood. So perhaps he made calls across Detroit. Maybe he made calls to Washington and manipulated to keep the interference with Eartha's career focused on the United States, on the domestic threat, by slyly reminding LBJ's team that Miss Kitt was insignificant, that a global effort was not warranted because Kitt wasn't a global citizen. Maybe Stepp also fed those lies into the ear of the president of the United Auto Workers, Walter Reuther, who then fed them to the president of the United States. Or maybe Stepp fed them into the ears of lesser UAW executives with close lower contacts in the White House. Whatever he did goes with me to the grave. What we know for sure: Eartha's international career was saved.

And we know this: Eartha Kitt's American career was almost assassinated by the American president who signed the Voting Rights Act but wouldn't cosign on a Black woman's right to state what all Black Bottom knew: that youth violence in American cities had everything to do with poor young men being snatched from their mothers and sent to fight and die in Vietnam. I had done so much for my girls. Eartha came back from the White House to the only city with enough audacity to shelter her audacious self — Detroit — and she let me cosign on doing one last something important for our boys. Marc Stepp gave me the big, inky, blue-black pen needed to sign that check and keep it good.

Eartha didn't stay long. Jetted in. Jetted out. Soon she will be in Europe. She will get back to the White House and she will sing "Santa Baby" in an East Room triumph — and for a Republican president. I predict that. And I predict this: The country will come to understand that Vietnam is an unjust and unwinnable war, fought by the poorest of the American poor, raining hell on poorer, Asian poor. Americans will come to know that in the year Eartha spoke loud and proud, more boys would die in Vietnam than in any other year. When the country understands that shame, Eartha will be one of the few who make us proud to be human *and* American.

Marc drove Eartha to the airport. A few hours later, just before midnight, Marc came back to see me, for what will be our last visit. He doesn't know this. I do. He cracked the hospital room window and had a smoke. Refused to give me a cigarette, but he let me have one puff off his. Wouldn't let me talk about Eartha, he wanted to talk about us.

"Zig, you and their daddies and mamas are getting them ready to go someplace other than a plant. I'm trying to make sure when they get there, and get to be teachers, nurses, policemen, doctors, lawyers, and preachers, they won't have to be paying for parents that lifted them up. I want Chrysler Highland Park to be paying even when these factories are torn down. I'm making sure they don't have to fly with lead in their shoes. One day, the breadwinners will deserve a retirement and their children will deserve to see their parents comfortable in it." My retirement plan is death. I don't say that. I say, "You keep working your end of the street and I work mine, and these kids gonna be alright." I say, "The circus may only come to town once a year, but it don't only come once. We'll win."

LIBATION FOR THE FEAST DAY OF MARC STEPP:
Union Card

1 jigger of bourbon

1 sugar cube
1/2 pony of water
Mint

In the bottom of a julep cup or jelly jar,
place the sugar cube and water and
slightly muddle. Next add six or seven
mint leaves and the bourbon, and stir
briefly. Top with crushed ice. With a
spoon, slowly churn the crushed ice to
chill the vessel. Be careful not to pull the
mint up off the bottom of the cup or jar.
Finally, place a mint bouquet into the top
of the ice, along with a straw.

WEEK 44
FORTY-FOURTH SUNDAY
AFTER FATHER'S DAY

After 1968, the psychologist Shirley Ann McNeil, PhD, became increasingly involved with Transcendental Meditation by introducing to Detroit public schools that New Age panacea for stress and a possible cure for addiction. Until her death in 2001 at the age of seventy-three, McNeil stayed in touch with many of Ziggy's former students, giving advice when asked and keeping track of their more-public successes. She kept a scrapbook of newspaper clippings as an evolving memorial to Ziggy's work, documenting the dozens of doctors, lawyers, professors, ministers, and teachers who had roots in his School of the Theatre. One of the doctors who attended Shirley during her last illness was a former principal dancer in the 1965 Youth Colossal, which Shirley herself had written.

501

Shirley McNeil

PATRON SAINT OF: *Teachers, Psychologists, Meditators, and All Manner of Black Zen*

Like so many people I love — especially Lloyd Richards, Artis Lane, and Bob Bennett — Shirley McNeil had a Canadian connection. She was born in Toronto. She arrived in Detroit not long after she graduated from the University of Dayton where she was the first Black majorette, and, in '51 or '52, the first sepian English teacher at Eastern High School.

I love a schoolmarm. If Mama is from Natchez, I am from Wendell Phillips High School, from 244 East Pershing Road, Chicago, Illinois. My first great girl crush was on Mrs. Borogf, my French teacher at Wendell Phillips, where I was president of the French Club. And my true side woman, my work wife, is Shirley McNeil.

Shirley has been with me a good long while. Others have helped me in a hundred different ways to mount the Youth Colossal, but Shirley McNeil was my secret weapon. Whether it was "Youth Moves In" or "Youth Accepts a Challenge" or "Youth Travels the World" or "Youth Designs for Tomorrow" or "Youth Builds a Bridge" or any one of the other Colossals, Shirley wrote the scripts for my Father's Day shows and she wrote them smart.

When I was a boy in Chicago, I read every issue of a magazine for children, called *The Brownies' Book,* that the NAACP put out back then. That magazine entertained me and it taught me; it uplifted me while overturning stereotypes that were designed to hold me down. From jump I wanted every Colossal to do that same work — to do what the Y Circus didn't manage to do, but what the old Negro pageants did. I don't get that done without Shirley McNeil, PhD. Shirley found faded scripts for *Star of Ethiopia, The Pan-American Kermiss,* and *The Answer to Birth of a Nation,* my favorite pageants, and she studied them. She begged, borrowed, and stole old issues of *The Brownies' Book.* She dipped into all of that when she was writing the Youth Colossal scripts.

Then Shirley went above and beyond. Shirley wrote my scripts to be more than pageants; she called my shows "play therapy." She talked about Carl Jung's sandboxes and Jean Piaget's stages, talked about all of that, something nobody cared about except Shirley, Katherine Dunham, Bob Bennett, and my aunt Sadye. Shirley declared, for all of them and for me, "We are creating antidote and answer."

I didn't follow half of what Shirley said. Sometimes listening to her was like trying to drink water from a fire hydrant. She had so many big ideas and talked so fast. Be it tickets to see Nureyev dance, View-Masters, playbills, encyclopedias, or just a book about African dance that she tucked into the little library she set up in the waiting area of our school, she was always tracking down and serving up that little something extra that just might engage the imagination or curiosity of a child we hadn't yet truly reached. To engage her own curiosity, she spent time over at the Freer House sitting up under the folks from the Palmer-Merrill Institute and started work on her doctorate in psychology.

By 1963 I was continuing to publish an entertainment and gossip column and she had begun publishing scholarly articles. She would always give me a carbon copy of any article she was working on, then badger me into reading it. Her articles would be studded with words like "bibliotherapy" and would discuss dance school as "dance therapy." The articles were a lot like Shirley's bar conversations where she would assert that "our" purpose was not teaching dance or teaching citizenship, but improving self-image.

Shirley believed better self-image led to sharper motivation and more self-discipline, though she preferred the phrase "self-direction." I teased her and told her James Brown thought hunger led to sharper motivation and more advanced self-direction.

If two people could be exact polar opposites but about the same business, it would be James Brown and Shirley McNeil. James spent an inordinate amount of time trying to figure out what you do to get a band to do its best; Shirley spent the same whole lot of time trying to figure out how you get a classroom to be its best. They both were all about maximizing potential. Their biggest difference? Shirley loved the carrot and James loved the stick.

It was Shirley who first called my School of the Theatre a citizenship school. Working with Shirley was half-party, half–road race. It was fun and sweaty, and you discovered something about the other person and something about yourself. We had us a big time, infusing my small fry with a life-changing love of an art and a willingness to create and go their own way.

All that was important to Shirley, but that wasn't all there was to the woman. Shirley was a good singer who performed weekly on the House of Diggs radio show — but my students knew, because we let them know, that Shirley's being teacher, psychologist, and writer was more important than being Shirley the singer, but only because brown psychologists, writers, and teachers were few and far between in our world.

We figured this out in the middle of the night over rye: Crying with your guitar, or in your voice, or in your dance, or on paper is almost the exact opposite of crying salt tears. Crying in art prepares you to do something other than cry. When Shirley announced to a gathering of educators at a dinner in the Ebony Room of the Gotham that the Ziggy Johnson School of the Theatre was the perfect place to teach students how to dance, not just to live the blues — how "a body can bear articulate and soul-elevating witness," I cosigned on that.

Igniting the will and the skill for my students to cry with their taps, with their toes, with their guitars, with their songs, and not with their eyes was our goal.

Father's Day 1968 will be the Colossal of Colossals. Shirley and I have decided the theme will be: YOUTH BUILDS A TIME CAPSULE. We're plotting two Hannibal strong numbers: "When the Saints Go Marching In," and "They Got the Whole World in They . . ."

"Saints" will play right before the first-act curtain. We're bringing in students from the Eastern marching band to play the music. They will stride across stage in a procession that will be a cross between a cakewalk and second line. Our best dancers will follow behind the musicians, performing the Black Bottom dance. My students will be costumed to pay homage to individual and specific greats of Black vaudeville. Leading the line? Butterbeans and Susie!

The final number, "Whole World in My . . . ," is an extravaganza that will include every child in the school. Voices and taps will provide all the music. There will be no instruments. Students from the Ballet Babes up to the Jazz Workshop will be singing a new version of that old Sunday School standard "He's Got the Whole World in His Hands." And each student will improvise their own dance steps, so it's like this: "They got the whole world in they PAUSE SNAP SNAP, they got the whole world in they PAUSE SNAP SNAP; PAUSE SNAP SNAP"; everybody will be singing and tapping to "They Got the Whole World in they PAUSE" but only one dancer will perform each of the SNAP SNAP beats except on the fourth-line climax when everybody will dance their own original dance on the SNAP SNAP and together they will make a whole new polyrhythmic sound. And every few verses there will be three solo lines: "I've Got the Whole World in my PAUSE SNAP SNAP" and followed by the original fourth-line climax.

The seed for my choreography came from one of the Ballet Babes. She said, "I got the whole world in my . . ." and then she rolled her hips like she was hula hooping, and then another girl sang back at her, "I got the whole world in my . . ." and she popped her fingers. Those girls snatched that fine AME church song back from Lawrence Welk and all those straight-beat Lutherans. And now they are going to share their truth loud, large, and syncopated.

Shirley has a lot to say about a time capsule's being about the past *and* the future. It includes what you want to take with you because you treasure it; and also what you want to take with you so the future knows who you were; and maybe, just maybe, if you don't make it to the future, someone not yet born when you bury your time capsule can start to become some of who you used to be.

Shirley calls that Black Bottom reincarnation. She wants me to choreograph a dance that involves a modern shout circle with girls and boys in the lotus yoga position with the only visible movement being their chests heaving and deflating and maybe their fingertips fluttering. I said, "NO!" to that. Then I started thinking about how I might-could make it work if we incorporated Lionel Hampton vibraphone music. My unofficial associate dean of the dance school can get out there. "Out there" is contagious.

That's why Gladys Knight and the Pips, the Contours, and the Fantastic Four are backstage every year helping the young performers get ready. They admire how out-there we get. In '66 I worried if I would have a big act. Didn't know for sure that I did until two weeks before the show. Anna came through with The Temptations and they were thrilled to join our students on-stage because, as David Ruffin said, "Y'all all the way wild!"

When I am gone, Mari will edit and publish my book and remind the world that the very first Youth Colossal was held in June of 1952. It was before Brown v. Board of Education, before the Civil Rights Act. It was before a lot of things. I almost closed the school in 1957. I felt like maybe my job had been done. Brown was part of it. Then I realized if our kids started going to integrated schools, they would soon need now more than ever a sacred brown, black, and

tan space, where the past could be remembered in ways that were useful to us, and a
future could be dreamed that reflected our
wishes.

I once confessed to Shirley that I didn't
believe in integration.

I said, "All the integration I need is
already in me. Mulatto. I've had that word
spat at me. We can be fully integrated
without many, or any, from the other side of
the tracks. We are Black and white already."
Shirley laughed and declared me a radical,
"red to the bone, short, pretty man." And I
laughed back and said I couldn't afford to
be anything but what I was, yellow and
Black as the ace of spades. Life was too brief
and I was too vulnerable to play to anything
but to my strength.

It takes will and skill to get to that. We got
to that. Thank you, Shirley.

LIBATION FOR THE FEAST DAY OF
SHIRLEY MCNEIL:
The Will and the Skill

1 pony of bourbon
1 pony of sherry
2 chunks of pineapple, juiced
1/2 lemon, juiced
1/2 pony of simple syrup

Fill a highball glass 3/4 full of ice. Add all ingredients. Stir. Add additional ice, if necessary, to fill glass.

Fill a highball glass ¾ full of ice. Add all
ingredients. Stir. Add additional ice, if
necessary, to fill glass.

WEEK 45
FORTY-FIFTH SUNDAY
AFTER FATHER'S DAY

In January of 1967 Ziggy treated students
at his school to a Monday night pizza party
to celebrate John Bubbles. Ziggy's small
fry crowded around the television in his office to watch Bubbles execute a few "impossible steps" and sing "The Town Where
I was Born" on *The Lucy Show.* The
students applauded so loudly for Bubbles
(wearing an understated baby-blue
sweater, gray slacks, and an open-collared
shirt) that their thunder drowned out some
of the details of Bubbles and Buck's history that Ziggy was imparting. Soon as the
credits had run, the phone on Ziggy's office desk rang. A hush came over the
room. The call was hoped for, but not
promised; the students were prepared
"just in case." Soon as Ziggy said, "John,"
he held the receiver out and the students
yelled, "Best dancer in the history of the
world!" When Ziggy hung up the phone he

loudly proclaimed: "There are three things I never want you to forget: Ziggy loves you. Detroit is your hometown. And John 'Bubbles' Sublett is a genius."

Bubbles and Buck

PATRON SAINT OF: *Dynamic Duos and Unbreakable Teams*

Sweetest people I have ever known: Bubbles and Buck. It was a long and loyal love. Bubbles and Buck, alias John Sublett and Ford Lee Washington, started working together in their teens. They danced together for going on forty years, till Washington died, in 1955. Exactly what the flavor of the love was, nobody who knows will be telling. We tell this: Bubbles can still write his name in chalk on a stage with his feet.

They were closer than close. Brothers. Lovers? Something sweet. Something strong. Something that lasted. Something white folks could not pry apart, and they tried. Gershwin. Eleanor Powell. Everybody wanted Bubbles, fewer folks wanted Buck. You wanted Bubbles, you got Buck, too. That's how Sublett do.

John William Sublett was the original Sportin' Life in *Porgy and Bess* on Broadway.

513

Bubbles could sing. When he brought the character of Sportin' Life into flesh-and-blood being, he injected nuances of meaning into "It Ain't Necessarily So" that the composer, George Gershwin, didn't put there, that the lyricist, Ira Gershwin, didn't put there, that the director didn't catch. His sepian audience heard it. And generations of actors after him who played the role Bubbles created, they heard it. *I* heard it. But you won't hear Bubbles on those early albums. They got white singers from the Metropolitan Opera to sing "best of *Porgy and Bess.*" Now that's a bold-face, ugly-as-homemade-sin lie. No matter.

Bubbles had a voice. And it was in no way ordinary. His voice didn't change until 1920. When he was eighteen. Then he couldn't get and keep his notes for a while. Said he would slide right off them. So he started dancing. Practicing all night long and crying when he couldn't get a step, he lived on coffee and donuts while he invented tap as we know it.

Everyone who came after echoed him. We thought he danced better than Bill "Bojangles" Robinson. Bubbles, everybody says, everybody knows, he invented rhythm tap dancing. Others danced on their toes. He danced on his heels. Dropped those heels, exploding Western ideas about the length of a bar and bars to the beat. Bubbles didn't read music. He *was* music. Complex music. Evolving music, improvising music. Music that expressed his understanding of the power of fluidity wrapped in snap. Just like Buck.

Ford Lee Washington, Buck, doesn't get the acclaim he deserved as a serious jazz pianist. Buck played the left hand of a dangerous and loving God — and that's a good God worth knowing.

In 1934 when I was picking up stateside dates with Butterbeans and Susie, Bubbles and Buck were on one of the Blackbirds tours, an extravagant and sophisticated musical revue that played London and all over Europe, attracting a cosmopolitan-cool ofay audience, they met a music-loving aristocrat we called The Dane.

The Dane thought Buck played like Earl Hines. Actually, he compared Buck to everybody great. Buck played like nobody but himself. He *was* great; that, the Dane was right about. The rest was, he was as in love with Buck as Bubbles was. We all were — but only Bubbles got him.

They come up hard. Starting in 1919 too many times, both men put on corkface to perform. They played Europe, Broadway, in the big-ticket drama shows, not just musical reviews. Real dramas with real music including the big one: *Porgy and Bess.* Bubbles and Buck were the first Black entertainers to appear on a television show. They were on a BBC show in 1936. Stars of the white circuits, they played the Palace, the Keith, the Orpheum, and the most prestigious houses on the white circuits, but they were made for film — it captured their details and they had so many gorgeous details.

Bubbles and Buck did a number called "Love Is in the Air Tonight" in the 1937 film *Varsity Show.* I love this bit. They are in long, light tails and top hats. And Bubbles is singing a love song to Buck. It's strange, they promised to kill people for the love of the other, and nobody noticed. What was *that*?

I thought they would always be together, die in each other's arms. I would have thought Bubbles would have gone just after Buck. He didn't. He rose from those ashes. Started showing up on teevee more often. Became one of the most powerful acts I ever did see on teevee. Loved seeing Bubbles dance in a sports jacket and dark pants. Bubbles dancing with Judy Garland. "Me and My Shadow." Judy Garland was the shadow. Bubbles was Me.

I want Bubbles to tap at my funeral, write my name in the Michigan snow, with his low-dropped heels. I want that man who cried like a baby when he couldn't get a step, and stepped like a man when it was achieved, to write my elegy with his well-dropped heels, and with the tips of his toes.

LIBATION FOR THE FEAST DAY OF
BUBBLES AND BUCK:
Something That Lasted

1 jigger of cognac
1 sugar cube
1 lemon peel
Hot water

Place sugar cube and a couple of tablespoons of hot water into a vessel suited for a hot beverage. Muddle the sugar and stir briefly. Add cognac and 4 to 5 ounces more of hot water. Twist lemon peel over the top, then drop into the cocktail.

WEEK 46
FORTY-SIXTH SUNDAY
AFTER FATHER'S DAY

In 1969, Moms Mabley's recording of "Abraham, Martin and John" reached number 35 on the pop charts, making her, at age seventy-five, the oldest person ever to crack the Top 40. She still holds that record. Moms Mabley died in 1975. In 2013 Whoopi Goldberg directed a documentary, *Moms Mabley: I Got Somethin' to Tell You.* Rumor has it that a Detroit Red biopic is in the works.

Detroit Red and Moms Mabley
PATRON SAINT OF: *Dandies, First Robins of Spring, and Candid Daughters*

Let this happen again. What do I have to give to get this day back? Nothing. It is here with me now.

I was wearing my still-new pink silk tie and puffed up like the first robin of spring when I came across my mirror image on the sidewalk outside the Gotham Hotel.

It would have been 1953, sometime after Easter but before the hullaballoo of the second Youth Colossal turned into the holler it would become in late May. It would have been late April when the hullabaloo was still a low rumble of ascending murmurs.

The sound and sight of exceptionally fancy footwork offered up by the girls and boys in the dancing classes rolled round my head, thrilling me. The April efforts of my students to get the attention of my dance teachers in hopes of being cast in a starring turn in the big show charmed and delighted, but rarely changed our casting. We knew, long before spring, who would be front and center come the first Sunday in June. But those flashes of April excellence sometimes stretched my dancers in ways that meant that the next year one of the dancers on a second or third row would spend more time center-stage front. Sometimes they high-kicked themselves into a new caliber of creativity. I was thinking about all that when I knotted the Easter tie around my neck.

And I was thinking about letting the neighborhood take a gander at me. When I passed through the front door of the Gotham Hotel, I wasn't so much thinking about going somewhere as going out to perambulate my personhood. I set out to strut as an especially favored dandy having an especially good day. I am unapologetic about this truth: I am a dandy.

I knew Moms through Butterbeans and Susie. Born in 1894, Moms was about fourteen years old when she untied the babies she had birthed after rape from her apron strings. Shaking off some of the dust of Brevard, North Carolina, she set off in a hurry to find someplace she could forget her daddy dying, trying to save folks from a fire, her mama dying on Christmas Day, and some young white sheriff raping her and some old Black man doing that same violent thing.

The girl from Brevard ran straight to Butterbeans and Sue, then wept in Sue's arms till the rest of the dust of Brevard was mud on Sue's dress. And when they together had washed that salty mud away, the girl who would one day be called Moms, who was then called Loretta, took the name Jackie Mabley after a man, Jack Mabley, who she would later say, truth or lie, had been a boyfriend who took so much from her she had to take something from him, and settled on his name, first and last. Moms was something.

Sometime around 1921, before the world and I learned to Charleston, Butterbeans and Susie took Moms to New York City, where soon she was playing Connie's Inn. When I met her, she was headlining at the Apollo. That was the 1930s. She was on the bill with dancer Honi Cole, and she wrote a play with Zora Neale Hurston.

Good Moms lines: "Anytime you see me with my arms around an old man, I'm holding him for the police." "I don't know no jokes, but I can tell you some facts." "Right church but the wrong pew." "Laugh yourself to death." Folks say her brother wrote some of her lines. I never believed that. Moms's off-the-cuff, late-night improvised verbal jabs directed at fools and rivals were sharp, hard proof of her comic genius. Shirley McNeil was smart. Moms was a genius.

Moms was my favorite political speaker. She talked about segregation. She talked about racism. She talked about power. She told me the power of the dandy was to know when, and when not to, hide your candy. She told me that the most audacious Black American wish, in terms of Black and white, was not to be useful.

The ugliest uncommon thing she had ever heard one of us be called was "Obsolete Farm Equipment" or "OFE." She heard that more than one time and in more than one place, but she thought she heard it first somewhere in Memphis about the same time the Black world was busy talking about Brown v. Board of Education. Some cotton brokers were busy talking about mechanical cotton pickers. Moms listened carefully. Later she cursed a man she called John Daniel Rust because he had invented the machine that made sepian life in the Arkansas and Mississippi delta a hotter and dryer version of the hell it already was. But the way she cursed the man, the cotton broker thought Moms was praising him.

She knew how to confront people and get away with it.

She told the warden of Sing Sing to go home and die. Those boys in that college laughed till they cried. Loved it, too, when she called the warden "son." Because it was her way of calling the warden "boy" right in front of the inmates. "I did that for them every year," Moms boasted. When she stood on the stage in that frumpy housedress with her toothless grin beside a well-dressed white man in a suit, she made the white men look like liars. Moms was the unvarnished truth.

Moms hardly knew a joke that wasn't filthy blue. Not just blue — filthy blue. She loved sex. And loved talking about it. She was Rabelaisian. Bricktop said that. Her mouth was her billboard. She wanted the world to know she had goodies and she had the goods and she knew all about what some folks tried to deny: that she was an erotic flower, that she was a sexual power. Others did not see her as she saw herself. She didn't let that matter. Moms, Moms. She came up hard, and she came up wide, she came up doing everything any woman ever did in the dark that she wanted to do or she didn't want to do, and she stayed so wide open she discovered that some of what she wanted to do she didn't like, but some of what she didn't want to do she quickly acquired a taste for. And when she met Red, she found one of her grand passions.

Moms danced in a cloche hat and flat shoes. She played the woman nobody paid attention to. Red played the reviled dandy. They both played the underdog. Moms made the maid relevant. Detroit Red made the dandy respected. I was thrilled they found each other.

I usually saw Moms just like me, with pretty showgirls on her arms. But this was different. She had found her true pal. Another artist of the highest caliber. I loved to walk between those two stars.

Moms was a trigger. So was Detroit Red. They took deadly aim. Moms with her teeth out. Lord, who wouldn't want to know the inside of that powerful mouth? And who wasn't afraid that she would kill you dead for just thinking about it? That woman was powerful and confounding.

Onstage, Moms lost her job, she lost her lover. In life, people hung around to love on her, feast days or famine. Me, I was one of them. And Detroit Red was another. Loved being in that bold person's fan club. She taught me how to be more than a man, or a woman, more than a category that was created and expected. She taught me to be the first robin of spring. Moms gave good gift. I'd give up going straight to heaven and spend two weeks in purgatory if it means I get to hear the joke she tells when she hears that I am dead.

LIBATION FOR THE FEAST DAY OF DETROIT RED AND MOMS MABLEY:
Fan Club

1 jigger of applejack
3/4 pony of lemon juice
3/4 pony of simple syrup

Place ingredients into a cocktail shaker.
Shake well and serve in a sour glass.

Place ingredients into a cocktail shaker.
Shake well and serve in a sour glass.

WEEK 47
FORTY-SEVENTH SUNDAY
AFTER FATHER'S DAY

In a 1988 interview for an article in the *Detroit Free Press,* Clifford Fears said he was "discovered" by Ziggy dancing at an amateur dance contest when he was eight years old. He claims he was teaching at Ziggy's school by the time he was eleven. This contradicts Ziggy's report. Fears concluded the interview by saying the only hope for Ziggy's dance company was either Fears or Baby Doll hitting the lottery. Clifford died of pneumonia in 1990 at the age of fifty-four.

Clifford Fears

PATRON SAINT OF: *Protégés, Prodigies, Mentors, and the Forgotten*

Tick-tock. Who am I leaving out? One of my teachers noticed Clifford Fears first. Saw him at some performance at Eastern High and brought him to my attention.

Soon Clifford was a student at the Ziggy Johnson School of the Theatre, and I was changing his class time from Friday to Monday so that he could be both a drum major at Eastern (Shirley McNeil lobbied for that) and a principal dancer for my company.

Looking back, he was in my company for just a hot minute. Too soon it was 1956 and Cliff was headed down to Miami. Then he was with Katherine Dunham in Paris, followed by Stockholm, always sending postcards home. I bet Lucille Ellis bought the stamps and put those scraps in the mail. I was puffed-out proud when he became director and founder of Katherine's school of the cultural arts in East St. Louis. Before the advent of the miniskirt, he was a mini-me.

In 1959 he was in Edinburgh. In 1960 he was dancing in Russia with a girl from K. D.'s troupe, which had finally disbanded.

When I'm gone, if there's one person who could for sure keep my school going, it would be Clifford. In my will I have instructed Baby Doll to appoint Clifford dean of my school. I want to honor him and provide for her. To accept the school, Clifford will have to release the world and return to Detroit. I pray Clifford rises to

527

the occasion.

And if that prayer is answered, I hope Clifford honors me as I have honored him — never crossing the lines that separate those who were once your students from those with whom you can play with abandoned delight. This is what honor requires.

I loved Cliff across unblurred lines so that he would fly. So he could dance for MLK in Stockholm. When he rises above the stage in dance flight, there is love and loss in my eyes. But there is only joy in his eyes. I have seen that. That is my better-than-Kilimanjaro.

LIBATION FOR THE FEAST DAY OF CLIFFORD FEARS:
Love Requires More

- 1 pony of brandy
- 1 pony of Venezuelan or other South American rum
- 1 pony of curaçao
- 1/2 lemon, juiced
- 1 sugar cube

Place sugar cube and juice into the bottom of a cocktail shaker and muddle. Add brandy, rum, and curaçao and ice

cubes. Shake. Strain into a rocks glass
filled with ice cubes.

WEEK 48
FORTY-EIGHTH SUNDAY
AFTER FATHER'S DAY

Arthur "Daddy" Braggs was from Saginaw, Michigan, where he established a compounded reputation as a patron of musical artists, a "Duke of Digits," and an excellent, if erratic, amateur baseball pitcher. In Idlewild, Braggs owned and ran the Club Paradise, with its famed Siesta Room.

At the peak of its popularity, some 25,000 people came to vacation in Idlewild in a single summer. The Idlewild Resort Company, or IRC, was formed in 1912 to market waterfront and water-access land to African-Americans. A Black surgeon, Daniel Hale Williams, purchased land from the company in 1915 and began persuasively talking up the virtues of vacationing in a Talented Tenth enclave, as a means of both providing respite from everyday racism and advancing the race through community building. W. E. B. DuBois was one of the original lot owners. By 1922 the

530

African-American Idlewild Lot Owners Association took control and ownership of the resort from the original IRC. All the classic Black beach towns — Oak Bluffs, Sag Harbor, and Highland Beach — had their particular and spectacular attractions. Highland Beach hosted no fewer than twenty-five descendants of Frederick Douglass; Oak Bluffs was perfectly perched to look out across the Atlantic back to Africa. On any given summer Saturday night in Ziggy's time, Idlewild hosted some 1,000 breadwinners and sweet soul sounds bouncing across a blue-black lake.

Arthur Braggs

PATRON SAINT OF: *Ringleaders, Circus Masters, and CEOs*

A new nurse came in today, pert starched cap on her head, thick white stockings on her legs, modest uniform. But I recognized her as a girl who wore one of the first bikinis in an Idlewild fashion show.

Around my way, we say Idlewild was the brainchild of Arthur Braggs. Most Black folks say Idlewild was actually the brainchild of a Chicago surgeon, Dr. Daniel Hale Williams. That Williams was the first man,

Black or white, to operate on the human heart. Williams imagined a place where Negro professionals could rest after all the work and trouble of being Negro in America. Arthur Braggs saw all the different shades of Black folk gathered and decided to take them in a new direction — not away from the evils of whiteness and white folk but toward the joy of being Black on the planet. The magnet he used to pull his bronze audience along: amazing shows.

Using the excellence of Black performance art, Arthur Braggs did a big thing: He created hours that were immersions in the pleasure of Blackness. Williams imagined hours that were an antidote to race-hate. Braggs imagined something far more radical. Or maybe he imagined nothing at all. He built. He created. He altered the landscape of soaring pine, aspen, and birch, adding shine: showgirls, rhinestones, and a multihued spotlight.

Braggs was born in Oklahoma but he spent the filet of his life in Saginaw, Michigan, living first on Myrtle Street, then at 710 North Franklin Avenue.

His first wife, Leodell, was ten years older than Arthur. She had completed high school. Arthur had only completed sixth grade before landing full-time in the working world as a janitor, but he had ambitions. He called himself a Dance Promoter and also a Sports Promoter. He used to be a terrific softball pitcher and when he was right, he was right, but when he wasn't, everybody walked. Look at me. I'm quoting myself to get the Braggs word portrait painted before my time runs out. In Saginaw the musicians called him Uncle Arthur. Later in Idlewild he was called Daddy Braggs. But Braggs started out running the numbers in Saginaw. In Idlewild he did something very different.

Williams dreamed up day-Idlewild; Braggs dreamed up night-Idlewild.

I love them both.

Loved them best in '55 when it was like this: Idlewild starts as soon as I slam the car door and start pulling away from the Gotham Hotel. But it gets good as soon as I stop by a certain ice cream emporium for five scoops of ice cream for fifteen cents. Five scoops! That's rich. That's abundance. There's a little old Indian woman who waves at me to stop when I am just on the outskirts of town and I always stop because I always have a gift for her, a paper sack with a new 45 chosen just for her at Joe's Record Shop. And she always has a gift for me, a tiny jar of local honey. Some folks bring all their own food. I don't. I'm always too eager to get out of the city, and with Holmes, Wilson's, Gibson's, Rittle's, and Hoskin's markets all nearby there's no need to tote groceries up from town when you can shop in Baldwin or on the island.

When I pull in to park in front of whatever little cabin is welcoming me any particular weekend, what's the first thing I see that makes me smile? All the license plates from places other than Michigan. I don't have to travel far to hear the coast-to-coast news of my world. Next big smile? Thinking about the show I will see later. First night and every night, I hit a show. Some nights I work a show.

A rooster crows at 6:00 a.m. and the day begins again. Some mornings there's a Bermuda shorts breakfast party. At 11:00 a.m. Sarge comes through with his young equestrians. At noon boats start humming up and down. The dinner bell rings at 6:00 p.m. Lottie Roxborough, Lela Wilson, and Lucille Winfield, my Idlewild mothers, see I get fed. If you kick off the month of August by giving one big party and inviting everyone over for a feast, for the rest of the month you can be free of cooking duties.

One of the things I love about Idlewild parties is just watching folk arrive. Some come by car, some on foot, and some on horseback. They come in yachts and in little motorboats. And sometimes they come in small planes.

We come and we get loud and happy and messy. Island hullabaloo is different from all other hullabaloo. Instead of the sounds of car horns and police sirens, we have island noise: crickets, buzzing of bees, birdsong. We have the whispering sound the pine needles make when the wind moves through, that proves what the older ladies say: that even angels gossip.

Instead of the smells I associate with well-run showbars in the city, walking toward the Club Fiesta, a showbar in the country-side, you catch the scent of flowering spurge, black-eyed Susans, woodland sunflowers, wild bergamot, horsemint, and Carolina rose. Eclipsing the bright neon — and there *is* a bit of bright neon in Idlewild — on the roads leading into town we have all the vivid colors of Allegheny plum, blazing stars, and bird's-foot violet. The plum tree flowers start white and turn pink. Like so many little-girl ballet slippers.

I tell the little girls of Idlewild that the plum tree blossoms are the ballet shoes for fairies, and they believe me. The dark, lovely plum fruit is just the color of a beautiful

535

tanned girl.

The wild bergamot begins to bloom in May. The leaves smell like mint. We call this bloom what the grandmothers call it: bee balm. The Ziggarettes tell me you can use it to clear up all kinds of lady problems. Some even use it on wounds or burns or tummy aches. In September, when the bergamot is finished, it is time to pack up our tents and leave. Nature's pharmacy has closed.

The lavender flowers have crazy, tube-like petals that come to form one spiky head. I can't walk a block without some little girl or old woman putting one in my buttonhole.

Flowering spurge is delicate, pretty, and poisonous. Idlewild black-eyed Susans have bright yellow petals and dark-dark centers. Butterflies are as strongly attracted to these flowers as single indebted doctors are to the rich island widows, and slick musicians to the bachelorettes. Our common rose, the Carolina rose, requires a long-tongued bee to get pollinated. The ladies of the island have turned this into a code. "I'm a Carolina rose" is a cry that requires the response of specifically well-endowed Romeos.

The best cooks on the island make jellies from the island fruit. And they add the petals of the flowers to salads. They have a luscious taste. Some put the petals in ice cubes, one of the many niceties of our Eden.

The roses bloom early and are followed by the rose hips. Sometimes we see ring-necked pheasants, bobwhites, or cottontail rabbits nibbling on the rose hips. Some of the matrons keep cats as mousers. Others of the matrons keep dance school proprietors as mousers. I prefer those matrons.

Late at night things are different. We make, uninvited, trans-Atlantic phone calls to Bricktop, while our host is busy making drinks. We make love to people we shouldn't be talking to. I run into Milt Winfield and he presumes to call me "Stanley" and I presume to call him "Livingstone." We laugh and revive. In the winter during the day at Idlewild men hunt deer. In the summer during the night they hunt dears.

There were some magnificent Idlewild summers. Let this be known, tell it twice if need be, some years, many weeks, there were more Black doctors in Idlewild on a single weekend than had ever practiced in the entire state of Texas! This rarely gets stated. It was well known in Black medical circles that the conversations those doctors, many men and just a few women, had with each other, inspired medical innovations and interventions, furthered best practices. And meeting those doctors inspired boys and girls to consider the profession.

For this and so much more, we all needed to shout Hallelujah! in the direction of Arthur Braggs, who well deserved to be praised for taking the rubber band off his bankroll to give the vacationers a floor show to eclipse Las Vegas, a somewhere so special there was no need to ever leave the orbit of Detroit, only a need to bounce into Idlewild, Detroit's satellite town.

Dr. Williams might have gotten the doctors coming. Braggs kept them returning. At night at the Club Fiesta or at the Flamingo there would be a midnight show. And it would be world-class wonderful.

There's a place we call "the house by the side of the road," and that place is always jumping. There are new cottages on Paradise Lake that are as swank as city digs, but there are still a few old cabins with outhouses.

When the Chicago Belles invade the island, it looks like opening night at the Rhumboogie, except we have all the best seats. How it inspires a Black body to see Gladys Chipchase, Julianne Buckner, Julia Pitts, Janie Marshall, or Mrs. Freeman Barnes ringside! And it is great to read about all the doings the morning after or the weekend after in *The Challenger,* Idlewild's Black newspaper. Always more women's names than men's names. Women outnumber men three to one.

In 1954 my mother came up. It was the first time she had been in a decade. When she comes I have a curfew. Mother still thinks she can spank me. Some of the very happiest hours of my life occurred on that happy island, when my grandson, my mother, and my daughter were all up at Idlewild disturbing my peace, complicating my routines, and deepening my happy.

I take Mama and the grandson to Mildred Sharber's eatery. We get a real home-cooked meal. We go back every morning she's here. In the afternoon I take the boy out and we kickboard across the lake and back.

Usually I manage to get in some golf. It's harder when my mother, grandson, and daughter are up, but I manage to on most days. Everybody is not as lucky. I've seen Charles Nelson, Joe Louis's bodyguard, roaming around in circles, looking for a golf game he didn't find. Strange golf bets abound on the island. Marcellus Wilson once bet his horse on a golf game. Every trip, it takes me a moment to get into the rhythm of playing golf on the island. But every trip, somehow, someway, that happens.

Life on the island is not perfect. There are

days I try to fish and all I catch is a cold and I am left buying five pounds of perch.

There's always romantic drama on the island, and it is always starring Black folks. People up here with the wrong people, being spotted by relatives with the ones they are not engaged to. Fortunately for some, there are so many white convertible Cadillacs up there in Idlewild you can't tell where folks spent the night — unless you get a good look at the license plates.

One July a certain gentleman drove thirty miles an hour in heavy holiday traffic to get to Idlewild to see a girl. When he got to Idlewild, five other guys were waiting for that same girl. There is a place on this island called Heartbreak Hotel. Someone suggested writing a book about the place. Nobody's going to do that, but I'm doing *this,* and it makes me happy.

What else makes me happy? People who can afford carpenters who are doing their own carpentry work on their own homes. Matey Stewart chartered a plane to get his wife, my Cordie King, to Idlewild in time for the annual fashion show. Daughter Nancy getting her eye busted open just before the show but getting it stitched up, by a visiting doctor, perfectly, and in time to strut. Hippy Dippy wearing one of her self-styled hats and ordering Champagne from her ringside table. Dinah Washington in her robin's-egg-blue four-door Imperial wearing a full-length fur in the cool of the late June night. White folks getting lost and finding their way into our town and looking utterly flummoxed with "Am-I-Really-Seeing-This?" written all over their faces as they discover our wonderland.

And in the aftermath of Idlewild, when autumn leaves (the heart-shaped birch leaves with their jagged edges, and the rounder aspen leaves) begin to fall, when it becomes harder and harder to tell an aspen from a birch, it also becomes harder and harder to tell which marriages will survive Idlewild summer and which won't. Back in Detroit, divorce courts stay open late. The town is a different kind of hot. And so am I. It is no joy to leave Eden consoled by memories from summer shows at the Club Fiesta, by souvenir matchbooks and cocktail napkins scribbled over with numbers, by dreams of and postcards from Ziggarettes, Zanzibeauts Fiesta Dolls, and Braggettes — love those gals! — Eleanor, Yvonne, Ines, Clineice, Val, and Arlene, but love best the Ziggarettes — they are smoking hot, in my memories of my idle and wild island days. Thank you, Arthur. And thank you, Butter-

541

beans and Susie, for giving Arthur his very first job in Chicago.

But best this: spring. Good Friday 1955, Milt Winfield and I rode out to Idlewild, planning to camp in his parents' house all Easter weekend, sustained by Campbell's Soup, while swinging hammers and wielding paintbrushes, wearing denim pants and jackets, getting the Winfield home ready for the season, far away from the expense, floss, and glory of Easter in Detroit.

Saturday, we saw a man about a boat, which Milt didn't buy, and a little cottage, which I didn't buy. We were both broke and happy. We tinkered with eaves, door sashes, fences, and whitewash, shedding layers as the temperature creeped up to almost-record-breaking highs. On Easter the sun rose in the noon sky on the warmest quiet day I would ever spend on the island. We were unprepared for the heat. We stripped down to our boxers and took out a canoe. As the temperature approached eighty, ours was the only vessel on an empty lake. No one looked back at us as we looked to the empty shore. Everything was to come. Everything was possible. We began to brown-up early under the Michigan sun in '55. We mused aloud that the angels with fiery swords must have fallen asleep on the job. We had slipped back into Eden.

LIBATION FOR THE FEAST DAY OF ARTHUR BRAGGS:
Idlewild Blooms

This recipe makes 2 1/2 gallons, enough to get an Idlewild weekend started.

1 quart of brandy
1 bottle + 1 glass of sherry wine
1 bottle + 1 glass of Madeira wine
5 bottles of Champagne, approximately 4 quarts
6 lemons, peels only
1 lb. of bar sugar
1 box of strawberries, rinsed and trimmed
2 lemons, sliced
6 oranges, sliced
1 pineapple, cut into small pieces
2 quarts of soda water

Bruise the peels of 6 lemons in 1 lb. of bar sugar. Put the flavored sugar in a punch bowl. Add all your fruit and still liquors. Stir well, then empty into another bowl in which a block of clear ice has been placed. Add Champagne and soda water when ready to serve. Include a piece of fruit in each serving.

WEEK 49
FORTY-NINTH SUNDAY
AFTER FATHER'S DAY

Dr. Alf E. Thomas Jr. graduated from Meharry Medical College in 1937 and was serving as a trustee on the Meharry Board when he died in July of 1968. More than once he served as chairman of the Detroit chapter of the NAACP's Fight for Freedom Fund Drive. In 1956 the annual dinner raised $31,000. Roy Wilkins credited the efforts and success of the Detroit branch with inspiring other cities to raise legal funds. Before Emancipation, Marion Island, like nearby Boblo Island, had sheltered people headed to freedom on the Underground Railroad. It has been estimated that over 30,000 Underground Railroad passengers passed through either Marion or Boblo. In the 1960s there was an amusement park on Boblo. War resisters, some few of them Black, would take the ferry to Boblo, then flee from there to Amherstburg, Canada.

545

Alf Thomas

PATRON SAINT OF: *Homemakers, Utopia Makers, and Stepparents*

Once, when the Alf Thomases were off to the West Indies and to Mexico, where they hoped to see Bricktop, Alf's brother Sam Thomas motored me out on his Boston Whaler to see Alf's island. "I have a boat; Alf has a yacht and an island," laughed Sam.

Sam believes he got the better deal. I got the better deal, still. Guest not host: No taxes to pay, no lawn to mow, no slip fees, and I still get tastes of the exclusive splendor that is Marion Island.

Sam and I sat on Alf's front porch and fished from our chairs. Caught bass and perch. Cooked our perch for dinner. Ate them by steno light. Marion Island — Alf had named the place for his wife, Marion Stubbs Thomas — is a private island owned by a single Negro doctor. It is in Canada. The island is green and beautiful and smells like freedom. There's milkweed, horsetails, and silverweed. The occasional American lotus blooms. Alf's house on Marion Island is graceful. It is one of those rare places where we escaped and got away safe. This is my island in the sun. This is where I play best. The only shows ever staged on this island were two of his daughters' weddings — Patricia's in 1958 and Fredericka's in 1961.

Mama Marion married well twice. First, she was married to Dr. Frederick D. Stubbs of Philadelphia, a big chest-surgeon. Freddie died at forty, leaving Marion plenty pretty money. Then she married Alf.

Freddie, a stiff real Philadelphia-style colored person, and Alf shared a profession and little more. Marion delighted in Alf's Detroit ways, gushing on about his "warmth, love, and kindness" in the pages of *Ebony* magazine. This is also where she explained that she hated the word "step," as in stepfather. She called Alf the "new" father; her children called him "Daddy."

Patricia Stubbs and Fredericka Stubbs weren't Alf's seed, but he gave them weddings of the century. I gave my daughter life, advice, a variety of trinkets, a good-enough name, and access to the limelight without having to work in it.

They said Alf was one of America's 100 richest Negroes. I always wondered how many of the hundred were in Detroit. Alf owned two hospitals: the Edyth K. Thomas Memorial Hospital and Haynes Memorial Hospital. His daddy was a doctor, too, Dr. A. E. Thomas. Alf started the national

547

NAACP Freedom Fund banquet. He had a real estate company and served on community boards and served as a trustee of his beloved Meharry Medical College. He loved music but he didn't get to spend that much time with it. But when he could, he did: He married a concert pianist and took me to be his friend. At the girls' weddings, the entire Detroit Symphony played as Alf's horses frolicked in their paddock.

I was there for the weddings. With 800 guests, they could sneak me in, but at small parties, such as the one they threw for the Gay Northeasterners on Marion Island, there was no place for me. I would see that crowd at Idlewild.

It is only from the outside that we don't see class. Black folk who want to say, "There is no class, just all of us are Black," usually say that because they have been hurt by siddity Blacks and think it's a way to get their own back, and it is.

But life is lived different than that. Inside the Black world there are circles and circles, and circles, and some I can enter into and some I can't. Inclusion and exclusion are not just a white and Black thing. And it is not just a rich and poor thing.

A rich white man's daughter has as little chance of getting into the Jack and Jill as mine does. It may not matter to the rich white man. But it mattered to me. I did not enjoy thinking there were verdant and exciting spaces inhabited by Negroes where I was not welcome. I liked it even less that such places might exclude my Josette. I was thrilled by the aloneness of Alf's island. We were not "other" there; we were only there.

I love Idlewild. It's a place where there are so many other people a lot like me that I have an opportunity to feel, live, and breathe the subtle differences between me and not-me, without experiencing those differences as chasms. I have had a space to sharpen my edges, discovering my ever-changing boundaries. The boundary between living and dead is thin and getting thinner. I hate thin. Alf's island and heaven are fat new frontiers. That's better.

In my early showbiz years, so much time was spent in places so not like me, so unappreciative of me, that all I could feel were the basics of Ziggy with much of Ziggy lost. Then I found my way to Detroit and into the Gotham Hotel.

It was in the lobby of the Gotham that I first met Alf and Marion, then Sam. Today, when Alf visited, he gave me a copy of the key to the front door of his island house and a key to Sam's boat. Left them on the

549

tray that fits across my bed. I've got the keys to a boat that will take me to a little territory where everything is beautiful and everything that is not serving or performing is Black. A place where I never had to perform. After the wedding, one or two, not many, of the guests sent their children to my dance school. I remember thinking, if more of you did, we would change this world. Some did. I let that be enough. The keys are everything.

LIBATION FOR THE FEAST DAY OF ALF THOMAS:
Married Well Twice

1 jigger of Jamaican rum
1 pony of Spanish brandy
1/2 lemon, juiced
1/2 lime, juiced
1 pony of simple syrup
1/4 lemon, cut into half-wheel slices
1/4 lime, cut into half-wheel slices

Place liquid ingredients into a cocktail shaker with ice and shake. Place lemon and lime half-wheel slices in the bottom of a rocks glass. Add ice. Strain contents of shaker over the ice. Serve with a straw.

WEEK 50
FIFTIETH SUNDAY
AFTER FATHER'S DAY

Baby Doll, described by the *Chicago Defender* as a "Mississippi ingenue," married Ziggy in Natchez, Mississippi, in February of 1965. In the wedding photograph Ziggy looks approvingly at his auburn-haired, gap-toothed bride with her dark and slanting eyes. She wears a tailored day-dress with a portrait neckline, nipped-in waist, and full gathered skirt. Around her neck on a thin gold chain is a cross. Even in heels and wearing a veiled pillbox hat, she's shorter than Ziggy, who wears a dark suit. Her gloved hands hold a small bouquet of roses as tailored as her dress.

Ziggy was not buried by his friend Congressman Diggs, but by the McFall Brothers Funeral Home. If Diggs had had charge of Ziggy's body, it is improbable the body would have ended up in his mother's Catholic Church. Most likely it would have arrived at the First Church of the Deliverance. Baby Doll knew the only way for the women, the mother, the daughter, and the wife to have the biggest say in the last show of Ziggy's life was to take the performance out of the hands of Ziggy's closest male friends. Later, Diggs thanked Baby Doll for giving McFall the job, saying, "You gave me the freedom to weep."

After Ziggy's death in 1968, Baby Doll converted to Catholicism and started wearing out Ziggy's rosary.

Working on Ziggy's Saints Day Book, Colored Girl flew to Detroit to interview Baby Doll. Baby Doll still lived in the Lafayette Towers, with a water view. After Ziggy's death she stopped working in the white world and started working at Ziggy's, first alongside Clifford Fears and after he died, without him. She married a widowed Black doctor. She carried on for a dozen years but eventually Baby Doll closed Ziggy's school. Boxes and boxes, overfilled with Ziggy memorabilia that had once lived in the dance school, were relocated to Baby Doll's way-past-cluttered apartment. She had to move stacks to give Colored Girl a place to sit down on the couch. When they each had a glass of wine in their hand, Baby Doll jumped in.

"On the phone you said that Bette burned Ziggy's book. And you've been trying to create it again, using his columns and interviews and the Internet. You wanted to know if I had read it."

"Did you?"

"Not read it — typed it. I was trying to make you a list of who was in it, from memory. I only came up with thirty-three of his Saints. Then I came up with this. Gloria had it for a while. Then her daughter, the doctor, wanted to read it. It's been passed around, scribbled over, some of the pages have been retyped. Here."

Baby Doll pulled an old vinyl dance case (the kind that little girls carry their leotards in to ballet class) out from under the chair where she was sitting, then pushed it toward Colored Girl with her foot. In the case was a carbon copy of Ziggy's manuscript.

"Little Miss Bougie Beige Office Worker" was Ziggy's other name for Baby Doll. There was a carbon-on-onionskin copy of Ziggy's book and Baby Doll let Colored Girl have it. Call. Response. Mari's words zagging with Ziggy's. And some other folks', too.

Baby Doll

PATRON SAINT OF: *Young Wives, Younger Wives, and Office Workers*

And I still kiss with pleasure. My tongue has become more discerning with age. At least that's what I tell Baby Doll — aka Yvette Mills — and what Baby Doll tells the world.

My first and only wife is nearby in the visitors' waiting room entertaining my guests. Would you like to meet her? She comes from Mississippi, like my mother. We were introduced at a party. I thought I would see her the next night, that she would be a new fixture on our circuit, but we didn't cross paths for weeks. Rushing downtown one afternoon to buy a tie, I came upon her peering into the window of Hudson's Department Store, looking as fresh and tidy as a woman can look in a cheap suit and cheap heels, and as lively as a creek fast-rising in April.

She came into Hudson's and helped me pick out the tie. She had a good eye. She knew what she liked and she seemed to know what she wanted to see on me. Soon we were sitting in Sanders's ice cream parlor and she was having her first encounter with the joys of Bumpy Cake while I drank black

554

coffee, savoring long looks at the woman I was quick deciding to marry.

Baby Doll is beautiful. She could have been a showgirl. She isn't tall but she's striking. She's what we call in the business a "pony," a short, curvy, trim girl, the kind of dancer they had at the Copacabana in New York City, except all those dancers were white pony girls. I never put white women in my shows. Never slept with a white woman. Not one. I have slept with a woman or two, in my time, but none so full of Spring as my gap-toothed, red-headed Baby Doll.

In the ice cream parlor, she shined in a way that made me think she had the slick of birth still on her. I had her show me her driver's license to prove she was over eighteen years old. As she pulled out the little square and waved it under my eyes, squealing that she was twenty-three, it struck me strong I had never seen more potential and pluck, pound for pound, walking the Earth in size-five shoes. She had a direct gaze, a fast mind, and a slow Mississippi drawl that stretched the three-beat name she told me to call her, Baby Doll, to a full six beats.

Her story was classic. A male cousin had moved her to Detroit. He had a job at Briggs, a three-bedroom two-family flat, one baby in a crib, one baby in his wife's belly, and an extra chair at the kitchen table. Baby Doll either could have "three hots and a cot" in exchange for helping with the cleaning, cooking, and baby watching, or she could get a job and help with the mortgage. The way she told the story gave all the glory in the tale to the cousin who sent for her, and the grandmother who let her go. She playfully described herself as "an ignorant, industrious adventuress of integrity." I almost cut and ran. Instead I queried. She seemed worth a question.

"What's that mumbo-jumbo you just used to describe yourself?"

"Lewis College, vocabulary quiz. I'm working on my 'I's.' "

She was enrolled in Lewis College of Business, located in a two-story colonial revival mansion house, with green shutters and a two-story solarium, and four white pillars, at the corner of John R. and East Ferry, an institution that had been sending "pert browns" out in the world to create lives for themselves with stenographer pens, typewriters, adding machines, and balance sheet ledgers since 1928. It was short blocks from my school on Warren.

The very next afternoon after our by-accident-Sanders-date, I picked her up on the front steps of her college, for our first official date — drinks at the Hobby Bar. I wanted to see how she handled city grit.

She was unfazed. "When Lord Jesus calls me home, I'm dead. Nothing's going to stop that. And nobody white or colored can take me before colored Jesus with woolly hair calls."

"Jesus has woolly hair?"

"Yes! I arrived in Detroit knowing only three things: my Bible, myself, and my movies. You and the Lewis College of Business are going to have to teach me the rest. But what I know, I know real good. And when I learn something, I don't forget. You going to find that out."

Truer words were never spoken to me. I fell in love with that woman against my will, against all odds, and against my general inclinations. She had banished fear of death from every inch of her brain with a raked-dirt-yard theology that provided her with an enviable inoculation against fear of mortality. She didn't have to tell me she knew a thousand wrong ways to die. She was from Mississippi. She was in Detroit. And suddenly she was exactly who I wanted on my arm to stroll with me to the end of time.

Not being afraid of death didn't protect Baby Doll from being afraid of other things.

She was afraid of spiders; afraid of mice; afraid of bumpy fruit and fabric; afraid of Fridays when they fell on the thirteenth; and afraid of sex. Baby Doll, in fact, named herself for the character played by Carroll Baker in the movie *Baby Doll* — an ingenue who marries a much older man and gets him to agree not to have sex with her while she gets some time to grow up in the shelter of his falling-down plantation house. I had seen the movie but I still wasn't exactly sure what Baby Doll was getting at by calling herself "Baby Doll."

The third night I saw her, I think it was at the Phelps Lounge, I asked about her name. She told me it was a message to future husbands.

"That you look good in short-short loose-fitting nightgowns and bloomers?"

"That I want to be married and not be touched — until I'm ready."

"But married?"

"I want my own house. I want a new name. I want someone to take care of, who will take care of me. I want to sleep safe, and pretty, and fed, in a crib, until I have had enough of sweet and sleep."

"Will an apartment do?"

It was a short courtship. Soon she was "the eldest of the new young brides married to the senior celebrities." Some of it was that I had begun to miss Mississippi. Not the hateful state that belonged to Governor Eastland and that ilk, but the Mississippi filtered through the lens of proud Black women's hearts, the Mississippi I knew as a boy in my Chicago that was filled with new arrivals from that state. The Mississippi that belonged to the Natchez Belle. Everything I missed about Mississippi was percolated and circulated in Baby Doll's blood.

Some of my pull toward her was this: The one thing she was afraid of, sex, was the one thing I wasn't afraid of. If I couldn't make her toes curl, I suspected my sexual courage might-could be contagious. If I could infuse my spouse with shamelessness, I would go out a lover for the ages. And yes, this once, I kiss and tell: Baby Doll is shameless.

Shameless is a miracle in this 20th century. More and more, our bright sepia city becomes conventional. Once was, a man who was not married could be the dean of a children's School of the Theatre and no one would think twice of sending their son or daughter to that man. As the fifties bled into 1960, people were starting to think twice. If I was around too many different women, they didn't want to send their daughters. If I wasn't around enough women, they didn't want to send their sons. When I lived in the Gotham, the whispers were "Ziggy's Ziggy." When I lived in a hotel, no one was surprised I was single. Live in an apartment, or a house, or even start talking about an apartment or a house, live any place with no maids and no restaurants, and everyone expects you, even me, the dean of the Ziggy Johnson School of the Theatre, to have a wife, to cook and clean.

It was convenient to marry Baby Doll, but I did not marry her for convenience. I married her for love, and for delight — the delight of surprising myself in the evening of life. She was more love and convenience than I had ever known. It is possible, if not likely, that I have known more desire. Yet this is true: I desire Baby Doll more than I desire anyone living. And I desire Baby Doll. There is a lid for every pot. She is my pot and lid; I am her lid and pot. Now.

We surprise some people. They make jokes about how she took her name from a movie about a sexless marriage. I tease louder and say we don't have "real sex" because I am too old to do it — but not too old to look. I say we have "eye sex." That gives folks a laugh.

You want folks to remember something

560

you've got to make them laugh or cry. Baby Doll makes me laugh. She will be the last thing I remember. Something I can't forget. How sweet it is, when death reaches out to embrace you, to have your arms full-up with love memories.

When I go, it will change her. She has already changed. Married these years, business school and I are not her only interests. She moved out of the crib and into the bed. She started working at a white company, but the longer I've been in here, the ten weeks, the more trouble they have started giving her about getting time off to visit with me. Sometime soon she will start running the school. And she's more than any of that: She's a golfer and a songwriter, as well as a wife. She has a set of beige Lady Palmer golf clubs, a complete and lovely set, along with a bag and a cart. She likes to golf with Gwen Gordy Fuqua, who also has a complete set of clubs, except Gwen's are a fine shade of light green. When Baby Doll's not golfing, she's coming up with song lyrics.

Baby Doll says she's an adopted daughter of Black Bottom. She circles back to the past to secure the future she desires; then she rejects the past to protect the present she enjoys. She knows when to do one thing, and when to do the other. She is city-gal strategic and country-girl strong.

In my end, I have returned to my beginning. I am bequeathing Baby Doll a younger second husband and a longer second marriage, as a matched set to our gold rings that shined.

LIBATION FOR THE FEAST DAY OF YVETTE MILLS:
Baby Doll

1 jigger of Puerto Rican rum
1 pony of grenadine
1 lime, juiced

Place ingredients in a cocktail shaker.
Shake well and strain into a
cocktail glass.

WEEK 51
FIFTY-FIRST SUNDAY
AFTER FATHER'S DAY

Dreams come true. They do not always stay true, but sometimes they come true. Colored Girl had known that since her first appearance on a Ziggy Johnson School of the Theatre Youth Colossal stage in a blue satin cowgirl skirt with fringe.

Colored Girl forgave her mother. If the mother had not burned up Ziggy's pages, she would not have been as prepared as she was to edit those pages when they were restored to her. If Colored Girl had had a less vicious mother, she would not have had the two best mothers, George and Ziggy.

She did not think she would get back to venturing out into nature, unafraid, naked, and unarmed. She was wrong. Weaving together, untangling, reembroidering the lives of the saints she found in Ziggy's book, Colored Girl got back to that.

She lives downtown in Nashville overlooking the river. In the early morning she shoots eighteen holes of golf almost every day God sends. She carries a full set of clubs and she doesn't use an electric cart or a caddy. By ten she's at her laptop with her coffee, writing. In the afternoon she's behind the bar. It is a good life. This is a clean train. She held the fort. She won the war in her head. And when all that was done, she lay down her sword and shield. Colored Girl embraced a Ziggy-taught love takeover, conceived in language, born in the five senses of her body, strong enough to rise toward the pleasures of now.

When Tiger Woods won the Masters Tournament in 1997, he was the greatest golfer in the world. In that hour he publicly acknowledged aloud that his way had been prepared for by Ted Rhodes. Tiger was a Ziggy dream come true, at long last. It didn't stay true, but it came true.

Ted Rhodes

PATRON SAINT OF: *Sportsmen, Old Friends, and Dreamers*

When I get upstairs, this is who I hope will be waiting for me at the gate: Saint Ted.

Truth be told, my favorite performances occur on golf links, not stages. And my very favorite performer is Mr. Ted Rhodes. I got a date with Teddy upstairs. Someday soon we're going to play eighteen holes. Half of being happy today is knowing something good is happening tomorrow. And if you don't know that, it helps to know that something good happened some yesterday. What's happening now is not always good. But now can always be good if you choose right how to think about tomorrow and yesterday. Teddy got me choosing right.

I taught Marie Thompson the chick-a-boom; Marie Thompson taught me to golf. I think I got the better part of that deal. Thompson was a national champion golfer. She won the very first United Golfers Association Open Women's Championship in 1930 and successfully defended that title in 1931. For the next decade, until 1941, she consistently finished in the top ten in that National. Fortunately for me and other sepian Detroit duffers, she fell in love with Samuel O. Jones, one of Detroit's first sepians to be employed in Detroit as a US postal mail clerk. Marie married Sam in 1936. She set up house, then set about expanding the Detroit Amateurs Golf Association.

Joe Louis was the first people's choice and then it was Sugar Ray Robinson. I love

Sugar Ray Robinson, but Joe Louis changed my life, and not in the way he changed a lot of folk's lives. Joe Louis was how I met Teddy Rhodes, or at least how I came to know him. For a minute Teddy worked as a valet for Joe Louis. Billy Eckstine met him first when Rhodes bounced out of the army and landed in Chicago. Soon we were all friends.

A good time for our little gang of duffers? We traveled west to see Teddy golf at the Riviera Ranch Country Club in Los Angeles. Those were halcyon days. Golfing with "Rags." He was proof we lied when we hollered, "The sharper you look the better you play golf." Teddy didn't care what he wore out on the course. He was from Tennessee, caddied at those Nashville country clubs to have a place to play. When he got good enough to play in tournaments, they kept him out by changing tournaments to invitationals. But it didn't keep him out. Not completely. And then he was back in Nashville, bringing along Lee Elder. And Lee Elder will bring along somebody. Nobody knows it now, but one day we will *own* golf. I feel that. Teddy Rhodes was something. Given a fair chance, he'd be acknowledged as the best golfer in the world.

But he wasn't given a fair chance. One

year it's Teddy Rhodes married my former chorine Claudia Oliver. Another year it was, Teddy Rhodes has a pro shop in the Pershing Hotel. Now, it's Teddy Rhodes is back in Nashville and not doing good. I put his name and his address in my "Zagging with Ziggy" column, along with a coded SOS, "Ted is in a sand trap down Nashville way," hoping folks would send him cards and money. Not sure which one he needed more. When you are sick and old and Black, Nashville is no place to be. Black Bottom is the place to be.

When I lived in the Gotham Hotel I would lie in the scented water of my tub with the tokens, with the soaps and oils that the chorines and barmaids and schoolmarms had given me, trying not to think of bills I hadn't paid or drapes that were needed for the opening of the school or business cards, or of record players, and wigs and suits, and so much else that has been stolen. I get in the tub and I can banish all of that with a waking dream that banishes all the bad thoughts that invade my head on dry land. I get in the tub and I dream of just after dawn, of Palmer Park, golf links, all mine, the way it is at 6:00 a.m.

Now I lie in my hospital bed and banish thoughts of high blood pressure readings

567

and low kidney output and hard pulse with my dream of 6:00 a.m.

Six a.m. is a land of second chances as good as the first. I drop a second ball and sometimes a third. There is no witness. No one coming up from behind to rush me. No one wishing to share the tee. In my golf dreams I have no place to be later in the day. No one looks over my shoulder as I tally my score. In my dreams I always play eighteen holes. And it is eighteen holes of serene.

In my reality it is nine holes. And there is somewhere I have to be. And so I dash to the park in the clean gleam of fresh and early morn. I look at the mansions on the border of Palmer Park that stand sentry, and I want to blind their eyes, throw rocks into the windows that spy on me. Then I remember the rich folk are sleeping. They don't play golf at dawn.

I see a Black lady folding herself out of a car; she is being dropped off for work. She is in a white shirtdress with an apron. I hope her grandchild goes to my school. I am in my uniform too: a mohair golf sweater, twill pants. I have a full set of clubs and a cool little cart. In my life I have never had a caddy and probably never will. I am too good a friend with Ted Rhodes to have a caddy. Teddy came up caddying for good men and bad men but it was the bad men he remembered, the stride of the meekly vicious men, some slim, some with paunches, who played while he worked and were jealous of his swing, and his walk, his loose and jangling sway that he hid behind on those segregated greens. He did what he needed to do to keep folk employing him, but no more than was absolutely necessary. Coming up in country clubs is a particular kind of coming up hard. Teddy Rhodes first knew the weight of marvelous golf clubs because he handed them, for years, to lesser golfers to swing.

In one of my golf dreams, Teddy let me caddy for him. I walked behind him over the links. It is the best golf lesson ever. And he has marvelous clubs. I am his caddy and he owns a perfect set of MacGregor clubs and they are engraved with his name.

In my best golf dream, I shoot my best game of the season and there are none there to see. The triumph is completely mine, without audience, and utterly undoubted. I love golf more than I love the theater. I love the theater but the theater is, for me, work.

Just because a man doesn't have a full set of clubs, or even one lonely golf club, didn't mean he couldn't be my friend. You can have a new set of Tommy Armour's clubs just in time for the Duffers tourney and be my friend, too. I'm not jealous. And you don't have to be good. I love the hit-and-hope-boys who extend the season and their learning time by jetting down Kingston, Jamaica, way. Some of my buddies hit so many into the trees they call each other Tarzan. And others — Billy Eckstine, Althea Gibson, Joe Louis, and Sugar Ray — are in demand on the Pro-Am circuit because they are so good.

My Anna Gordy is a good golfer. Played so well with her Lady Palmer Clubs that I called her Patty Berg. People will remember Anna far longer than Patty. That seems impossible to some ofays now, but it is true and I know it. People will remember Anna. And they will remember her, in part, because Mari got snatched out of Detroit as Detroit was imploding and she landed in a spot where she will discover the tools necessary to preserve my Saints as my Saints will have preserved her. One day that I won't live to see, I predict my Mari will play golf almost as well as my Anna.

Golf is my 21st century arriving early. Something I couldn't imagine as a boy in Chicago. At Wendell Phillips I ran track, I played basketball, I danced, they called me a slick trick. All of these were expected things. We danced in slavery. We did not golf. This door has been the hardest one to walk through: The one that leads to leisure, an hour of leisure, a day of leisure, a half day of leisure, a round of leisure, not all of us ever arrive at that. With golf I have achieved this.

Life is a club; you pay your dues over and over. Paying your dues. Doing the things you don't want to do, the grubby work, so that you can do the thing you want to do. There's not one secret to life, there are two: Pay your dues, and have a thing you want to do.

My last day on the links was in September 1967. There had been nineteen consecutive rainless days, and then there was bad weather that threatened the baseball pennant race. The teachers were out on strike, 300,000 strong. Our little school became a kind of day camp and daycare once the big school didn't open. The day that the teachers went back with their raise, I called Marc Stepp to holler "Hallelujah!," then I headed to the links.

I had never seen such a dry September in Detroit. Old-timers said that the heavens decided not to cry. Invisibly, the fires of the summer rebellion continued to burn. It was dry and hot and then it wasn't. The last day of the month it was in the forties and we had started September at 90 degrees. Autumn leaves were in the air. Ten miles out of the city it snowed.

Winter was coming early. Only I knew that was a good thing. Summer is the season of roots. Fall is the season of threats. Winter is the season of resources and renewal. Spring is the season of blooming. This year, winter needed to come soon.

When I put up my golf bag after that outing on the links, I cleaned my clubs, not like you would clean them to put up a golf bag for the season, but to take enough time to decide just who I should gift my clubs to. Baby Doll wouldn't let me give my clubs away. She said we'd just need to buy a new set the next year. She didn't know what I knew, that when I put my old Nat King Cole 45 of "Autumn Leaves" on the hi-fi, I couldn't lift my right foot to drag myself around the room. Chick-a-boom! My leg was dragging. I knew where I wanted to step but I couldn't do it. Dr. Bodywork says that was a ministroke.

I have stayed too long at the fair.

It is 1968. Father's Day is coming soon. And there will be a Youth Colossal with or without me. But it won't be in Detroit. The

Gotham has been blown up. Twelfth Street has been burned down. Paradise Valley has been forgotten. Idlewild has been fatally wounded by integration and television. One performance seen by millions eclipses live shows. Little German Beetles and Japanese Datsun Bluebirds are popping up all over the road. They do not need hundreds of thousands of us. We were needed in Detroit. This is *not* Detroit. Detroit is yesterday. Detroit is tomorrow. Detroit will come again.

All the leverages have changed. Except one: God gave me a body, and I had used it with zeal. Now that body is mysteriously slow. Too slow for the stage, but not too slow for the links. My legs are heavy but my arms are strong and my eyes are good and my hands don't tremble. My pulse is starting to slow. I will get a new caddy cart and shoot a fine round. And if not on Earth, then in heaven.

LIBATION FOR THE FEAST DAY OF TED RHODES:
A Full Set of Clubs

1 jigger of Old Tom gin
1/2 lime, juiced, or 1/2 pony of lime juice

1/4 orange, juiced, or 1/2 pony of orange juice
1 chunk of pineapple, juiced, or 1/2 pony of pineapple juice
1/2 pony of rock candy syrup

Fill cocktail shaker with ingredients, add ice, shake, and strain into a cocktail glass.

WEEK 52
FATHER'S DAY

Colored Girl and her friend Sophia left the fancy dining room in the Hermitage Hotel and took a cab to Opryland. They spent the afternoon at Opryland amusement park eating Dippin' Dots, freeze-dried ice cream bites, and riding the roller coaster, which gave them an excuse to scream. Colored Girl was upside down on the cyclone clutching Sophia's hand when she made a promise she would keep.

Ziggy Johnson

PATRON SAINT OF: *Ballet Babes and Other Small Fry with Taps on Their Heels and Toes*

Joseph "Ziggy" Johnson invented a word, "mistery." It was his name for lost historical facts and lost cultural wisdom that he believed only dance, drum, song, and poem could reclaim. He designed, choreographed, and produced a hit show, *Dream Mistery,* celebrating the concept in 1942. To give you a taste of "mistery," here's a bit of a contemporary review highlighting the finale he had built around the hit song of the show:

In the wings a fringe of moonlit palms suggested a tropical setting. The company, in carnival attire, dimly seen behind a scrim, swayed to faint music. Down front on the darkened stage a bright spotlight focused on T-Bone in top hat, white tie, and tails. Very softly he intoned the opening stanzas of the song meant to evoke nostalgia and grief. Weaving through verse after verse was a leitmotiv inspired by the mystery and magic of night. Reaching the finale, he addressed himself to the guitar and allowed his voice to sink to a whisper again. With a dynamic sequence of chords, he commenced an arresting cadenza. Electrified, the enchanted audience rose to its feet to applaud.

The hit song was called "Evenin'." When that review came out, Ziggy was at once a nationally recognized choreographer, dancer, producer, and emcee. Based in Detroit, he spent weeks on the road, landing most often in Chicago, St. Louis, New York, and Atlantic City. He was not yet the political man he would become once he abandoned that peripatetic life and embedded himself in Detroit's Black Bottom neighborhood and expanded his vocation list to include syndicated weekly columnist and founder of the Ziggy Johnson School of the Theatre.

According to the census, 39,679 "Negro females" under five years old lived in Detroit in 1960. There were also 36,086 Black girls under the age of nine but over five; 27,750 Black girls between nine and fourteen; and 19,293 older Black teen girls. All in all, there were 122,808 Black girls in a single city. In contrast, in that same city, Detroit, in that same year, 1960, there were 525 Black women over eighty-five. Detroit was a city of Black girls. Ziggy Johnson was a man who paid attention to this fact.

I write from Bullock's Black Bottom Bar in Nashville. I am Mari, Ziggy's former student, Ziggy's last editor.

My parents enrolled me in Ziggy Johnson School of the Theatre for five years, from 1962 until the fall of 1967. I was three years old when I walked through his doors, the age his friend Sammy Davis Jr. was when he first went to work onstage. I was eight years old when I abruptly left the school, the same age Ziggy's friend Tim Moore was when he was touring Europe without parents or guardian in a Black juvenile duo billed as the Gold Dust Twins.

Ziggy had tremendous respect for and unusual awareness of the capability of our youngest sepian citizens to create art of significance. For Ziggy, a central significance of all Black art is that it increases the capacity of both artist and audience to restore self and to know self. By the late fifties, Ziggy was focused on a particular group of artists — Black girls. He turned his energies to nurturing our ambitions, our art, and our "mistery," or, as it is called today, magic. And he got more than a few grown folk, his Black Bottom Saints, committed to that.

A cradle-to-grave Catholic, and an altar boy, Ziggy grew up reading *Butler's Lives of the Saints.* Originally published in twelve volumes in the 1750s, 200 years later when Ziggy was planning, in the summer of 1952, for the opening of his Ziggy Johnson School of the Theatre in Detroit, Michigan, four-volume sets of *Butler's Lives* were almost as common as rosaries in Black Catholic American homes. On his deathbed, Ziggy wrote his own *Lives of the Black Bottom Saints.* In it he lays out the unexpected roots of both Motown music and Black girl magic, as well as fifty-two paths from trauma to transcendence.

Some have cautioned me about this book, warning that within Ziggy's pages lies the wisdom that has allowed us to survive a vicious world, and that we should not share that wisdom so widely, as it may come into the hands of those who have made Black lives harder. I say, Tikkun. I tell a different story, because of the stories Ziggy told me. I say, women, you got some allies upstairs in heaven you don't know you have. I say, even if there *is* no heaven, your worst day is behind you and I will teach you a dance that lets you know in your clean bones that your worst day is behind you — a dance Ziggy taught me.

I say you can't steal Black girl magic but it can be gifted. I say we live in a moment so broken we must risk sharing the mistery even if those we share it with don't "get it" and try to shame us for sharing. Ziggy called, I responded. You are holding something originally created by Ziggy, lost for decades, altered and added to, miraculously found, and finally annotated by me. I say mistery provides new paths out of misery.

Ziggy wrote his *Lives of the Black Bottom Saints,* beginning in the fall of 1967 and completing it, according to Baby Doll, about two days before his death in February of 1968. He didn't keep a diary, didn't have access to his newspaper columns in the hospital, so there are inconsistencies. Ziggy was working from memory with a brain fogged by illness, assisted by a variety of friends who popped in and out of his room, each with their own memories of dates and events. Some of these have seeped into Ziggy's text. While the draft was in Baby Doll's possession, it was amended by at least two different hands, and a variety of magazine articles, newspaper clippings, obituaries, and letters were found stuck between the pages. The pieces create chords. There are two versions of creation in Genesis: In one version the world is created in seven days, in the other the world is created in one day. Both stories illuminate. And so it is, for me, with Ziggy's variations. I have been honored to serve as his last editor.

> Is there a place that hides from sight
> Where daytime never turns to night?
> Somewhere, somewhere?
> There must be, else we could not bear
> The pain, the anguish we have here.
> Tell me! Tell me! Is it not true?
> A place exists where we're made anew,
> Somewhere, somewhere?
> — WILLIAM FRANK FONVIELLE (1866–1903)
> African-American poet and memoirist

For Ziggy Johnson, that place was an inner-city Detroit dancing school. Someone needs and asks. Someone hears and helps. Folks witness and give testimony. In Ziggy's Black Bottom, God does not make saints, *people* do. That's another Ziggy truth.

Ziggy died February 7, 1968. His last column appeared in the *Michigan Chronicle* on February 10, 1968. He was buried in Chicago after a requiem mass three days later. Father Tolton is still waiting to be officially recognized as a saint by the Catholic Church. And Baby Doll's still kicking.

LIBATION FOR THE FEAST DAY OF ZIGGY JOHNSON:
Zig's Zag

1 magnum of Champagne
1 lemon, juiced
1/4 cup of bar sugar
1 jigger of strawberry syrup
1 orange, sliced
3 slices of pineapple

In a large glass pitcher place sugar and lemon juice. Stir until dissolved. Add all other ingredients. Pour into eight Champagne flutes. Toast! Another round! And another for an end sweet, high, and nigh!

ACKNOWLEDGMENTS

I want to thank Joseph "Ziggy" Johnson for writing columns in the *Michigan Chronicle* that inspired me to want to be a writer and for founding the Ziggy Johnson School of the Theatre, where I was once shoved onto a Youth Colossal stage and pointed toward hard-won happy — come rain or shine.

Marie Brown and Patrik Bass have been my publishing dream team. After reading the manuscript, Marie *knew* that Patrik Bass at an Amistad helmed by Tracy Sherrod under a HarperCollins umbrella held high by Judith Curr was the ideal home for *Black Bottom Saints*. Marie was right! She always is.

Long before I had HarperCollins behind me, I had Vanderbilt University. I am proud to have served Vanderbilt as a writer-in-residence for the entirety of "the Zeppos era," an era committed to excellence fueled by diversity. I was awarded a paid, year-long sabbatical for 2017–2018 that made writing this novel possible. I thank Chancellor Emeritus Nick Zeppos, my dear friend; Acting Chancellor and Provost Susan Wente; and Chair of African-American and Diaspora Studies Tracy Sharpley-Whiting, each and often, for their outstanding institutional and personal generosity. The publication of *Black Bottom Saints* coincides with the first days of Daniel Diermier's tenure as Vanderbilt's ninth chancellor. I'm proud to be one of the first Vanderbilt authors and first novelists published on his watch.

Nathan Huggins was the first scholar to assist me significantly with my writing when I was an undergraduate at Harvard University, enrolled in his course on the Harlem Renaissance authors. Others who have provided emboldening theory and encouragement have been Houston Baker, Glenda Carpio, Thadious Davis, Skip Gates, Lovalerie King, Tiffany Patterson, and Hortense Spillers. Kenvi Phillips, Curator of Race and Ethnicity of the Schlesinger Library, acquired my papers for Harvard as I was finishing this novel. I grew up in the shadow of Howard University; that Kenvi, a Howard-trained scholar of American history and public history, brought my pages back to the place I first began to imagine I

could support my life with my imaginings
— true sweet. I am grateful to all the many
scholars who have critically engaged my
novels and songs, yet I must note three, two
of whom I've never met, whose work at various times inspired me to keep on keeping
on: Patricia Smith Yaeger, Barbara Ching,
and Cameron Leader-Picone.

Julieanna Richardson and the History-
Makers digital oral history archive provided
invaluable inspiration for this project: a
work of printed fiction that dances with that
digital archive's profound works of oral history.

I teach a course at Vanderbilt called "Black
Detroit" in which I get to teach the work of
Herb Boyd's *Black Detroit* and Tiya Miles's
The Dawn of Detroit. I want to thank them
for writing those informed and informing
histories.

I am indebted to all my early readers,
some from the academy, some from the
music world, some from publishing, some
with roots in Black Bottom, some from old
Black Bottom. But I am most indebted to
these particularly brilliant and generous
folk: Thadious Davis, Basil Egli, Justin
Townes Earle, Debra Gaskin, Derrick Har-
riell, Reggie Hudlin, Randall Kenan, Callie
Khouri, Carter Little, Tracy Sharpley-

Whiting, Liz Van Hoose, and Caroline Randall Williams. Their critiques did much to help improve and evolve the manuscript. Liz gave multiple drafts of the manuscript exceptionally close and rigorous scrutiny; her suggestions, questions, and quibbles were invaluable.

Dr. Wally Clare, cardiologist, provided historical information on the treatment of cardiac disease in the early 1960s, becoming the fictional Ziggy's only real doctor. Jimmy James Greene worked to translate my novel into a deck of cards. Louis York is committed to helping that card deck get out into the world. All this is profound gift.

I was fortunate to attend the very first book club meeting to discuss *Black Bottom Saints* where Audrey Bowie, Tammy Bryant, Phyllis Cain, Michele Dowdy, Freida Outlaw, Marlene Sanders, and Kathy White gifted me with insightful readings and powerful questions.

The summer Marie was helping BBS find its way home to Amistad, I was making and directing a four-minute film, *Blue Blazer* (based on the Thomas Bullock chapter of the BBS series) as the capstone of a summer filmmaking intensive at the NYU School of Professional Studies. That doesn't get done without the following cohort: Gary

Gasgarth, my film-making teacher; Alan Arkush, my filmmaking coach; Larry Banks, my DP; my two luminous stars, Joseph Edwards and Bjorn DuPatey; and my two favorite fellow student filmmakers, Olga Ivanova and Meki Seldana. Thank you each and all.

There is one Black Bottom Saint who didn't make it into the novel whom I would like to acknowledge — David Williams. David championed my novel writing, in the world, in the larger academy, and within the Vanderbilt community, from jump, when it was neither popular nor safe. I went out on my first book tour with armed guards because of violent threats. The way he stood by me in 2001 was one part George Stanley standing by Colored Girl, one part Lawrence Massey standing by Dinah Washington, and one part Dave standing by Alice. I called David "the Motown Mountain." In the winter of 2019 David succumbed to an unexpected acute medical crisis and died. David loved everything Detroit, and is now buried in that city. David; his wife, my play-sister Gail Carr-Williams; and her mother, Malissa Carr — who makes an appearance in these pages — are the three people who made an amazing island of Motown Magic for me on the Cumberland.

A best that is left for me in Detroit is my half sister, Debra Jean Gaskin. She is a retired attorney, a wife, mother, grandmother, church activist, and most excellent friend. An alumna of Ziggy's, she is living proof of the fortitude, integrity, and beauty that rose within Ziggy's walls. As a young public defender in Detroit, Debra sought justice and mercy for the grandchildren and great-grandchildren of Black Bottom. As a stalwart supporter of Hartford Memorial Baptist Church and its pastor, the Rev. Charles G. Adams, she is part of an audacious plan, Hartford Village, a senior living facility within Detroit City limits that has enabled some who literally grew up in Black Bottom to return to city living in their eighties.

Yvonne Johnson, Mr. Johnson's widow, graciously allowed me to interview her at length for this project. Dianne Bland, one of his most legendary teachers, also generously granted me an interview. Norma Fambrough gave me a critically important interview. Alex Albritton and Jiam Desjardins shone light into old Detroit. I thank them each and all.

My living Detroit family: Cousins David and Keenan (who also attended Ziggy's), Uncle Jimmy, half brother Stan Randall, and all my Alabama family, including especially Michael Johnson and all our Alabama Johnson kin, share with me a connection to Black Bottom and inspire me with their strength and beauty.

I was my mother's only child, but Black Bottom loves a fictive kin bond: I adopted some siblings, cousins, and second cousins over the years, and these and theirs I claim as kin: Alex von Hoffmann, Amanda Little, Anita Joyce-Barnes, Ann Hammock, Anton Mueller, Betsy Wills, Brad Gioia, Bill Collier, Bill Harbison, Bob Doyle, Bud Baker, Carter Little, Chelsea Crowell, Courtney Little, Chuck Harmony, Claude Kelly, Danny Glover, David Feinberg, Debra Martin Chase, Diana Fisketjon, Elena Byrd, Elizabeth Dennis, Edwin Williamson, Forrest Talley, Gail Williams, Helen Bransford, Jim Cooper, Julie Frist, Jun Makihara, Kate Ezell, Kimiko Fox, Kirk Barton, Kumiko Makihara, Laura Lea Bryant, Lee Pratt, Leslie Weisberg, Lisa Campbell, Lissa Smith, Marc Fishman, Marq Roswell, Mathew Clark, Mary Jane Smith, Mimi Oka, Neil Krugman, Perian Strang, Randy Tarkington, Ray Kennedy, Reggie Hudlin, Rex Hammock, Rhiannon Giddens, Richard Patton, Robin Patton, Sam Strang, Siobhan Kennedy, Steve Earle, Tanya Watson, T-Bone Burnett, Tommy Frist, Tracy Sharpley-Whiting, Vandana Abramson, Volney Gaye, and Warrington Hudlin. A modern joy is my having "mothers of choice": Joan Bok, Edith Gelfand, Florence Kidd, Leatrice McKissack, and Philomena Maher. Quincy Jones was my champion and God-daddy in the LA film and music world — and the only one I ever needed. Little in life is better than a big brood of brilliant, feisty, and beautiful sibs, cousins, playmamas, and an amazing God-daddy.

While I was writing this book, Dr. Vandana Abramson and Dr. Ingrid Meszoly literally saved my life. It was my dear friend Reggie Hudlin who said that sometimes, to save the boat of life from sinking, a bodacious set of tattas has to be thrown overboard. He was right. Vandana is my Bob Bennett. Reggie is my Reggie.

Tandy Wilson's City House, Margot, the bar at Etch, and Josephine's — these are the restaurants that fed this novel. And David Ewing is the person with whom I shared most of those meals. David's love of history dances with my love of literature. Tandy's and Margot's love of food has infused my own love of life. Sometimes the only way I made it through a week was knowing I would land at Tandy's on a Tuesday.

590

Matt Tocco, also born in Detroit, was the inspired barkeep who helped me test and refine my spins on Thomas Bullock's cocktail recipes. I thank Matt and the generosity, insight, and support of the Strategic Hospitality team.

My godchildren, Kazuma Makihara, Takuma Makihara, Cynara Fox, Charlie Feinberg, Lucas Mueller (whose father, Anton Mueller, edited my first four novels), and Aria Little are all deeply loved by me. Kazuma has promised to be the walking stick of my old age — I could not love him more.

My daughter's godmother, with her husband, Jun Makihara, have been patrons of all the arts that matter to me most. They established numerous scholarships at Harvard University — including one for my father, George Randall, a denizen of Black Bottom. Mimi Oka and I have been best friends for over forty years. No one has taken more steps beside me on my long walk to hard-won happy than Mimi. No one has been more generous than Uncle Jun.

No one has read more of my pages, listened to more of the raw stories, gazed at more of the photographs, or given me more cause for joy than my daughter, Caroline Randall Williams. It is a rare pleasure to be part of a family of writers. That pleasure is mine. In no small part, writing this book was an attempt to gift Caroline the world my father, George, gifted me. Without George's storytelling, this book would not be.

The Black Bottom Saint Sammy Davis Jr. had Big Sammy and Will Mastin, and I had George and Ziggy. That has been enough for me to rise from the ashes every time I got burned down.

ABOUT THE AUTHOR

Alice Randall was born in Motown and migrated to Music City after graduating from Harvard. She began her writing career as a songwriter and is an award-winning songwriter who has had over thirty cuts including the #1 smash hit "XXX's and OOO's (An American Girl)" recorded by Trisha Yearwood that has become a country classic. A respected screenwriter, she has sold screenplays to major studios including Paramount, Warner Bros., and CBS. *Black Bottom Saints* is her fifth novel. Her earlier works include the *New York Times* bestseller *The Wind Done Gone, Pushkin and the Queen of Spades, Rebel Yell,* and *Ada's Rules.* With her daughter, Caroline Randall Williams, she coauthored the acclaimed cookbook *Soul Food Love,* winner of the NAACP IMAGE award, and the young adult novel *The Diary of B. B. Bright, Possible Princess,* winner of the Phillis Wheatley Prize. Randall

593

is on the faculty of Vanderbilt University, where she teaches courses on Black Detroit, soul food, African-American children's literature, African-American film, Black country, and country lyric in American culture.